D0790528

7/98

The Romance World Raves About
Barbara Dawson Smith!

Once Upon A Scandal

"Every time Barbara Dawson Smith writes a book, she creates a beautiful, heartwarming masterpiece that fills the soul and stimulates the heart. ONCE UPON A SCANDAL is a marvelous love story . . . This future classic is a keeper that is destined to be reread many times, especially when the reader needs an emotionally uplifting experience."
—*Affaire de Coeur*

"Barbara Dawson Smith is an author everyone should read. You'll be hooked from page one." —*Romantic Times*

Never A Lady

"Timeless romance that will keep you turning the pages." —Kat Martin

"It's time for the rest of the world to discover what Barbara Dawson Smith's fans have known all along—this is a can't-miss author." —*RomEx Reviews*

"A treasure of a romance . . . a story that only a novelist of Ms. Smith's immense talent could create. Barbara Dawson Smith continues to be a refreshing, powerful voice of the genre. A must read." —*Romantic Times*

More . . .

"A brilliant and daring tale."   —*Affaire de Coeur*

"This is a multi-faceted story with deep secrets and many forks in the road to true happiness. Ms. Smith constructs a passion-filled story draped in suspense and danger. An action-filled story set in the Regency period."
                                              —*Rendezvous*

"NEVER A LADY is an outstanding Regency historical that keeps the reader in suspense right up to the end . . . the sexual tension is beautifully handled . . . a winner! Barbara Dawson Smith is a romance writer to watch!"
                                         —*Romance Forever*

A GLIMPSE OF HEAVEN

"Superb reading! Barbara Dawson Smith's talents soar to new heights with this intense, romantic and engrossing tale."   —*Romantic Times*

"Excellent . . . a triumphant and extraordinary success . . . a master writer."   —*Affaire de Coeur*

"Fascinating storytelling!"
                            —*Atlanta Journal & Constitution*

**St. Martin's Paperbacks Titles
by Barbara Dawson Smith**

A Glimpse of Heaven
Never a Lady
Once Upon a Scandal
Her Secret Affair

HER SECRET AFFAIR

BARBARA DAWSON SMITH

KINSMAN FREE PUBLIC LIBRARY
6420 CHURCH STREET
P.O. BOX 166
KINSMAN, OHIO 44428

DISCARD

St. Martin's Paperbacks

NOTE: If you purchased this book without a cover you should be aware that this book is stolen property. It was reported as "unsold and destroyed" to the publisher, and neither the author nor the publisher has received any payment for this "stripped book."

HER SECRET AFFAIR

Copyright © 1998 by Barbara Dawson Smith.

All rights reserved. No part of this book may be reproduced in any manner whatsoever without written permission except in the case of brief quotations embodied in critical articles or reviews. For information address St. Martin's Press, 175 Fifth Avenue, New York, N.Y. 10010.

ISBN: 0-312-96507-9

Printed in the United States of America

St. Martin's Paperbacks edition/May 1998

10 9 8 7 6 5 4 3 2 1

/

*With love to Greg and Alisa Dawson and
their two heroes in the making,
Christopher and Will.*

Acknowledgments

As always, my gratitude goes to Jennifer Enderlin, editor extraordinaire, for believing in this book and making it even better . . .

To Helen Breitwieser, for being a superb advocate of my work . . .

And to my fearless and peerless critique group, Susan Wiggs, Betty Traylor Gyenes, Christina Dodd, and Joyce Bell, for providing the very best in advice, support, brainstorming, and most of all, friendship.

Author Note

In my last novel, *Once Upon A Scandal*, an excerpt from this book appeared under the title of *The Venus Touch*. I wanted you to know that *Her Secret Affair* is that very same book; only the title has been changed. Enjoy!

✑ Chapter 1 ✑

*H*e would teach her a lesson she would never forget.

Standing in the gloom beneath a plane tree, he scrutinized her house. It didn't look like a brothel. Situated on a quiet street, the town house was built of the same pale stone as its neighbors. Rain scoured the tall windows and sluiced down the fluted columns that flanked the porch. Three granite steps led up to a discreet white door, its brass knocker gleaming in the twilight. From time to time, the lace curtains showed shadows of people moving inside the lighted, ground-floor rooms.

According to his spy, the harlots would be eating dinner. Upstairs, the closed draperies shut out all but a glimmering of candlelight in one room.

Her room.

A cold sense of purpose consumed him. He wanted no witness to their meeting. He would wait in her boudoir and use the element of surprise . . .

He pivoted on his boot heel and crossed the wet cobblestones. Raindrops flew from his caped overcoat. A carriage rattled past, harness jingling and wheels clattering. He averted his face, then ducked into the mews behind the row of town houses.

Shadows darkened the narrow passage, and the odors of rubbish and droppings tainted the damp air. The stamping of a hoof came from inside a stable. At the third house, he spied the plain wooden door that marked the servants' entrance.

The knob turned easily and he stepped inside. He paused, orienting himself in the murky corridor. A faint, musky aroma hinted at decadent pleasures. From the front of the house came the clink of cutlery, the whining complaint of a woman, and the shrill laughter of another. To his left lay the door to the basement kitchen; he could smell the stench of boiled cabbage and fried fish. The door to his right hid the stairwell, and he mounted the steep steps in the unlit shaft.

In the second-floor passageway, lewd paintings cluttered the walls. A golden arm of light beckoned him toward an open doorway.

He walked quickly, quietly. He would take her unawares when she returned from dinner. He would put an end to her plans once and for all.

Stepping through the portal, he stopped dead.

She was *here*.

At the dressing table, his quarry sat on a gold-fringed stool. The hissing of the coal fire must have masked his footfalls, for she did not notice his presence. Or perhaps she was too absorbed in grooming her hair.

She looked young, no more than eighteen. Not that her age mattered; she was old enough in the ways of corruption. And like others of her calling, Miss Isabel Darling was an expert at controlling men.

But for once she had met her match.

She admired herself in the oval mirror, turning her head this way and that, her eyes half closed as if she were entranced by her own beauty. Russet strands blazed amid the rich brown mass that curled down past her waist. Each stroke of the brush lifted her hair, teasing him with glimpses of a curvaceous form clad in a copper silk wrapper.

His body responded with untimely appetite. His blood heated and his loins tightened. With senseless greed, he wanted to abandon his mission, to avail himself of her services instead.

Damn her.

He flexed his fingers and walked into the boudoir, his boots making no sound on the plush rose-pink carpet. An opened door in the far wall revealed a room dominated by a four-poster bed with a mirrored headboard and gaudy gold hangings. The bed where she serviced her customers.

He stopped directly behind her. His thin, black kid gloves descended to her shoulders, his fingers curling lightly into her tender flesh. Her skin felt like a babe's, warm and satiny and unblemished.

Her brush froze in mid-stroke, and her startled gaze flew to his in the gilt-framed mirror. Her eyes were wide and sherry-brown, fringed by thick lashes.

. She gasped, her bosom lifting, luring his attention downward. He leaned closer, drawn to the feast of her breasts. Though it might earn him a place in hell, he wanted to taste her—

With a wild cry, she pivoted on the stool. The hairbrush flashed out and whacked him in the ribs. The blow thundered through his chest. Her face fierce with savagery, she whipped her arm back for another strike.

He seized her wrist. "I wouldn't do that, Miss Darling."

"Who are you?" she demanded. "Who let you in here?"

"I showed myself in."

She jerked against his grip. "Get out. Before I scream."

"Go ahead. The other women are too far away to hear."

He could sense her fear. It was there in the flaring of her slim nose and the trembling of her lips. He relished his power over her. One sharp twist and he could break the fragile bones of her wrist. He could punish her for what she had done. For what she intended to do.

He pried the brush from her fingers and set it down on the dressing table. Then he planted his hands on either side of her and murmured into her ear, "That's no way to treat a guest. It's bad for business."

Isabel Darling reared back and blinked warily. "I don't know who you are, but I did not invite you here. This house is closed."

"Not to the Duke of Lynwood."

"The duke—?" Brazenly direct, she looked him up and down—white cravat and caped greatcoat, tan breeches, and polished Hessians. She gave a toss of her head, causing her long, wavy hair to shift around her shapely figure, brushing places that iron control denied him. "You're too young to be His Grace. Too . . . too . . ."

"Civilized," he said with a note of derision. She couldn't begin to fathom how different he and his sire were.

Isabel Darling sat watching him. "You're Lynwood's son," she said slowly. "You're Justin Culver. Earl of Kern."

He stood back, acknowledging her words with a mocking bow. "I see you've done your research."

She looked into the mirror and deftly wound her hair into a loose topknot, securing the luxuriant dark curls with tortoiseshell pins. The utter femininity of her action bewitched him. The urge to press his lips to her soft skin warred with his sense of purpose. "Go away," she said. "My business is with Lynwood."

"Your business is with me. My father is indisposed, and I am handling his affairs."

"This is a matter of some delicacy," she said, clasping her hands on the dressing table. "I'm willing to wait until I can speak to the duke."

"No. We'll settle things now."

"On the contrary, I must insist—"

"Insist all you like, Miss Darling. It will do you no good." Kern spoke in an uncompromising tone. "I've read those bogus memoirs—or at least the portion you sent to him."

She countered his gaze with a frigid glare of her own. "Do you always open letters marked 'Private and Confidential'? It is not the honorable thing to do." Turning from him, she fussed with her hair again. "Now go away."

Kern's chest throbbed with bottled-up rage. She would never see his father. Nor would anyone outside his family.

Controlling his temper, he leaned down, scowling at her in the mirror. "Heed me well," he stated. "You'll deal with me, and me alone. I'll wager you didn't bargain on *that* when you put together your vicious little scheme."

For the length of several heartbeats, Isabel Darling stared at his reflection. An aura of startled purity haloed her. Then a sultry smile transformed her face, banishing the illusion of innocence.

She rose gracefully from the stool, a dainty woman who barely reached his collarbone. As she walked away from him, her hips undulated with subtle sensuality. The coppery sheath did not reveal so much of her slim figure as he'd expected. Yet Isabel Darling embodied male fantasies.

His fantasies.

"Say what you have come here to say, then," she murmured.

"You are in possession of an obscene work involving my father. If you dare to publish it, I shall see you arrested for libel."

"Prove the memoirs false, then. That will make for a lively court case indeed, m'lord."

He stood very still, hating her audacity and hating even more to admit she was right. Isabel Darling possessed the means to sully his good name, to make his father a laughingstock, to subject his family to gossip and ostracism. And her proposition could not have come at a worse time.

"His Grace misused my mother," Miss Darling went on, picking up a pink feather boa from the chaise and caressing the plumage. "Everyone shall know of his vile behavior. Unless, of course, you comply with my request."

"Request." Kern let out a harsh laugh. "Extortion is more the word."

"*Is* that the word?" She tapped her forefinger against her small chin. "Hmm. I should call it justice."

"Justice? You think to coerce my father into sponsoring you. To pass *you* off as a lady. To present a strumpet's bastard to the *ton*."

Her gaze was unwavering, shameless. "Yes."

Kern paced the over-furnished boudoir, loathing the dissipated life it represented. The carnality *she* represented— the pain of broken lives, the stigma of degradation and dishonor. "That is ludicrous. You have no breeding. You don't belong in polite society."

"It is no more ludicrous than *your* father mincing about at the royal court, pretending to be respectable."

"His Grace of Lynwood has the blood of kings flowing through his veins."

"And the lust of a lecher flowing through his . . ." She paused delicately. "Well, you know what."

Her reproachful demeanor angered him. She acted as if she—and her mother—had been wronged. Kern slashed his hand downward. "Your mother was a whore. She did what whores are paid to do."

Miss Darling paled, but held her chin high. Her small white fingers gripped the feather boa. "And who pays *you* to be a self-righteous snob, sir?"

"Very amusing. How much gold will it take to buy your silence?"

"I do not want your money. Entree to society will suffice."

"Where you can dupe some rich fool into marrying you? I think not."

Though she gazed steadily at him, he had the impression of some deeper purpose in her, secrets he could not fathom. "Why shouldn't I marry well?" she asked. "I want the life that was denied to my mother. She was a penniless gentlewoman seduced by Lynwood. And then abandoned to her fate."

"Melodramatic nonsense," Kern said dismissingly. "She moved on to another customer quickly enough. In fact, I would venture to say she was servicing a procession of men even while she and my father were involved."

Miss Darling's gaze wavered, and he knew in cold triumph that he'd surmised correctly. There *had* been other men. Many of them. No doubt she knew all about them from reading the memoirs.

And how many gentlemen had Isabel Darling beguiled? How many customers had run their hands down that exquisite body? How many men had shared her bed?

And for God's sake, why did *he* want to share it, too?

He strode toward her. "Don't pretend ignorance, Miss Darling. You doxies are all alike. You entertain whomever is willing to pay your price."

"Oh? No amount of money could induce me to have *you*."

"Suppose I were to agree to sponsor you. To let you into society so that you can work your trickery. What would you give me in return?"

He saw her eyes grow round as he stopped before her, mere inches away. She seemed not to notice that the boa slipped from her fingers and pooled at her feet. The air felt charged, as if he'd been struck by lightning. He had come here expecting to confront a coarse, well-seasoned strumpet, not this dainty girl with dark eyes and fine features. As much as her scheme enraged him, he had to admire her pluck. She did not cower, not even now.

His body was on fire for her. But he kept his hands at his sides, even when her lashes fluttered slightly, a sign of submissiveness. She had a soft, willing mouth, and her lips were parted, revealing the gleam of pearly white teeth and the dark promise of pleasure.

Never in his life had Kern propositioned a common whore. Yet she goaded him beyond control. He recklessly bent his head to her, tilting up her chin with one fingertip. "Witch," he muttered. "You've gone about this all wrong. It would be far more profitable for you to seek *my* favor."

Sparks of gold glittered in her brown eyes. He could feel her quivering like a mare scenting her mate. Then she spun away from him and retreated.

She took up a position behind a gilt chair. Her rigid stance conveyed anger, yet when she spoke, her voice was calm. "You're as disgusting as your father," she said. "You'll introduce me to society—or I shall publish the memoirs within one month's time."

Kern clenched his teeth. What a bloody fool he was for letting her charms distract him. There would be the devil to pay if his father's randy exploits were printed for all the world to read. The scandal would taint his entire family, including his fiancée, the naïve Lady Helen Jeffries. God knew, the disgrace might destroy their betrothal.

Yet he would not—could not—succumb to this black-mail. It went against every principle he held dear.

Kern stalked toward Isabel Darling. She held her ground like a defiant martyr standing up to a lion. No, like an amoral bitch. Her physical beauty masked the ugliness of her character.

This time, he gave rein to his fury. He encircled her delicate neck with his hands. Through his thin gloves, he could feel the swift beating of her pulse. "You play a dangerous game, Miss Darling. But you'll have to find yourself another dupe."

"You daren't refuse me," she said in a low tone.

"On the contrary." He scanned her in contempt. "It would be easier to turn a leper into a lady than you."

A hiss of displeasure escaped her. She stared boldly up at him, defying his insult. Even now he was seduced by the softness of her flesh. He was disgusted by his urge to bear her down to the floor and take the release she sold to other men . . .

"Well, well," drawled a husky female voice from the doorway. "Here's a charming little scene."

That accusing tone snapped Isabel to her senses. She stepped back so fast the room spun. Or perhaps it was the giddy effect from gazing too long into Lord Kern's merciless green eyes. She had been transfixed by his towering presence, by the smell of rain mixed with the dangerous scent of man.

The epitome of arrogance, he calmly turned toward their visitor, as if he hadn't just wrapped his fingers around Isabel's throat. She could still feel the pressure of those hands, smooth and menacing, capable of snuffing out her life. Subduing a shudder, she watched Callie stroll into the boudoir.

The exaggerated sway of her hips called attention to her voluptuous figure. The years had been kind to Callandra Hughes; few lines marred her face and the brassy blond of her hair hid any gray. She adored men—or rather, she adored the attention men afforded her.

Like a performer in a music hall, she made a show of removing the lace fichu from her bodice and exposing the low cut of her maroon gown. "Shame on you, Isabel," she purred, without taking her smoke-blue eyes from Lord Kern. "You oughtn't have kept such a handsome buck all to yourself."

Isabel stiffened. "This is a private conversation."

"I'm sure it is." Callie sidled up to Lord Kern, leaning forward to give him a better look at her breasts. "And who might you be, sir?"

He ignored the question. "Excuse me, madam. I was on my way out."

"So soon?" Pouting prettily, she slid her arm through his. "Perhaps you'd prefer the company of a woman more experienced in the fine art of pleasuring gentlemen—"

"Aunt Callie," Isabel broke in. "There's a matter I wish to discuss with you."

"Later—"

"Now. My guest can find his own way out."

Sullenness drew down the corners of that ripe cherry mouth. But Callie released his arm. The earl made a formal bow to both women. His sharp gaze pierced Isabel for a moment, and again she felt that strange pressure in the pit of her stomach. He had alarmed her from the moment he had first appeared behind her in the mirror, frightening her half to death. Without a backward glance, he strode out of the boudoir.

It would be easier to turn a leper into a lady than you.

Isabel closed her fingers around a scent bottle, tempted to hurl it after him. She hated the way he made her feel, as if she were a worm he'd like to squash beneath his elegantly shod foot. Let him think her a fortune hunter, an adventuress. He was nothing but a rich snob, believing himself superior toward those less fortunate.

He might think their quarrel resolved, but she knew better.

"So," said Callie, drawing Isabel's attention away from the empty doorway. "What is this all-important matter you wish to discuss?"

Isabel fought the wash of warmth in her cheeks. "There's nothing. I only didn't want you to go with him."

"I see." Looking thoughtful, Callie sashayed around Isabel. "So Aurora's little girl has a gentleman caller at last. Who is he?"

"He's an arrogant nod-cock, that's who."

Callie arched one perfect eyebrow. "Well, aren't all

men?'' She pranced to the dressing table and primped her golden curls while watching Isabel in the mirror. ''I've been wondering why you've been acting so secretive lately. Now I know. You finally have yourself an admirer.''

Isabel scrambled for an explanation. ''His father was a friend of my mother's, that's all.''

''How amusing. Now the son is taken with the daughter.'' Callie regarded Isabel as if seeing her with new eyes. ''I shouldn't be surprised. You've grown up to be quite as pretty as Aurora, you know.''

Isabel's throat closed. She wanted to deny it. Though she could look at herself and glimpse an uncanny resemblance to Aurora Darling's dark beauty, she still felt like the awkward child who'd been taunted by bullies about her bastardy.

''Our Isabel has a charm all her own,'' declared the short, round woman who swept into the boudoir. Aunt Minerva, or Minnie as Isabel liked to call her, bustled around the room like a ball of energy, her aproned gown swishing purposefully as she plumped the pillows on the chaise and tidied the jars of cosmetics. ''And I, for one, should like to know what Lord Kern was doing in this house.''

''Lord Kern?'' Callie said, her lips parting in surprise. She pointed at the empty doorway, where the earl had disappeared. ''Lynwood's heir? That was *him*?''

''Aye.'' Scowling, Minnie plucked the boa from the carpet. ''I saw him walking out—he told me he came in the back entrance. And 'tis your fault, Callandra Hughes, for neglecting to lock the doors again. Any manner of riffraff might've caused us harm.''

Callie stuck out her lower lip. ''I'm no servant to be checking doors and windows.''

''You'll do your fair share, Miss Hoity-Toity, or you'll be finding yourself turning tricks on a street corner in Whitechapel.''

''Oh no, Miss Almighty Minnie.'' Callie stalked toward

the older woman. "On her deathbed, Aurora promised I'd always have a home here."

"*If* you abide by the rules of this house. And that means tending to your chores instead of lying abed till noon and primping till eventide."

"Listen, you old witch. Just because you were never as pretty as me—"

"Stop it." Isabel stepped between the two women, who stood nose to nose in the center of the room. "Stop this quarreling at once. It's beneath the both of you."

Minnie glared at Isabel for an instant. Then she lowered her head, her graying ginger hair sticking out of her mob-cap. "Forgive me. 'Tis this plaguey Irish temper what gets the best of me sometimes. Your dear mama always did chide me for it."

"Well, *I* see no need to apologize," Callie said with a toss of her blond ringlets, "since Isabel broke the rule about entertaining men in the house. She's the reason the rest of us ladies pledged to quit whoring. But perhaps our little girl isn't so innocent anymore."

Even as Minnie sucked in an angry breath, Isabel raised her hand to prevent another argument. "I sent his lordship away and that's the end of it."

"He'll be back," Callie said. "I recognize that look in a man's eyes. You've made a conquest, you mark my words." She flounced out the door and vanished with a twitch of her skirts.

"Cheeky baggage." Minnie shook her fist. "You'd think she was the Duchess of Lynwood instead of a hoary old lightskirt." The stout woman tucked the feather boa into a drawer of the highboy. "Don't mind her, dearie. I'll have a talk with her later for upsetting you."

"Please, leave it be."

"Now, now." Minnie paused in her tidying to regard Isabel. "You're as dear to me as my own daughter. I won't have anyone slandering you."

Isabel managed a distracted smile. Though they were no relation, she had grown up regarding Minnie and the other "ladies" as her aunts. Minnie had come often to visit Isabel in the country, where Aurora had sent Isabel to live under the care of a governess, far from the brothel. And when her mother had died the previous year, Isabel had returned here to London to live. She'd had no other choice. Extravagant to the end, Aurora Darling had squandered her earnings and died a pauper.

Minnie polished an alabaster goddess with a corner of her apron. "Now tell me. Why did Lord Kern come to call on you?"

Isabel opened her mouth, then closed it. She hadn't intended her aunts to find out, not yet. Now, the earl had exposed her secret.

The enormity of her dilemma struck her with shattering force. Her wobbly knees gave way and she wilted onto the chaise, hugging herself in a vain attempt to keep the pain at bay. But the effects of the vicious encounter with Lord Kern rolled over her again, and she felt her eyes heat with bitter tears of frustration.

"Holy Mother of God." Minnie clapped her hand to her cheek. " 'Tis true we need money, but surely you didn't sell yourself to his lordship."

"Of course not!" Isabel remembered that appalling moment when he had accused her of being a whore and she had wondered—ever so briefly—what it would be like to disrobe for Lord Kern, to let him touch her in all the ways she'd heard about, eavesdropping while the aunts gossiped.

"Did he insult you, then?" Sounding outraged, Minnie sat down beside Isabel on the chaise and placed a comforting arm around her. "Say the word and I'll go after that fancy bloodsucker."

"It wasn't anything like that."

"Then why did the man steal in here to see you?"

"Because . . ." Isabel considered lying, but the keen

look in those hazel eyes demanded the truth, just as it had since she was a toddler and had taken one of her mother's shiny diamond earbobs. Minnie's familiar scent of musk washed over Isabel, and she was tempted to blurt out the fears and suspicions that had goaded her since reading Aurora's memoirs. "Because I'd written to his father."

"To Lynwood? And what would a wee girl like you be wanting with that randy old goat?"

Struggling against an imprudent confession, Isabel shot to her feet. "Excuse me. I-I really don't wish to talk about this anymore."

She half ran into the bedroom—her mother's old bedroom—and opened drawers randomly until she found a square of embroidered linen amid the array of scanty undergarments. With shaky strokes, she wiped her cheeks. Blast Lord Kern for coming here. Blast his haughty, interfering hide!

It would be easier to turn a leper into a lady than you.

Isabel tilted her head back and stared at the ceiling with its fancy gilded cornices. His insult lodged like a thorn in her breast. He couldn't know how deeply, how painfully, he'd struck. He couldn't know how many years she had dreamed of being accepted by the society that would scorn the love child of a courtesan.

Seeing Lord Kern reflected in the mirror had been like viewing the devil himself: those eyes an uncanny shade of green, his hair as black as sin, his expression so fierce it could curdle milk. Big and bold, he had loomed over her, catching her off guard and laying ruin to weeks of planning.

She had anticipated bargaining with a man of weak disposition, an aging aristocrat without scruples, a man easy to sway to her purpose. All noblemen wanted to protect their precious reputations. They had visited her mother under cover of darkness and had left before dawn, the cowards.

Now Isabel cursed her own naïve lack of foresight. She should have gone to Lynwood House unannounced. She should have demanded an interview with the duke. So much depended upon her acceptance into the *ton*. It was the first step to determining the truth. Heaven help her if the duke took that truth with him to his grave.

" 'Tis the memoirs, isn't it?" Minnie said from behind. "You've found Aurora's memoirs. And you're using them to some foolish purpose."

Isabel spun around to see the middle-aged woman standing in the doorway, her hands on her ample hips. "How did you know about Mama's journal?" Isabel blurted. "I only just discovered it a month ago."

Minnie shrugged. "I remember she did a lot of writing in that little book. Though she never would talk much about it."

Isabel had come across the slender volume hidden deep within the clothespress. "I'm sorry. I should have told you when I found the memoirs, but . . ." She paused, biting her lip. For once she hadn't wanted to share her thoughts with her "aunts." The diary had been too scandalous, too explicit. And too revealing of her mother's follies.

Minnie stood motionless. "What overblown nonsense did Aurora describe in her book?"

"She related stories about . . . the men who had shared her life over the years. That's all." In her typical giddy style, Aurora had been vague on dates while waxing poetic on her torrid love affairs with a series of noblemen.

Isabel had read the book from cover to cover while locked in the privacy of her bedroom. She had been stunned by the eye-opening peek into her mother's risqué life. It was one thing to imagine her mother entertaining gentlemen callers; it was quite another to learn the details of her sexual exploits. And when Isabel had turned the last page, her queasy fascination had been eclipsed by the shock of that final, damning entry . . .

"Are you blackmailing his lordship, then?" Minnie's broad features looked somber, disapproving. "Have you threatened to publish those memoirs unless he pays up?"

Minnie had guessed only part of the truth—the wrong part. Isabel hedged. "Mama didn't leave much else of value. You know how thoughtlessly she spent money. It would be wonderful if we could move out of London— you and Aunt Callie and Aunt Di and Aunt Persy. Aunt Persy especially needs the fresh air of the country. And the rest of us . . . we need to be free of all *this*." Isabel waved her hand at the frivolous room with its rose-pink satin and gilt doves and lacy frills. It was like living atop a wedding cake, a dismal reminder of her mother's lost dreams.

"That's not the whole of it," Minnie said slowly. "I wonder if you're curious about your father. What did the diary say about him?"

Isabel's stomach gave a sickening lurch. Walking to the window, she parted the curtains and gazed out into the dusk-darkened street. "Mama called him Apollo. She didn't give his real name—she only said he was a gentleman." Despising the twinge of yearning inside herself, she asked in a low voice, "Are you sure Mama never spoke of him to you?"

"No." Minnie loosed a heavy sigh. "Aurora could keep a secret, I'll say that much for her. She lived alone here till the time of your birth. By then, he'd abandoned her— and you." She paused. "But Lynwood is not your father, if that's what you're thinking. Aurora didn't meet the duke until after you were born."

Isabel had known as much from the memoirs. She kept her face averted, for Minnie had always been able to read her so well. "Thank heaven for small favors."

" 'Tisn't wise, this course you're following, girl." Minnie's mournful voice came from behind, along with the sounds of her shuffling around the bedroom, rattling the quill pens on the desk and then thumping the pillows on the bed. "Your father isn't interested in you. He never once bothered to visit you—or even to tell you his name."

"He sent money to Mama for my schooling."

"Humph. The minute Aurora died, he stopped those paltry payments. But we're not in the poorhouse yet, so you needn't go looking for him."

"I never said I was looking for him," Isabel retorted.

She kept a firm grip on the velvet drapery. Long ago when she had been young enough to believe in fairy tales, she had fancied her father the king of a magical realm. When the village children jeered at her, she yearned to prove she was indeed a princess. She waited until a rare visit to London, waited until the moment Mama enfolded her in a perfumed embrace, and then she let her questions pour forth.

She would never forget the way Aurora's face had crumpled. Weeping, she had retired to her bedroom. Watching her vivacious mother overtaken by melancholy had shaken Isabel, and her youthful pain hardened into a lasting scorn for the man who had forsaken them. She had no interest in him as a father—not now or ever.

But she had another reason for wanting to find him. A reason that had nothing whatever to do with money. If all went well, soon he would know she had deduced his identity from reading the memoirs.

"You still look overwrought, child." Minnie's voice intruded, her gaze sharp and searching. "Did Aurora by chance write about her final illness?"

Isabel's mouth went dry. "Only one brief passage."

"And what did she say?" Minnie ventured closer. "Tell me, dearie. You can trust your auntie. I've always had your best interests at heart."

That soft, coaxing voice soothed Isabel's misgivings. She hadn't told Minnie the whole truth, lest her aunt try to stop her. She hadn't admitted that one purpose made her determined to enter the upper echelon of society no matter what the risk. She had made her vow upon reading that last, frightful entry in the memoirs.

Yet perhaps she *should* tell. Aunt Minnie would find out soon enough, anyway.

Resolutely, she turned to face her aunt. Minnie stood with her mobcapped head cocked to the side, her doughy features radiating concern. Taking a tremulous breath, Isabel put her terrible suspicion into words. "Mama wrote . . . that someone wanted to stop her from completing her journal."

Minnie's eyes narrowed to slits. "Stop her? Who?"

"One of her gentlemen lovers." Willing away the quaver in her voice, Isabel voiced the horror that had haunted her day and night for the past month. "You see, he poisoned Mama. She was murdered."

Zeus came to me last night.

His impromptu visit to my boudoir startled and delighted me, for it was as if no time had passed since our dreadful quarrel all those years ago. Like myself, His Grace of L—— has endured the ravages of age. Yet he seemed eager once again to play the bull to my Europa, and I was most happy to lead him on a merry chase. Only after he had conquered me most gloriously did his true purpose come clear: he ordered me to cease writing these memoirs.

I cannot fathom how L—— learned of my secret pursuit, for I had not spoken to him in many years. Perhaps I might have found out the name of his spy had I not been so angered. Like Hera in her highest fury, I sent my Zeus away with a wicked cuff to his ear.

And now that one has learned my secret, the others may well follow. They will not care to see their exploits in print, these naughty old lovers of mine. They are men in high places, as mighty as the immortal gods on Mount Olympus for whom they are named—and as lusty a mélange as any woman could ever hope to know.

Indeed, the longer I ponder the possibilities, the more ardently I anticipate a reunion with each and every one of them.

—The True Confessions of a Ladybird

ᜳ Chapter 2 ᜰ

*I*t was *her*.

Staring out the window of the Lynwood coach, Kern leaned forward, his body charged with awareness. Only moments ago, he had exited Westminster Palace, having left the Lords Chamber during a debate over an agricultural bill. Unlike the heirs to other titles who idled away the hours at gaming tables, Kern believed in preparing for the time when he would take his rightful place in Parliament. But today a restlessness had made it impossible to sit still. Today his mind kept wandering from politics. With irritating persistence, he found himself thinking about *her*.

As the coach started out of the government complex and into the neighboring slums, he reached by habit to close the curtains. When the vehicle slowed at the intersection of two narrow streets, he saw her.

A woman strolled the pavement beside the ramshackle brick buildings. A slanting shaft of late sunlight set fire to her dark hair.

Though he could see only the woman's back, he recognized that slender form and hip-swaying gait. It was the same figure that had haunted his dreams for the past three days and nights.

She veered toward a husky, bearded man who beckoned from an alleyway. The lout offered her a bottle. As she snatched it up and drank greedily, he yanked her to him and fondled her backside.

Kern grasped the door handle. His legs tensed from the urge to spring to her aid. Then the coach passed the couple, enabling him to see her face. She had the coarse, sallow skin of a slattern. Gin dribbled from the corner of her thin mouth. Shadows robbed the glory from her hair.

The talons of tension eased, releasing Kern. He forced himself to relax against the leather cushions. How ridiculous to mistake a common streetwalker for the beautiful and cunning Isabel Darling.

Moodily, he gazed upon the teeming masses of people; the thieves and coiners and beggars; the whores who prowled for customers within sight of Westminster Abbey. Miss Darling had no reason to ply her trade here in Devil's Acre. She owned a fancy brothel several miles away. And she stood to make a tidy profit by publishing her mother's memoirs.

Scowling, Kern shifted position on the seat. He could well imagine the sensation such a book would cause. All of London would scramble to purchase a copy and read about Aurora's noble lovers. The scandal would rock society. It would bring shame upon the time-honored name of Lynwood. As head of the family during his father's chronic illness, Kern braced himself for the coming crisis.

And there was something he must do. Now. Before he was tempted to put it off again.

Kern dreaded the task. Yet he felt duty-bound to warn George Jeffries, the Marquess of Hathaway. All of his life he had regarded Lord Hathaway as the model of propriety and gentlemanly behavior. Hathaway was a venerable statesman who had the ear of the prime minister. Over the years, he had been more a father to Kern than the Duke of Lynwood.

The ties between the two families stretched back for generations. Kern's grandfather had fostered Hathaway and his infant brother as orphaned youths, and later Hathaway had returned the favor by providing Kern with the guidance sorely needed by a boy whose father disappeared for weeks—even months—at a time, squiring one mistress after another, reappearing only long enough to get another child on his beleaguered duchess.

Kern remembered his mother as an unsmiling madonna who had kept to her chambers. She had wept at the slightest provocation, and he'd known, even as a lad in leading strings, not to bother her. Yet still he had adored her, and he had lived for the rare times when she'd half-smothered him with attention. He could understand now the sorrow that had ruled her life. She had endured a worthless lecher for a husband. And Kern was the only one of her six children to survive infancy.

She had died when he was ten years old. He had the hazy memory of seeing her lying in the coffin, her slim hands crossed over her white bodice. When it came time to close the lid, he had panicked, imagining her shrouded in darkness, defiled by worms. He had thrown himself against the vicar. He had kicked and screamed, and Lord Hathaway had borne him outside, holding him until he cried himself to exhaustion.

Lynwood had not been present. He had been off on a jaunt to the Continent, and though he'd rushed home upon receiving news of his wife's grave illness, he had arrived a week too late for her funeral.

Likewise, on the morning Kern was to set off for his first term at Eton, his father had been insensible after a night of carousing. Hathaway had stopped by to slip Kern a purse of gold coins and to wave adieu as the coach set off.

Kern had always known he would wed Hathaway's only daughter when she came of age. Like him, Lady Helen Jeffries had lost her mother at a tender age. Helen was eighteen now, and he was twenty-eight. They were to marry in two months' time, near the close of the Season. The match was utterly satisfying to him, for Lady Helen was both genteel and sweet-tempered, and the alliance would join two great dynasties.

If Hathaway still considered him an acceptable son-in-law. *If* Kern could weather the storm whipped up by one Isabel Darling.

His fingers tensed around the tasseled hand strap as the carriage turned the corner into Grosvenor Square. Curse the blackmailing purveyor of smut. If ever he saw her again, he might be tempted to strangle the bitch, to put an end to her scheming once and for all.

The horses came to a stop in front of a stately town house built of pale stone. A footman carrying a lighted torch opened the door of the carriage. Donning his hat, Kern stepped out onto the paving stones and paused a moment, breathing the cool evening air scented by the ever-present tang of coal smoke. He braced himself to face Hathaway.

Discretion was the marquess's most valued trait. Now Kern had to inform him that his daughter, by virtue of her betrothal, could be made an object of ridicule. And Kern was honor-bound to offer to withdraw his suit.

His steps leaden, he mounted the stairs to the pillared doorway where a servant ushered him inside the elegant entrance hall. He knew this place as well as his own house, from the marble stairway to the ancestral portraits on the paneled walls. He said to the footman, "Is Hathaway in?"

The man took his cloak and hat. "Aye, m'lord, but his lordship is engaged with an out-of-town guest."

Blast. Kern was impatient to see the unpleasant task over with and done. Now he would have to cool his heels. "Show me in, then." Hearing the hum of voices, he motioned the servant forward, following him into the high-ceilinged drawing room with its green-striped chaises and gilt chairs.

"Lord Kern," the footman intoned.

Kern's gaze was drawn to the mantelpiece where his host stood. A small yet imposing man, Lord Hathaway exuded the prideful presence of a war hero. His bushy white eyebrows were drawn into a frown, his salt-and-pepper hair unnaturally rumpled.

Nearby sat his younger brother, the Reverend Lord Raymond Jeffries, pastor of St. George's Church. Beneath his fine clerical garb, his shoulders were slumped. With both hands, he gripped the ivory knob of his walking stick, keeping the blunted tip planted in the rug. His hawk-nosed face wore an uncharacteristic look of sullen resentment.

The charged animosity in the air startled Kern. He had the distinct impression that his presence vexed Lord Raymond. That in itself baffled Kern, for he had always been welcomed as a family member.

On a chaise angled away from the door, two ladies perched side by side, their backs to him. The fair-haired Lady Helen Jeffries turned to grace him with a smile, her face so guileless he felt a surge of determination to fight for her hand.

But one glance at her companion struck all tender sentiment from him.

She alone did not pivot to face him. A gray leghorn bonnet hid her features from his view. The late-afternoon sunlight set fire to the dark ringlets that draped one shoulder. She held herself like a princess, her shoulders squared and her neck straight. Just three days ago, he had placed his hands on that smooth white skin . . .

No. He must be hallucinating. Again.

Kern walked closer, rounding the corner of the chaise. She sat with her hands demurely folded in her lap. A lace modesty piece was tucked into the décolletage of her sober gray gown.

And then he found himself staring into the slyly sensual brown eyes of Isabel Darling.

Denial clawed at his chest. How the devil had a whore's bastard finagled her way into one of the most respected houses in England? What lies had she told to Hathaway? What truths to Lady Helen?

The fire hissed and spat as if in evil amusement. Her smile tinged with triumph, Isabel Darling rose from the chaise and came toward him, dipping into a graceful curtsy at his feet.

"Lord Kern," she purred. "What an honor. I've been hearing so much about you from my cousin."

"Cousin," he repeated numbly.

"Why, yes. I am Lady Helen's cousin. Miss Isabel . . . Darcy." She paused delicately, gazing up from beneath the fringe of her lashes as if daring him to challenge her false name.

A scathing denunciation seared his throat, but before he could speak, Helen hurried over to link arms with Isabel. "Isn't this a wonderful surprise, Justin? I never even knew I *had* a cousin. She's only just arrived in the city."

"And already introducing herself to the gentlemen," the Reverend Lord Raymond said acidly, flexing his fingers around the ivory head of his cane. "Someone had best teach the gel how to behave."

"Oh dear, have I committed a *faux pas*?" Isabel lifted her hand to her cheek, blushing at will. "Pray excuse my rustic manners."

"For shame, Uncle Raymond—embarrassing our guest." Helen escorted Isabel back to the chaise. "Dear Isabel. I may call you Isabel, mayn't I?"

"Nothing would please me more."

"You mustn't take offense," Helen said, patting Isabel's hand. "We're all family here. And it is most uncivil of Uncle and Papa to act so grumpy. Why, you've scarcely shaken the traveling dust from your clothes."

"I fear I'm imposing upon you—all of you." Isabel bowed her head, revealing the tender curve of her neck.

"As I was saying, the untimely death of my parents has left me in rather reduced circumstances. Perhaps if you could recommend a respectable boardinghouse somewhere . . ."

"Heavens, no. We won't hear of you staying with strangers." Helen giggled. "That is, we're strangers, too, but I hope not for long. I hope we shall soon be fast friends."

"How very kind you are," Isabel murmured. "It's a comfort to have a safe place to stay . . . among people who care about me."

She lied so prettily. Kern felt the ugly rise of rage. "You'll be wanting a post as a governess or companion," he said. "Allow me to help you secure one. Immediately."

"Thank you, m'lord. But surely my travails can be of little notice to one so exalted."

"On the contrary, I admire those who seek gainful employment. Do you perchance have any special *skills*?"

Her skin paled at his innuendo. Her gaze locked with his, and he saw the resentment there, the obstinate determination to push her way into the *ton*. She flashed him a brilliant smile. "I regret you're too late in your offer of aid, m'lord. When you walked in just now, my cousin was proposing I accept a place in her household."

"Not just a place—you'll have a home here." Helen's eyes glinted with sympathetic tears. "Isabel will be *my* companion. She'll accompany me into society. Won't she, Papa?"

The marquess's granite countenance gave away nothing of his thoughts. "Of course," he said tonelessly. "Miss Darcy must remain here with us for the Season. I insist upon it."

Kern scowled from another jolt of shock. Why would Hathaway accept her trumped-up tale? Surely he knew better . . .

In the throes of denial, Kern gripped the back of a chair

and wished it were her throat. "Where exactly do you hail from, Miss Darby?"

"Darcy," she corrected, her direct gaze taunting him. "I've come by mail coach all the way from Northumbria, a journey of nearly four days."

"Strange. By your accent, I would have taken you for a Londoner."

"My dear, departed mother spent her childhood here. No doubt I learnt my speech pattern from her."

And your loose morals. He was tempted to call her bluff. But Helen was biting her lip in anxiety, and he couldn't bear to hurt her—at least not until he got to the bottom of this entanglement.

He swung toward her father. "Hathaway? You've never mentioned a Darcy branch of your family."

The older man stood rigidly at attention. A troubled light flared in the steady darkness of his eyes. "The connection is somewhat distant. But we welcome Miss Darcy nonetheless."

"I see. And did she provide a letter of reference?"

"That isn't possible. Her family is gone now." The warning note in his voice invited no more questions.

Kern subjected him to a hard stare. Hathaway knew her true identity. How? Surely *he* could not have consorted with Aurora Darling. Hathaway could not be one of the men described in the memoirs.

Could he?

Impossible.

Then Hathaway cast a guarded glance down at his brother, whose smile had the fixed quality of a man gritting his teeth. Ten years the younger, the Reverend Lord Raymond Jeffries had been a rake in his youth. He limped from the effects of a long-ago duel that had been hushed up by his elder brother. The incident had induced him to settle down with a proper society wife and to obtain a living through Hathaway's patronage.

Lord Raymond. *Of course.*

At one time, Lord Raymond must have engaged in an illicit affair with Aurora Darling. And, as always, Hathaway was protecting his younger brother from scandal.

The churchman got to his feet with the aid of his cane. "Would that I had time to spare for idle chitchat. But I've a sermon to prepare for the morrow."

"And it had best be a lively one," Helen said, shaking a teasing finger at him. "Cousin Isabel and I shall be listening from the family pew."

" 'I am the good shepherd, and know my sheep.' That will be the subject of my sermon. None of us can fool the Almighty, for He always knows what secrets lie within our hearts." He cast a dark look at Isabel, then excused himself.

"I'll see you to the door," Hathaway said.

The two men left the drawing room, the sharp tap-tapping of Lord Raymond's cane conveying an unspoken anger. Their heads were bent together, and Kern restrained himself from marching after them and demanding answers.

He would have his interview with Hathaway. He would press for an end to this charade. This time, Hathaway must not protect his brother from scandal. A greater wrong could be done if Isabel Darling succeeded in her scheme to wed an aristocrat.

Kern felt a soft touch on his arm. Lady Helen smiled up at him. "Will you be staying to dinner, Justin?"

She had the clear eyes and porcelain skin of a girl straight out of the schoolroom, but for once, her naïveté annoyed him. "Am I invited?"

Helen's expression took on a quizzical, wounded quality. "Certainly. You're always welcome."

His sharpness shamed him. Of course she could not fathom the source of his ill-humor. She had no darkness in her, only light.

He placed his hand tenderly over hers. "If it pleases you, of course I shall stay to dinner."

"Are you sure?" she asked doubtfully. "If you're otherwise engaged . . ."

"I'm not."

Isabel Darling stood watching, one of her eyebrows arched. *She* saw everything. And judging by the curve of her beautifully shaped lips, she enjoyed his struggle. "I daresay *I* am the cause of his lordship's hesitation, my lady." She leaned forward conspiratorially, and for one frozen moment he feared she meant to spill her secret, to contaminate Helen's innocence. Then Isabel went on blithely, "No doubt he fears your country-mouse cousin might embarrass him by using the wrong fork."

Helen giggled. "Oh, Justin is not so fastidious as *that*. And you are certainly not a mouse."

"I'm dressed as one, that much you cannot deny." Those sultry dark eyes laughed at him, and against his will, he felt the pull of her wicked attraction. "What say you, m'lord? Would it be easier to turn a leper into a lady than me?"

The chit had thrown his own words back at him. With a stiff bow, he conceded her diabolical cleverness. "You exaggerate, Miss *Darcy*. I wouldn't dream of playing Pygmalion, though I suspect you'll do well enough on your own."

Their gazes held, his hard and hers mysterious . . . enticing . . . alluring. He could not take his eyes from her, though he was aware of Helen standing beside him, oblivious to the deep undercurrents.

"The Season is off to a grand start," Helen said with a clap of her hands, her face shining. "Oh, how I'm looking forward to it. We shall all have such fun together in the weeks to come."

* * *

She had done it. She had captured a place in the inner circle!

Her knees weak, Isabel sank onto a padded stool in Lady Helen's spacious dressing room. It was a relief to escape the volatile atmosphere of the drawing room and Lord Kern's hostile presence. When he had walked in, Isabel had feared for the first time in her life she might swoon. She had waited for him to expose her, braced herself to hear him denounce her as a fraud.

But he had kept his own counsel. Clearly he would protect his fiancée from unpleasantness no matter what the cost to his pride. His devotion threw Isabel off balance. What would it be like to inspire such love in a man?

She crushed the wistful sentiment. Lord Kern had merely been practicing the gallantry of a gentleman toward his lady. Hathaway had been no less protective of his only daughter.

The marquess had been furious this afternoon when she had showed him and his brother a certain damning entry copied from her mother's memoirs. Hathaway's face had grown so red she feared he might suffer an apoplectic fit. To his credit, he had not blustered or tried to deny the truth as Lord Raymond had done at first. Instead, Hathaway had stared at her for the longest time, his thoughts hidden behind his flinty features. Then, just as her spirits had begun to sink, he had agreed to her terms. To protect his brother's reputation, Hathaway would take her into his own house and present her as a distant relation.

Unlike Lord Kern. *He* had refused to sponsor her. He would have throttled her for certain if he knew she suspected his father of murder.

A rightness of purpose burned within Isabel. Minnie had provided further confirmation of the suspicion her mother had written about in the memoirs. Isabel's mind leapt to the proof she had learned three days ago.

After she had told Minnie about the murder, the older

woman had sunk down onto the bed and stared at the floor for a long moment before lifting her stunned gaze. "You think 'twas Lynwood who poisoned Aurora?"

"Or one of her other lovers." Agony gripped Isabel's throat. "Who else could it have been?"

Minnie said slowly, "I never thought to mention this to you before, dearie. But now . . . I wonder if I should."

"What?" Isabel hastened to Minnie and grasped her work-wrinkled hands, hands that had once been soft and white. "Do you know who he is? Do you know who did this to Mama?"

"The night before Aurora took ill, I saw a gentleman go into her bedroom. 'Twas too dark to see his face, and I thought little of it at the time, for she liked her privacy . . ." As if emerging from a trance, Minnie gave a sharp shake of her mobcapped head. "Nay, you must be mistaken. Your mama died of the ague, that's all."

"I'm not mistaken, and what you saw proves it," Isabel said fervently. "That man must have administered the poison. And I'm going to find him."

Dismay widened Minnie's eyes. Her hands squeezed Isabel's. "Don't do anything rash, child. You can't fight such powerful men. Leave it be."

"I cannot. Somehow, I'll track him down. I'll make him pay for his crime."

From that emotion-charged moment, Isabel had refused to listen to any further remonstrations from her aunt. Nothing could stop her from seeking justice. Not the daunting task of infiltrating the *ton*. Not the prospect of posing as a lady. Not even the threat of facing arrogant aristocrats like Lord Kern.

"Dear cousin, you look lost in thought," Lady Helen said on a merry laugh. "Do stop woolgathering and tell me, what do you think of these?"

Isabel blinked at the girl who stood before her. Helen held her arms outstretched to display a pair of gowns, one

of dotted white net over a pale green underskirt, the other
of ivory silk with azure ribbons threading the short, puffed
sleeves. Both gowns were demurely fashionable. Both
were perfectly suited to a debutante of Helen's fair coloring
and slender form. By her bright eyes, she seemed to expect
a comment, so Isabel said, "They're quite pretty."

"They just arrived this morning from the dressmaker.
So which one?"

"Which one what?"

Helen giggled. "Which one would you like to wear to
dinner, of course?"

"Oh." Isabel's throat tightened. She reached out to caress the cool softness of the ivory silk. How generous of
Helen to share her wardrobe. Isabel had prepared herself
for opposition, for pacifying a spoiled, snobbish lady. But
Helen had welcomed her with open arms. Somehow, that
made the deception all the harder. "Can't I just wear what
I have on?"

"Heavens, no. Papa is most insistent on formal attire at
dinner." Helen turned to rummage through the huge ar-
moire, where a variety of frocks hung from hooks. "So is
Justin. We daren't displease them."

Isabel bristled. "Lord Kern cannot dictate how you
dress. He isn't your husband yet."

"But he will be soon." Helen whirled around, clutching
a pale-blue gown to her bosom. "Oh, doesn't he stir the
most glorious awe in you? He is so handsome, so clever,
so *perfect*, I never quite know what to say to him."

I can think of a few choice phrases. "Speak your mind,
that's all. Make him heed your opinions."

"You make it sound so easy. But I confess to fearing
I'll bore him with chatter about parties and gossip and mat-
ters of no consequence. He spends many of his days at
Parliament, you know."

"He can't be a member," Isabel blurted in surprise.
"His father is still alive."

"Justin says he's educating himself for the time when he will join the House of Lords. And I am a paper-skulled ninny when it comes to politics." Helen sighed, as if her high spirits had plummeted. "How did *you* manage to speak to him so readily?"

Helen seemed genuinely worried, and Isabel bit her tongue to keep from denouncing Lord Kern as a priggish bore. "*I* am not betrothed to him," she said. "Perhaps that's why I'm not overwhelmed by his almighty greatness."

"You must be a few years older than me, too," Helen said, before hastily adding, "Oh piffle, I don't mean to say you're on the shelf, only that you've likely had more experience with the world than me. I've been confined to the schoolroom these past eighteen years, learning the accomplishments of a lady." Her face lightened and she smiled winningly. "I am to be married on my nineteenth birthday, June the tenth. Did you know that?"

Eighteen going on nineteen. Isabel sat unmoving. Her own birthday was June the twelfth. Helen was mistaken—by strange coincidence, they were the exact same age, born two days apart. Yet how vastly different their lives had been, she growing up with a courtesan for a mother and whores as her aunts, while Helen had known the security and respect due a high-born lady.

"No," she said softly, "I didn't know."

"I am to have the most splendid wedding. It will be the pinnacle of the Season." Holding the blue gown, Helen twirled around the dressing room. "Only imagine, me walking down the aisle of St. George's, the choir singing, the roses blooming, everyone smiling. It will be as wonderful as a fairy tale."

Watching her, Isabel felt the tug of wistful yearning. A long time ago when she was five, she had dreamed of being a princess. The fantasy lured her, sweeping over her again in a warm, compelling wave. She would grow up to have silky blond hair and sky-blue eyes and skin as soft and white as the petals of a lily. She would live in a palace and never have to eat mashed turnips. She would have a dog to romp with during the day and to cuddle with at night. After all, her father was the king.

By the time Isabel turned eight, she knew the fallacy of fairy tales. She had plain reddish-brown hair and dirt-brown eyes, and her skin freckled if she ventured too long into the sunshine. She lived in a rustic country cottage and dutifully ate mashed turnips. Dogs were dirty creatures and she mustn't beg for one. After all, she had no father, only a distant mother who couldn't be bothered with selfish requests. Thus proclaimed pinch-mouthed Miss Dodd who lectured her on the accomplishments of young ladies.

By the time Isabel turned twelve, she knew she was no lady, either. She had been born, not in a fine mansion, but on the wrong side of the blanket. She endured the jeering of village gossips because she had been banished from the city. After all, her mother was busy doing wicked acts with rich gentlemen.

But on rare occasions Aurora sent for her daughter, and oh, what visits those were! In a mad flurry of extravagance and kisses, Mama would dress Isabel in laces and silks as if she were a fashion doll. In the afternoons they would watch the lords and ladies promenade in Hyde Park, and at night they would stroll past glittering mansions where the gentry dined on cream and cake, with nary a mashed turnip in sight.

Isabel had sighed along with her mother, caught up once more in the yearning to be a princess. As she grew to womanhood, her fancies expanded with the hope of meeting a prince. He would fall in love with her at first sight and carry her away on his noble steed to the castle where they would live happily ever after. She would bring Mama there. Together, they would be great ladies admired and adored by all the people in the realm.

Of course, her mother had died and reality had intruded. It always did. And here Isabel sat, at long last a resident of the palace. Except that she was not the princess. Lady Helen filled that role.

Beautiful, sweet, naïve Lady Helen, who whirled around the dressing room as if waltzing with an invisible prince.

"It's dangerous to believe in fairy tales," Isabel felt compelled to say. "You might suffer a rude awakening someday."

"Oh, my dear." Her face full of sympathy, Helen danced to a halt in front of Isabel. "You've had so many terrible things happen, what with your parents' passing and you being left all alone. But I'll show you how wonderful life can be. And to make things even more perfect, you shall be one of the attendants at my wedding."

"I don't think that's wise—"

"Please, Isabel, you *must*. We'll start shopping first thing on Monday. And while we're choosing my bride clothes, we'll purchase a new wardrobe for you, too. My things are too insipid for your vivid coloring. If you're to set society on its ear, you'll need ballgowns and shoes and fans and all manner of fine bonnets."

That was precisely the offer Isabel had hoped for, having little money of her own to squander. Her drab gray gown was left over from her days when she had studied under a governess, and the dresses she had inherited from her mother were far too risqué for a young lady who supposedly had been rusticating in the country. "What will your father say to the expense?"

"He'll be pleased. Papa is the finest and most generous of men—you'll see."

No. She couldn't believe that of Hathaway—or any nobleman. His pious brother had used her mother, had played on Aurora's craving for affection.

Yet a wave of dark longing stole Isabel's breath. All her life she had ached for a father. She had wanted him to hug her when she was hurt, to tuck her into bed at night and tell her stories, to listen to her hopes and dreams and fears. She'd wanted the protection, the closeness, the *love* she heard in Lady Helen's voice.

Isabel's triumph over the success of her ruse dissipated, leaving a sour churning in her belly. Had Hathaway acceded to her demands only to protect his own sterling reputation—and his brother's? Or had he acted for his daughter's sake, to shield his precious princess from scandal? The answer made Isabel feel dirty, as if she had tainted this happy home.

"I'm so glad you've come to live with us." Helen's eyes shone as she knelt before the stool and grasped Isabel's hands. "We'll be the best of friends. You'll be the cousin—nay, the *sister*—I've always wanted."

The feel of those warm, trusting fingers increased Isabel's discomfort. Only with effort did she force a smile. Lady Helen didn't know the real reason Isabel had come here. Yet the truth might come out. And soon, if she managed to prove Helen's Uncle Raymond had poisoned Aurora Darling.

In the meantime, Isabel had another villain to investigate. Aurora had attempted to conceal his true identity, but Isabel had spotted the clues written in the memoirs. She had guessed the identity of her father.

Now she meant to track him down.

❦ Chapter 3 ❧

*T*onight marked her first excursion into Society.

Descending from the Hathaway coach, Isabel accepted the assistance of a young footman. For a moment she held his gloved hand as she lifted her gaze to the stately stone mansion, where the candlelit windows glowed with the aura of a fairyland castle. A dreamlike panic made her heart thump faster. Tonight she would join the *ton*. Tonight she would dance with the upper crust. Tonight she would leave behind the common masses who gathered across the street, oohing and ahhing as an endless stream of carriages discharged their stylish occupants.

The discreet tugging of the footman's hand snapped her back to reality. She was holding up the line of guests. Releasing her tight grip, she graced him with a warm smile. "Thank you, sir."

Ruddy color mottled his cheeks as he bobbed a bow. "Aye, m'lady."

M'lady. The respectful address gave her a rush of guilty delight. With Helen's help, she had spent the past fortnight preparing herself, memorizing the strict rules of proper behavior. She had practiced dance steps with a tutor. She had enjoyed fittings for an array of new gowns, the finest of which she wore tonight. Donning the outer trappings had been the easiest part of her masquerade. But now came the test—could she fool these aristocrats?

Isabel joined the parade of guests mounting the stairs to the columned porch. Her braided gold spencer warded off the evening chill. She could hear the rustling of her jade silk skirts, the swirl of conversations, and the gay trill of laughter. Despite her fears and doubts, exuberance bubbled up inside her. Her father had come from this world.

Holding her head high, she walked up the steps. She had a right to be here. Yes, she did. Finally she would be treated like the daughter of a gentleman instead of the bastard of a whore.

Cold, gloved fingers closed around her upper arm, squeezing hard. Jolted out of her reverie, she looked up into Lord Kern's scowling face. The joy inside her twisted into a knot.

The white cravat set off his swarthy skin and black hair, and the light from the torchères cast a sinister darkness into his green eyes. In contrast to the amiable man who had chatted with her and Helen in the carriage, he radiated hostility.

His harsh voice rasped into her ear. "For pity's sake, show a little more discretion."

He was a master of disguise, concealing his brutal side from all but Isabel. She didn't like being hated—though after years of being teased by village bullies, she'd learned to hide the hurt. In her haughtiest tone, she said, "I beg your pardon?"

"If you insist upon flirting with the servants," he hissed, "at least have the courtesy to do so in private."

"Flirting?" Realizing he referred to the footman, she bristled, lowering her voice when she caught the curious glance of a stout lady ahead of them. "I don't suppose *you've* ever offered a charitable word to a servant. Else you would have recognized my kindness for what it was."

"Your kindness is legendary," he muttered. "Especially toward *wealthier* men."

"And your boorishness is showing." She glared down at his big hand, his fingers pressing into the sleeve of her spencer. "Release my arm. You can find someone else to escort."

His grip remained firm. "Helen is the only other woman in our party. And she's walking behind us with her father. So I'm afraid you and I are forced to play your game."

"Marvelous," Isabel said through gritted teeth. "But once we're inside the house, I'll thank you to stay far away from me."

"Your gratitude is premature." He bent nearer, and she caught a whiff of his cologne, a musky male tang that caused an involuntary melting sensation inside her. "Rest assured, Miss Darling, I don't intend to let you out of my sight."

She resisted a shiver. What did he mean by that ominous remark? Lord Kern had the power to ruin everything. A word from him, and she would be exposed for a charlatan.

The closeness of the crowd made further private conversation impossible. Caught in the crush of guests, they moved through the massive double doors, relinquished their wraps to a servant, and started toward the receiving line. She heard Helen chatting with her father; then Lord Kern joined in their conversation, chuckling at one of Helen's sprightly remarks. In a dramatic transformation, he smiled at his fiancée, his stern features softening with charm and warmth.

Watching the two of them, Isabel felt a hollow ache inside herself, a queer sense of aloneness. Everyone else here *belonged*, by the simple and unattainable gift of birthright.

"Miss Darcy?"

Lord Hathaway extended his arm, offering to escort her to their host and hostess. She searched his majestic, aging features for the animosity Kern had exhibited, but found only cool politeness. It made her feel all the more guilty for using him and his daughter as pawns. When she had first joined his household, the marquess had subjected her to stony silence. Yet his granite facade had shown small cracks of late. Yesterday, he had gruffly praised her manners at dinner. Tonight, on the way to the ball, he had inserted several droll compliments into Helen's monologue about Isabel's transformation. Perhaps he truly accepted her . . .

"You're hesitant," he observed. "Never fear, the Winfreys won't bite."

Taking his arm, Isabel smiled with heartfelt warmth. "Thank you, my lord." She impulsively added, "You've been more than welcoming. I want you to know how much I appreciate it."

The marquess didn't smile back. Blankness veiled his coal-dark eyes, as if he regretted showing gallantry to his blackmailer. "Any courtesy on my part has been done for Helen's sake," he said curtly. "You would do well to remember that."

"Of course." The brief sense of affinity shriveled inside her. How foolish to think otherwise, Isabel chided herself. How foolish to hunger for true acceptance. Though she wore the garb of a lady, she had the soul of an outcast. And a heart shadowed by a deadly purpose.

The consummate gentleman, Hathaway guided Isabel forward, presenting her as a long-lost relation from the country. Lord and Lady Winfrey bade Isabel a cordial welcome, setting the seal of their approval on her presence and sparking a guarded relief in her. She had passed the first test. Afterward, Hathaway joined a group of men in a political discussion while Lord Kern escorted Isabel and Helen up the grand staircase to the ballroom.

The long chamber was decorated like an Egyptian bazaar, the walls festooned with tentlike draperies. Clusters of palm trees filled the corners, and the crystal chandeliers sparkled like stars against the dark arch of the sky. In an alcove at one end, the musicians were tuning their instruments. Footmen dressed in Arabian robes offered drinks to the company. A sense of expectancy filled the air, renewing the gaiety inside Isabel and quickening her pulse.

She was here, truly *here*. She was one of the favored few admitted to a society ball. She tapped the toe of one dancing slipper on the polished wood floor. Anything could happen tonight. A myriad of new experiences lay before her, as enticing as the treasures in Aladdin's cave.

Not even Kern's glowering presence could dim her anticipation. At last she had the chance to set her plan in motion, and she meant to enjoy herself in the process. But she would not forget her goal. Against the side of her thigh, she could feel the slight weight of the pocket hidden inside her petticoat, the pocket containing the slim diary written by her mother. Isabel kept it with her at all times, prudently tucked away with a small dagger for protection. Starting tonight, she would finagle a few encounters with certain gentlemen named in the memoirs.

Her stomach gave an involuntary lurch. She would begin with the cad who just might be her father . . .

Lord Kern bowed to her. "I should like to request the second dance."

"Thank you, but that won't be necessary," Isabel said firmly. "It's understandable that you'd prefer the company of your fiancée."

"Oh, but Justin has already promised me the opening quadrille and a waltz later," Helen said with an airy wave of her gloved hand. "*You* must allow him two dances as well. That way, the other gentlemen will grow jealous of his good fortune and come flocking to your side."

Isabel feigned a shy laugh. "Truly, this is all so overwhelming for a country miss like me. Perhaps it's best that I remain in the background for a time—"

"And hide among the palm trees?" Helen giggled. "Don't be silly, Isabel. I vow, you're one of the prettiest ladies here. Don't you think so, Justin? Isn't my cousin a beauty beyond compare?"

She's a viper. A sleek, seductive serpent in the guise of a lady.

Kern compressed his lips around the retort. How could Helen be so blind? Isabel Darling mocked the ideal of frail, virtuous womanhood.

Although youth lent her a certain freshness, she looked far too bold and exotic in a jade gown that hugged her bosom and skimmed downward over womanly curves. She needed no jewels to call attention to the fullness of her milk-white breasts. The frock set off her vivid coloring, the sherry-brown eyes, the hint of fire in the cascade of dark curls. Surely no one could mistake *her* for a blushing maiden.

No one but Helen. Sweet, naïve Helen. He far preferred her delicate blond beauty to Isabel's garish sensuality.

Turning to his fiancée, he took up her gloved hand and kissed its dainty back. "My dear, I confess to admiring only you." Glancing at Isabel, he couldn't resist adding, "However, I've no doubt Miss Darby may appeal to certain types of gentlemen."

"Miss *Darcy*," Helen corrected with surprising sharpness. "Really, Justin, you might make an effort to get my cousin's name right. And you'd share my admiration for her if you'd come 'round more to visit. Now, I want you two to be the very best of friends."

Irked that Isabel Darling already commanded Helen's loyalty, he forced out an apology. "I beg your pardon, Miss Darcy."

"It's quite all right. I, too, have trouble remembering names." She edged toward an oasis of palms, where chairs provided seating for those too old or infirm to dance. "The music will be starting, so I had better find a place to watch.''

"Quickly, Justin," Helen said, tugging on his sleeve. "You must introduce Isabel."

The sparkle in her blue eyes gave him a bad feeling. "Introduce?''

"Of course. You know as well as I that she cannot dance without a proper introduction to her partner. We must find the most eligible man here." Helen turned to survey the crowded ballroom, where guests were beginning to line up for the first set.

"Really, I don't want to put you to any trouble," Isabel said. "I'm perfectly happy to wait—''

"Oh, famous!" Helen said, peering across the chamber. "Mr. Charles Mobrey is standing alone by that pillar. You went to Eton with him, didn't you, Justin?''

"Unfortunately so," Kern began.

"Not only is he heir to Viscount Eslington, he has twenty thousand a year," she confided to Isabel. "He's a bit reserved, but you'll draw him out. Come along now, both of you, and hurry.''

Helen, a matchmaker? Kern didn't care for this new impudence in his otherwise docile fiancée. It must be the influence of Isabel Darling, he reflected grimly as he followed in their wake. She was corrupting his beloved, putting inconvenient ideas in her head. And Isabel's show of reluctance didn't fool him. It was all part of her ruse to make people believe she was a meek little rustic rather than a greedy opportunist in search of a rich husband.

At least Charles Mobrey was too much the elitist to be taken in by her spurious charms. Kern remembered him as an intense sort, fancying himself a poet and given to bouts of brooding. True to form, Mobrey lifted a fair eyebrow at Isabel, his chin jutting regally above his elaborate cravat and rather stout chest. Kern performed the introductions, then stepped back to watch as Isabel smiled and flirted. To

Kern's unpleasant surprise, Mobrey's aloofness melted like candle wax, and he asked Isabel to partner him.

The orchestra launched into the opening strains of a quadrille. Kern led Helen toward the long line of ladies and gentlemen assembling on the dance floor. She curtsied before him at the start of the dance, smiling merrily, her cheeks flushed with success.

"Isn't it grand?" she whispered. "Mr. Mobrey often comes to these affairs and never deigns to squire a lady beneath his social standing. Only our Isabel has been able to catch him."

"He's a snob, not a fish. And no doubt he'll dodge the hook when he finds out the bait has nothing to her name."

Instead of leaping to Isabel's defense, Helen frowned thoughtfully. "I've been worrying about that very thing," she said. "I do believe I shall have a word with Papa on the matter."

Kern only half heard her, glowering as Isabel performed the complicated steps with style and refinement, as if she'd danced at society parties all her life. The candlelight caught the copper strands in her dark brown hair, and the lush green gown caressed her feminine figure. Mobrey no longer looked bored, nor did he stick his nose in the air. His condescending features wore the newfound fervor of a smitten lover. Whenever the dance steps brought them together, she inclined her head toward him in conversation. Her lips were curved into a sultry smile, and her eyes caressed him as if he owned her heart.

A tightness squeezed Kern's chest. Damn the slut. It only went to prove that expensive clothing and fine manners couldn't disguise her basic nature. Yet were he a betting man, he would never have wagered on her first conquest being Charles Mobrey.

As he watched, she leaned forward and whispered into Mobrey's ear. The gentleman clutched his hand to his heart.

God! Was she already arranging an assignation? Surely not even Isabel Darling would be so brazen. So what the devil was she saying to him?

"I never dreamed I'd dance with a man of your rank," Isabel murmured, injecting a note of awe into her voice. "You must be acquainted with every member of the *ton*."

"They're a brood of cackling hens, every last one of them." Charles Mobrey's ash-gray eyes flitted to her breasts before returning to her face. "You, on the other hand, are a bird of paradise. A brilliant sun washing away the tedium of this dull assembly."

Isabel judged it imprudent to point out that he had mixed his figures of speech. "Fie, sir, you'll have me blushing. I would sooner speak of you than dwell upon myself."

"Modesty only enhances your beauty. 'O my luve's like a red, red rose, / That's newly sprung in June: / O my luve's like the melodie / That's sweetly play'd in tune . . .' "

A promenade drew him away, granting Isabel a respite from his cloying attentions. Curbing her impatience, she considered how best to find out what she needed to know. As she was pondering, her gaze strayed over the multitude of dancers and clashed with Lord Kern's keen eyes.

Rest assured, Miss Darling, I don't intend to let you out of my sight.

His vigilance made her feel flushed and guilty. Drat him. Did he expect her to commit a *faux pas*? She didn't plan on venturing outside the bounds of propriety.

At least not while he was around.

The dance pattern brought her back to her partner. The instant Charles Mobrey again grasped her gloved hand, she smiled winningly at him. "If I may be so bold as to say so, you've been blessed with an amiable nature," she said. "You must have dozens of admiring friends."

His portly chest puffed with pride beneath his plum-colored coat. "Many appreciate my finer qualities. Yet you, Miss Darcy . . . you are perceptive beyond compare."

A curl of sandy hair rested above his burning gaze, and his fingers clutched at hers. He was ready, quite ready to do her bidding. Her pulse surged at the thought of her goal. Artfully lowering her lashes, she murmured, "How generous you are. Perhaps . . . oh, I dare not ask you."

His gloved hand pressed tighter. "What? What is it? Tell me!"

"I would beg a favor of you, but our acquaintance has been too brief."

"Ask away, my red, red rose. I will fetch a coal from Mount Vesuvius if it pleases you. A jewel from the crown of the tsar. A star from the very heavens—"

"It's nothing so heroic," Isabel said hastily. "Being newly arrived in the city, I am at a disadvantage. I wondered—since you know so many members of the *ton*, perhaps you might introduce me to someone."

His fair eyebrows lifted in distress. "If my company displeases you—"

"Oh, that is not the case at *all*! You are the finest of gentlemen. No, I am merely interested in finding several old acquaintances of my dear departed mother . . ."

The dance steps separated them for a few moments as they changed partners. Though she was deliberately trying to engage his sympathies, a lump filled Isabel's throat. Oh, how her mother would have loved dancing at a ball like this one, basking in the attentions of a handsome gentleman and knowing he returned her affections.

But none of her lovers had offered respectability to her. When Aurora had threatened to expose their dirty secrets, one of them had killed her. Quite possibly, Isabel knew, the murderer had been her father.

With each thud of her heartbeat, the old pain battered at her self-control. She wanted to turn and run, to flee this ballroom and return to the familiarity of the brothel.

Coward, she chided herself. She needed to get this encounter over with and done, like a draught of bitter medicine. She had lived in a dream world for far too long. It was time to confront reality.

Isabel felt a squeeze of her fingers and found herself once again gazing into the ardent, aristocratic face of Charles Mobrey. "My dear lady," he said, "if you allow me to arrange an introduction to any person here, you'll make me the happiest of all men."

Success lay within her grasp. The quadrille was drawing to a close, and she had no intention of waiting around for her dance with Kern. Doubtless he would be glad to rescind that duty.

Rest assured, Miss Darling, I don't intend to let you out of my sight.

Shaking off her misgivings, she flashed Mobrey a brilliant smile. "Then let us take a promenade to the card room, shall we? I've a suspicion the gentleman I wish to meet may be there. But you must promise to let me bring up the topic of my mother in my own way and in my own time . . ."

As Mobrey led her off the dance floor, she steeled her nerves. If all went as planned, she was about to come face-to-face with her father.

The bevy of dancers milled at the end of the set, blocking Kern's view of Isabel and Mobrey. He hid his impatience while Helen exchanged greetings with the venerable Duchess of Covington.

It was customary for a young lady to return to her chaperone at the end of a dance. But Hathaway had objected to engaging a chaperone on the grounds that a female relation might scrutinize Isabel's connection to the family and discover the scandalous truth. For shopping expeditions and social events when Hathaway could not escort his daughter, there was old Miss Gilbert, who had been

Helen's governess for many years and valued her post too much to ask questions.

Miss Gilbert had remained home tonight. And Hathaway was ensconced with his political cronies in the library. Kern would have liked to have been there, too, had not circumstance left him to act the nursemaid.

The throng dispersed. Other dancers took their places on the floor. He could not see Isabel or Mobrey anywhere. Where the devil had they gone?

Helen and the duchess were debating the proper height of a lady's plumed headpiece. Flashing his most charming smile at the duchess, Kern made an apology, cupped Helen's elbow, and drew her away.

"But Justin," she protested as they wended their way through the crowd. "I wasn't finished talking. I was just making my point that if the feather worn by a lady is longer than her face, she looks ridiculously out of proportion—"

"The music is starting again. You've promised this dance to young Blakey, have you not? Ah, there he is now." The orchestra struck up a lively reel. Suppressing a twinge of guilty relief, he handed her over to the gangly, blushing Earl of Blakey. "Do excuse me," Kern said with a bow to Helen. "I must find your cousin for our dance."

Isabel and Mobrey had left the ballroom; that much Kern determined after making a circuit of the huge chamber, exchanging greetings with a number of acquaintances and dodging several others who were known to be long-winded. He strode into the corridor and scanned the people there. Two middle-aged women glided up the stairs to the ladies' retiring room. In the dining room across the passageway, servants were laying out a midnight supper. He peered over the balustrade and spied a few late arrivals in the foyer below. Others went in and out of the lower reception rooms. Had Isabel maneuvered Mobrey into a dark corner somewhere?

His steps quick with tension, Kern descended to the

ground floor, glanced into the library where his political cronies gathered amid the pleasant odor of cheroots, and then proceeded to the drawing room. The furniture had been moved aside so that small tables could be set up for card playing. A number of games already were in progress, with gentlemen and a few ladies who preferred not to dance.

Then he saw her.

At the far end of the room, dark as sin against the pure white marble mantelpiece, stood Isabel Darling. Charles Mobrey was making an ass of himself, bowing as he seated her and then scrambling to fetch her a drink. Another man unknown to Kern already occupied the table. Stout and bewhiskered with a scar bisecting his cheek, he had a gouty leg propped up on a stool.

Kern should have been pleased to see Isabel engaged in so public a pursuit as card playing. But her attention was focused on the stranger, and her too-charming smile made Kern mistrust her motives.

He negotiated the maze of tables. "Ah, Miss Darling," he said. "I hope you need a fourth?"

Isabel looked up sharply, a scowl flitting over her gypsy features. Either she disliked the sight of him or she was up to no good. Both, he decided. Then her lips quirked into a polite smile and he knew she was about to refuse him, so he pulled out a chair and sat down.

At that moment, Charles Mobrey returned with two glasses of champagne, one of which he handed to Isabel. "Kern, old boy. Never knew you to be one for gaming."

"Surprise," said Kern. "I found myself at loose ends when my dance partner vanished."

Isabel's cheeks took on a pink flush. "Fancy that, a lady daring to spurn you. I'm sure if you return to the ballroom, my lord, you'll find dozens of others who would be happy to fill her place."

"Is she not kindness personified?" Mobrey asked of no

one in particular. His lapdog eyes softened on her. " 'Beauty is truth, truth beauty.' "

Isabel lowered her lashes. "Sir, you are too flattering."

" 'Beauty provoketh thieves sooner than gold,' " Kern countered.

"Then make haste and depart lest you be tempted into thievery," Isabel countered with a sly curve of her lips. "I'm certain we can find a more experienced gentleman to complete our foursome."

Her smile stung his loins. He imagined her in bed with a gossamer gown draping her curves and her unbound hair flowing across the pillows. He despised this effect she had on him. Though unlike other men, he could control his base instincts.

"Now, now, my impish Queen of Hearts," Mobrey said. "Lord Kern might be a newcomer to the tables, but he'll even the odds in our little game of whist. Kern, if I may present your partner, Sir John Trimble?"

Kern nodded to the man sitting opposite him. Trimble's nose was large and misshapen like that of a pugilist's. A thick scar ran across his cheek, and bushy brows squatted above his beady eyes. His lips slit the weathered wrinkles of his face. " 'Tis a pleasure," he grunted. "Though you might not care to join our game. You see, I lack the funds to play deep."

"Fine," Kern said. "We'll play for the satisfaction of winning."

Trimble shuffled the deck, his stubby fingers deft. Isabel studied him covertly, intently, and Kern couldn't fathom her interest in Trimble. By his own admission, he lacked riches. Unless . . .

No. He couldn't have been one of her mother's lovers. Aurora Darling had chosen her men based on their wealth and rank. She wouldn't have bothered with a lesser being like Sir John Trimble.

Kern abandoned the speculation. Isabel's true interest

lay in Mobrey. The card room gave her a better chance to work her strumpet's wiles on him than the ballroom, where convention permitted her only two dances with the same partner.

Trimble dealt the cards, and Kern studied his hand. He knew the rudiments of the game from his days at school, back in that brief time when he'd thought if only he embraced sin he might win his father's approval . . .

He locked the door on those dark memories. They meant nothing now, nothing but a hard lesson learned at the expense of his integrity.

"Diamonds are trump for this hand," Mobrey told Isabel, tapping the card lying in the center of the table. "That means the diamond suit takes precedence over the others."

"I know a little of the game," she said, lifting her white shoulders in a shrug. "Enough to muddle my way through."

Indeed, she played adroitly, though Kern sensed a certain distractedness in her. He felt the brush of her skirt beneath the table as she tapped her toes on the floor. She made several blunders, losing the game for her and Mobrey. When, at the end of an hour, they had won only two hands, she lay down her cards with a regretful smile. "Thank heavens we didn't play for money," she said. "I would have beggared myself—and my long-suffering partner."

Mobrey reached across the table and patted her hand. "Jolly good show, Miss Darcy. With you as my partner I am always the winner."

"It takes time to learn the fine points," added Sir John. "I myself have played for some thirty or more years."

She leaned toward him, her breasts straining against her bodice. "Then perhaps you would be so kind as to teach me those fine points?"

Clearly puzzled over the attention of a beautiful young lady, he studied her, his bristly brows drawn together. He couldn't know, as Kern did, that Isabel Darling liked to bewitch every man she met.

"Why, that would be an honor . . . Miss Darcy," Trimble said gallantly. "However, I'm leaving tomorrow to visit a friend in the country for a week or two. Perhaps when I return?"

She pursed her lips. "That will be fine."

"Your cousin will be wondering at your absence," Kern said. "We should return to the ballroom."

Rising, he offered his arm to her. She hesitated, glancing at Trimble one last time before accepting Kern's aid. Her hand felt small yet firm in his, capable rather than fragile. He wondered how many men those fingers had caressed, what liberties she used to arouse them, how long she teased them before lifting her skirts . . .

Tortured by dark fantasy, he realized Mobrey knelt on one knee before her, gazing up at her in adoration. "May I call on you, Miss Darcy?"

She smiled. "Certainly you may—"

"Another time," Kern snapped. With a tug on her arm, he pulled her out of the drawing room.

Her warm smile chilled to a frosty glare. "Is it quite necessary to behave like a cretin?"

"It is when you behave like a courtesan," he said in a low voice.

"I've done nothing unladylike."

"You make a conquest of every man you encounter."

"Oh? Have I made a conquest of you, then?"

She was laughing at him. *Laughing.* As they started up the grand staircase, he caught her womanly scent, a light perfume of roses with a hint of dark musk. He wondered if her skin tasted so delicious. He muttered for her ears alone, "This is no matter for jesting. I will personally see to it that you do not bring shame upon Hathaway or his family."

Isabel returned his challenging stare. "Is that a threat, my lord?"

"It's a promise. You see, I intend to foil your plan to trap some wealthy fool into matrimony."

Her dark eyelashes fluttered downward, hiding her thoughts. "If you say so, my lord."

Damn her artfulness! Why did he sense she hid secrets behind that fine-boned face, secrets he could not fathom? She hid nothing. Her purpose was easy to read and as old as time. She was a fortune hunter who wanted to snare a rich man as her husband. She aspired to join a rank far above the one earned by her disreputable life. And she didn't care who she manipulated or who she hurt.

Drawing her into a deserted alcove, he seized hold of her chin, bringing it up and forcing her to look at him. Her skin felt warm and soft, made to tempt a man. "Be forewarned, Miss Darling. Should you lure some unsuspecting gentleman into an indiscretion, I'll be there to stop you. A few choice words, and he'll see you for what you really are: a whore, a smut peddler, and a blackmailing bitch."

Music lilted from the ballroom. His denunciation hung in the air as if to mock the merry tune. Isabel Darling stood motionless, her brown eyes wide and steady, her lips tight and bloodless. His arrow had struck its mark. Yet he felt no triumph, only an uneasiness akin to shame. For all that he knew he was right about her, a part of him wanted to reach out and stroke her cheek, to kiss the softness back into that sulky mouth.

Without uttering a word, she brushed past him and glided toward the ballroom, leaving her scent to haunt him. Somehow, the dignity of her bearing made him feel less of a man.

And he was hard-pressed to remember why he hated her.

One of the first lessons a courtesan learns is to endure the disdain of Society. This Truth came clear to me early in my career.

While I was trying on a hat at a milliner's on Bond Street, Mr. Terrence D—— entered the shop. Having enjoyed his company only the previous week, I smiled and started to walk toward him. He turned away and spoke to the shopkeeper, who then approached me, snatching the hat from my head and shooing me out the door.

I departed in a fury for home. How dare one of my customers set himself so far above me! I was still in a distraught state when Sir John T—— came to call, my face stained with tears of rage. He held me in his arms, making no carnal demands and showing me the tender regard of a friend. Without a word for his own needs, he listened to me rail against those who scorned me.

Yet no man and woman can lie close without the rise of certain yearnings. And so, after my tears were spent, I invited him on a glorious trip to Elysium. His gentle touch made me feel like a goddess created for his adoration.

Those who think him ugly have not looked deeply into his soul; they do not see how perfectly he understands a woman's heart. Alas, his penury forced him to marry well, yet I take comfort from the fact that he loved me first. He is a man of honor who will be greatly distressed for me to reveal our private affairs. But I cannot record in these pages the story of my life without saying that Sir John T—— is the only man I can truly trust. He alone knows my secrets. He alone knows the heart-breaking truth about my child.

The truth I will take with me to my grave.

—The True Confessions of a Ladybird

๛ Chapter 4 ๛

"*I*t's high time you returned," Callie called out. Her mantle flapping like crimson wings, she swooped through the large, shadowy bedchamber at Hathaway House.

Isabel closed the door. The pleasant haze of weariness from her first ball vanished as she took a sharper look at Callie. Brassy blond hair tumbled around her shoulders. Mud spattered the hem of her gaudy yellow gown. Her bosom nearly overflowed her scandalous décolletage.

"You're dressed like a gentleman's fancy piece," Isabel chided. "Why are you not wearing your servant's garb? Don't tell me you've gone out."

Callie caressed the shapely curve of her hips. "And so what if I have? It isn't fair that *you* make merry at a party, while *I* molder here all alone."

"You're supposed to be posing as my maid. That is what we agreed upon."

"Only because I want to help you find out who killed Aurora." Callie reached out and fingered Isabel's green silk skirt. "But maybe you've told a Banbury tale. Maybe what you're really planning is to land yourself a rich, respectable husband."

Isabel peeled off her kid gloves. That was the same accusation Lord Kern had flung at her only hours ago. "I told you, Mama wrote in her memoirs about her fear of poisoning. I'd let you read so for yourself, but . . ."

"But I don't read so good," Callie finished with a shrug. "Still, from what you said, Aurora didn't give any real proof."

"Several of Mama's former lovers visited her in the weeks before she died. There was ample opportunity for one of them to administer arsenic in something she ate or drank. Aunt Minnie saw a man going into her bedchamber the night before she took ill."

"She did?" Callie blinked in surprise. "But he was likely a customer."

Isabel gave an impatient shake of her head. "Mama's symptoms fit poisoning—even the doctor I consulted said it was probable."

"Hmmm. Her symptoms also fit a terrible case of the ague." Callie blew out a sad sigh. "Whatever it was, the poor soul did suffer. I was there—I saw her."

Isabel remembered, too. She remembered her feeling of helplessness as her mother wasted away to wraithlike frailty. The doctor had been unable to ease her suffering, to restore the vitality that had once made Aurora Darling the most dazzlingly beautiful woman of the *demimonde*.

Her throat taut, Isabel walked to the fireplace. Red coals glowed on the grate, though the flames had died. Despite the scoffing of those around her, she would never let the fire of her conviction go out. *Never.*

At tonight's ball, she had begun her battle for justice. She had secured an introduction to Sir John Trimble. The encounter had left her shaken, uncertain. She'd wanted to be consumed by contempt for him. She'd wanted to hate him for ignoring her all these years. She'd wanted to look into his eyes and see the cold cruelty of a killer.

But instead he had treated her with politeness, even kindness. And she felt an aching emptiness, a yearning she despised. She reminded herself that she had no more reason to suspect him of murder than any of the other men in her mother's life.

Was he her father? The memoirs had been coy on the matter, forcing Isabel to read between the lines. In several entries, Aurora had referred to Isabel's father as Apollo. Yet oddly, Sir John Trimble was the only one of her mother's lovers who had *not* been assigned a god's name. He was the only man who had truly loved Aurora Darling. He was the only man who knew her mother's secrets.

Just what were those secrets?

The question frustrated Isabel now more than ever. She wondered bitterly if he had planned to leave town, or if he'd decided on the spur of the moment, unwilling to face his bastard daughter. When he returned, she would confront Trimble in private. She would determine once and for all what he knew about Aurora's death.

A few choice words, and he'll see you for what you really are: a whore, a smut peddler, and a blackmailing bitch.

Like blight on a rose, Lord Kern's threat spoiled the bloom of her confidence. He could destroy her reputation, ending her chance to find the murderer. Worse, she had to admit that his blunt assessment hurt. His words reminded her that she would never, ever be accepted in his world. No matter how many parties Isabel attended, no matter how many aristocrats she duped, her presence in society could be only temporary.

Callie's arm encircled Isabel in a quick hug, washing her in the scent of heavy perfume. "Ah, don't look so glum," Callie said. "If it makes you feel better to ask questions of these lords, then I won't stop you. But take care. When you stir up a bee's nest, you're liable to get stung."

"I have to find justice for my mother," Isabel said. "And *you* have to behave like my servant. Please, auntie, it's only for a few weeks."

"Don't you fret. Nobody will catch me slipping in and out of this house. And anyhow, I only went back home for a little visit—" Callie pressed her hands to her carmined cheeks. "That's what I wanted to tell you. Persephone's taken a turn for the worse. She's been asking for you."

"Aunt Persy?" The news drove all other thought from Isabel's mind. She seized hold of Callie's shoulders. "Tell me. What's wrong with her?"

"She's had a terrible stomach upset, and that miserly Minnie won't call the doctor. Says the old leech won't do any good."

"Oh, *dear*."

Hastening across the sumptuous bedchamber, Isabel stripped off the fine gold spencer that had she had worn to the Winfreys' ball. In the dressing room, she snatched a cloak of dark-blue merino from a hook. She flung the satin-lined garment over her shoulders and drew the hood up to conceal her hair. Then she ran back to Callie, who had found a pair of embroidery scissors and sat trimming her nails by the light of a candle.

"Come," Isabel urged. "You'll have to show me the back way out."

"Oh, so now you *want* me to go sneaking around this fancy house."

"Only long enough to point me out the right door. And then you'll return straight here and wait for me."

"It isn't safe for a lady to go gallivanting through the city at night." Callie gave a delicious shiver. "Who knows, a man may accost you."

"I have my dagger," Isabel said, patting the pocket tied inside her skirt and feeling the thin, reassuring shape of the blade. Until the murderer paid for his crime, she would carry the weapon with her at all times—along with the small, precious book of memoirs. "Now don't delay."

Callie arched her painted eyebrows, but she wriggled off the bed, picked up the candlestick, and minced to the door.

Out in the corridor, Isabel held her forefinger to her lips. Callie rolled her eyes, then led the way toward the rear of the house. Gloom veiled the portraits and statuary along the stately passage. The thick broadloom carpeting muffled their footsteps. As they passed Lady Helen's bedchamber, Isabel could hear the muted trill of Helen's voice. She must be telling her maid all about the evening.

Thankfully, no sounds emanated from downstairs. Upon their return, Isabel and Helen had left Hathaway and Kern in the foyer. A groom had gone to fetch Kern's mount from the mews, and Lord Kern's hostile gaze had followed Isabel up the stairway.

How he would relish the chance to catch her in a transgression. How he would love to expose her masquerade to the world.

She rubbed her bare forearms beneath the cloak. Really, she had naught to fear. More than a quarter hour had passed, so the officious earl should be long gone.

In the library downstairs, Kern curtly shook his head as Hathaway held up a crystal decanter. The smaller man poured himself a glass of amber liquor. Then he settled into a wing chair by the hearth, took a sip of his drink, and tilted his head back.

"Ah, I'm growing too old for these parties," he said. "Give me a glass of fine brandy and a good book and I'd be contented of an evening."

Restless, Kern roamed the room with its shelves of leather-bound volumes. "I don't see how you can have a moment's contentment while that interloper lives under your roof."

Hathaway's relaxed countenance turned chilly. "Stop your pacing," he commanded. "And cease this nattering about my houseguest. What's done is done, and there's no turning back."

Kern threw himself into a leather chair. "You *can* turn

back. Send her away. Make up a story about how she had to return to the country. No one will question her absence.''

"And allow the memoirs to be published."

"Yes." Kern clenched the arms of the chair. "It isn't your fault that Lord Raymond got himself tangled up with a whore."

"We've been over this before. No scandal must touch him. He would lose his chance for the bishopric of London."

At one time that granite glare would have daunted Kern. But not now. Not while he felt this festering resentment. "Then think of Helen. Miss Darling is hardly suitable company for my future wife."

"Miss *Darcy* comported herself well tonight. She is intelligent and well-educated—her mother sent her to the country to be schooled by a governess. And she has promised to be gone by the end of the Season."

"You put great faith in the word of a blackmailer. She'll trick some fool into offering for her. You cannot in all conscience allow any gentleman to marry her."

"Should such a situation arise, I will deal with it then."

"It *shall* arise, you mark my words. And that is all the more reason to send the chit away now—before someone uncovers her true antecedents. Before people know how you've jeopardized your own integrity."

"Do not question my honor, Justin."

Seeing Hathaway's knuckles whiten around the glass of brandy, Kern abandoned the ill-advised line of attack. "I mean no disrespect. But Isabel Darling doesn't belong in our world. She's the bastard of a whore."

Hathaway drained his glass and set it down with a sharp click. "None of us can change the circumstances of our birth. Nor can my brother change his past misdeeds. We can only go on from here."

"Then let Lord Raymond pay for his sins. As I shall let Lynwood pay."

"Don't be so unforgiving, Justin. All men make mistakes." His expression flinty, Hathaway turned his gaze to the hearth. The firelight cast his weathered profile into sharp relief. "In truth, it is better to give in to passion than to deny its existence."

Shaken, Kern sprang to his feet. "You would say that? You, who have led an exemplary life?"

"I am no marble hero to be displayed upon a pedestal." As Kern was about to snap out a protest, Hathaway passed his hand over his face, looking suddenly old and weary. "I've no stomach for quarreling tonight. Be off with you now. I'll not hear another word on the subject."

Kern knew from experience that once Hathaway made up his mind, there was no changing it. Swallowing the bitterness of frustration, he bade Hathaway good night and left the house.

But as he mounted his horse, Kern did not feel obliged to accept Isabel Darling. Quite the opposite. She had invaded his ordered life, brazenly pushed herself into a respectable position, and now sought to make a conquest of an unsuspecting gentleman. The very idea incensed Kern, and he could no more ignore her scheming than he could walk away from a crime being committed on the streets.

His sense of conviction strengthened as he guided his mount through the patchy mist. He would stop Isabel Darling, keep her from finagling a permanent place in the *ton*. As he neared the deserted corner, he glanced down the side street. His preoccupation vanished into alertness.

A small, shadowy figure had emerged from the darkness of the mews.

A few minutes earlier, by the uncertain light of the candle, Isabel had crept down the cramped staircase. Young ladies being forbidden to enter the servants' domain, she had not ventured this way before: "Where does this go?" she whispered to Callie, who led the way.

"Pantry. Watch out for the butler. He sleeps in front of the silver."

"He . . . why?"

"He guards the silver plate." Callie's grin flashed through the darkness. "And makes sure none of the staff escapes at night."

"Then how can we—?"

But Callie was already opening the door at the bottom of the stairs. She poked her head out and motioned to Isabel, who tiptoed forward, peering over Callie's shoulder.

The pantry was a narrow, oblong room lined with tall cabinets. The feeble light of the candle picked out the dull gleam of dishes and silver on the shelves. In contrast to the silence of the stairwell, the air rang with rhythmic snoring: a snorting intake of breath, followed by a loud, whistling exhale.

Isabel could see the outline of the cot and the stout form of Botts, the butler, beneath the blanket. Breathing a prayer for mercy, she stole past him, trailing Callie, who sauntered along as if she hadn't a care in the world.

Once they were safely beyond the pantry, Callie unerringly led her through a maze of dark rooms. In the servants' hall, the tang of jellied eels lingered in the air. One more short corridor and they slipped outside, into the chilly night.

Callie pointed to a footpath winding through the small, misty garden. "Go through the gate there, then turn right. Mind you watch your step—there's muck about." She paused, her hand cupped around the wavering candle flame, her pouty lips firming with belated concern. "Oughtn't I go with you?"

"No. You'll stay here, in case someone knocks on my door. If I'm not back by morning, tell everyone I'm sleeping late."

Isabel hastened along the flagstones. A gust of wind fluttered the leaves of a beech tree and swirled the scent of damp earth. Wisps of fog curled like ghostly fingers around the darkened shrubbery. She opened the garden gate, thankful the hinges didn't squeak.

A horse snuffled in the stable; then all lay quiet. The grooms and coachman would be sleeping by now. She picked her way through the shadows, heading toward a lighter square marking the end of the mews. The flimsy dancing slippers provided little protection against the occasional sharp pebble.

Though her feet already hurt from dancing and it was well after midnight, Isabel knew she wouldn't rest until she had assured herself of Aunt Persy's health. In half an hour's swift walk, she could reach the town house, lend aid and comfort, then return before sunup.

She turned the corner of the alleyway and hastened along the side street toward the square. Here, the erratic mist hung deeper and denser than in the mews. Tree branches poked like black, skeletal hands out of the fog. The hollow clopping of hooves echoed from the distance and then faded. How eerie to walk the deserted pavement, to see no carriages or delivery drays rattling along, no servants hurrying on a master's errand. A sense of utter aloneness made her shiver.

Quickening her steps, Isabel slipped her fingers into her pocket and gripped the handle of the dagger. She kept her gaze on a misty yellow beacon at the far corner of the square. The gas lamps would light her way through the darkness. Her thoughts jumped ahead. Had Aunt Minnie remembered that Aunt Persy always felt better after a tisane of peppermint and sage? Had she administered sufficient drops of laudanum?

Isabel reached the gas lamp. Strange, how a little circle of light could lend reassurance. Though tempted to linger, she stepped down from the curbstone, lifting her hem to avoid dragging it in a puddle. The clatter of hooves startled her.

Out of the gloom of the side street burst a rider on horseback. He came straight at her.

Isabel loosed a choked scream. She whipped out the dagger and leapt backward, bumping into the iron lamppost. He reined to a halt just beyond the gaslight, his figure tall and menacing, cloaked in black mist.

"Miss Darling," he bit out. "So it *is* you."

Lord Kern. She would know that sardonic voice anywhere. Now she could discern the arrogant thrust of his jaw, though the night obscured his expression. The ball of shock inside her exploded into anger. "What do you mean, frightening me like that?"

"I saw you sneaking like a thief out of the mews." His horse pranced; he controlled it with the reins. "Put the knife away."

Wanting to plunge it into his cold heart, she sheathed the dagger in her hidden pocket. "I'm not a thief. So you can be on your way."

"Why are you out here?"

"I couldn't sleep," she lied. "So I'm taking a stroll."

"No *lady* walks the streets alone." He looked her up and down. "Of course, old habits die hard."

"I've had enough of your insults for one night."

"And I've had enough of your folly."

As he started to dismount, she seized the opportunity to stride across the street. "Don't trouble yourself," she called over her shoulder. "If I come to grief, you should be happy to be rid of me."

He spurred his horse forward and kept pace with her. "If anyone sees you, there'll be gossip. You wouldn't risk your diabolical plan for a promenade in the park."

She tensed, her step faltering. For the barest instant, she feared he had found out about her investigation of murder. But no, he thought she wanted a rich husband. She continued briskly along the pavement. "If you're concerned about scandal, then ride away and quit calling attention to me."

"I want to know where you're heading."

"Nowhere in particular."

"Indeed." His voice hardened, deep with suspicion. "Have you an assignation with Mobrey? The least he could have done was to send his carriage for you."

She fisted her fingers beneath the cloak. Damn Lord Kern for always thinking the worst of her! "How astute of you to guess my secret," she said scathingly. "His carriage awaits me in the next street. So you may leave me now in good conscience. I'll ruin myself and be gone from your life without an ounce of effort on your part."

Keeping her gaze focused ahead on the misty row of town houses, she marched along with her chin held high. There, that should satisfy the earl. If he had any sense in that haughty head of his, he would abandon her to her fate.

He swore viciously under his breath. Then his big dark shape swooped at the edge of her vision. She started to turn, but his muscled arm clamped around her waist as he hauled her up into the saddle.

She found herself wedged sideways in front of him, her legs dangling high above the ground and her bottom squashed between him and the pommel. The twisting of her cloak lashed her in place within the circle of his arms. Any attempt to move only nestled her more intimately against his hard body.

Her rage at his audacity burned deeply, sizzling low in her belly. She tilted her head back, intending to demand her freedom. But the caustic words died in her throat. His face was stark and compelling in the shadows. Against her shoulder, his heart beat a strong rhythm. With every breath, she drew in his male scent: leather and musk, darkness and danger. She felt consumed by the impulse to lift her arms and draw his face down to hers, to touch his smooth-shaven cheek, to taste his masculine lips . . .

She stopped herself in dismay. This was sexual desire, the carnal longings she had heard her aunts discuss when they thought she wasn't listening, the secret ache she'd felt alone in her bed in the dark of night. She had sworn not to follow her mother's path, sworn not to give herself indiscriminately. She had vowed to save her passion for the man who earned her respect and trust.

So how could she desire this blue-blooded brute?

Isabel punched his arm. "Let me down."

His embrace tightened to the verge of pain. The horse pranced along, jolting her forward against the pommel. "Stop your squirming," Kern snapped. "You'll frighten my mount."

"Where are you taking me?"

"Back to Hathaway's. So you won't bring shame onto him or Lady Helen."

She thought of Persephone, weak with illness, calling for her. "Wait! You don't understand."

"If you're worried about Mobrey, I doubt he'll give up on you so easily. He'll be groveling at your feet come morning, bringing you posies and begging for your favors."

"If you must know," she said through gritted teeth, "I'm not off to meet him. So release me."

Kern reined the horse to a halt. The palatial facade of Hathaway's town house appeared through the mist. Other than a faint, flickering light in her own second-story window, the house loomed like a dark and silent sentinel. But it was not so imposing as the man who held her hostage.

The very real danger of her situation gripped Isabel. If he knew the memoirs lay only inches from his grasp, he would wrest up her skirts and seize the book. She caught her breath at the image of his hand sliding over her thigh . . .

His gloved fingers tilted her chin up. His eyes glittered

through the gloom. Again, she felt that heated quivering inside her, the shocking desire to melt against him, to turn in the saddle and wrap her legs around his waist.

"You're lying," he said flatly.

She had to think a moment before remembering he referred to her meeting Charles Mobrey. "I'm not."

"I can prove it by seeking out Mobrey's carriage right now."

"Then do so if you like. You won't find him."

"So where were you going, then? And don't repeat that nonsense about taking a stroll."

Desperate to be shed of him, she blurted out, "It's my Aunt Persy. She's taken ill and she needs me."

"Where does she live?"

"At the brothel—with my other aunts."

"Ah, your *aunts*."

"Yes. *You* might scorn them, but they're all the family I have." To her chagrin, a telltale heat stung her eyes. Jerking around before he could notice, she strained against the iron fetters of his arms. "Now let me down so I can be on my way. There's no time to waste."

"For God's sake, sit still." He snapped the reins and the roan gelding set off at a trot. "I'll take you there."

"I don't need your help."

"You're getting it, anyway. So quit arguing."

He shouldn't believe her, Kern told himself as he guided his mount through the foggy streets. Isabel Darling was a liar, an extortionist, a fortune hunter. But no matter how immoral her character, he couldn't let a woman strike off alone in the middle of the night.

Curse his sense of decency.

And his soft heart. For a moment there, he could have sworn she'd had tears in her eyes. *Tears.*

Her close proximity dissolved his powers of reasoning. Even though she sat as stiffly as a tailor's mannequin, her feminine form drove him mad . . . the cradle of her hips

. . . the lushness of her bosom . . . the friction of her soft bottom rubbing against him. For once, just once, he wanted to be free of scruples. He wanted to whisk her off to an inn and make violent love to her. He wanted to take her again and again until she ceased to plague him, mind and body.

It is better to give in to passion than to deny its existence.

Devil take it. He didn't deny the existence of passion. How could he, when his loins burned like the fires of hell? But if he let his animal urges rule him, he would become like his father.

His breath made harsh plumes into the chilly air. His palms were sweating inside his thin riding gloves. It had been far too long since he had tasted the forbidden ecstasies of the flesh, that was all. He needed a wife, and soon. He needed gentle, innocent Helen. Then he could rid himself of these dark fantasies. Fantasies filled with the witchy Miss Darling.

By the time they reached the town house in a quiet neighborhood west of Regent Park, Kern had worked up more of a lather than his horse. He lifted Isabel down to the ground, and she went dashing away even before he dismounted. With a twitch of her midnight-blue cloak, she opened the front door and disappeared inside the house.

With no groom available, Kern walked the horse in the darkness, seeking to cool himself down as well. "There now, what do you think of that?" he growled, rubbing the horse's neck. "She's run off without so much as a thank you for my pains."

The roan blinked its dark eyes and snuffled as if in sympathy.

"No doubt she expects us to wait out here in the cold for half the night. As if we've nothing better to do."

The horse shook its silky mane.

Kern secured the reins to the iron fence rail. "Deuced

females," he muttered. "You're lucky you're gelded."

This time, the horse stamped a hoof and snorted.

After giving the animal one final pat on the neck, Kern strode up the front steps and rapped on the door. He paced the small porch until the latch rattled and the white-painted panel opened a crack.

A tall, willowy woman in dishabille glared out at him. A waterfall of red hair curled down to her silk wrapper, and her brown eyes snapped with hostility. "Who are you?"

"I've come for Miss Darling."

"Haven't you heard? Miss Darling is dead."

For an instant, his mouth went dry with horror. Then he caught her meaning. "The younger Miss Darling."

"She's busy."

The redhead started to slam the door, but he blocked it with his foot. "I brought her here just now. Let me in at once."

The woman sullenly obeyed, admitting him into the gloomy foyer. By the light of the candle in her manicured hand, she glowered as if he were the devil himself. "Minnie won't like you being here. This house is closed to rakehells."

It struck him as amusing, to be mistaken for a libertine. If only she knew, he wanted to howl out his frustration at the moon. "You're Diana, aren't you?"

"Who gave you my name?"

On his first visit here, the person he'd paid to leave the door unlocked had told him all about the women who lived in this house. "Never mind. Tell Miss Darling that Lord Kern awaits her."

"Tell her yourself. She's up there." Diana shrugged her shoulder in the direction of the stairway. "Just don't get underfoot—we've a sick woman in the house." Taking the candlestick with her, she mounted the stairs, her hips undulating in an exaggerated sway.

Kern paced the dark foyer. He had no intention of invading a strange woman's bedchamber. Of course, such qualms hadn't stopped him the last time he'd been here, when he had confronted Isabel in the boudoir.

Despite the lateness of the hour, he felt restless, charged with energy. He glanced upstairs, but saw no sign of life in the gloom. An indistinct murmuring of voices came from the upper floor. Hands on his hips, he roamed into the darkened parlor.

No coals glowed on the hearth, and the grate had been swept clean. Although night shadowed the room, he could see that it was decorated with the same gaudy lack of taste as the rest of the house: statues of half-clad gods and goddesses, pink and gold draperies on the windows, chaises arranged in coy groupings—for orgies, no doubt. His mind conjured the image of himself reclining there beneath Isabel. Her skirts would be drawn to her waist, her slim white legs straddling him, her skin silken to his exploring touch . . .

Muttering a curse, he threw himself into a gilt chair and stretched out his legs, crossing his boots and loosening his cravat. On the mantelpiece the clock tick-ticked into the silence. By strength of will, he subdued his inner beast. He would not torture himself with carnal reverie. He would not imagine the lecherous pleasures indulged in this house. He would discipline his mind, concentrate on nothing at all . . .

"Asleep at last," Isabel whispered.

Weary, she gazed down at the woman lying in the bed. Aunt Persy looked shockingly old, her pale cheeks sunken and her closed eyelids laced by spidery blue veins. A nightcap half swallowed her thinning gray hair. Her shallow breathing barely stirred the quilted counterpane.

Aunt Minnie beckoned Isabel toward the door. Picking up the candlestick and an empty teacup, Isabel tiptoed out of the room and joined Minnie in the gloomy corridor.

The plump, middle-aged woman shook her head. "The first rest she's had in two days, the poor dear. And all the while calling for you."

"You should have sent word sooner," Isabel murmured, fighting a deep-seated guilt. "I would have come immediately."

"What, and leave your fancy friends while you cared for a shopworn ladybird? I thought you'd forgotten all about them who helped to raise you."

"Of course I haven't forgotten. I've been gone for only a fortnight."

Minnie took the teacup from her and set it on a small table beneath a painting of Cupid and Psyche. "Hmph. And not a single visit in all that time. Methinks you've tasted the good life and now you're getting ideas far above your station."

"I want to find the man who killed my mother." She swallowed hard, wondering if Trimble's kind temperament masked a soul as ugly as his face. "I want to make him pay."

"Now there's a foolish notion. How many times must I tell you so?"

"It isn't foolish. You yourself said you saw the murderer enter Mama's bedchamber."

"I saw a man, that's all. I would never have told you so if I'd known you'd go haring off like this, chasing after shadows." Minnie tugged disapprovingly on the fringes of her black shawl. "Supposing some nob really did do her in. Would he confess to the crime just because you asked? 'Tis more likely he'll murder you, too."

Isabel defied a shiver. "I must find out the truth," she said.

"Mother of God, show some sense. No court of law will take *your* word over the Quality. And don't think to fool anyone, either. You are who you are, a trollop's daughter, and no fashionable lady's gown will change that.''

The words stabbed into Isabel's unguarded heart. For a moment, she could not speak. She would expect such a denunciation from Lord Kern, but not from Minnie, who had often visited Isabel in the country, when Aurora was too caught up in pursuing her own dreams. Steadily, trying not to resent Minnie, Isabel replied, ''I know who I am, Aunt.''

''Do you, dearie?'' Minnie embraced her, imparting a faintly musty scent. ''Oh my sweet girl, forgive me for being so blunt, but I worry about you. I want to protect you from the cruelties of the world, that's all.''

Resisting comfort, Isabel pulled away. ''I'm a woman now. I can look after myself.''

''Can you? I think you'd best come home, back where you belong.'' Minnie sighed. ''I've been thinking about those memoirs. If you're bent on collecting a little blackmail, I'll turn my head the other way. We could use a bit of money to buy us that house in the country. It might be your Aunt Persy's only hope for recovery.''

That knowledge sat like a stone in Isabel's stomach. ''I'll get the funds somehow. But first I must find Mama's murderer.''

''As stubborn as Aurora you've become.'' Her hazel eyes narrowed with displeasure again, Minnie looked Isabel up and down. ''You'll be wanting to return to Hathaway's. I'll fetch that laggard Diana to sit a turn with Persy.''

''No. I-I'll stay a bit longer.''

''Do as you like, then. I pray we'll be seeing you again ere another fortnight passes.'' Minnie marched down the darkened passageway and vanished into her chamber.

Isabel wanted to call her back, to make amends for leaving again. But why should she apologize? Her purpose was commendable. She wanted justice done; she would not let an evil nobleman get away with murder. With Trimble gone for a while, she would focus her investigation on the Reverend Lord Raymond Jeffries, the Duke of Lynwood, and one other likely suspect.

Going back into the bedroom, Isabel placed the candlestick on the bedside table. She smoothed her palms over the jade silk ballgown, now sadly rumpled. Somewhere, she'd lost a few pins from her upswept hair, and curls dangled down her back. *You are who you are, a trollop's daughter . . .*

Kern never let her forget her past, either. He had taunted her about walking the streets alone; he had accused her of meeting Mobrey on the sly. And when he had taken her up on his horse, she had hungered for the devil, hungered to know the feel of his hands and the taste of his mouth.

Desire burned like a steady flame deep within her. She refused to believe her flesh was as weak as her mother's. At least she could be grateful Kern had left her off here and had gone back to his insulated world.

Her legs trembling from exhaustion, Isabel sank down onto a stool beside the bed. Aunt Persy slept peacefully, though dark circles bruised the pale skin beneath her eyes. Her thin arm lay upon the counterpane, her ruffled sleeve hitched up to her bony elbow. Years ago, when Isabel was a child, Aunt Persy had always hidden a sweet or two in her sleeve for Isabel to discover. The memory of that little kindness now brought tears to her eyes.

Blinking hard, she reached out and gently felt the aging woman's wrist. Her pulse still raced, as quick and light as a bird's heartbeat. A cold prickling of panic crept over Isabel. Only a year ago, her mother had lain like this, too ill to awaken . . .

Isabel shook off the uneasy feeling. Aunt Persy had not been poisoned. She suffered from a disease contracted from her profession, a disease which caused these interludes of poor health. This was the worst spell yet.

Unexpectedly, her skinny fingers curled around Isabel's

hand. Aunt Persy made a breathy sound in her sleep as if she took comfort from the touch.

Isabel took comfort, too. Leaning forward on the stool, she lowered her head to the counterpane. She had been away in the country when her mother had taken ill, and she had arrived almost too late. Now she prayed it was not too late for Aunt Persy. Just for a few moments, she would hold her old auntie's hand.

The clock chimed five times.

Kern blinked into the darkness. He must have dozed. Cold and uncomfortable, he stood up and stretched, his muscles stiffly protesting. It would be dawn soon. In the great houses of London, the servants would be laying the morning fires.

Damn. What was taking Isabel so long?

He walked to the stairway and stood there a moment, gripping the gilded newel post. He should abandon her, let her find her own way back to Hathaway's. Let her make her own explanations as to why she'd come in at midday, disheveled and still wearing her ballgown.

But Helen would suffer. For all his brash words to Hathaway, Kern hated for his fiancée to discover the grim truth about her "cousin."

Isabel was leaving here. Now. Whether she liked it or not.

He quietly mounted the stairs. Remembering the layout of the house, he turned down the corridor. A faint illumination guided him to an opened doorway.

Inside, a candle guttered in a pool of wax on the bedside table. An old woman lay asleep in the four-poster. She looked as delicate as a wren, the nightcap huge on her sparse gray hair. Were it not for the almost imperceptible movement of the counterpane, he might have thought her a corpse. One birdlike claw was stretched out, clinging to Isabel's hand.

Isabel, too, was asleep. She sat on a stool beside the bed, her cheek pressed to the mattress. Her eyes were closed, her lips parted slightly. A stream of untidy dark hair spilled down her back. The vulnerability of her pose stirred an unguarded softness in him.

Denying the feeling, he crossed the room and touched her bare shoulder. Her skin felt deliciously warm. She sighed in her sleep, a seductive sound from his darkest imaginings. He gave her a hard shake.

Her lashes fluttered and lifted. She stretched languidly as if seeking a more comfortable position. Then she turned her head and gazed up at him.

Her eyes widened, deep dark pools against the milky paleness of her face. She looked vaguely puzzled by his presence. Kern had never seen Isabel without her mask of defiance, and he found himself leaning closer, drawn to her in spite of himself. She embodied the cuddly sweetness of a girl and the sleepy sensuality of a woman. Lured by a temptation greater than lust, he wanted to take her into his arms, to kiss her awake.

"It's time to go," he muttered.

"Sshh." Sitting up, she glanced at the woman lying in the bed. "I can't leave Aunt Persy."

"You have no choice. Unless you're prepared to give up your scheme."

She carefully disengaged her hand from those clawlike fingers. He'd known that argument would work. Isabel Darling wanted only to protect her own interests. Bending over the bed, she tucked the coverlet around the aging woman's sleeping form. He wondered cynically why Isabel bothered with a show of loving compassion.

She motioned him to the doorway. "I'm staying here a while longer," she whispered. "I'd have come downstairs and told you earlier, but I didn't realize you'd waited."

The announcement jolted him. "Everyone will wonder where you are."

"I'll think of an explanation later." Isabel bit her lip, her gaze on the slumbering woman. "I can't leave her just yet. Not without knowing if the doctor will come . . ."

"What ails her?"

She raised her chin as if daring him to jeer. "It's the French pox. She suffers from these bad spells now and then."

"I see."

"Do you?" Isabel asked, her mouth twisted with bitterness. "A gentleman tainted her—someone from your perfect world. Yet we can't get a competent doctor to visit here. The one who *will* deign to come only wants to bleed her, and she's too weak already."

"I'll send for my father's physician, then. There's no better medical care to be had." Kern spoke without thinking, and he wanted to call back the words—until Isabel's face lit up with disbelief and cautious hope.

She reached for his hands and fervently clasped them. "My lord. You would truly do that for her?"

For you, he thought. *For you.*

Shaken, Kern pulled his hands free. "Do not mistake my purpose," he said coldly. "I want you back to Hathaway's straightaway. Before you cause a scandal."

∽ Chapter 5 ∽

*W*here was Kern?

Anxious for news about her aunt, Isabel aimed a distracted smile at yet another caller who cut a determined swath toward her through the crowded drawing room. It was late afternoon, the height of the visiting hour, and two score of the *ton* sipped tea and sampled an array of cakes proffered by liveried footmen.

The skinny, red-haired gentleman halted before her and bowed. He looked familiar, but for one horrid moment she couldn't recall his identity. Beside him loomed his stout mother, clad in brown chintz and glowering like a guard dog.

"My dear Miss Darcy. It is a pleasure unparalleled to see you again." He thrust out a ribbon-tied bunch of white lilies. "Please accept my humble offering."

Taking the bouquet, she cast about for his name. "Why, thank you . . . Sir Woodbane."

As Isabel made the obligatory curtsy, his mother lifted her gold lorgnette and gazed through it. "We did not speak but a moment at the ball last evening," she said, "and I find myself curious as to your background. I've a cousin in Northumbria and do not recall the name Darcy among any of the better families."

"My father cared little for mingling with society," Isabel lied glibly. "He was content with his scholarly studies. We had quite the extensive library at our manor house."

"Manor house? In what part of the county did you live?"

"Oh, to the north, far from any village." Isabel artfully lowered her gaze. "I fear I am quite the rustic, not nearly as cultured and sophisticated as yourself, my lady."

"On the contrary, you are enchanting," the baron effused. "Utterly delightful. You add a flare of the unconventional to our insipid society."

"And who were your mother's people?" the dowager broke in. "I should like to acquaint myself with her lineage."

If they knew the truth, Isabel thought, they would run screaming from the room. For a moment she was tempted to do just that—to see the shock on their snooty faces when she brazenly revealed that her mother had serviced some of the most respected lords of the *ton*, that one of them had fathered her bastard. And one of them had murdered her. Perhaps the same man . . .

Helen glided forward, a vision in ivory muslin. "Oooh, what pretty lilies." She leaned toward the flowers, inhaling the scent with her dainty nose. "I confess, I'm torn between choosing roses or lilies for my wedding. And there are gardenias to consider. It is a horribly difficult decision to make."

"Try a mixed bouquet," Isabel suggested dryly, grateful for Helen's blithe chatter. "Sir, it is most considerate of you to bring me flowers."

" 'Tis but a paltry gift to express my ardent admiration for you, Miss Darcy," he said in a rush. "When we danced last night, you made me the happiest man in all London." His mother gave an audible sniff, and he clamped his mouth shut, his face flushing the same brick-red hue as his hair.

The elder lady lifted a shrewd eyebrow at Isabel. "Those lilies were plucked from my conservatory. They should be put immediately in water lest they wilt and go to waste." She turned to her son. "Timothy, I should like to sit down now."

"Yes, Mama." With one last soulful look at Isabel, he guided his mother toward a group of gossiping matrons.

The moment he and his mother were out of earshot, Helen whispered, "Woodbane is positively lovesick."

"And his mother is positively frightening," Isabel whispered back, handing the aromatic bouquet to a footman, who bore it toward the display of posies and nosegays already decorating a side table. "I fear she doesn't approve of me."

"She doesn't approve of any lady who eyes her precious son."

"I danced with him but once. That hardly makes me a fortune hunter." Isabel didn't add that it worried her to be scrutinized by an old biddy with nothing to do but poke her nose into other people's antecedents.

"Well, he *does* have ten thousand a year," Helen said in a breezy undertone. "But his grandfather was in trade, and you can certainly do better. Let's take a turn around the room." Linking their arms, she drew Isabel past a pack of fashionable gentlemen. When one swain made a move to join them on their promenade, she waved him away with a charming smile. "Viscount Lipscomb," she murmured dismissingly. "Even if he *would* make you a viscountess, he's too short. You'd look ridiculous standing at the altar with him."

Isabel stifled an irreverent laugh. "Helen, really," she whispered. "I've no interest in snaring a husband."

"Oh, piffle. Every lady wishes to marry well. What else is there for us to do?"

Faced with those innocently sparkling eyes, Isabel felt a fond smile rise to her lips. She had never had a true friend before. In the village where she had grown up, she had been taunted about her bastardy, and had learned to keep to herself. At least here she felt safe among these people who thought her a lady. Indeed, she could grow used to this comfortable life of visits to the modiste and drives in the park and cozy bedtime chats—*if* she could forget her secret worries about her aunt. She could scarcely wait to ask Kern for the doctor's report. "Speaking of marrying, where is your fiancé today?"

Helen lifted her shoulders in an airy shrug. "Oh, Justin doesn't care for these affairs. He considers them a waste of time."

"Will he be coming later to dinner, then?"

"He said as much." Helen scanned the throng of guests. "But like Papa, he's often delayed at Parliament."

"And your uncle?" Isabel prodded. Over the past fortnight, the Reverend Lord Raymond Jeffries had avoided her like a curse, never once coming to Hathaway House. "Did he accept your dinner invitation this time?"

Helen shook her blond curls. "He declined again. I don't see why you want Uncle Raymond to visit. He's a dull fellow, always lecturing about spiritual matters. Listening to him quite puts me to sleep."

"I did notice your eyes close in church last Sunday."

"Did you? I hope no one else saw." Helen blinked in dismay, then laughed. "Oh, you're teasing. Do be serious. We're supposed to be looking over your prospects." Her face alight with zeal, she squeezed Isabel's arm. "Isn't it exciting? I daresay every gentleman you met last night has come to call on you."

Except one, Isabel thought as they strolled the length of the palatial drawing room. None of these young noblemen had known Aurora Darling, and Isabel chafed at the delay in her plans. "Yesterday evening, I played a round of cards with Sir John Trimble. *He* isn't here."

"Sir John—?" Helen screwed up her pretty features into a frown. "I don't believe I know him."

"He seldom gets about in society—he suffers from the gout."

"Ye gods, he must be my father's age, then. You can't possibly be interested in someone so old."

"Oh, I prefer older men." The fib tasted sour on Isabel's tongue, but she would need the excuse in the coming weeks. "They're more settled, less inclined to gaming and wildness."

"Like Justin. He is the paragon of propriety."

The comparison startled Isabel. "Lord Kern isn't old. He can't be quite thirty yet."

"He's twenty-eight. I suppose I've always seen him as an elder brother. He's ever so kind and caring, ready to correct me if I dare to set a toe out of place." Helen sighed, slowing her steps. "I've a confession, dear cousin, but you must promise never, *ever* to breathe a word of it to him."

"As you wish."

Helen bent closer, murmuring in Isabel's ear, "I sometimes find myself dreaming of wicked rogues. Not any of these gentlemen here, mind, but men of stories and legends. Oh, to be abducted by a dashing pirate. Or swept away by a handsome highwayman on horseback."

Isabel bit down hard on her lip. Last night, she had been carried off into the night by a man cloaked in black. By Helen's fiancé.

You don't know Lord Kern. He is dark and dangerous, as bold as any pirate.

Her breast ached from a knot of shameful longing. How could she lust after Helen's intended husband? The notion was appalling, disloyal, reprehensible. Yet there was no denying she had desired him. She had grown hot with yearning when he had hauled her onto his horse—and then struggled against the same secret fire on the ride home at dawn.

Her passion could only have been a momentary aberration, the natural reaction of female to male. In the light of day, it seemed incredible that she could want a man who despised her.

"Being abducted isn't so romantic as it sounds," Isabel pointed out. "A highwayman would act crude and vulgar. You would more likely detest him than fall madly in love."

Another sigh fluttered from Helen. "Dear Isabel, always so practical. You mustn't think I'm displeased with Justin. We've been promised to each other since we were children. He is so fine and handsome, and very dear to me." They turned at the far end of the drawing room and strolled back toward the gathering, passing the opened doors to the entrance hall. "Hsst. Do you see that?"

"What?" Isabel glanced toward the fashionably dressed aristocrats, who were idling away the afternoon.

"There in the corner. Mr. Charles Mobrey is staring at you again."

At the other end of the room, the stout man sat alone and aloof, his stiff cravat bracing his weak chin and his fair hair curling around his brooding features. Mobrey had been the first to arrive today. He had pressed a posy of violets into her hand, along with a syrupy poem extolling her beauty.

"Ah," Isabel said. "It's the man who compared my lips to ripe cherries and my eyes to chocolate bonbons."

Helen giggled. "It only goes to prove how violently he's in love with you. No doubt he'll be offering for you soon."

"Offering what?" spoke a low-pitched voice from behind them.

Isabel whirled around. A flush surged through her body when she saw Lord Kern looming over them. He exuded perfection from his polished leather Hessians to his groomed black hair. His burgundy coat outlined the breadth of his shoulders and showed off the elegance of his white neckcloth. One would never guess that only hours ago, he had swept her up on horseback and held her as close as a lover.

"Justin," Helen squealed, lifting her hand for his kiss. "What a delightful surprise. Why are you not at Parliament?"

He made a formal bow. "I couldn't stay away from you." His lip curled slightly as he turned to Isabel. "Besides, I thought Miss Darcy might need looking after."

Rest assured, I don't intend to let you out of my sight.

Her heart tripped over a beat. Did he know she felt a wretched tug of attraction to him? His eyes were the cool green of a woodland pool. Not even a shaft of sunlight from a nearby window could penetrate his thoughts. One fact was certain. *He* felt no attraction to *her*.

"How thoughtful you are," Helen said with a smile. "But we've a roomful of men anxious to fill the role of champion to my cousin."

"So I see." He scanned the throng. "Now who, pray, is offering for whom?"

"No one," Isabel said quickly. "It is only idle gossip and not worth repeating."

"And premature as well." Giving Isabel a secret wink, Helen looped her arm through his. "Oh, Justin, I'm glad you're here. I did so want your opinion on a matter of grave importance."

He cast a suspicious glance at Isabel, then returned his attention to Helen. "Is something wrong?"

"It is a most vexing dilemma. Perhaps you can solve it for me. Do you prefer lilies or roses to decorate the church at our wedding?" Helen frowned earnestly at him. "Cousin Isabel suggests I might use a variety of flowers— and that is a very fine compromise—but I wanted to discuss it with you first, in case you have a preference."

"Whatever you decide is perfectly agreeable with me,"

he said, patting the back of her hand. "I defer to your excellent taste."

He smiled down at her with a fondness that defied his cold, forbidding nature. Gazing at them, the darkly handsome prince with his dainty blond princess, Isabel felt like an outsider. They were born to this privileged world while she only masqueraded as a lady, infiltrating the inner circle of society, yet never truly belonging. Eventually, whether she liked it or not, she must go back to her old life.

You are who you are, a trollop's daughter . . .

She denied a pang of regret. It wouldn't do to covet fashionable clothes and fancy balls. Or to wish she might truly belong in this sheltered world as Helen did. At all costs, Isabel must remember her purpose in being here—to find the nobleman who had murdered her mother. And Kern's father ranked high on the list of suspects.

With iron determination, she addressed Kern. "How does His Grace of Lynwood fare?"

The warmth left the earl's features, chased away by chilly arrogance. "Well enough. And are you having a fine time, entertaining your admirers?"

"My cousin has more suitors than the daughter of a duchess," Helen murmured proudly. "Is it not wonderful, Justin? She's a dazzling success. We've received *piles* of invitations to balls and soirees and dinner parties."

He gave Isabel a hard stare. "It is a wonder, indeed."

"Perhaps I may ask," Isabel persisted, "why we are never invited to dine with *you*, my lord? If your father is improved, then it seems ill-mannered for us to stay away. And now that I think on it, I do believe my mother once knew him. I should like to renew the acquaintance."

"You never mentioned that before," Helen said in delight. "Fancy, what a small world this is—"

"My dearest, we're keeping you from your duties as hostess," Kern broke in, his tone pleasant but firm. "You mustn't let us monopolize you. I'll occupy your cousin."

"As you say, my lord." Helen squeezed Isabel's hand. "I do so want the two of you to be friends." Smiling, she hastened toward their visitors.

Ignoring the curious glances from the throng, Kern took Isabel's arm, directing her to a quiet niche near the pianoforte. He despised himself for noticing the silkiness of her skin. Anger seethed inside him, though he maintained a bland expression. Releasing her, he kept his voice low and said, "I'm onto your game, Miss Darling."

"I do not play games, my lord." She rubbed her arm where he had touched her. "Games are for idle people prone to silly amusements."

"You want to badger my father about the memoirs. You still hope to blackmail him. I will not permit it."

She lifted her chin and asked the question that had been nagging at her. "I wish to speak to Lynwood's doctor. Did you send him to Aunt Persy?"

"Yes."

"And?" A hint of anxiety laced her voice. "What did the doctor report? How is she faring?"

"As well as can be expected under the circumstances. Dr. Sadler professed to be puzzled by the sudden severity of her symptoms. He could only surmise she isn't a very strong woman."

"She was healthy at one time," Isabel said with a trace of bitterness. "Did he prescribe any medication or tonic?"

"He gave her a dose of morphine to ease her pain. He'll return to her on the morrow. I'm afraid there's nothing else to be done but wait for improvement."

No matter how little respect he had for Isabel Darling, Kern hated being the bearer of bad tidings. Slim and lovely in a willow-green gown, she leaned against the satinwood pianoforte as if unable to stand without support. A small pucker marred her brow, and she worried her lower lip with her white teeth. He felt a dangerous softening inside himself, the urge to draw her close and offer comfort. He didn't like knowing she could care for someone other than herself. It was easier to condemn the crafty female who dared to blackmail her betters.

"Smile, Miss Darling," he said in a silky undertone. "Lest people say we're quarreling."

That did the trick. Her spine went rigid, her shoulders squared. She curved her lips into the parody of a smile. "Pardon me if I embarrass you by showing concern for my aunt. Now, if you'll provide me an address for Dr. Sadler, I'll send him his fee."

His brief tenderness vanished. "The matter has already been settled."

"I don't want your charity."

"Then consider it a gift to my future *cousin*-in-law."

The keenness of her stare made his skin prickle. "You don't wish me to contact Dr. Sadler, do you?" she said slowly. "You think I'm planning to ask him questions about Lynwood."

"Leave my father out of this."

"Tell me, then, what ailment does he suffer from? The pox, same as Aunt Persy? Is that why you suggested *his* doctor examine her?"

"*No.*" Taking several deep breaths, Kern willed away the pressure in his chest. Only he and a few trusted servants knew his father experienced spells of madness. He bent closer, speaking for her ears alone, "Heed me, Miss Darling, and heed me well—"

A shrill voice interrupted him. "Whatever are you two whispering about there in the corner?" called a fleshy woman squashed into a gilt chair halfway across the long drawing room. "I vow, my lord, you and Miss Darcy have been behaving like conspirators."

Lady Woodbane, damn the cow. Behind her hovered her

son, staring with lovesick eyes at Isabel. "Ah, you've spoiled my surprise," Kern said easily. "Miss Darcy has been advising me on a bride gift for Lady Helen."

Even from across the room, he could see Helen blush with pleasure. She clasped her hands to her small bosom. How sweet she was, as excited as a child. And how undeserving he felt for lying. He vowed to make it up to her by purchasing the finest bride gift money could buy.

"Oh, I beg your pardon," said the baroness. "I merely wished to ask if perhaps Miss Darcy would play a song for us on the pianoforte."

He stepped back to allow Isabel space to walk to the bench, but she stood unmoving. Her face had gone pale. "I'm afraid I don't play," she told the baroness.

"Not play?" The older woman arched an eyebrow. "Come now, you are being modest. Every lady plays and sings."

"No, ma'am. I never studied music. It was not considered important by my parents."

"Well! That is a strange upbringing." The dowager cast a veiled, I-told-you-so glance at her son. "Very strange, indeed."

"Not so strange an upbringing as that of those who never learned manners," Kern said. "Helen, will you play for us?"

Lady Woodbane sat blinking, her lorgnette dangling from her pudgy hand as if she were unsure whether or not she'd been delivered a setdown. Isabel Darling stood with her chin held high and defiance sparking in her fine dark eyes.

Helen glided forward, seating herself at the pianoforte. Kern didn't understand the impulse that had prompted him to rescue Isabel. He felt damnably drawn to her again, drawn to this upstart who put him in the ignominious position of defending her character. She would as soon lay waste to his honor as thank him.

As the tinkling strains of the pianoforte brightened the air and all eyes turned to Helen, Kern bent closer to Isabel, speaking for her alone. "As I was saying, I forbid you to contact Lynwood."

"Forbid?" she whispered, edging a coquettish glance up at him. "Fie, sir, you speak strongly for a man who has no jurisdiction over me."

He gritted his teeth. "Nevertheless, you'll listen well. Should I find you anywhere near Lynwood, there'll be hell to pay."

The lustiest of my lovers was Zeus.

Unlike more circumspect gentlemen, the Duke of L—— was not one to take his indulgence in my chamber and then depart under cover of darkness; ofttimes he liked for us to venture into the very fringes of polite Society, and as for myself, I enjoyed the secret jest we played on those who would shun a lady of my vocation.

On one such memorable occasion we attended the Opera, situating ourselves most comfortably in the Duke's private box. There, while seated in the shadows cast by lamplight from the stage below, Zeus reached beneath my skirts and pleasured me to the accompaniment of a robust tenor and a pretty soprano. I then took liberties with his manly person, and thus we passed a delightful hour. No one could guess at our naughty occupation, for Zeus and I pretended a respectful interest in the opera even while our busy hands worshipped those regions sacred to Cupid.

In time we knew each other in such diverse places as beside the lake in St. James's Park on a moonlit night and in the dressing room of a snobbish modiste on Bond Street in the middle of the afternoon. Once he even bribed a watchman at Westminster Abbey, and this story would not be complete without a narration of how we took our joy by the tomb of the Virgin Queen . . .

—The True Confessions of a Ladybird

∽ Chapter 6 ∾

"Are you certain Justin will approve?" Helen said as the Hathaway coach turned a busy corner in Mayfair.

Bracing her gloved hands on the leather seat, Isabel fabricated a smile. "He's always pleased to see you," she said. "Wouldn't you like it if he came to call on *you* unexpectedly?"

"Yes. Oh yes, indeed." Helen's brow furrowed beneath the wide-brimmed bonnet with its pink satin trim. "Still, he likes surprises very little. He's a stickler for arranging events in advance—he set our wedding date nearly a year ago."

"Then it would do him well to learn the joys of spontaneity."

"Perhaps so." Helen's face took on a glow of determination. "Yes, you're right. I must teach him to avoid schedules and to relish the moment."

"His lordship despises impulsiveness in a female," Miss Gilbert ventured in her tiny, high-pitched voice. "A lady comports herself with decorum. She does not go where she is not invited."

The governess sat opposite them, a shy mole of a woman wrapped in a plain brown cloak. Her dark eyes darted back and forth between the girls, and she dabbed a handkerchief to her bloodless lips.

"Oh Gillie, don't fret," Helen said, leaning across the carriage to pat the older woman's hand. "My cousin has a point—Justin *will* be happy to receive us. It's the perfect occasion to go over the guest list for our wedding. You and I must soon begin the task of addressing the envelopes to ensure the invitations go out on time . . . "

As the women launched into a discussion of the wedding plans, Isabel turned her mind to a more pressing matter. For the past two days, Kern had hovered close by, escorting them to soirees and dinners and musicales. He had a way of glowering that made her intensely aware of his dislike for her, though in front of Helen he was all gentility and politeness. Isabel recalled the odd pleasure in her breast when he had defended her. But of course, he had done so only because they were in public. What he said to her in private was another matter entirely.

Rest assured, Miss Darling, I don't intend to let you out of my sight.

Isabel absently tugged at the tight blue ribbons securing her bonnet. Today, though Helen didn't know it, he had an engagement at Parliament. Isabel had lain awake half the night trying to devise a clever scheme for interviewing the Duke of Lynwood. It was impossible to escape during the day; young ladies did not wander around London on their own. Even if she did manage to get away and steal in through a back door of Lynwood House, a servant might catch her as she wandered around looking for the duke's apartment. And she could think of no excuse that would get her past the front door, let alone upstairs to the family quarters. In the end she had decided to quit trying to be clever and embrace boldness instead. She had persuaded Helen to call on Kern.

The coach swayed as it pulled into the curved drive in front of Lynwood House. Stepping down from the carriage, Isabel caught her breath in awe at seeing the enormous stone residence that faced Hyde Park. With its high windows and stately cornices, it looked like a palace. The tall pillars of the porch dwarfed her. "You're to live here soon," she murmured to Helen as they walked up the broad front steps, Miss Gilbert trailing behind them. "Are you looking forward to the day?"

Helen sighed. "Yes, but I shall miss Papa very much. The old duke is rather a frightful man."

"How so?"

Helen glanced back at Miss Gilbert, then whispered in confidence, "When I was a girl, he would pinch my cheek and slap my bottom. If I shied from him, he would bray with laughter." She shuddered. "I cannot fancy living in the same house with such a man, though Justin assures me the duke keeps to his rooms these days."

"When did he become ill?"

"Last autumn. He suffered a seizure and hasn't received visitors these past six months."

Isabel clenched her fingers into fists. That meant the lecher had been healthy while her mother was alive. Was he the one who had poisoned her?

A young, white-wigged footman opened the front door. "My lady," he said, jerking into a surprised bow. "I fear Lord Kern has gone out."

"Gone out!" Helen said, a pout of dismay on her fair features. "When will he return?"

"His lordship didn't say. He left no instructions—except . . ."

"Except what?"

"He said that you and Miss Darcy are not under any circumstances to wait upon him here."

Helen frowned. "What an odd message. He wasn't expecting us."

Isabel understood—too well. Kern had outwitted her, anticipating this visit. *Should I find you anywhere near Lynwood, there'll be hell to pay.*

But she wouldn't give up without a fight. "You surely

misunderstood,'' she said. ''Lady Helen is his lordship's intended bride. He would never forbid her admittance.''

Looping her arm with Helen's, she ignored Miss Gilbert's squawk of dismay and marched past the astonished footman. Isabel found herself in the soaring elegance of the entrance hall. A domed window set high in the ceiling let in filtered sunlight, keeping the place from being gloomy. ''One must never be bullied by a servant,'' she murmured to Helen. ''Now, which way to the drawing room?''

''Up one flight,'' Helen said, leading the small party toward the grand staircase with its white-and-gold balustrade. ''How magnificent you are, Cousin,'' she added in a whisper. ''I would have obeyed without question and fled home.''

''Oh dear, oh *dear*,'' wailed Miss Gilbert, twisting her handkerchief. ''His lordship will be *furious*. He will take me to task for your undisciplined behavior.''

''Nonsense, Gillie,'' Helen said as they mounted the wide, marble steps. ''He is not your employer. And besides, I am a grown woman now. You are my friend and my companion, but I do not answer to a governess any longer.''

''Or to any man,'' Isabel added, determined to prevent Kern from dictating to his future wife. He would domineer a sweet girl like Helen unless Isabel took steps to protect her. ''A woman should exercise an independence of mind rather than blindly follow the directives of others.''

''I quite agree. And I will tell Justin so the moment he arrives home.''

''Perhaps not the very moment,'' Isabel cautioned. ''One must sometimes allow men to *believe* they hold the upper hand. Even if they do not.''

''Oh, I see. How clever you are.'' Helen blinked her admiring blue eyes. ''How did you become so knowledgeable in the ways of the world?''

"From reading and the study of human nature." To distract Helen, Isabel exclaimed, "What a perfectly lovely room. I vow, it will be your favorite retreat once you're married."

Its walls hung in yellow silk damask, the drawing room radiated a cheery warmth. There were groupings of chaises and chairs, elegant bric-a-brac on the octagonal tables, and a delicate French writing desk near the white marble mantelpiece. The long windows provided a breathtaking view of Hyde Park with its green trees and riding paths.

As Helen ordered tea and handed their wraps to the footman, Isabel wandered to a window. The light aroma of beeswax perfumed the air, and a fire snapped invitingly on the hearth. She couldn't deny a moment of longing to think of living in such splendor, relaxing in this room with a book or gazing out upon the magnificent vista of the park. But to gain a position here, Helen must shackle herself to the haughty Lord Kern.

A shiver unsettled Isabel. So much for envy.

Restlessness kept her from sitting with her companions. Now that she had breached this fortress, she needed to fabricate an excuse to slip away. If her luck held, she would require no more than a quarter hour to accomplish her purpose.

Pressing her palm to her lower back, she approached Helen. "My lady, I fear an exigency is upon me. I must seek out the retiring room."

Helen jumped to her feet. "What is it? Are you ill? We'll return home at once."

"My need is immediate." Isabel modestly lowered her gaze. "It is my monthly visitor, you see." It was not entirely a lie; she expected her courses to begin in a day or two.

"Oh! You poor dear. I'll ring for a servant."

Helen started toward the bell pull, but Isabel caught her arm. "No, please. I'd be mortified to ask the footman for assistance. I'll go upstairs and find a maidservant.''

"You cannot go alone. Gillie, kindly accompany my cousin.''

Isabel motioned the aging governess to remain seated. "Please stay and enjoy your tea, both of you. I insist upon it. I'm perfectly capable of tending to my own needs.''

Before they could voice further objections, Isabel hastened from the drawing room. Her senses thrummed with anticipation. At last she had her chance, and she would make the most of it.

Should I find you anywhere near Lynwood, there'll be hell to pay.

Lifting her dark-blue skirts, she ran lightly up the staircase. Kern could go to the devil. She wouldn't waste any time being frightened of him. What could he do to her but rave and rant?

"Prostitution is the bane of our society,'' proclaimed Mr. Bertrand Sweeney, who had stopped Kern outside the Commons Chamber to solicit his support for a new bill. "One cannot stroll along the Strand without being accosted by a hussy ready to sell her services for a shilling's worth of gin. Why, the bawdy houses in this city must number in the thousands. They must be closed, all of them, to preserve the moral integrity of our great nation.''

A fortnight ago, Kern would have agreed with Sweeney's conservative politics. Now he thought uneasily of the old whore Persephone, lying ill of a disease contracted in the pursuit of her profession. "And what would become of the women? How would they earn their bread?''

"That is no concern of ours, m'lord.'' Grinning, Sweeney clapped Kern on the arm as if they were social equals. "Indeed, let the trollops wallow in the gutter where they belong.''

"I cannot consent to any proposal that will increase by vast numbers the destitute who wander our city.''

Sweeney's jaw dropped. "Surely you of all men should champion my bill with your friends in the Lords Chamber. Your father, the duke, being a renowned reprobate—"

"Say no more," Kern broke in icily. "This city needs stronger policing to enforce the laws we already have in place. Show me a bill for that, and I will gladly endorse it. Good day, sir." Leaving Sweeney sputtering, Kern strode toward the main doors, his footsteps ringing on the stone floor.

The disagreeable encounter fed his inner turmoil, and after a morning of listening to long-winded speeches, Kern was tempted to abandon civic duty. He felt a yearning to hike the hills of his boyhood home in Derbyshire, to breathe the clean air of the country, to escape the problems of the city and concentrate on the familiar business of his estate. His wedding loomed six weeks away, and Helen surely would forgive him a brief absence. Perhaps then he could rid himself of this persistent restlessness.

But an iron-fisted purpose held him in London.

Isabel Darling.

She and Helen intended to spend the day selecting bride clothes, and Helen said laughingly that the bridegroom mustn't tag along. Far from eager to make the tedious rounds of milliners and glovers, Kern had heeded the announcement with a sense of relief. Isabel couldn't embroil herself in too much trouble while on a shopping expedition.

Or could she?

She might meet up with a besotted swain like Mobrey. Those dark, come-hither eyes would flash seductively. Her lush lips would curve into a siren smile. She would sway her hips and beckon to him, luring the unsuspecting fool into an indiscretion . . .

Kern balled his fists. Isabel Darling would never secure herself a respectable marriage. Never.

And he must heed the danger represented by her mother's memoirs. Though at present Isabel dared not publish the filth without endangering her masquerade, Kern knew she *would* attempt blackmail should the opportunity arise. This very morning, he had instructed the footmen against such an event. So why did he feel so uneasy?

He exited the Commons Lobby to find his carriage waiting outside, the smart black equipage drawn by a pair of matched grays. As the footman leaped down to open the door emblazoned with his coat of arms, Kern snapped out a single word to the coachman.

"Home."

Isabel glanced over her shoulder at the long, elegantly appointed passageway. She saw only a maidservant staggering under a pile of linens and heading in the opposite direction. A tomblike silence lay over the upper floor.

Removing her bonnet, Isabel looped the ribbons over her arm. She pressed her ear to a white-painted door. Within, a querulous voice rose and fell, though the words were muted. The duke?

There was only one way to find out.

Taking a shaky breath, she turned the gold handle and crept inside. She found herself in a gloomy sitting room that smelled sharply of medicines. The voice came from the next room, and she tiptoed toward the open portal.

A fire blazed on the green marble hearth. No expense had been spared in furnishing the room with the finest in ottomans and chairs and gilt-framed paintings. Dominating the cavernous chamber was a massive four-poster hung with bronze velvet. The ornate ducal crest adorned the gold-fringed canopy.

A liveried manservant stood beside the bed, attempting to coax the white-haired invalid into swallowing a spoonful of tonic. With a sweep of his gnarled hand, the duke struck away the spoon. Syrupy brown liquid sprayed the wall, and the utensil fell to the carpet.

"Get away, you mangy dog! Poison me, will you? Bring me my dueling pistols, by gad, and fight like a man."

Poison? Isabel's ears perked up. If the duke suspected others of foul play, might it not point at his own guilty conscience?

"Your Grace, Dr. Sadler says this medicine will improve your health." The servant retrieved the spoon, then picked up a brown bottle from the bedside table.

This time, the duke opened his mouth and took the tonic. And promptly spat it back into the servant's face.

The man lurched backward, scrubbing his sleeve over his eyes. Dark spots marred the front of his pale-blue livery with its waterfall of white lace.

The duke tipped back his head and cackled with laughter. "Think you can get the best of Lynwood, eh? That'll teach you. Keeping me confined to this demmed bed."

Isabel saw her chance and hurried forward, the bonnet swinging on her arm. "You'll be wanting a change of clothing," she said to the servant. "I will sit with His Grace until your return."

The servant pivoted, a look of alarm on his ruddy features. "No strangers are allowed in here, miss."

"It's quite all right. I'm a friend of the family, cousin to Lady Helen Jeffries."

"Cousin, eh?" the duke said. A broad smile showed his yellowed teeth, and he patted the bed. "Sit down, my pretty."

"I wasn't told of any visitors." The hulking servant peered suspiciously at her. "Sorry, miss, but I'll be ringing for help."

"Yes, do that," she bluffed. "Tell the whole staff you're not competent in your post. Tell everyone you couldn't properly care for His Grace." When the man hesitated by the velvet bell rope hanging near the wall, she put on her most severe countenance and added, "Run along now. With luck you'll only be gone for a few minutes."

"Be off, you scurvy rat," added the duke, who sat glowering in the bed. "You can't have her—she's mine." He snatched up a silver cup from the bedside table and hurled it at the lackey.

The manservant caught the vessel, but not before liquid drenched him. Scowling, he backed away, shot a suspicious glance at Isabel, and then scurried from the chamber. The door banged shut behind him.

Isabel was alone with the Duke of Lynwood.

He looked old and cross, a man far past his prime. Like a map of dissipation, spidery red veins lined his nose and cheeks. He wore a voluminous nightshirt with ruffled cuffs, the collar open to show the gray hairs on his broad chest. Rumpled white curls framed the strong bones of a once-handsome face. His eyes glinted a shrewd shade of green.

Kern's eyes.

But this man possessed not a jot of his son's iron-willed honor. This disgusting lecher had been intimate with her mother. The thought made Isabel slightly queasy. Although she had loved her frivolous, pleasure-seeking mother, she herself could never embrace such a wicked life, could never put her happiness in the hands of a man who refused to marry her, who thought himself her superior simply by virtue of his birth.

"Don't stand there gawking," the duke said. "Come closer. Let me have a better look at you."

Isabel advanced one step. "I've come to ask you a few questions, Your Grace."

"Questions, bah. I'll ask the questions. Are you the one I sent for?"

"Sent for?"

"Never mind, never mind. Just tell me your name."

"Isabel." Watching him closely, she added, "I'm Isabel Darling."

Letting out a dry laugh, he slapped the gold-embroidered counterpane. "Then come, *darling*. Come to me, you brazen hussy." His forefinger crooked, he beckoned to her.

PROPERTY OF
KINSMAN FREE PUBLIC LIBRARY

Her skin crawled as she looked into his uncomprehending eyes. "You misunderstand—I wasn't being forward. My given name is Darling. I'm Aurora's daughter."

"Aurora?" He blinked in confusion. "Aurora Darling?"

Isabel nodded. "She called you Zeus. She described you in her memoirs."

His lip curled in disdain. "I remember now. The brassy bitch wrote about me without my consent. And when I told her to stop, she sent me away with a cuff to the ear. As if I were a stable boy."

The resentment contorting his face startled Isabel. Was he the one, then? Was this half-mad invalid her mother's murderer?

Isabel chose her words with care. "You must have been furious. What would you do to a woman who made you angry?"

"I have my ways of dealing with headstrong females." A lewd grin curled his lips and he motioned to her again. "Come here and I'll show you."

Isabel remained at the foot of the bed. She was conscious of the damning memoirs, tucked into the little pocket beneath her skirt. "So you visited Aurora about a month before her death last spring. Did you go back to see her after that one time?"

"Death?" He shook his head. "What sort of blather is this?"

"Surely you knew. She became gravely ill several days after you visited her." Isabel's throat caught, and her voice grew whispery. "Perhaps you gave her something to eat or drink."

"Eh?" He cupped his ear. "What have you brought me to drink? Not more of that accursed medicine."

Was he deliberately acting obtuse? Time was wasting. The servant would return soon, and Helen waited downstairs. Isabel decided to reveal what Minnie had reported.

"A man was seen going into my mother's chamber late on the night before she took ill. When was the last time *you* saw her?"

"Ill," he muttered. "I've had enough talk of illness. Fetch me my backgammon set. You and I shall play."

"I've not come here to play games, Your Grace. I'm simply curious. Did you bring my mother a gift? A box of sweets perhaps? Or a bottle of wine?" If he was determined to stop her from completing her memoirs, he could have added arsenic to any food or drink.

"Stop your babbling. Never did like a female who rattled on too much." He pointed across the room. "It's over there."

It? She whirled around, half expecting to see a flask of poisoned wine or a signed confession. But there was only the backgammon board sitting upon a marble-topped table.

"Bring it here," the duke ordered testily. "Or I'll send you away."

What did he hope to accomplish by playing a game? Why not simply deny his involvement in the death and be done?

Deciding to humor him, she walked across the fine oriental carpet and picked up the heavy board, carrying it to the foot of the bed.

"Not there," the duke said. "Here." He patted a place beside him.

Cautiously, Isabel approached him. He looked harmless enough, his shoulders slumped and his hands loosely linked in his lap. And he was an invalid, confined to his bed. Still, she was glad for the dagger hidden in her pocket along with the memoirs.

"Perhaps you'll at least tell me how you learned Aurora was writing her memoirs," Isabel said as she set the game on the counterpane. "Did one of her other lovers alert you?"

He made no reply. She glanced up to catch a wicked

glint in his eyes. With a cry of conquest, he pounced.

His arms snaked out and dragged her onto the mattress. Her hip struck the backgammon board; the dice and playing pieces scattered. She fought him, wriggling and straining, but he held her pinned, his muscles surprisingly strong.

"Got you!" he snorted. " 'Tis a fine jest, Aurora. Did I play along well enough to suit you?"

He thought she was her mother? He must be mad, utterly mad. "You're mistaken," she cried out. "I'm Isabel. Release me at once."

He grinned. "You always did fancy a chase. Remember the time I pretended to be a brigand and ran you down in the mews behind Carleton House? We're lucky your moans of pleasure didn't awaken the Regent."

"I am *not* Aurora."

"Of course not. You're a coy virgin and I shall ravish you."

Laughing in macabre delight, the duke shifted his hand to her breasts. She lashed out, but the bonnet ribbons hampered her arm. Seeing her dilemma, he only chortled the louder.

Bile choked her. If only she could reach her dagger.

"Demme," he exclaimed. "You're wearing a frigging corset. Roll over."

Fighting panic, Isabel feigned compliance. This might be her only chance. As he shifted himself away, she plunged her hand into her pocket. And her shaking fingers closed around the haft of the knife.

∽ Chapter 7 ∾

*T*he chit had invaded his house.

Peeling off his gloves, Kern took the main stairs two at a time. He had arrived home a few moments ago to the news that Lady Helen Jeffries and Miss Isabel Darcy awaited him in the drawing room. The luckless footman had earned himself a rebuke, though Kern intended no further castigation.

He, too, had known the power of Isabel's dark, hypnotic eyes. If anyone required punishing, it was her. Only her.

Holding a teacup, Helen met him at the opened doors of the drawing room. Her mouth wore a naïve smile. "Oh, Justin! How good it is to see you."

"My lady." Affording her a brief bow, he stepped into the long chamber and glanced around. But Isabel wasn't sitting by the tea tray with its plate of cakes. She wasn't hidden in a window seat or perusing a book in the corner.

The only other occupant of the room was Miss Gilbert. She scrambled off her chair and made a curtsy. "My lord!" she squeaked, dabbing at her lips with a handkerchief. "Oh dear. Oh dear me."

Kern pivoted toward Helen. "Where is Miss Darcy?"

Her cheeks reddening, Helen bent down to place her teacup on the silver tray. "She needed a moment alone."

"Where?"

"She had a . . . a pressing need."

In a flash, he comprehended Helen's blush—and Isabel's diabolical cleverness. "How long has she been gone?"

"Perhaps fifteen minutes. I'm certain she'll be back straightaway."

Hell. *Bloody hell.*

He tossed down his gloves and started toward the door, but a small hand alighted on his coat sleeve. "Justin, do take a seat," Helen said. "I'll pour you a cup of tea, then we can go over the guest list for our wedding."

"Later."

"Now," she said with uncharacteristic firmness. "No doubt you're angry that I ignored your wishes and came to call on you. However, as an independent woman, I must insist upon exercising my right to make my own decisions."

This was more of Isabel's doing, he realized grimly. She had used her influence to dupe a sweet, impressionable girl. All for the purpose of infiltrating his house and creating havoc.

All for the purpose of pursuing her scheme of blackmail.

"Rest assured, I'm not angry at you," he said, patting Helen's small hand with a gentleness that belied the violence churning within him. "Now if you'll excuse me, I, too, have a pressing need."

Isabel crouched on the bed and watched the Duke of Lynwood. His green eyes were rounded with bafflement, like a child whose toy has been snatched from him. In contrast to the gleeful rapist of a moment ago, he lay perfectly still.

And for good reason.

She held the knife to his privates. "Touch me again, and I'll unman you."

Praying he wouldn't challenge her, Isabel slowly scooted backward on the mattress, never taking her gaze from him. Her heart drummed against her ribcage. The only sounds were the hiss of her quick breaths and the rustling of her skirts. When she reached the foot of the bed, she angled her legs toward the floor. Shakily, she stood up and backed away, brandishing the dagger. She could still feel his ghostly hands on her, groping, pawing, violating. Hands that had once pleasured her mother.

But Isabel wouldn't let herself think about that. Better she should use this opportunity to question him further. Yes. She should take advantage of his docility.

A deep breath failed to calm her. She could hear the quavering in her voice as she asked, "Now that I have your full attention, Your Grace, perhaps you'll admit the truth. You added arsenic to some food you gave my mother, didn't you? A box of chocolates perhaps."

He stared blankly. "Chocolates? When did I give you chocolates?"

"Not me. My mother. Aurora Darling. She was poisoned—"

Behind her, the outer door clicked open. A draught of cool air eddied into the room. Quick, sharp steps approached through the sitting room.

The manservant.

Isabel's knees nearly buckled, though she kept her watchful gaze on the duke. If only she had another moment. "Go away. His Grace and I are having a private conversation—"

"Take care!" Lynwood yelled, flapping the voluminous sleeves of his nightshirt. "The wench has a knife."

A hand shackled Isabel's wrist. The painful pressure wrested a cry from her. The dagger dropped from her numb fingers and thumped to the floor. And she found herself gazing up into the icy features of Lord Kern.

He held tightly to her arm. Her protest came out a dry, muted croak. Marshaling her scattered defenses, she returned his bold stare. For a moment they were locked in a silent battle for dominance. Then he released her so suddenly she stumbled backward and bumped into the wall. Unable to support herself, she sagged against it.

Lord Kern picked up her dagger and tucked it into an inner pocket of his coat.

Dear God. *Dear God.* She'd been caught. And yet strangely she felt safe now. Safe from the mad duke.

"The chit threatened to cut my balls off." Slapping his hands over the nightshirt, Lynwood cupped that portion of his anatomy. "I don't understand it. She enticed me, she toyed with me."

"Miss Darling does like to play games," Kern said, giving her a chilling look.

With effort she lifted her chin and glared back. "'Tis lucky you arrived when you did, m'lord. Else your papa would be a soprano by now."

But Lord Kern didn't appear to be listening. He walked to the bed and helped the old man slide beneath the coverlet. "Calm down, Your Grace. She won't trouble you anymore. I shan't allow it."

"You won't ever allow me a strumpet," the duke whined; then abruptly he pounded his fists on the bed. "Bloody prison guard! This is *my* house and I'll entertain whomever I please."

At the bedside table, Kern calmly poured out a dose of liquid from the brown bottle and put the spoon to his father's mouth. "Swallow."

"No."

"Swallow," Kern repeated.

"It will castrate me swifter than any knife."

"It's your illness that's castrated you. Now drink for the sake of your health."

The duke took the spoonful and swished it around in his mouth. He slid a sly glance up at his son, who promptly pinched the duke's nostrils shut, forcing him to swallow. Lynwood gulped and coughed, wiping his mouth on his sleeve. "Cold bastard. *You* never let your cock rule your wits."

"Now there you're wrong." Lord Kern paused, his face hidden from Isabel as he looked down at his father. "I most certainly am not a bastard."

She had but a moment to wonder at the animosity between father and son when the door opened, and the manservant came rushing inside, clad in clean livery embellished by spotless white lace. On seeing Lord Kern, he bobbed up and down like a jack-in-the-box and apologized to the point of groveling. Kern spoke a few words of instruction to him before turning from the bed.

Isabel straightened, concealing a shiver as the earl strode toward her. His face was stern, implacable in its handsomeness. He took her arm and hauled her out of the bedchamber, through the gloomy sitting room, and into the passageway. She stumbled along at his side, her petticoats tangling in her legs and her ruined bonnet bumping her hip.

He couldn't intimidate her, she wouldn't let him. With Helen waiting downstairs, he could only rage at Isabel and then let her go. What did a tongue-lashing matter when she had achieved her purpose in speaking to the duke?

Not that she had learned anything useful. She would have to return here . . .

"Lynwood is half mad," she said. "That's why you keep him confined to his chamber. You can't trust him in public."

Kern cast a dark glance at her. "At present, *he* is not the madman."

On that ominous statement, he thrust open one of the many doors along the passage, escorting her into another enormous bedchamber. The closed draperies barred the sunlight. Dust sheets covered the chairs and bed, giving the illusion of ghoulish watchers.

He released her, pacing with restrained anger to the unlit

hearth and back again. The click of his heels resounded on the wood floor.

Isabel's skin prickled, and her bravado wavered in the face of cold male fury. "I should like to rejoin Lady Helen," Isabel said. "She'll be wondering what's keeping me."

She edged toward the door, but he stepped into her path. "Let her wonder. I'm sure you'll come up with another lie."

"It's improper for the two of us to be alone. We'll cause a scandal."

"You should have considered that when you enticed an old man." Kern looked her up and down as if he found her utterly contemptible. "No doubt you tried to sweeten your blackmail by offering yourself. Let it be known, I have legal control of Lynwood's business affairs. So your efforts were for naught."

"I wasn't blackmailing him."

"No? Then did you hope to take your mother's place in his bed?"

She held tight to the bedpost. Why did it hurt to suffer Kern's misguided opinions? "I never enticed your father. He only imagined it. You know his foibles better than I."

"I know your cunning as well. You'd peddle your body to anyone in breeches."

"Then your memory is faulty, my lord. At our first meeting, *you* propositioned *me*."

"So I did," he said, his voice low with menace. "A pity I've never availed myself of what you give so freely to other men."

He stalked toward her, and a wave of acute awareness rippled through Isabel. He exuded power like an angry god come down from the heavens to punish a defiant mortal. The dark determination on his face should have frightened her, but a curious fascination held her in place. Swept up in the throes of a strange thrill, she could not have fled if her life had depended upon it.

His arms imprisoned her and his fingers roughly caught her chin, but before he could use force, she lifted herself on tiptoe and met him halfway. He groaned out her name, and she shut her eyes, the better to savor the closeness of his muscled body. His kiss melted her until she felt flushed with fever, and his tongue penetrated her mouth with aggressive intimacy. The divine bliss of passion made her more conscious of the emptiness inside herself, the need to be filled by this man.

Kern. Dear God, she was kissing Lord Kern. Wildly. Thoughtlessly.

"No," she whispered, turning her head to the side and inhaling the alien male scent of him. "We must stop. This is *wrong*."

"To hell with right or wrong," he muttered, and kissed her again with coaxing intensity.

Isabel caught her breath as his big hand cupped her breast, exploring her with the reverence of a connoisseur. The familiarity that had been so disgusting with an old lecher now enflamed her senses. She should not allow Kern such liberties, yet she, too, wanted—*needed*—him to go on touching her. She wanted to know the feel of his hands on every part of her body. A dark excitement unfurled within her. She wanted what she had heard the aunts whisper about . . . she wanted flesh on flesh.

As if privy to her fantasies, he reached behind her and worked at the buttons of her gown. All the while, their lips clung in a series of frantic kisses. His hands trembled— trembled as she herself trembled with the fury of her feelings. She slid her fingertips along his jaw and luxuriated in the roughness of his skin, the coarse silk of his hair. How extraordinary to inspire such passion in a man she'd believed to be heartless, hostile, unfeeling. How incredible to experience such arousal in herself. She felt as if another being possessed her body, a sensual creature who thrived on voluptuous indulgence.

Cool air wafted against her spine. Isabel shivered deliciously as he fumbled with the strings of her corset. The stiff garment loosened, and she helped him push down her bodice, their eager hands bumping until only a scrap of thin lawn covered her above the waist. With one arm he caught her to him, then peeled her chemise downward. He cradled one bare breast in his palm and gazed at her with hooded eyes.

"Beautiful. My God, you are beautiful."

The harsh awe in his voice filled her with wanton pleasure. Bending his dark head, he suckled her until her legs melted like candle wax and she felt herself tumbling backward, taking him with her. They landed in a tangled heap on the feather bed. His body came down on hers; his weight knocked the breath from her lungs and jolted Isabel to her senses.

Even through the folds of her skirts, there was no mistaking the hard rod pressing against her thigh. Often enough she'd heard the aunts describe a man's physique and his driving urge to copulate. Given her own pulsing need, she realized how close to disaster they loomed.

She braced her hands on his shoulders, but it was like pushing against a granite wall. "Kern, *no*. We mustn't do this. We cannot."

"We can, indeed," he muttered against her throat. "I want you. I need you."

They were the words she had dreamed of hearing, whispered by a nameless, faceless lover in her lonely bed. He moved his mouth down to her bosom, and the heat of his kisses threatened to melt her resolve. And then he reached down to draw up her skirts.

The memoirs. He could discover the memoirs. The little book lay at her side . . .

The thought galvanized her. He was her sworn enemy,

the one man who could ruin her plans. The one man who could ruin *her*. "Listen to me," she urged. "This cannot go any further."

"For God's sake, stop talking." And he nipped the tender bud of her breast.

She sucked in her breath, resisting the erotic pleasure of it, resisting the reckless desires inspired by his closeness. Cupping his hard jaw in her palms, she drew up his face and forced him to look at her. The primitive passion there was terrifying . . . and incredibly tempting.

She forced out the words. "Helen is waiting downstairs."

He stared with half-closed eyes, his fingers caressing her skin and sending ripples of pleasure through her. She saw the moment when realization dawned in him. His eyes widened, the wildness releasing its hold on the civilized man. His hands tightened on her, but only for an instant. Uttering a groan of frustration, he jerked himself off the bed.

He strode across the dim bedchamber and flattened his palms on a table, his back bowed. His uneven breaths disturbed the air as he struggled to master himself.

Like dry autumn leaves blown by a cold wind, regrets piled high in Isabel. She felt bereft . . . empty . . . alone. Her reaction made no sense, for there was nothing to lament. Better she should rejoice in thwarting Kern. Better she should take satisfaction in his obvious discomfort.

Better she should stop feeling so distressed herself.

"Don't lie there gawking," he growled over his shoulder. "Cover yourself."

His command jolted her into sitting up on the bed. She tugged at the twisted chemise, then wrestled with the corset. Out of the corner of her eye, she saw him stalk to a mirror and straighten his cravat. When he turned around, he looked the fine nobleman again, with nary a hair out of place or a wrinkle in his forest green coat, while she felt mussed beyond repair.

"You might offer to help me," she snapped, straining to reach behind her back. "I can't get these strings untangled."

His lips thinned in arrogant disapproval as he approached the bed. "Turn around."

She obeyed—only because the minutes were ticking away. She crossed her arms to hold the undergarment in place. As he pulled on the laces, his fingers brushed her back, and she drew in a breath to extinguish the damnable flame kindled by his touch.

"Too tight?" he asked.

Seized by an inexplicable shyness, she shook her head. It felt strange to be tended by a man, especially this aristocrat. What must he think of her? Though her throat ached, she held her chin high. No doubt she had confirmed his ill opinion a hundredfold. He would be blaming her for leading him astray, while absolving himself from any sin.

He kept his thoughts to himself. Cloaked in impersonal silence, he buttoned her gown and waited while she tidied her hair and repaired her bonnet. Then he went to the door and held it open, the consummate gentleman.

His cool control irked her. It was as if their passionate encounter on the bed had never happened. Isabel wanted to shatter his haughty self-discipline, to remind him he was a man like any other man. She wanted to prove his civilized manner was only a veneer.

Walking to him, she tracked her fingers along his clenched jaw and over his warm lips. "Never fear, my lord. Your little secret is safe with me. For the moment, anyway."

The slight flaring of those green irises betrayed his alertness. "I have no secrets."

"You do now." She curved her mouth into a wicked smile. "Who knows, someday I might just write my own memoirs."

Icarus always came to me under cover of darkness.

The most furtive of all my lovers, the Reverend Lord Raymond J—— took his pleasure after hours, when inquisitive eyes would not witness his lapse from grace. When he could indulge his penchant for dressing in my underclothes and pretending to be a fallen angel.

One nocturnal visit in particular stands out in my mind. I had passed a pleasant evening with a gentleman from Cornwall, and upon his departure, took myself back to bed, only to be awakened in the wee hours by the stealthy groping of my flesh and the whispering of naughty proposals in my ear. Icarus wore my best feathered boa, a silk shift, and a pair of my gartered stockings, but it mattered little to me, for the tool beneath these feminine trappings was all man. What delights we shared in the darkness, what joys of Eros! When at last our passions were spent, he slunk away as if our heated encounter had melted his angelic wings.

You might wonder, Dear Reader, why did I tolerate a lover who was ashamed to be seen with me? Perhaps, being the daughter of a stern country vicar, I liked the jest of luring the good cleric into sin. Or perhaps—oh, yes!—perhaps it was the prospect of soothing my broken heart, of filling the void left by the loss of my first true love.

My dearest Apollo.

—The True Confessions of a Ladybird

✺ Chapter 8 ✺

*K*ern walked into his father's bedchamber the next morning and found him with a lapful of housemaid.

Stripped linens from the bed strewed the floor. Sunshine streamed past the opened draperies and haloed Lynwood, clad in a dressing gown and enthroned in a wing chair by the window. Two giggling maidservants vied for his attention. He delved his hand beneath the skirt of one and buried his face in the bosom of the other.

Kern thought he'd grown inured to his father's lechery. But after a night of brooding about his own lapse of moral restraint, he lost all patience.

He strode toward the trio, took firm hold of the maidservants by their apron strings, and brought them stumbling to their feet. Their giggles turned to gasps. The plumper of the two fell to her knees, wailing, "Don't sack me, m'lord. We didn't mean nothin'."

"Don't turn me out on the streets!" cried the other. "I'll starve."

"Never venture near this room again," Kern said. "Now get out."

They made a wide berth around him, snatched up the dirty linens, and scuttled out the door.

Lynwood crossed his arms over his rumpled green dressing gown. His bare, withered legs stuck out from beneath the hem. "Don't glower, boy. There's no wrong in having a bit of fun. Truth be told, another taste of pussy might make you less of a prig. You haven't had any in how many years? Fourteen, eh?"

Looking into the dark pit of memory dizzied Kern; with iron effort he stepped back from the edge. Rather than let himself be drawn into a quarrel, Kern stalked to the leaded casement window and leaned against the sill. There had been alarming episodes of late when his father had had trouble recalling his own name, times when he did not recognize his own son, but from the sharp gleam in his eyes, Lynwood appeared lucid this morning. For that, at least, Kern could be thankful.

"Where is Mullins?" he asked. "No maid is allowed in here without him present."

Lynwood bared his teeth in a grin. "My prison guard had a trifling accident just before the maids arrived. I fear I missed the chamber pot and pissed all over him instead."

Kern stifled a startled laugh. His father needed no encouragement in his tricks. "Henceforth, he'll store a spare set of clothing right here in this room. Now, I wish to ask you about your visitor yesterday. Miss Isabel Darling."

"Fine-looking piece of ass, eh? Pity *you* don't go for whores."

But Kern did—at least this one in particular. For half the night, the memory of her lush body had tortured him, the sweetness of her kiss, the softness of her breasts, the incredible moment when he had covered her on the bed and felt her hips cradle him. Even now the witch roused him to throbbing torment.

Yes, he had the same base urges as any man—but until yesterday he'd possessed the discipline to control himself. God! How could he have forgotten Helen?

His fingers dug into the windowsill. "Something Miss Darling said has been troubling me. She claims she did not attempt to blackmail you. Is that true?"

"Blackmail?" Lynwood blinked as if confused. "How could the chit extort money from me? I've never bedded her. Even if I had, she'd be lost among the masses."

"She has Aurora's memoirs. Are you certain she didn't threaten to publish that filth?"

"I can't remember her saying so." The duke passed his hand over his wrinkled face. "Strange, for a while there, I believed the young one *was* Aurora—till she pulled that knife on me. Betimes, I can't keep my own wits straight."

Resisting a surge of pity, Kern concentrated on the discrepancy that nagged at him. "Then she must have tried to entice you. You said so yourself." Yet that didn't make sense, not when there were younger, wealthier, more accessible noblemen to gull. "What other reason could she have for coming here?"

"I'll tell you what. She asked if I'd put arsenic in a box of chocolates." Lynwood snorted in derision. "I never gave a woman chocolates in my life. The rod in my breeches is treat enough."

"Arsenic." Despite the sun beating on his back, Kern went cold. What deadly game was Isabel playing now? "Tell me exactly what Miss Darling said to you."

"The chit said she'd cut my balls off, that's what! Just because I mistook her for her mother."

Kern hunkered down on his heels in front of his father. "Never mind that. I want to know about the arsenic. Who were you supposed to have poisoned?"

"Her mother, I think." The duke's imperious features crumpled into horrified sadness. "But I wouldn't have hurt Aurora. We had many a good time together. Many a good time." He hung his head in the guise of a dispirited old man.

Stunned, Kern sat back on his heels. *Isabel believed her mother had been murdered.*

Impossible.

Yet like an icy fist, the thought gripped Kern. It cast a

new light on her determination to infiltrate the *ton*. Perhaps Isabel wasn't a fortune hunter intent on snaring a husband.

Perhaps she wanted to trap a killer.

"Will you be stealing him for yourself, then?" Callie asked.

She appeared behind Isabel in the dressing-table mirror. The glass reflected her china-doll face with the servant's mobcap perched incongruously atop her saucy blond curls. A shrewd grin revealed her stained teeth.

Isabel paused in the act of pinning her hair. She had been smiling dreamily into the mirror, lost in the fantasy of primping herself while her bridegroom watched from the bed. She deliberately had kept him nameless, faceless, a big shadowy man waiting to love her. But today his features took on a decidedly familiar look... "Stealing who?" Isabel asked cautiously.

"Lord Kern, of course. You've been flitting around here this morning, sighing like a lovelorn maiden."

"I have not," Isabel protested. Or had she? She picked up a pin and jabbed it into her chignon. "Whyever would I spare a thought for him? He and Helen are to be wed in June."

"Nevertheless," Callie said in a singsong voice, "Lady Helen might have the legshackle ready, but it's you he really wants."

"Don't be absurd. He despises me. He'd like nothing more than to toss me out on my ear."

"He'd like to toss you on your back right there in the bed," Callie said. "I know, for I saw the two of you together yesterday."

Isabel's fingers froze around the silver brush. No one knew of her erotic encounter with Kern at Lynwood House. "Saw us? Where?"

"Lord Kern escorted you and Lady Helen home. I spied you alighting from the carriage." Hips swaying, Callie strolled to the window and gazed down at the sunlit street, then slid a sly smile at Isabel. "I was watching from right up here. The earl may have been holding her ladyship's arm, but he was looking at you. Nay, he was *staring*, as if he'd like to rip off your gown and do all manner of wicked things—"

"That is quite enough," Isabel broke in, as an unwelcome heat seared her body. *He already undressed me. He touched me and caressed me and it was not wicked at all, but wonderful.* "You're imagining rather a lot into a mere look."

"Oh, I don't think so," Callie purred. "By the by, have you noticed the size of his hands?"

"No." *Yes. I remember the warmth of his fingers around my breast.*

"Well, *I* certainly noticed. It's been my observation that the bigger a man's hands, the bigger his cock." Callie sauntered closer as if in confidence. "Trust me, his lordship is built like a stallion."

"I wouldn't know or care." *But I remember lying beneath him. I remember how he moved against me . . .*

"Such a sweet little virgin you are. It's time a man initiated you into the arts of passion. And take my advice, his lordship would make you a fine lover."

Lover? Isabel's insides clenched with dreadful longing. In denial, she turned toward the mirror and snatched up an amber hair ribbon. "I don't want a lover. So you can stop your silly speculations."

"My, my. Aren't we the milk-and-water miss today?" Callie plucked the curling wand from its stand, took a lock of Isabel's hair, and deftly fashioned a ringlet that draped her shoulder. "I do hope you aren't really becoming a snooty lady. You'll soon be thinking yourself too good for your aunties."

Guilt washed over Isabel. Pivoting on the stool, she gave Callie a hug around her curvy waist, relishing the warmth of her cushiony body. "Forgive me for speaking so sharply. I would never, ever put myself above you or the other ladybirds." Drawing back, she regarded the older woman. "Have you heard how Aunt Persy is faring today?"

Callie smiled with motherly affection. "She's still on the mend. Di sent a message. She and Minnie are taking good care of her, so don't you fret."

"If only I could be there, too." That was Isabel's one regret about the masquerade, having to maintain the fiction of being a gentlewoman who didn't know of such evils as bawdy houses. How gratifying it would be if she could stop there today when she and Helen went on their round of visits.

But Helen would be appalled. She would regard Isabel with shock and disgust. Their fledgling friendship would come to a swift and bitter end.

That and worse would happen were Helen to learn of the intimate encounter with Kern, Isabel knew. How could she have lost herself so completely in his arms?

Drawing a shuddery breath, she studied her reflection in the mirror. The image of a gentlewoman, she had fine bones and a milky complexion unmarred by freckles. The delicate arch of her eyebrows accentuated her brown eyes. Yet despite her demure amber gown and the fashionably upswept curls, she was no lady. Perhaps, deep down, she was like her mother . . . a woman of easy virtue, a frivolous romantic who thrived on male attention.

You are who you are, a trollop's daughter . . .

Unwilling to let Minnie's pronouncement darken her spirits, Isabel jumped up from the dressing table. No, she hadn't forgotten who she was, nor would she ever forget. How could she, when Kern had aroused her passions with remarkable swiftness?

Isabel left the bedroom and headed down the corridor. Upon reaching Helen's chamber, she paused for a moment to prepare herself. The role of innocent country cousin seemed harder and harder to maintain these days. Coaxing her mouth into a pleasant smile, she knocked on the white-painted door.

Miss Gilbert opened it. The old governess was all a-twitter, fluttering her handkerchief like a flag of surrender. "Oh, my. It's a dreadful turn of events. Simply dreadful."

"I beg your pardon?" For one horrible instant, Isabel thought she'd been found out. She feared that her imprudent tryst with Kern had been exposed. Then she saw to her surprise that Helen was still in bed. She was sitting up and sipping a cup of tea, the covers drawn to her chin and her golden hair spread over the pillows.

Isabel hastened to the bed. "What's the matter? Are you ill?"

Setting the teacup on the bedside table, Helen managed a wan smile. "Dear Isabel. My throat is sore and my head aches most awfully. I would have sent word, but I kept hoping I'd improve. I'm so sorry, but you shall have to do without me today."

"I'm not going anywhere," Isabel declared, laying her hand on Helen's smooth brow. "You're feverish. Shall I send for the doctor?"

"No, it's merely a case of the sniffles. A few days of rest and I'll be fine."

"I'll read to you, then. Perhaps that will soothe you."

Helen smiled. "You're the dearest, kindest cousin. But to be honest, I feel more like taking a few drops of laudanum and sleeping the day away." She patted Isabel's hand. "You and Gillie can leave me. Justin will join you. It's a fine day—perhaps the three of you might take a drive in the park."

The prospect of a day free of obligation lured Isabel. This was the chance she'd been awaiting, to pursue the investigation. Tamping down a secret thrill, Isabel hastily considered her options. "You mentioned stopping at

church to discuss the details of the wedding ceremony with your Uncle Raymond. I'd be happy to go in your stead."
And question the randy goat about the murder.

"Oh, but I couldn't ask you to perform such a tedious task," Helen demurred. "It can wait until I'm well."

"Planning a wedding is always a thrill. So long as you trust me to see to the particulars."

"Of course I do," Helen said with a warm smile. "I would trust you with my life."

And your fiancé? Isabel bit back the question—and the incumbent guilt. She had no designs on Kern. In truth, she would rejoice to know she would never see him again. Now, if only she could slip out of the house before he darkened the foyer with his unwelcome presence.

She bade Helen farewell and escaped downstairs with Miss Gilbert. Isabel cautiously glanced into the drawing room, her senses alert for his tall, haughty form. The elegant green room was deserted, praise God, so she made straight for the front door.

"Oughtn't we wait for Lord Kern?" Miss Gilbert asked, trotting faster to keep up with Isabel.

"Good heavens, no. He won't care to escort us without Lady Helen."

An impassive footman opened the door. Isabel swept through the portal—and stopped on the porch as a phaeton drew up behind the Hathaway coach at the curbstone. Lord Kern sprang down from the driver's seat and tossed the ribbons to a groom.

Her heart did an inglorious leap. So much for luck.

The spring breeze ruffling his dark hair, he strode up the steps. An aura of angry purpose lengthened his strides. "Where is Helen?" he asked, glancing beyond the opened door behind them.

"Oh, my lord, we must be the bearer of bad tidings!" Miss Gilbert piped. "The poor dear has taken ill."

"Is it serious?"

"A cold," Isabel said, "but severe enough to confine Helen to her chambers. I might suggest that you go straightaway to the florist and order a posy to cheer her spirits. If you'll excuse us, Miss Gilbert and I have an errand."

He stepped into her path when she would have gone past him. Lethal suspicion narrowed his jade green eyes, the same eyes that had blazed with unbidden passion the day before. "What errand is that?"

"I promised Helen I would tend to a few minor details in regard to your wedding. We shall return in an hour or two." Again she tried to step around him, but this time Miss Gilbert's high-pitched voice thwarted her.

"Miss Darcy and I must call on the Reverend Lord Raymond Jeffries," said the governess. "That is, if you think it is perfectly proper for two ladies to visit a gentleman, considering that he is a clergyman."

Kern's sharp gaze pierced Isabel. "It is perfectly proper for a gentleman to escort the cousin of his betrothed to church. Miss Gilbert, you shall remain here."

As the governess sputtered a protest, he took Isabel by the arm, marched her down the steps and toward the phaeton. The pressure of his warm fingers made her skin prickle and her pulse tremble. His male scent hinted at darkness and danger, and she noticed a turbulence seething in him like a storm about to break. No doubt he blamed *her* for their kiss.

She held her chin high. Really, he was the one who should be ashamed of his conduct. He was the one who had acted the aggressor and precipitated their encounter.

And he was the one who had wrecked her plan for today. How was she to interrogate the minister with Kern hovering over her?

"Release me at once," she hissed. "I've no intention of going anywhere with you."

"Make a scene, then. If you dare."

Before she could retort, his hands encircled her waist. His big, strong hands. The hands that signified his prodigious proportions elsewhere.

Hot and flustered, Isabel lost her chance to object as he lifted her up into the open carriage, then vaulted beside her onto the seat. She scooted to the edge of the narrow cushion, but her amber skirt still brushed his tasseled Hessians. With a piercing glance at her, he took hold of the ribbons and guided the fine bay horse into the traffic around the square.

"So," he said in a clipped tone. "Tell me what business you have with Lord Raymond."

"Helen asked me to go over the wedding ceremony with him."

"The real reason," he said impatiently. "I'm privy to your tricks. I suspect that you intend to pester him as you did my father—"

"And you," she broke in. "Don't forget that I flaunted myself before *you*, too." If Kern wanted to believe her depraved, then she may as well parade her depravity.

His gaze fell to her lips, and she shivered from more than the cool breeze. Then he jerked his attention back to the busy street. "That regrettable incident has nothing to do with what I want to know now."

His ill opinion of her hurt, and the pain made her angry. "Oh, yes it does. That *regrettable incident* demonstrates the sort of woman I am. I lure men into my clutches. I tempt them into sin. I cast a spell on them and then milk them for their money."

He cocked a black eyebrow. "You certainly have a bee in your bonnet today. I must have spoiled your plans for the afternoon."

"Indeed you did. I meant to have a tryst with the Reverend Lord Raymond." Determined to rattle Kern's self-control, she flashed him her most sensual smile. "Though if you're interested, m'lord, perhaps we could make it a threesome.''

She had the satisfaction of seeing a muscle tighten in his jaw. "Don't trifle with me, Isabel. I know what mischief you're planning."

"Of course—'tis blackmail. I seduce gentlemen and then extort wealth from them. It's an easy way to make a living."

"You told me yesterday that you hadn't come to Lynwood House to blackmail my father."

"I did?" Caught off guard, she managed an airy laugh. "Well, I must have been lying. You know you can't trust a word I say."

"I wonder." While they were stopped behind a delivery dray, he gave Isabel a long, measuring stare. It made her uneasy, as if he could see through all the falsehoods to the truth of her quest. "I had a rather enlightening visit with my father this morning. He made a startling statement."

"What might that be? Did he tell you how I climbed into bed with him? How he refused to pay the price I demanded, and so I drew my dagger in an attempt to make him yield?"

The earl cast another grim, knowing look at her, and she felt the jittery urge to squirm. "He said you accused him of murdering Aurora Darling."

∞ Chapter 9 ∞

*K*ern watched the color wash out of Isabel's cheeks. Her sherry-brown eyes rounded with unguarded shock. A chill ran through him. By damn, she really *did* believe Aurora Darling was the victim of foul play.

And she thought his father had done the deed.

Blinking her long lashes, Isabel slid her gaze toward the crowded pavement, where servants and tradesmen hurried about their business. "Murder? I can't imagine how the duke formed such a notion," she said in a too-innocent voice. "He must be madder than I'd thought."

"He was parroting your words."

"How do you know? You weren't there."

Her pert denials fed his frustration. She deserved to be punished for harassing a sick old man. He seized her chin and forced her to look at him. "Don't try to cozen me, Miss Darling. If you continue to persecute my father on false grounds, I shall see you thrown out of society and tossed back into the brothel where you belong."

She drew a shuddery breath; her bosom rose and fell beneath the silk spencer. "You wouldn't dare. I would publish the memoirs."

"Would you? Or is your true purpose to unmask a murderer? A man you believe is a member of the *ton*."

Isabel set her mouth in an obstinate line. "I am under

no obligation to tell you my business. So why don't you stop the carriage and let me off here? I'd sooner walk to church than endure your company.''

"Oh no," he said through gritted teeth. "You are staying with me. Until you give me the entire truth."

She stuck her nose in the air. "Prepare yourself for a dull afternoon then, m'lord."

He wanted to shake her. Instead, he snapped the reins, setting the bay to trotting smartly, the harness jingling as they headed out of Mayfair. She *would* tell him everything. And Kern knew just the way to extract the information from her.

Isabel sat up straighter as the refined neighborhood gave way to common shops and smaller houses. "This isn't the way to St. George's Church."

"No."

"You're heading toward the Strand. Where are you taking me?"

"You'll see."

Within minutes they passed the Covent Garden Theatre. Kern drew the horse to a halt in front of a plain, paltry brick building. People went in and out of the front door: an official in a white wig and black suit, a weeping woman with a handkerchief pressed to her nose, a disreputable knave hauled up the steps by a runner in his distinctive scarlet waistcoat.

Isabel blinked. "The Bow Street Office," she murmured. "Why have you brought me here?"

"Since you won't be honest with me, you can tell your story to the magistrate instead." He leaned toward her, determined to have his way. "And be forewarned, Miss Darling. The gossip will spread and all of society will find out where you hail from."

Her mouth opened, then closed. She heaved a frustrated sigh, stopping him with a hand on his arm when he would have stepped down from the carriage. "All right, then," she said, her voice vibrating with emotion. "You want the truth? Leave here and I'll tell you."

Kern snapped the reins, and the horse went trotting down the street. "Go on."

"One of your kind poisoned my mother. One of your kind killed her so that she could not complete her memoirs. And no matter how you threaten me, I will find the culprit and see justice done."

The conviction in her tone shook him. He despised himself for wanting to draw her close, to ease her anguish. "Where is your proof?"

"A few days before she died"—Isabel paused to stare down at her clenched hands—"my mother recorded her fears in her memoirs. And her symptoms corroborate with poisoning."

"If you're saying she accused my father, that's utter nonsense," Kern said flatly. "Lynwood may be guilty of many sins, but he isn't a murderer."

"She didn't specify him by name. But the duke is one of several . . . former lovers who learned she was penning her memoirs. One by one, they came to call on Mama, to order her to stop." She spoke slowly, as if the admission were painful. "And Minnie saw a gentleman entering my mother's bedchamber late on the night before she took ill."

"Why did you not present your suspicions to the magistrate?"

"Do you think anyone back there"—she gestured at the building now half a block behind them—"would believe me? Or even care to investigate the death of a courtesan?" She gave a brusque shake of her head. "The law would rejoice at one less whore plaguing the city."

At her bitter tone, Kern felt a flash of compassion. She sat upright and proud, her fine eyebrows drawn in worry. For the first time, it was clear to him that she had loved her mother—and suffered from her loss. Yet he could not allow himself to soften toward her. "So you decided to

investigate on your own. You blackmailed your way into
Hathaway's house. And now you're sneaking out to see
the Reverend Lord Raymond. You intend to badger him
with your questions, too.''

She laced her gloved fingers in her lap. ''If I am, it is
no concern of yours.''

''I beg to differ. He happens to be the uncle of my betrothed. He is a fine, God-fearing gentleman devoted to the
church.''

''Strange, my mother described him as a cunning lecher
who harbors dirty secrets.''

On a few occasions, Kern had caught Lord Raymond
eyeing the women in his congregation with something less
than reverence. But Kern would not give Isabel any am-
munition for her little war. Besides, Lord Raymond was
not a murderer. Long ago, he had tutored Kern in his studies and offered a friendly ear whenever Hathaway had been
unavailable. Lord Raymond was a decent, warmhearted
man, a man who had tenderly set the broken wing of a
sparrow Kern had found as a boy.

''Dirty secrets?'' Kern scoffed. ''If you're referring to
the duel that caused his limp, that is an old scandal. And
it exonerates him from having the capability to murder. He
fired into the air rather than pull the trigger on his oppo-
nent.''

''I'm not alluding to *that* incident.''

''Then what possible secret could he hide?''

She pursed her lips and stared straight ahead, her spins-
terly primness at odds with her sensual beauty. ''It is not
for me to divulge.''

Her aura of mystery maddened Kern. He wanted to kiss
the truth out of her, to caress her beautiful body until her
defenses came down and she bared herself to him, body
and soul. He wanted to find the nearest lodging house and
finish what they had started yesterday.

God help him, he deserved to be horsewhipped. Despite

his betrothal to Helen, he still lusted after Isabel.

Turning his attention to the street, he clenched the reins. The wheels of the carriage clattered over the cobblestones. "We shall question Lord Raymond together, then."

"No!" she objected. "I do not want your interference."

"I'm involved whether you like it or not," he said. "Now tell me, what other gentlemen are named in your mother's diary?"

"I've told you quite enough."

"You've told me too little. I wish to read the whole of these infamous memoirs. Where the devil are they?"

She jumped as if he had pricked her with a pin. "The book is hidden away in a safe place—where no lordly snob like you might be tempted to dispose of it."

"So I am to take your word on this allegation of foul play. You must think me a colossal fool."

Isabel subjected him to a scathing once-over. "On the contrary, my lord, I don't think of you at all."

Damn her audacity. *He* had lain awake half the night thinking of *her*.

For all her prickly defiance, he remembered her ardent response to his caresses. He remembered how she had met his kisses halfway, how she had helped him draw down her bodice so that he could stroke her soft breasts.

Holding the reins in one hand, he placed his fingers over hers in her lap. The warmth of her flesh penetrated his thin driving glove. A warmth he desired beyond all reason and prudence. "Liar," he said silkily. "You tempt me to disprove your claim of indifference. Admit it. You want to engage in a tryst as much as I do."

His challenge rendered Isabel breathless. Though sunshine washed Lord Kern in brilliance, highlighting his perfect white cravat and haughty cheekbones, he exuded a wild aura. He drove the carriage with idle ease while taunting her with words as a pugilist would wield his fists. And to her utter mortification, her body responded to his aggressive male allure. A pulse beat low in her loins. Even here, in plain view of all the world, she wanted him to shift his fingers to her leg. She wanted him to slide them higher . . . higher . . .

She wanted to be his whore.

Isabel thrust his hand away. "Heed your driving. Lest you kill the both of us."

He chuckled darkly. "My driving is not what will bring you to harm. It's your audacity in making criminal accusations against powerful men."

She seized the change of subject. "Then you admit that one of these aristocrats killed my mother."

"I concur that certain depraved villains are capable of murder. But neither my father nor the Reverend Lord Raymond are among them." He directed the horse and carriage to the curbstone. "Be forewarned, I intend to prove that to you."

Curse him for prying. How could she coax reliable answers from Lord Raymond with Kern glowering at her, defending the very man she was interrogating? She must try, though she was shackled to Kern as surely as a prisoner to her gáoler.

They had arrived at St. George's Church with its lofty Corinthian portico and fine steeple. Kern leapt down and secured the horse, then came around to Isabel's side. She didn't want to accept his aid, and he knew it; she could tell by the mocking gleam in his eyes. Arrogant clodpole. But she had trouble descending gracefully from the high perch. Clasping her waist with his big hands, he swung her down to the pavement. His touch burned and she moved quickly down the footpath, disdaining the ladylike affectation of leaning on the gentleman's arm.

The church smelled of beeswax and damp stone. Their steps echoed in the nave. The pews were empty, the chandeliers unlit, though sunlight streamed through the window over the altar.

They found the pastor writing in his small, tidy office, a leather-bound copy of the Bible opened before him. His ivory-topped cane stood propped against the desk.

Spying them, the Reverend Lord Raymond Jeffries gave a bleat of surprise. The scratching of his quill pen ended abruptly. His curly brown hair and startled expression lent an incongruous boyishness to his hawk-nosed face.

He pushed back his leather wing chair and rose, gripping the edge of the desk for support. The wariness thinning his lips altered to a pleasant smile, as if he were donning a domino. "Justin. And Miss . . . Darcy. This is most unexpected."

"I trust we're not disturbing you," Kern said.

"Of course not. I was merely taking notes for Sunday's sermon." Lord Raymond gestured at two hard chairs. "Please, sit down. Tell me, to what do I owe this visit?"

Seating herself, Isabel suffered the force of his stare. She banished any intimidation by picturing him draped in a pink feather boa and a silk shift and pretending to be a fallen angel. "Lady Helen asked me to come here," she said sweetly. "It seems you've refused a number of her dinner invitations. She was concerned about you."

He resumed his seat. "Parish duties have kept me busy," he said stiffly. "Do convey my regrets to my niece. And assure her, there will come a time when I am again able to visit Hathaway House."

"I see." Stung, Isabel caught his meaning. He would not darken their doorway so long as she was in residence. The self-righteous pansy. "Helen also asked me to go over the particulars of the marriage ceremony with you. But since you are so *busy* these days, perhaps that can wait for another time. For now, I should like to ask you a few questions in regard to my mother."

Disapproval pinched the smile from the clergyman's face. He leaned forward in his chair. "Questions? I ended my regrettable association with that female many years ago. There is nothing more to say.''

"On the contrary," Kern said from his stance by a bookcase, his arms folded negligently across his burgundy coat. "Miss Darling believes her mother was murdered . . . by means of poison. She wishes to know whether *you* did the deed."

"*I?* Murder?" Sputtering, the Reverend Lord Raymond fell back in his chair. Sunshine through a small leaded window cast his middle-aged features into sharp relief. "This is madness . . . an outrage!"

Blast Kern. Isabel had meant to be subtle, to judge the cleric's reactions by degrees. "It is the truth," she said, flashing Kern a furious warning to keep silent. "Lord Raymond, I should like to know your whereabouts on the night of May tenth last year."

"How would I recall my activities of a year ago? I was probably at home with my wife." He shook his head, his face twisted with horror. "I . . . I thought Aurora died of natural causes later in the month, God rest her sinful soul."

He had gall, to judge her mother more a sinner than himself. Isabel thought of Mama's bright laughter, her generous nature. But this man had never bothered to know the goodness in her. "That was the night she took ill," Isabel prompted. "And that was also the night one of the other ladybirds saw a man visit her very late. Just as *you* used to do. For reasons we both know."

His face went as pale as the parchment on the desk. He glanced at Kern, then looked at her in a rage. "It wasn't me. And may I remind you, in exchange for my brother taking you in, you promised not to mention my visits to her ever again."

"I won't. So long as you answer my questions today."

For a moment the only sound was the harshness of his breathing. "I never went near Aurora, nor any other whore, these past fifteen years. I swear it." He pressed his ink-stained hand to the Bible. "As God is my witness, my life has been devoted to the church."

"But you did go to her, at least once more," Isabel said. "Just like Lynwood and the others, you warned her not to publish her memoirs."

"That was no assignation," he insisted. "I called on her for all of five minutes. In April, not May."

She scrutinized him, detecting resentment and something more—something dark and tortured. Desperation? Fear? "A murderer would feel no qualms about lying. Therefore, I must have evidence that you are telling the truth—"

"Enough," Kern said, pushing away from the bookcase and stalking toward her. "Lord Raymond has told you all he knows. You will not badger him any further."

"His answers are vague. I need proof of where he was on the night of May tenth."

Kern took firm hold of her arm. "You have his word as a gentleman. Good day, sir."

The clergyman got to his feet, leaning on the ivory knob of his cane. "I trust she'll say nothing more about this outrage. Should even the breath of scandal taint me, not even Hathaway will have the power to procure the bishopric of London for me."

"She'll hold her tongue. I'll see to that." Without further ado, Kern propelled her out of the church and into the sunshine.

His arrogant assumption of control infuriated Isabel. She shook off his grip and stopped in the dappled shade of an oak tree. "You far exceed your authority," she snapped. "You should not have interfered in there."

"You should not have treated Lord Raymond as if he were a criminal. I've known the man since childhood, and I say he's innocent of any alleged murder."

"I see. *You* require proof that my mother was poisoned. But *I* am not afforded the same privilege in regard to Lord Raymond's integrity."

"No, you are not. Now come along before all of London sees us quarreling."

Isabel realized that people strolled the byways, servants and tradesmen going about their business, fine coaches passing by. And who knew what curious eyes peered out the windows of the neighboring town houses?

Swallowing her ire, she accompanied Kern to the phaeton, where he helped her up into the high seat. Only as the horse began trotting and the carriage rolled smoothly down the street did he turn to her and say, "Tell me the names of the other men you are investigating."

As if she would allow him to interfere again! "At the risk of repeating myself, that is confidential information."

His jaw tightening, he frowned at the traffic. "I suppose they are all described in the memoirs which you refuse to show me."

She pressed her lips together. Let him stew in his own ignorance. He did not wish to help her, but to warn the others. Men of his kind formed a closed circle, protecting one another's reputation.

He peered at her, so keenly that she feared he would guess the small book lay within his reach, tucked inside the hidden pocket beneath her skirt. He couldn't know; no one knew. She took care when she changed clothes so that not even Callie suspected.

Kern said, "One of the gentlemen on your list is Sir John Trimble."

Isabel stiffened. Trust him to remember that card game at her first ball. But he couldn't pry into Trimble's past. He mustn't. She couldn't bear for Kern to find out that her own father had not wanted her.

At his level stare, a flush flooded her cheeks. Her palms felt clammy inside her gloves. "You can't be certain of that."

"No. But the truth shouldn't be too difficult to ascertain." He returned his attention to the road, and she soon noticed that he guided the horse south onto busy Regent Street.

"Where are you going?" she asked.

"I recall Trimble belonging to one of the clubs. It should be a simple matter to track down the man."

Appalled, Isabel said, "But he's out of town. You heard him say he was going to the country for a while."

"Then we shall see if he's returned."

Damn Kern. She considered insisting he return her to Hathaway House, but feared more that he would interrogate Trimble himself and ruin the element of surprise. At the very least, she wanted to be present to hear what excuses Trimble had to offer in regard to her mother's murder.

On St. James's Street, Kern stopped the carriage in front of what looked like a graceful country house, though it sat in the midst of the city. He beckoned imperiously, and the doorman came hurrying down the steps.

In answer to Kern's query, the servant lifted his top hat and scratched his balding pate. "Short man with a hidjus scar across his cheek? Think I've spied such a gennelman over at Boodle's from time to time. Shall I find out for you, m'lord?"

Nodding, Kern flipped him a coin, which the man snatched nimbly. He dashed across the street to another elegant club, and within moments he'd returned with an address. Sir John lived in a rather seedy neighborhood off Haymarket.

Kern concealed a surge of triumph and set off in pursuit of his quarry. Though Isabel sat as stiff as a governess's ruler, her gaze focused straight ahead, he sensed a powerful agitation in her. The breeze fluttered dark wisps of curl around her face. Undoubtedly she had known where Trimble resided. But she was determined to thwart Kern however she could.

He was just as determined to thwart *her*.

In short order, he drove through the crowded streets and located the dwelling in a row of small, undistinguished town houses. Kern wondered how a man who lived in such reduced circumstances had been able to afford Aurora Darling. That was one question Kern intended to pose.

But Trimble wasn't in, and the brisk housekeeper who answered the door said he'd not yet returned from his trip. Kern had to settle for leaving word that he would come back on the following Friday morning.

"See? I told you he wouldn't be here," Isabel said with an air of triumph as they descended the front steps. "And you are not to return here without me. This time, *I* will direct the questioning. Lord Raymond might have revealed more had *you* been shrewder in making your accusations."

Setting his jaw, Kern stopped beside the carriage. "Forget him. He isn't the guilty party."

"Oh? He had ample cause. And if you mean to take so careless an attitude toward Trimble, too, you must leave the interrogation to me."

"Like hell," Kern bit out. He never swore in front of females, but Isabel Darling pushed him to extremes. "I intend to keep a firm leash on you lest your lack of breeding land you into trouble."

"*My* lack of breeding? *Your* father is Lynwood."

Refusing to snap at her bait, Kern gritted his teeth. "Your lack of breeding," he repeated. "If anyone of consequence should see you visiting gentlemen without a proper chaperone . . ." He almost said *you'll ruin yourself*, but amended, "You'll bring shame down on Lady Helen and her father."

Isabel drew herself up with dignity. "I am perfectly aware of how a lady comports herself. I had a governess who taught me to curtsy and simper with the best of them—*oh!*"

Struck by the alarm elevating her voice, he followed her gaze across the street, where a group of urchins huddled on the corner, their attention focused on something small crouched within the center of their circle. Their shouts and taunts radiated a sinister brutality.

To Kern's astonishment, Isabel seized the whip from its stand inside the phaeton and then hastened toward the band of children. "Good God," he muttered, and strode after her. What ill-bred calamity was she involving herself in this time?

One flourish of her whip and the ragamuffins scattered in four directions, disappearing into alleyways and around corners. By the time he reached her side, she was scooping up the brown-and-gray animal that cowered on the ground.

She cradled it to her breast. "Oh, Kern. It's a puppy. Isn't she adorable?"

"He," Kern corrected, giving the tiny, quivering creature a cursory examination to make sure it wasn't hurt. Mats covered its floppy ears and short tail. "And he's filthy. You had better put him down."

"No." Isabel shot Kern a fierce frown. "Those boys might return and bully him again."

He had to concur with her reasoning. "And what do you intend to do with the animal, then?"

"I'll take him home. I'll care for him myself."

"May I remind you, Hathaway House is not your home. You've no right to impose a mongrel upon the marquess and his household."

Her face paled, but she did not release her hold on the dog. She cuddled it in her arms, stroking the dirty gray spot on its brow while the little creature grew calmer. "I have another home where I can take him eventually," she said. "In the meantime, I will not abandon this puppy."

Turning on her heel, she marched toward the phaeton. Kern followed, resenting her for making him feel like a first-rate cad. Who was he to obstruct her kindness? Did he despise Isabel so much he could accept no human decency in her?

He helped her up into the carriage, and she held tight to the puppy, though dirt smudged the amber silk of her gown. As she crooned to the dog, her expression softened and she smiled, absorbed in doting on her ragtag pet. The breeze flirted with her curls, and sunshine pinkened her cheeks. She might have been a lady bent on rectifying the harsh injustices of life. He caught himself wishing for half the attention she lavished on the animal.

Kern snapped the reins. How ridiculous to feel his gut twisted with jealousy over a godforsaken ball of fur. If anything, he should be bent on discovering who else she suspected of murder. What other men had she paid special attention to these past few weeks?

There had been Charles Mobrey, but Isabel had not solicited his friendship; she had used him to obtain an introduction to Sir John Trimble. Since then, a number of young gentlemen had courted her, but Kern could think of no one in particular who might have frequented an aging whore when there were younger ones to be had.

Why should he bother solving the mystery, anyway? So long as Isabel refrained from accusing his family members, her plotting shouldn't interest Kern. Let Isabel make her private accusations. Give her enough rope, and sooner or later she would hang herself. Sooner or later she would confront the murderer—and the murderer would deal with her.

Chilled to the core, Kern glanced at her. She giggled as the puppy licked her chin. Giggled like a carefree girl. A violent pressure built in his chest. He wanted to shake some sense into her. He wanted to rant at her, to forbid her from pursuing her dangerous course of action.

When she saw Kern watching, the light in her eyes dimmed, though a twinkle of defiance lingered. "M'lord," she said.

"Yes?"

"That is his name."

Had she guessed the identity of the murderer? Clenching the reins, Kern leaned toward her. "Who? Who is this man?"

"I'm not referring to any man. It's the perfect name for *him*." Smiling impishly, she hugged the homely stray dog to her bosom. "Henceforth, he shall be known as M'lord."

14 May 1821

> *Though my hand trembles with weakness, I take up my pen once more to record my thoughts . . . nay, my fears. Has it truly been a fortnight since I took ill? The malady has kept me abed, sapped my strength, made me aware of how frail a vessel is the mortal body.*
>
> *Alas! Until this vile sickness struck, I enjoyed the health and spirit of a woman far younger in years. I lived for pleasure. But now all prospect of pleasure has been robbed from me.*
>
> *I have been poisoned.*
>
> *Dear Reader, you may scoff at my suspicions, yet heed me well. These past weeks, my lovers have come here, one by one, to warn me against my writings. Now I fear there is a Villain among them who wishes me dead, a Villain who is determined to keep me from completing these memoirs.*
>
> *But I will not be stopped. Having squandered both fortune and love, I find myself weary and alone. God willing, the proceeds from my book will permit me to leave this house of assignation forever and join my dear daughter in Oxfordshire. There at last we shall live together, she and I. And perhaps there I might find a measure of the peace I never found with her father . . .*

—The True Confessions of a Ladybird

∽ Chapter 10 ∽

I sabel hesitated in the corridor outside the library.

M'lord wriggled in her arms and his cold nose nudged her chin. The dog had cleaned up rather nicely, she thought, though it would take a few more good meals to fill out his scrawny body. After a wild bath in the scullery sink that had rendered Isabel as wet as the frisky pup, his coat shone like honey dappled with milk. A footman had produced an old collar from the stables, and a kitchen maid had cleaned the leather lead. Botts the butler had wrung his hands and fretted over what the master would say. Isabel had assured them all she would obtain authorization from Lord Hathaway.

Now, having changed into her best aqua tea gown, she faced that very task.

Filled with guilty apprehension, she rubbed her cheek against the puppy's soft head. These past weeks, the marquess had been decent enough, considering she had blackmailed her way into his esteemed household. Hathaway had treated her politely while maintaining a circumspect distance. In truth, he might have subjected her to petty cruelties, but instead he had paid for her new wardrobe and accepted her—albeit reluctantly—as a companion for his only daughter. Just as reluctantly, Isabel was coming to believe him a true gentleman, honest and fair, even admirable. She had not thought such a man existed—at least not in aristocratic circles.

Lord Kern, on the other hand, exemplified the arrogant snob. Though he wanted people to believe him honorable, he lacked tenderness and integrity. Witness his angry kiss.

Her skin flushed with unwelcome heat. She cursed the feeling for what it was, sexual longing. Yet she wanted him with all the shameless hunger she had heard the aunts talk about—she wanted to feel his warm body cover her and to know the touch of his fingers on her naked flesh. She wanted to learn carnal knowledge with Kern as her teacher.

Only an idiot would desire the one man who could defeat her quest for justice.

Only a hussy would covet the fiancé of a dear friend.

Only a wretch would demand yet another favor from Hathaway.

Isabel faced the closed door of the library. This morning she had acted without thinking. Now that she'd had time to reflect, she knew she had rushed to M'lord's defense from more than the humane desire to rescue an abused animal. Although she never would have admitted as much to Kern, she had seen a phantom of herself in the puppy—the misfit taunted by village bullies about her shady past.

Isabel clasped the dog closer. He was so small, so vulnerable, as she herself had once been. She had intended to leave him in her bedchamber just now, but he had whined and cried, begging her with adoring brown eyes until her heart had melted.

No one would take him away from her. *No one.*

She raised her hand to knock. Before her knuckles met the white-painted panel, the door opened and the marquess stormed out.

She jumped back, bumping the door frame. Hathaway came to an abrupt halt. He reached out as if to steady her;

then he jerked his hand back. "You," he said in an ominous voice.

He stood as straight as a poker. Though not a tall man, he radiated so much authority he seemed to tower over her. His white caterpillar brows clashed in a frown. Not since she had presented him and Lord Raymond with the damning excerpt from her mother's memoirs had the marquess regarded her with such icy contempt.

Her heart sank. He must have heard about her stray mongrel, though he did not spare M'lord a glance. But she never gave up without a fight. "Good afternoon, Lord Hathaway. I should like a word with you."

"No. *I* should like a word with *you*, young woman."

He stepped back, a sweep of his hand bidding her to enter. She held the puppy and marched into the library. Never before had she been allowed into Hathaway's private sanctum. Comfortable chairs and rugs silvered by age decorated the long room. The masculine retreat smelled of tobacco and leather and the ineffable essence of old money.

At any other time, Isabel would have liked to explore the rows upon rows of books lining the walls. She would have liked to examine the family portraits hanging on the paneling above the bookshelves. But not now.

Now she had M'lord's welfare to consider.

Bracing herself to persuade the marquess, she turned around as he shut the door. "I know that my status as your guest permits me no further privileges," she began. "Therefore, I must apologize for upsetting you—"

"Upsetting?" he said in a tight voice. "Your actions today have been insolent and insufferable. You have far overstepped your boundaries, Miss Darling. And I will not tolerate it."

At his sharp tone the puppy growled, and Isabel stroked M'lord to calm him. Hathaway's fierce attack both wounded and angered her. Was he so opposed to allowing this little creature in his house? "Pray forgive me for not coming to you straightaway," she said. "You see, I didn't think it would be wise—"

"You didn't *think*." Pacing before the carved stone fireplace, Hathaway ran his fingers through his salt-and-pepper hair. "If there is one thing I can abide less than ill behavior, it is excuses. The least you can do is to own up to your actions."

"I'm offering an explanation, not an excuse," she said stiffly. "As I was saying, I didn't think it wise to come here without first giving M'lord a bath."

Hathaway stopped in his tracks. His face paled; then a ruddy color surged from his throat into his cheeks. "By God," he said slowly, clenching and unclenching his fists, "if you dare to consort with gentlemen in your bath, young woman, I shall thrash you within an inch of your life."

Stunned by his vehemence—and his mistaken assumption—she shook her head. "*No.* M'lord is my *dog.* I rescued him today from a band of bullies."

"Your dog."

"Yes. We've been talking about him—about whether or not you'll permit me to keep him here." Feeling as befuddled as Hathaway looked, Isabel tilted her head. "Haven't we?"

The marquess blinked at M'lord, and the puppy gave a fierce yap, though spoiling the watchdog effect by wagging his tail.

"Apparently we've been speaking at cross-purposes," Hathaway muttered. He stalked to the writing desk, picked up several sheets of vellum, and shook them at her. "I was referring to this letter, which was delivered a short while ago. In it, my brother told me of your vile accusations."

She wanted to laugh from giddy relief. Lord Raymond. Hathaway was referring to Lord Raymond.

Of course, that was hardly cause for cheer.

She set the puppy down on the carpet and held the

leather lead while M'lord trotted away to sniff the base of a dictionary stand.

The marquess glowered at her, his white-knuckled hands at his sides. "Have you nothing to say to this charge, Miss Darling?"

"Yes, I visited the Reverend Lord Raymond this morning," she said carefully. "I merely asked some questions in regard to my mother's death."

"Questions, bah! You hurled lies at him. You claimed Aurora Darling was murdered." His fist struck the desk, rattling the quills and silver inkstand. "It's nonsense. Cockle-brained, fanciful nonsense."

His vehemence jolted her, and she wondered if his reaction typified what would happen as more and more people learned the story of Aurora's murder. "No, it isn't nonsense. I was there at my mother's deathbed. I *know*."

"You know nothing." He coldly regarded her. "Had such a crime been committed, the magistrate would have been notified. The news sheets would have covered the story in sordid detail. All of London would have buzzed with the scandal."

"The truth was written in my mother's memoirs. She swore she was being poisoned by one of her . . . her former lovers." For some inexplicable reason, Isabel felt compelled to convince him and took a step closer. "Mama hid the book so well I didn't find it until many months after she died. By then, who would have believed me?"

"Who, indeed?" The marquess's voice rang with contempt. Tossing down the letter, he prowled back and forth in front of his writing desk. "To think Justin failed to silence you and your disgusting allegations this morning. By God, I shall have a word with him about *that*."

"It's no concern of his—nor of yours—if I choose to find the man who took my mother from me. Besides, can you prove Lord Raymond is *not* that man?"

Hathaway stood very still, yet she had the impression of

seething emotions in him. "I will hear no more of this folly." He pointed his forefinger at her. "Heed me now, and heed me well. So long as you are living in my house, you will behave like a lady. You will not go about like the common hoyden you are, accusing your betters of a capital offense. Do I make myself clear?"

Shocked to the core, she could only gaze at him. Then she managed a shaky nod as despair leapt out and sank its sharp teeth into her confidence. For a time she had felt accepted by him, a lady on equal social footing with his own daughter. How could she have forgotten that was all an illusion? In truth, he—like Kern—viewed her as an interloper. To them, she was no better than the tweeny who scrubbed pots in the scullery or the groom who mucked the stables.

Damn all noblemen.

Yet in the midst of her humiliation, she couldn't help puzzling over Hathaway's agitation. Why did he appear so white-faced and shaken, as if he had been delivered a shattering blow? Why did the shadow of some dark emotion lurk in his eyes?

Then the truth struck Isabel. Staring, she took a step backward.

Lord Hathaway was terrified. Terrified that his pious, conniving brother really might have committed murder.

"Murder, bah," Minnie said. " 'Tis a girl's fancies and nothing more. I don't know what else we can say, m'lord."

In the unforgiving light of day, the parlor had an air of tarnished vulgarity. The sun had faded the maroon upholstery on the chaises and turned the gilt fringe on the draperies to the color of dingy brass. A shawl was draped carelessly over a broken cane chair. Brighter squares on the gold-striped wallpaper showed where paintings had once hung.

The pictures likely had been sold, Kern thought, judging

by the squalid state of the house and the obvious need for funds. He hadn't noticed the defects on his previous visits to the brothel. Candlelight and darkness forgave many faults.

Was Minnie telling him everything she knew?

He studied the stout woman who sat enthroned on a high-backed chair. But for the low green bodice that flaunted a pair of bovine udders, she might have been a duke's dowager aunt. On the chaise across from her lounged Diana, idly twisting a lock of flame-colored hair while staring out the window.

The sooner Kern solved the mystery of Aurora's death, the sooner Isabel would vanish from his life. "A girl's fancies," Kern repeated. "Then you're saying Aurora Darling was *not* poisoned?"

"Who's to know the truth but God?" Bowing her mob-capped head, Minnie heaved a sigh that jiggled her impressive bosom. " 'Tis no wonder the sweet child is distraught. She did so love her dear departed mother. Not that Aurora deserved such loyalty."

"Explain yourself."

"From the time Isabel was born, her mum paid her little heed. She was only a babe in arms when Aurora sent her away to a wet nurse in Oxfordshire. Even as she grew older, Isabel only came back here for brief holidays. Of course *I* made a point to visit her whenever I could manage. Somebody had to look after the child's welfare." A look of earnest worry on her round face, Minnie leaned forward, her work-worn hands clasped in her lap. "Oh, do send her back home to us, m'lord. Don't let her go on this way, poking into people's secret lives. She can only come to grief."

Kern feared that himself. He knew he should focus on questions about the crime, yet he hungered to know more about Isabel's past. "And you," he said, turning to Diana. "Do you concur with this assessment of Aurora?"

Diana buffed her fingernails against the brown silk wrapper that hugged her sagging figure. A webwork of lines marred her white skin. "Aurora didn't want the chit raised around the men who used to come here. And I can't say as I blame her." She scanned him, her full lips pouting with hostility. "Too many toffs are keen on little girls. Men like you prefer to plow a tender field."

If she had kicked him, he couldn't have felt more jolted. Until now he had not considered Isabel as a young girl growing to womanhood with a company of harlots as her only family. But which version of her past was the truth? Had Aurora been a neglectful mother? Or was she to be commended for banishing her bastard daughter to the country? He was inclined to believe the latter, though it galled him to feel any admiration for a courtesan.

Careful not to let his composed features alter a whit, he circled the women, deliberately engaging Minnie's watchful gaze. "You claim that Isabel is prone to fancy. Yet late on the night Aurora took ill, you saw a man entering her bedroom."

"Aye, but that weren't anything out of the ordinary."

"Can you describe the man?"

Gripping the arms of the chair for leverage, she shifted her bulk. "No, m'lord. It was past midnight, and so dark I only caught a glimpse, enough to know he was a customer. At the time, I thought nothing of the matter. Aurora always liked her privacy."

He turned to Diana. "Did *you* see this man?"

"Don't you think I would have said so by now?" She gave a toss of her fiery hair, and the sunlight picked out dull gray strands among the red. "I was in bed, if you must know."

"Alone?"

"Yes. I do as little entertaining as possible, men being the swine they are." Her lip curled, making Kern aware of where Isabel had learned her scorn for gentlemen.

He closely watched both women. "Do either of you know where Aurora's memoirs are hidden?"

Diana shrugged. "That's a question for Isabel."

Frowning, Minnie shook her head. "She has the book with her, I suppose. And 'tis folly indeed, her going after all those society gents just because Aurora had some wild notion she'd been poisoned."

"Has anyone ever tried to steal the memoirs?" Kern asked.

"Steal?"

"Yes. It strikes me as odd that a man might have killed Aurora to stop her from publishing the memoirs. Then he left without the book."

Minnie inserted a finger beneath the mobcap and scratched her scalp. "I never thought of that before. But the diary was hidden for many months. Mayhap he looked but couldn't find it."

"Perhaps." But still, Kern wondered. Wouldn't the murderer have turned the house upside down in a search for the damning volume? And what would he do when he learned that Isabel now possessed it?

The thought shook Kern. A man who had killed once would not hesitate to kill again . . .

Diana crossed her legs, one of her slippers impatiently kicking the air. "Is that quite all, your lordship? I've plenty to do with Callie and Isabel gone and Persy still recuperating."

"Aye, we're too busy for this chitchat," Minnie said, her eyes narrowing on him. "For one, the cabbage soup will burn, and then what'll us poor old women do for dinner? It's not like we can afford to waste."

So that was the way of it.

Kern reached into an inner pocket, drew out two gold sovereigns, and placed them before a chipped statue of a naked nymph. Diana sat up straight, the boredom fleeing her fine-aged face. Minnie stared at the money and avariciously rubbed her thumbs against her forefingers.

"Now," he said, "tell me everything you know about Aurora's lovers."

Isabel arrived at the ball unfashionably early. Only a few guests stood chatting in the entrance hall, waiting for Lord and Lady Wilkins to form a receiving line. The butler stalked past, balancing a silver tray of wine bottles. A white-gloved footman took Isabel's pelisse and Miss Gilbert's cloak.

"Oh, dear, I do not think we should have come alone," Gillie whispered. Bundled in brown bombazine, she dabbed at her lips with a handkerchief. "We ought to have waited for Lord Kern to escort us."

That was precisely why Isabel *had* contrived to depart well before the appointed time. "Nonsense," she said. "It is perfectly respectable for a lady and her companion to attend a ball."

"Yet a gentleman would lend us his protection and gallantry."

"And we would be imposing on him. With Helen still abed with a cold, he surely will be thankful for being spared the obligation to escort us."

At least Isabel prayed so. She had no wish to spend the evening dodging her nemesis. Today, she had ascertained the arrival in town of another gentleman who had once consorted with her mother. She was banking on the hope that he, too, had received an invitation to this, one of the premier events of the season.

The last aggravation she needed was Lord Kern hovering at her elbow. Now that he knew she sought to punish one of his kind, he would thwart her at every turn. Unless she kept a step ahead of him.

Yet as she and Miss Gilbert mounted the grand staircase to the reception rooms, Isabel felt her worries float away. An irresistible excitement bubbled inside her, the thrill of living a favorite fantasy, of being a princess on her way to meet a prince.

Ever since she had joined the ranks of polite society, that youthful daydream had enveloped her again like a gossamer veil settling over her common sense. Though a part of her knew it was impossible, she still wanted—yearned for—what she could not have.

A passing gentleman bowed to her, and she inclined her head in regal graciousness. Living as a lady fed a hunger in her soul. Illusion or not, she liked being regarded with respect and honor. Here, removed from the cruelties of her base birth, she felt secure and safe. When the charade ended—as end it must—she would go back to her real life. Back to being the sensible and unsuitable Miss Darling, virginal resident of a brothel.

You are who you are, a trollop's daughter.

True though it was, she shut out Minnie's pronouncement. Closing her eyes, Isabel memorized the moment— the rustling of silk and lace, the cool smoothness of the marble balustrade beneath her palm, the sound of cultured voices echoing in the vastness of the entry hall. Someday she would appreciate the fond memories of a time when she had been a lady . . .

"I say, Miss Darcy!"

Her eyelids snapped open to the sight of Mr. Charles Mobrey, shooting like a cannonball down the corridor. The elaborate folds of his cravat nearly swallowed his double chin. A corkscrew of sandy hair bounced against his brow as he skidded to a halt and bowed deeply to her.

"Good evening, Miss Darcy." With nary a glance at the governess, he seized Isabel's gloved hands in a fervent grip. "I've been waiting for you in an agony of hope. Will you be so kind as to grant me the opening dance?"

Isabel curbed a rush of impatience. He hardly fit her image of a prince, but she had to occupy herself until her quarry arrived. "As you wish. So long as Gillie does not object."

Mobrey swung toward the older woman who hovered behind Isabel. "Pray, grant your approval, ma'am. Lest I expire here and now from a broken heart."

Miss Gilbert fluttered her handkerchief. "My dear young man. Of course you may dance with my charge. You are eminently suitable."

"Bless you for saying so."

They were both so earnest, Isabel wanted to laugh. "For now, Gillie, let us find a place for you to sit away from the crush of guests."

The immense ballroom was indeed beginning to fill with people. Golden candlelight from the chandeliers spilled over the assembly of dark-suited gentlemen and brilliantly gowned ladies, the unmarried girls clad in purest white. The musicians were tuning their instruments, and a palpable air of excitement eddied through the crowd. The scene looked like the staged rendition of a fairy-tale ball.

But Isabel wouldn't meet her prince tonight. She had other plans. More important plans. She had a dragon to slay.

She guided Miss Gilbert to a cushioned seat near a tall window, where chaperones and matrons were gathering to gossip. "Mind you return to me after every dance," Miss Gilbert said, her plain face screwed up in concern. "An unmarried lady always has her partners approved."

Poor, dear Gillie. She would be bamboozled tonight, there was no escaping *that*. Pricked by guilt, Isabel leaned down to kiss Miss Gilbert's aging cheek. "I shan't bring shame upon you, I promise."

She would try her level best to keep that vow. To do otherwise meant bringing disgrace not only on herself but on Helen and the marquess. And Isabel still felt shaken by Hathaway's harsh censure, and by her own yearning to prove herself worthy.

Mobrey took her by the arm and led her toward the

dance floor, where other couples were assembling. As they waited for the music to start and Mobrey cooled her with a breeze of overblown compliments, she found herself scanning the crowd for a certain tall earl too haughty for his own good. *Stay away, Kern*, she thought. *Don't you dare interfere with my plans for tonight.*

"Where, pray, is your guardian this evening?"

Isabel blinked at her officious partner. "I cannot know. Though with his fiancée ill, I'm sure he has no wish to attend."

"Fiancée?" Mobrey's mouth gaped open for a moment. "Ah, you speak of Kern. But I meant Hathaway."

"Oh." Isabel felt like the perfect fool. "I daresay the marquess is at his club."

"A pity. I was intending to ask him for an audience at his earliest convenience." Mobrey seized her hand and raised it to his lips for a kiss. "You can guess why, can you not?"

An inkling of alarm came over her, but she shook her head. "Perhaps you've an interest in entering politics? I'm sure Lord Hathaway would be happy to guide you through the intricacies of Parliament."

"My dearest Isabel, you mistake the source of my passion. Yet I cherish you all the more for your modesty." He pulled her closer in the crush of waiting dancers, and he whispered in her ear, "Precious lady, I can remain silent no longer. Permit me to express my most ardent love and admiration for you, the woman I have chosen as my own from among all others."

"Sshh." Feeling her cheeks flush, she glanced around to make sure no one had overheard. Then she drew him to an alcove where the tinkling of a small fountain masked their conversation. "Please," she hissed, "do not speak so recklessly in public."

"Then let us forego this dance, my love. Let us steal out to the garden, where we may declare our true feelings for one another. 'Drink to me only with thine eyes, /And

I will pledge with mine; /Or leave a kiss but in the cup/ And I'll not look for wine.' "

She wanted to box his silly ears, but she might scrape her hands on his high starched cravat. Oh, dear. *Oh, dear.* She hadn't anticipated that Mobrey loved her with all the emotion in his self-centered heart. His attentions could put a crimp in her carefully laid scheme.

"We shall stay here and dance," she said firmly, when he would have spirited her out of the ballroom. "And you need not address Lord Hathaway on my behalf. He has no jurisdiction over me."

"But he is your guardian. Your closest male relation."

"We share only a distant connection. Thus, I am mistress of my own fate." Striving to let him down easily, she decided on a measure of honesty. "Please understand, I am not at leisure to marry you or any other man. To put it bluntly, I lack the means to tempt any gentleman."

Mobrey reared back in an almost comical look of shock. "Hathaway has made no financial settlement on you?"

"None. And do not hold him to blame. He cannot be expected to endow every long-lost relation who appears on his doorstep." She bit her lip, remembering how cold and disapproving Hathaway had been that morning. Yet he had allowed her to keep M'lord, and she wanted nothing more from him. "It is enough that he has given me this Season. When it is done, I shall return to the country, where I have a little cottage and a small stipend on which to live."

It was a dreary tale, and too close to the truth for comfort. Predictably, Mobrey looked horrified—for all the wrong reasons. "I've income aplenty . . . but no marriage settlement? It is not to be borne."

"It must be borne—and by me, not you. I fear you shall have to choose a bride elsewhere."

"You are right! I must retract my offer until such time as I may ascertain why Hathaway thinks so little of you." He jerked a bow and scurried off into the crowd.

So much for undying love.

Isabel spared no time for cynicism. Lifting her chin, she moved slowly through the ballroom, past the lines of graceful dancers in the center of the chamber. Whenever she spied an acquaintance, she made a discreet inquiry about the man she sought. The man who might be her mother's killer.

Focused on her search, Isabel kept her ears open and her smile sparkling. She danced with a variety of partners and dutifully checked in with Gillie from time to time. More than once, she noticed Mobrey's sulking glare as he spoke with other guests. Each time he did so, ladies murmured behind their fans. Gentlemen bent low to hear their whispers. At first with puzzlement, then with chagrin, Isabel intercepted their speculative stares and pitying glances.

Had everyone assumed she had money? Just because Hathaway had sponsored her?

A sense of loss ached inside her breast. Too late, she realized the inadvisability of showing kindness to Mobrey. The man was a cad of the first order, spouting poetry one minute and scandal the next. She should have known better than to trust a nobleman.

She squared her shoulders and kept smiling. Let him gossip. It would provide a relief from maintaining her facade. If word of her reduced circumstances got around, she would have fewer suitors to distract her. No gentleman, no matter how well positioned, would wed a woman without tuppence to her name.

As she made her way off the dance floor, a man stopped before her and bowed. Tall as a lamppost, he had sparse graying hair and thin, autocratic features that showed the inroads of age.

"Miss Darcy, I presume?" When she nodded, his foxy eyes looked her up and down in a way that made her skin crawl. "Permit me to introduce myself. I am Mr. Terrence Dickenson. The man you've been seeking."

❧ Chapter 11 ❧

*K*ern spotted her across the crowded dance floor.

Wearing a sapphire gown that flaunted her fine white shoulders, Isabel blended beautifully with the throngs of aristocrats. She might have been born to hold court in a mansion like this one. The hint of fire in her dark hair mimicked the woman herself: elusive... mysterious... seductive.

And she was flirting again, damn her. Curving her lips in a come-hither smile, she touched the arm of a lanky, balding gentleman. He leaned closer to her, saying something that was lost to the noise of the ballroom, something that caused her to arch her throat and laugh.

Against his will, Kern felt drawn to her, his cool control decimated by the rise of desire. He wanted to spirit her away, to show her the advantages of choosing a younger man...

Recognition stabbed him. That old scoundrel was Terrence Dickenson, a former crony of his father's. According to Minnie, Dickenson had engaged in a flaming, on-and-off affair with Aurora.

No doubt Isabel knew that, too.

His jaw set, Kern started through the swarm of guests. He had to save the fool woman from her own folly. He had taken only a few steps when an insistent tug on his sleeve halted him. He found himself frowning down into the worried face of Miss Gilbert.

The governess bobbed a curtsy, then lifted a handkerchief to her pale lips as if to hide behind the scrap of embroidered linen. "My lord, thank heavens you are here at last. I've been hoping that you would attend tonight."

He patted her kid-gloved hand. "We'll have a nice chat in a while. For now, duty requires me to dance with Miss Darcy."

"But that is *exactly* why I must confide in you, my lord. You see, the most dreadful thing has happened." She glanced from side to side, then whispered, "Everyone has found out."

This time, Kern gave the governess his full attention. "Found out what?"

"I did not know it myself. Oh dear, what will Lord Hathaway say when he discovers how people are whispering?"

He balled his fists. "Tell me who's calling her a fraud."

"A fraud, m'lord? You misunderstand me." Her brow wrinkled, the small woman leaned forward confidentially. "They're saying our Isabel has no dowry. She is poor as a church mouse."

"Ah," he said, relaxing a fraction. So that was all. "The sorry scandal was bound to come out sooner or later."

"But not in so public a forum, and without you or the marquess here to quell the gossip. Oh, mercy! How will the dear girl find a husband now?"

She won't. Kern kept silent, unwilling to voice any platitudes. It was true; society could be cruel to those in need of money. And even crueler to those who lacked the proper bloodlines.

"It is all my fault for not keeping a closer watch on her," Miss Gilbert went on. "She is too unwise in the vagaries of the *ton*." Peering through the crowd, she shook her head with its prim mobcap. "They are all gossiping about her. While she smiles as if her future is rosy.''

Isabel was smiling, all right. She was smiling at that randy old goat. From Kern's preliminary investigation, he knew that a few years ago, Dickenson had wed a very rich and very jealous widow who kept him close to home. But his wife was nowhere in sight. "Calm yourself, Miss Gilbert. I'll take care of the matter. No one will dare to denigrate her in my presence."

"Bless you, my lord. Oh, bless you for a good, kind man.''

As he stalked away, Kern shrugged off a niggling guilt. Miss Gilbert wouldn't think so highly of him if she knew exactly *how* he intended to take care of her charge. But then, Miss Gilbert didn't have an inkling of Isabel's true background.

Or her reckless purpose.

Kern knew. The chit lacked the sense of a flea. Eventually, if she went on prying into the lives of powerful men, she might get herself killed. *Killed.* All to avenge the death of a wanton mother.

A band of rage and frustration tightened around his chest. He'd left the brothel today with a guarded tolerance for Isabel's spirit. Though he couldn't condone her boldness, at least he could fathom her determination. She too had been raised in an atmosphere of moral decay. She too had not been given a choice in her parentage. It was strange to feel this connection to her, as if they'd shared a similar background—when in truth they'd been raised in utterly different worlds.

An acquaintance beckoned to him; he nodded politely but continued to wend his way toward Isabel. He would not stand idly by while she invited mayhem with her heedless questions. If necessary, he would bind and gag her and send her back to the brothel where she belonged.

Or *did* she belong there? She looked perfectly at ease

here. She brought a fresh breeze of vitality into this otherwise tedious party.

She was laughing with her companion, her face shining
and her eyes glowing. Then she turned her head and spied
Kern across half the length of the ballroom. Their gazes
locked. Her smile died. Even the music seemed to hush
while violinist and flutist readied their instruments for the
next set.

I need you.

The incautious thought seized him, tortured him with
memory and fantasy . . . her lips softening to his kiss . . .
her arms drawing him close . . . her legs parting to accept
him . . . Ever since that interlude on the bed, he had
dreamed of Isabel to the verge of obsession. He had craved
the dark sweetness of her mouth, the wild passion of her
body moving beneath him.

He ordered himself to think of Helen. Helen, who in six
weeks would be his wife. But to his shame, he could not
conjure the likeness of his fiancée, not when he gazed upon
Isabel's vivid beauty.

She spun around, thrust her arm through Dickenson's,
and led the old roué toward a door at the opposite end of
the ballroom. Anticipating her retreat, Kern increased his
pace. He snubbed several acquaintances and whispers
buzzed in his wake, but he kept walking. On some vague
level, he surprised himself. He, who had always behaved
with the utmost propriety, was giving chase to a female
through a congested ballroom.

And he didn't give a bloody damn what people thought.

Leaving the chamber through the opened door, he spied
the couple in the deserted passageway. Dickenson had
paused to smooth his thinning gray hair before a gilt-
framed mirror, while Isabel tugged on his arm. "Miss
Darcy," Kern called out.

Her slender back went stiff. Dickenson frowned over his
shoulder. Kern closed the remaining distance and stepped

in front of them. "Before you run off, do allow me to pay my respects," he said, taking her small, gloved hand and kissing it.

She smelled faintly of roses and rainwater. He wished to God she *was* stalking a rich husband. It would be far easier to think ill of her.

Her lips taut, she withdrew her hand. "Lord Kern. I thought you would be at the Hathaways' tonight, keeping Lady Helen company."

"Helen is indisposed, as you know. It is her fondest wish that *I* keep *you* company." His gaze focused a challenge at Terrence Dickenson.

"Ah, I remember you now—you're Lynwood's heir," Dickenson said. "Last time we met, you were peering through the banister rails at one of Lynwood's parties." His thin face took on a sly humor. "A more disapproving little fellow I never did see. Nor one more fascinated by the goings-on."

Unwillingly, Kern recalled that night. He'd been home on holiday from Eton, still grieving the loss of his mother the previous autumn. Lonely and unable to sleep, he had ventured down the stairs only to see his father fondling a lady's bare breasts in full view of the other revelers . . .

"Oh, really?" Isabel said. "How old was he?"

"Ten, perhaps," Dickenson said with a shrug.

"And the duke allowed frolicking while his son was in the house?"

"Lynwood did whatsoever he pleased." Dickenson cast a crafty glance at Kern. "Many a boy would have liked such a father. Especially one who took such care with his education."

Darker memories pushed to the surface of Kern's mind, but ruthlessly he buried them. He had learned the hard way to cage his wild urges lest they leap forth to strangle him. "It is the goings-on here that fascinate me," he snapped.

"I trust you have an explanation for leaving the ball with Miss Darcy."

"We were discussing a private matter—" Isabel began.

"Pray allow Mr. Dickenson to answer," Kern said.

Dickenson lifted his slightly stooped shoulders. "The lady was feeling rather faint from the crush of guests. We merely wished to find a quiet spot for her to recover."

"Then by all means, let us do just that—all three of us."

At his harsh tone, Dickenson backed up a step. "Hold on, old chap. The lady don't need two escorts. Matter of fact, I'll just toddle on back to the party now."

"No," Kern said. "I'll have a word with you first. Both of you." He took Isabel by the arm and marched her to the end of the corridor, where he opened a door in the white paneling and motioned to Dickenson to lead the way.

In the doorway, Dickenson dug in his heels. "I say, Kern, what is this havey-cavey nonsense?" he blustered. "You're not Miss Darcy's guardian."

"An excellent point," Isabel said. "I think Lord Kern should mind his own concerns rather than meddling in ours."

"Then don't think," he stated in a voice that brooked no disobedience. "Just walk."

Isabel felt a shiver of apprehension as they went down the servants' staircase. She conceded the uselessness of arguing. If she wanted to interview Dickenson, she would have to do so with Kern standing guard.

Upon reaching the ground floor, they proceeded to a room lit by moonlight shining through a pair of tall windows. It was the morning room, judging by the small, pedestal table suitable for eating a private breakfast and the chairs arranged near the hearth for doing needlework and having cozy chats.

Not that there was anything cozy about *this* chat.

Isabel settled uneasily on the edge of a chaise. Kern

closed the door with a definitive click. He prowled to a desk in the corner of the room, where he took up a menacing stance in the shadows. Clearly he knew of Dickenson's connection to her mother. How had Kern discovered that fact without reading the memoirs? He must be guessing.

Dickenson stopped in the middle of the moon-silvered rug. He reached in his pocket, drew out a small box, and inhaled a pinch of snuff. "I don't understand your high-handedness. You can't have any interest in the lady. Word has it you're engaged to Hathaway's daughter, Ellen."

"Helen," Kern corrected oppressively. "Her name is Lady Helen."

"That is neither here nor there," Isabel said, determined to be the voice of reason. "Mr. Dickenson, you may as well know. We need your presence here for another reason entirely."

We. She'd included Kern unthinkingly, and yet she was suddenly very glad for his presence. Knowing that he stood nearby, she felt safe, protected, not so all alone.

If he had the sense not to spoil the investigation as he'd done with Lord Raymond. She tried to catch his eye, to convey the message that *she* would handle the questioning, but his attention was focused on the older man.

Dickenson grimaced. "Reason? What reason? I've never done you a harm. We've never even met before . . . have we?" He peered owlishly at her. "No, I'd've recalled meeting a lady of your grace and charm."

"You've met my mother," she murmured. Gathering her courage, she added, "You surely remember her. Aurora Darling."

Dickenson fumbled the snuffbox as if it were a live coal. It slipped through his fingers and thunked to the floor, spilling its dark powder. Paying no heed to the mess, he gaped at her. "Aurora—? Impossible. You are hoaxing me."

"It is no hoax." Kern leaned his elbow against the marble mantelpiece. "We know all about your past association with Aurora. She liked to call you Narcissus."

Now how did he know *that*, too? Chilled, Isabel surreptitiously patted the hidden pocket where the diary was hidden. It was still there, a small thin rectangle concealed within her petticoat.

Dickenson's eyes widened in the moonlight. Watching him, Isabel fisted her hands in her lap. She hated seeing awareness dawn in the eyes of a man, even this amoral man. She hated the moment when the trappings of a lady no longer concealed her base birth. She wanted to dash out of the room, to run as far and as fast as she could.

" 'Tis those demned memoirs." Dickenson swung toward Kern. "You've gotten your hands on the book," he said hoarsely. "By Jove, you should act the gentleman and burn it."

"He doesn't have Mama's book," Isabel said. "I do. And it is safely tucked away where no one will find it."

"So that's the way of it, eh?" Dickenson scowled first at her, then at Kern. "Never would have taken a stuffed shirt like you for a blackmailer. By gad, you're lower than Lynwood."

Kern's hands curled into fists; though he stood cloaked in shadow, Isabel could sense the fury radiating from him. Quickly she said, "We aren't interested in blackmail, sir. Only in your answers to a few questions."

"Questions? What questions?"

She took a deep breath. "Did you visit my mother in the month before she died?"

"Any time we spent together was private," he said testily. "I certainly paid her amply for the privilege."

Isabel winced inwardly to think of this lecher with her mother. Struggling for a calm expression, she repeated, "Did you visit her?"

When Dickenson stuck his aristocratic nose in the air, Kern growled, "Answer the lady. Did you or did you not go to see Aurora Darling in regard to the memoirs?''

Dickenson kicked at the tiny mound of snuff on the carpet. "So what if I did? If you're planning on tattling to my wife, she's off nursing her sister in Sussex. I won't have you upsetting her with old gossip.''

"We'll leave the tattling to the *Tattler*," Isabel said acidly. "Tell me, do you recall the exact date on which you last saw my mother?''

"Date? How the devil would I recall the date? 'Twas last spring sometime.'' Prowling to a mirror on the wall, he nervously smoothed his sparse hair. "April. Or perhaps May. Devil take it, I don't know. It's not something one records in an engagement book.''

Isabel controlled her frustration. "When you last visited her, did you bring her a gift? Flowers? Jewelry? Or perhaps . . . sweets?''

He shrugged. "Bonbons, I suppose. She liked the chocolate ones from Bell's Confectionery Shop.''

Her heart beating faster, Isabel leaned forward. He could have added arsenic to the chocolates. The poison was readily available in any chemist's shop. He could have acted out of desperation to stop Aurora from publishing the memoirs and getting him into trouble with his jealous wife.

"What is the point of all this questioning?'' Dickenson whined. "Truth be told, I should jolly well like to know how you came to be living under Hathaway's roof—and using a false name. You must have duped the marquess. Such a man would never condone a whore's get in his house.'' His upper lip curled in crafty disdain. "Come to think of it, if you don't destroy those memoirs immediately, I've a mind to go straight to him and alert him to your sordid little scheme—''

"You won't breathe a word.'' Kern strolled toward Dickenson. "You see, the point of this questioning is simple. We wish to determine who poisoned Aurora Darling.''

Dickenson staggered backward a few steps. He lifted a

hand to his cravat, his signet ring glowing in the moonlight. "P-poisoned? Are you saying . . . she was murdered?"

"Yes."

Another pause. Then he squeaked out, "And you think *I* did it?"

"That depends. Can you can verify where you were on the night of May the tenth last year? The night Aurora took ill."

Dickenson's mouth worked. "I-I-I told you, I don't keep precise accountings of visits to courtesans. What man would be dunderhead enough to do so?"

"Then we shall have to find out the information from another source," Kern said in an ominous tone. "In the meanwhile, I would advise you not to leave the city. The magistrate at the Bow Street Office may wish to question you."

"Magistrate! This is beyond absurd. You oughtn't to be helping this little tart—you owe allegiance to your own brethren." He started to shake his finger at Kern, then apparently thought better of it and lowered his hand to his side. He spun toward Isabel instead. "And you . . . you belong in the gutter. Not among decent folk. You're no more a lady than my laundress."

Isabel sat rigidly upright, her hands folded in her lap. She knew that outwardly, she was the image of a gentlewoman, and yet inside she felt like that little girl again, yearning to be a princess while knowing fairy tales could never come true.

Muttering self-righteously, Dickenson bent down to get his snuffbox and tucked it into an inner pocket. He straightened to his full height and swept her again with his spiteful gaze. "Furthermore, I'm not surprised Mobrey was gossiping about your lack of a dowry. Wait until everyone hears what *I* have to add—"

Kern surged out of the shadows and caught Dickenson by the throat, thrusting him up against the wall. A small table crashed over. A basalt vase slid to the floor and smashed into black shards.

Kern didn't appear to notice. "Say one word against Miss Darcy and you'll answer to me."

"I . . . won't." Dickenson made a wet, choking sound. "Let . . . me . . . down."

"First, apologize to the lady."

"I-I'm . . . sorry."

"That's better." Kern released his captive and stepped back. "Heed my warning," he said. "If you mention this meeting to anyone, I won't hesitate to reveal the filth in your past. Your wife will know every sordid detail."

"Y-yes, m'lord." Dickenson made a feeble attempt to straighten his mussed cravat. He edged toward the door and scuttled out, slamming it shut behind him.

The muted lilt of a minuet drifted from the upstairs ballroom. To hide the trembling of her arms, Isabel crossed them over her midsection. *Little tart . . . you belong in the gutter . . . you're no more a lady than my laundress*. The opinion of a jaded rake should hold no consequence, yet she stung as if she'd been slapped. Her only consolation was in seeing Dickenson trounced before he could expose her masquerade to all of society.

Not that she thought Kern meant anything personal in defending her. Understandably, he wished to protect his own interests—by keeping Lady Helen and Lord Hathaway clear of scandal.

Still, Isabel felt obliged to him. "Thank you for coming to my aid, m'lord. It was most kind."

"Kind," he repeated darkly.

"Yes." A faint aura of danger radiated from him. How well did she know him, really? Conscious of how isolated they were, she rose from the chaise. "I do appreciate your assistance in questioning Mr. Dickenson. It was foolish of me, I suppose, but I didn't expect him to threaten me."

Intending to return to the ballroom, Isabel walked toward the door. She had no sooner placed her hand on the brass lever when Kern came at her like a streak of dark lightning. She found herself in the same position as Dickenson had been—with her spine meeting the wall. Except that Kern's fingers did not circle her throat. They burned into her bare shoulders.

Intense emotion glittered in his eyes, and the awareness of his hard male form washed through her. The hot thrill of it left her breathless. She knew she ought to protest his cavalier treatment of her, yet no words came to her tongue. Instead of talking, she wanted to do something else with her mouth. She wanted to kiss him.

"Don't run off yet," Kern said. "I should like to know what you intended to do if Dickenson had confessed to the murder."

She struggled to focus her thoughts. "I'd have reported him to the magistrate, of course. I'd have seen him punished."

"Ah, but suppose you never reached the magistrate." He glided his hands higher on her shoulders, and his thumbs rubbed ever so lightly over her throat. "Suppose the killer silenced you first."

The chill she felt was part fear, part arousal. Her skin prickled, her breasts tingled. Afraid she might disgrace herself by embracing him, she flattened her hot palms against the cool wall. "You're assuming Dickenson *is* the murderer."

"Perhaps he is. Or perhaps not. My point is that I won't allow you to take the risk of meeting these men alone." His hands lay heavily upon her shoulders. His big hands. She wanted them to move lower . . . and lower . . .

"Well, that isn't for you to decide," she said. "And Dickenson wouldn't have dared to harm me. Not in the midst of a big party."

Kern chuckled, a low, mocking rumble in his chest. As if he were privy to her secret fantasies, his hands descended until they cupped her breasts. The heat of his skin penetrated the thin silk of her bodice. She caught a whiff of his scent, musky and male, and her knees nearly buckled from another warm rush of desire. She wanted to touch him, to feel his pulse beating beneath her thumb.

"How naïve you are, Miss Darling. Surprising for someone who has known the seamier side of life."

His insult shattered the erotic spell. Isabel gave him a hard shove that caught him off guard. She stalked to the center of the room and wheeled around to face him. "Let me get this straight. You push me up against the wall, fondle my bosom, and then *you* call *me* seamy?"

"I apologize for the slur. I merely meant that your upbringing—"

"I know what you meant. And you never miss an opportunity to remind me of my background, do you? As if being the son of London's most notorious lecher makes you my superior."

He stood watching her, the shadows hiding his face. What was he thinking? That she was less than the scrapings off his noble boots?

"Speaking of fathers," he said blandly, "I've been wondering about yours."

Isabel blinked in numb wariness. Her mouth went dry. "Wondering? About . . . *my* father?"

"He was a gentleman, a man of society. And your mother called him Apollo."

His tall, dark shape swam before her eyes, and the whole room seemed to wobble. What else had Kern found out? Did he know she suspected Apollo and Sir John Trimble were one and the same? Surely not. Without reading the memoirs, he couldn't have seen the clues . . .

Groping for the back of a chair, she held tightly to it. "Who told you?" she whispered. Then in a sickening flash, she guessed. "Aunt Minnie and Aunt Di. You've been to see them."

Kern shrugged. "Since you refuse to allow me to read the memoirs, it seemed the wisest course. I wanted to find out about the men in your mother's life. To determine who was around when Aurora was poisoned."

Isabel's chest ached with pent-up pain and fury. Only by digging her nails into the back of the chair did she keep from flying at him and clawing his aristocratic face. "I never gave you leave to meddle in my life," she said, struggling to keep her voice cold and composed. "Nor did I invite you to poke your nose into my private investigation."

"Only a few minutes ago, you were thanking me for helping you out with Dickenson."

"Then I withdraw my appreciation. Henceforth, you are to cease interfering."

He walked slowly forward until he stood in a shaft of moonlight. His unwavering eyes held hers. "No," he said, rather benignly. "My aim is to uncover the truth behind your mother's death. The sooner I do so, the sooner you can return to your own world."

"How admirable of you to drive an undesirable out of the *ton*. You're a service to your own kind."

He threw back his head and laughed. " 'Undesirable' is not quite the word I would use to describe you, Isabel."

In spite of her anger, she felt a little shiver of pleasure. It was bodily attraction, she told herself, not the desire to know him, to see into his heart, to confess all her fancies to him. Never would she become like her mother, a foolish dreamer who worshipped noblemen. "Arrogant is the word I'd use to describe *you*. You're nothing but a shallow snob. It's amazing that you were never taught good manners."

She started toward the door again. He stepped into her path and caught her by the wrists. A peculiar intensity radiated from him. "*You* were taught manners," he said. "You were raised by a governess in Oxfordshire. It's no wonder you've been able to fit in so well in society. Apollo paid for your genteel upbringing.''

His fingers shackled her wrists as tightly as the memories that imprisoned her heart. She had known about the quarterly payments from an anonymous patron; her mother had made much of the fact that her dear Apollo cared enough to provide well for his baseborn child. Yet the payments had ceased the moment Aurora died.

The bitter truth was, he had not cared a jot for Isabel. Sir John Trimble had shunned his bastard daughter. She was an embarrassment, a mistake to be swept beneath the rug of respectability. And she couldn't bear for Kern to find out how cheaply her own father had valued her.

She wrenched ineffectually against Kern's grip, but succeeded only in freeing the ancient hurt. ''Why do you keep talking about him?'' she asked. ''Are you suggesting I should be properly grateful? That I should venerate a man who never bothered to acknowledge me? A man who never came to visit me, who never told me his name, who only sent money now and then to assuage his guilty conscience? A man who left me to be teased by the village children for being a bastard?'' She gave a sharp shake of her head. ''He is not my father. I have no father. Don't speak of him again.''

''Isabel, I'm sorry. I hadn't realized he hurt you so much. But regardless, we must speak of him.''

She couldn't bear his gentle tone. She didn't want pity or sympathy from a lord. ''Why? So you can have another excuse to belittle me? To molest me while you point out how vastly superior your bloodlines are? Well, I don't intend to tarry here and endure the pompous opinions of a jackass.'' She tried again to twist free, and when he wouldn't release her wrists, she kicked him. The satin dancing slipper provided scant protection, and she stubbed her toe on his hard shin. ''Ouch!''

''For pity's sake, calm down,'' he said, pushing her to

arm's length. "You've misread my purpose. If you would heed me a moment, you'd understand that."

"I've heeded you long enough, and you've done nothing but attack and insult me. There's nothing you can say about my father that would interest me. Nothing at all."

"Unfortunately, there *is* something—perhaps something you haven't considered." Kern's eyes shone darkly in the moonlight, and he lowered his voice to a compassionate murmur. "We must find out who Apollo really is."

"*No!*"

"Yes. You see, he had reason to murder your mother."

His statement paralyzed Isabel. Though she herself feared that very thing, hearing it stated so baldly made sickness rise in her throat. Her mother, slain by the only man she had ever loved. Slain by the man whose blue blood coursed through Isabel's veins.

That she could be the offspring of such a monster was too hideous to contemplate. It made her feel dirty, degraded, when she had fought all her life to be a worthy person. That was why she didn't want Kern to find out her father was Sir John Trimble. If Trimble really was the killer, no one but Isabel need know his relation to her.

She shook her head in denial. "Apollo is never identified by his real name in the memoirs. So he had no cause to harm Mama."

Kern rubbed his thumbs along her inner wrists to calm her. "Are you certain there isn't a hint to his identity in the memoirs? His rank, perhaps? Or a description of where he lived?"

"There's nothing. So you see, you're wrong. You can forget all about him."

"You can't be sure of what Aurora said to him in private. He might have had reason to fear she would change her mind and tell the world about their bastard daughter. The scandal would ruin a man of rank."

Pulling away, Isabel crossed her arms over her breasts.

Her throat felt tight and her eyes burned. She wanted only to get him off the treacherous topic of her father. "You're grasping at straws. I'm sure one of the other men killed her. We just have to find out *who*."

"Isabel." Kern gathered her close, tilting her head into the lee of his shoulder. "Forgive me for upsetting you. I never meant to cause you pain."

She didn't want to be comforted by him; she wanted to hate him for prying into her secret past. Yet it felt so good to lean against a man for once, to draw strength from him, to relinquish the burden of her fears.

A breath whispering from her, she wrapped her arms around his waist, resting her cheek against his smooth coat. He held her close, folding her into himself, shaping her to his hard form. She welcomed the heat of him, the heady scent of man, the superiority of his size. She was so weary of fighting for the truth, so weary of being alone with no one to protect her. This embrace felt somehow different from that first time, in the deserted bedroom at Lynwood House, when lust had stolen her wits. Now she sensed a need inside herself that was deeper and sharper, a vulnerability of the soul.

She wondered if he felt it, too, and her question was answered when he tilted up her chin and whispered her name and brought his mouth down on hers. He kissed her with tenderness and feeling, and with a sigh she gave herself into his keeping. Never in her life had she imagined she could want a nobleman so much. Awash in pure sensuality, she blocked out the voice of reason and met the bold thrust of his tongue with her own shameless yearning. She moved her hands over him, learning the contours of his body, letting her palms absorb the strong beating of his heart.

He shuddered in response to her touch. His arms tightened and his hands slid downward to clasp her derriere, pressing their hips together so that she could not mistake the proof of his masculinity. The contact awakened her to the scorching desire to be filled by him, only him. She wanted to know his power, his vigor, his passion. She wanted his hands upon her naked flesh. No other man could satisfy her; no other man had ever even tempted her. Surely he was her destiny, the fairy-tale prince she had been waiting for all her life.

"Isabel." He spoke against her lips, as if he could not bear to release her. "God help me . . . I swore I wouldn't make this mistake . . . ever again."

She heard him through a fevered haze, and opened her eyes to his dark shape looming over her. *Mistake?* The ardor began to seep away, but she clung desperately to it, as desperately as she clung to his shoulders. "Please, Kern. Kiss me. I need you so."

She slid her hands around his neck to draw him to her, seeking the oblivion of his warm mouth.

But he might have been carved from granite. The hands that had touched her with tenderness only an instant ago now thrust her away. As if she were a whore he'd sampled and then deemed not worth his while.

"No," he said through gritted teeth. "We cannot do this. You know as well as I how wrong this is."

She did. Yet the forbidden attraction pulsed inside her, undeniable and alluring. "I don't care," she said on a moan. "I just want to forget . . ."

"No." He blew out a deep, frustrated breath. "We can't forget. We were discussing your father. It's imperative we find out who he is."

The chill in his voice froze her, as did the ice of reality. Kern wanted to find Apollo. He wanted to unearth all the sordid secrets of her past. He wanted to find the murderer so that he could send Isabel back to her own world. And she had been a fool to think he cared for her.

Gathering her shattered dignity, she stepped back, her fingers bunching the slippery folds of her silk skirt. "I told you, I have no father. And should you seek to prove otherwise, I shall never, ever forgive you."

To her mortification, her voice broke. Unwilling to let Kern see the tears stinging her eyes, she brushed past him. He called out her name, but she ran for the door, ran back to the gossips in the ballroom.

Back to the safety of her masquerade.

Like the god of myth, Narcissus loved only himself.

That much was apparent from the first time Mr. Terrence D—— came to me, and yet I found him amusing in his own way. Given his preening nature, he liked to gad about in public and thus escorted me to plays and concerts and art galleries. From the beginning of my career as a courtesan, I was determined not to be hidden away like a gentleman's naughty secret. I yearned to go out into public and experience all the varied amusements of life. So for this purpose, Narcissus proved useful, indeed.

He was a lusty fellow, too, always ready for a tumble, as keen for pleasure as I. We spent many an ardent hour in my bed, and 'twas he who placed the glass at the headboard so that he might admire himself at his play. In truth, had I allowed it, he would have positioned mirrors on the walls as well, so that no matter how we cavorted, he could still view the reflection of his beloved self.

Dear Reader, you might wonder why I tolerated such a coxcomb. You see, he came to me seeking a remedy in his struggle against the Solitary Vice. He might have indulged in this Vice even more often had not his physician warned him that the unnatural practice eventually causes insanity. Narcissus will not like me to reveal his confession. Yet there are those among you who also hide a fondness for this secret Vice, and perhaps will show pity toward him . . .

—The True Confessions of a Ladybird

⊷ Chapter 12 ⊷

"*I* see you've been allowed to stay," Kern said.

Pacing before the sunlit windows, he watched as the mongrel paused just within the doorway of the Hathaway drawing room. The pup looked much cleaner than it had the day Isabel had rescued it. The scrawny animal was a peculiar mix of spaniel and terrier, with a spotted gold coat and floppy ears along with short hair and a stubby tail.

"Well, come inside," Kern prompted. "You've nothing to fear from me."

The dog advanced slowly, then stopped again, cocking its head. Kern comprehended the creature's mistrust. In its short life, it had encountered many cruel humans on the city streets.

There were just as many cruelties within the finest houses in London, Kern knew. His fellow aristocrats might not torture an animal on a public roadway, yet some of them were bloodthirsty nonetheless. And one among them had committed murder.

He snapped his fingers. "Here, boy. I shan't hurt you."

The dog crept forward and halted a few feet away. Kern crouched down and waited patiently while the puppy worked up its courage and inched closer. When it was close enough, Kern gently scratched its ears. After a moment the dog rolled over so that Kern could rub its thin belly and see its prominent ribs.

"So where is your mistress this morning? Where is Isabel?"

The dog whined in reply, tail thumping the carpet as if it recognized the name.

"No doubt she is plotting to steal away from me." Kern felt somewhat foolish, talking to a dog. But the disquiet inside him needed an outlet. "You must help me keep a close watch on her. Lest she embroil herself in more trouble."

And she would do just that if he gave her half a chance. Isabel seemed determined to reject his assistance, determined to solve a mystery far beyond her capabilities. She didn't understand the danger. The thought plagued him as it had for the better part of the night. She was headstrong, impetuous, and far too vulnerable.

Last night, she had refused to consider Apollo a suspect. But Kern had a feeling she knew more than she let on. Her protests had been a little too vehement. Yet why would she not want him to investigate Apollo? Of all the men who had once shared Aurora Darling's bed, Apollo had the most at stake. The disclosure of a bastard daughter would rock society. He would no longer be welcome in the best homes or invited to *ton* events. Society might turn a blind eye to hidden improprieties, but it could be ruthlessly cruel to a man caught with the evidence of his indiscretion.

And Kern wanted to be the one to ruin the blackguard.

I have no father. Should you seek to prove otherwise, I shall never, ever forgive you.

When she had flung that warning at him, tears had glittered in her eyes. *Tears.* She had been furious, beyond rational behavior. She hadn't wanted to hear that her father might have killed her mother. "I can't fault her for not wanting to face him," he muttered. "But by God, I'm going to find the knave and wrest the truth out of him."

As if in agreement, the puppy licked Kern's hand. Absently, Kern petted the animal.

Before last night, he had not known Isabel possessed any human vulnerability. He had viewed her as a common upstart without a moral to her false name. She had blackmailed her way into this household. She had lied and flirted and masqueraded until he thought she couldn't possess a scrap of honesty in her beautiful body.

Please . . . kiss me . . . I need you so.

His throat tightened. He shouldn't feel this indecent tenderness toward her. Isabel Darling contradicted his ideal of womanhood—she was neither modest nor virtuous. But when he got near her, all sense left him. He had sworn not to kiss her again—and look at what had happened. At the first opportunity, he had been all over her, drinking the sweetness of her mouth, memorizing the curves of her body, caressing her with the ardor of a lover . . .

"Why, Lord Kern," spoke the object of his brooding thoughts. "It's so refreshing to see you groveling on the floor."

He looked up to see Isabel glide into the drawing room, arm in arm with Helen. Helen clapped her hands. "Oh, Justin, how famous! You've found Isabel's puppy."

Feeling awkward at being caught in conversation with a dog, Kern rose to his feet. "So it seems. Good morning."

They made a compelling pair, the one pale and blond, the other dark and sultry. The dog raced to Isabel, and she scooped him up, cuddling him to her bosom. "Naughty boy," she murmured affectionately. "I didn't know where you'd gone."

The sight mesmerized Kern. His gaze lingered on Isabel's lips, soft and rosy and far too tempting. Even in the amber muslin gown of a lady, she brought to mind the pleasures of the bedchamber.

Illicit pleasures. Pleasures he should not contemplate with any woman but his fiancée.

Curbing his licentious thoughts, he strode straight to Helen. By damn, she was the woman he wanted to marry. Sweet and tractable, she would make him the perfect wife. Determined to prove it to himself, he did something he had done only once before, on the occasion of their betrothal. He bent and kissed her smooth cheek.

He experienced a mild sensation of pleasure at her fair beauty, but no flash of sexual heat, no mad desire to press her down to the carpet and give vent to his baser instincts. To his chagrin, she inspired the gentle affection of a brother for a younger sister.

Shame dug its claws into his chest. He had no right to lust after a whore when his hand was promised to an angel. Helen had a pleasing figure and an agreeable disposition. But she was a lady, and he would never permit himself to fantasize about *her*. Once they were married, however, he was certain to find satisfaction in her bed.

"I trust you're feeling better?" he asked.

"A trifle. This wretched cold still has me sniffling." She daintily dabbed a handkerchief to her reddened nose.

He glanced at Isabel. She was watching him, and he wondered if she was reliving their scorching kiss—until her dark gaze frowned a message to him. Had she, too, learned that Sir John Trimble had returned to town?

He returned his attention to Helen. "Are you feeling well enough to go on a drive to the park?"

She shook her head. "Tomorrow, perhaps. You and Isabel shall have to excuse me again. Forgive me for being a stick-in-the-mud."

His heart gave a jolt suspiciously like exhilaration. No. It couldn't be exhilaration. He wasn't *glad* to leave his fiancée behind. He only welcomed this opportunity to solve the mystery.

"You could stay with her, m'lord," Isabel suggested slyly. "After a week cooped up in the house, Helen would appreciate your company. I don't mind going out with Miss Gilbert.''

Damn her for a trickster. She wanted to interview Sir John alone. ''Or perhaps *you* could remain here,'' he countered. ''You could see to Helen's comfort far better than I.''

Helen laughed. ''Please, neither of you stay. I do believe I shall be content to spend the day curled up with a book in the library. If you wouldn't mind, Justin, you can take me there right now.''

While Isabel went to fetch bonnet and pelisse, he escorted Helen to the library. He meant to take his leave of her and go out to wait in his carriage, but Lord Hathaway beckoned to him.

The marquess sat writing at the desk in the library. On seeing Kern and Helen, he set down his quill and greeted them.

''Papa,'' Helen exclaimed. ''I thought you'd gone out already. Will I disturb you if I read here awhile?''

He smiled as she leaned down to kiss him. ''Of course not, my dear. But I must ask you to wait outside for a few minutes while I have a word with Justin.''

''Then I'll have a cup of tea in the morning room. Perhaps you'll join me when you're through?''

Hathaway gave a distracted nod, watching while she glided out of the library and closed the door behind her. In the sunlight, lines of strain bracketed his mouth and eyes. He rose and went to the sideboard to lift a cut-glass decanter. ''Brandy?''

Kern declined with a shake of his head. He was surprised to see Hathaway pour a tumbler for himself. Always austere, the marquess never imbibed spirits so early in the day.

Hathaway abruptly inquired, ''Where is Isabel this morning?''

Kern hesitated. It was absurd to feel guilty. "She and I are going for a drive in the park."

The older man sipped at his drink. "I want you to keep a close watch on her. As you well know from that interview with my brother, she has some ridiculous notion that Aurora Darling was murdered."

Kern frowned. "Ridiculous? I've come to think she's telling the truth."

"Bah." Pacing, Hathaway took another swallow. "There would have been a hue and cry over such a crime. We're speaking of the wrongful death of a courtesan who serviced any number of gentlemen. By gad, the news sheets would have spewed the scandal all over London."

"Not without proof." Kern chose his words carefully. "I've taken the liberty of speaking to the other women at the brothel. One of them saw a man entering Aurora's chamber on the night she took ill."

Hathaway jerked around to stare. Brandy splashed over his hand, but he didn't appear to notice. "A man? Who?"

"The woman—Minnie is her name—didn't see his face. And I cannot shake the notion that something is wrong about the death. Apparently, Aurora wrote in her diary that she'd been poisoned."

The marquess's jaw looked set in granite. He drained his glass and slammed it onto the desk. "Truth or not, I won't have a young woman from my house gadding about London, making wild accusations. If you care a jot for Helen's reputation, you'll see to it that Isabel Darling comports herself as a lady."

"The mongrel stays outside," Kern said.

Descending from the carriage, Isabel held onto M'lord and frowned at the earl. His manner had been testy ever since they'd left Hathaway House. While driving, he'd stared straight ahead and offered little conversation. "Does that order include me?'' she asked tartly. ''Seeing that you consider *me* a mongrel, too.''

The rebuke caught his attention. Looking remarkably handsome in a dark green coat that set off his eyes, he stopped on the pavement and scowled at her. ''If I thought I could dissuade you from questioning Trimble, I certainly *would* make you wait outside. But you'd only sneak back here without me.''

''How astute of you, m'lord.'' Hearing its name, the puppy wriggled and licked her chin. All the annoyance inside her melted away and she found herself speaking reassuringly to him. ''Don't let the nasty earl frighten you, love—you're staying right with me. We can't have you running away in this bad neighborhood, can we? Those awful bullies might come back and hurt you.''

As she cuddled the puppy to her bosom, Kern watched with an odd expression on his face. It was a hungry look, one that inspired a breathlessness inside her. He regarded her as if he wanted to haul her into the dubious privacy of the nearest alleyway, lift her skirts, and have his wicked way with her. And to her shame, she longed for him to do so. The mere thought of giving her virginity to him left her flushed and weak.

Blast him for making her feel like a trollop!

She slanted a look at Kern. ''I wouldn't expect you to understand my attachment to this dog. I daresay you had dozens of pets while you were growing up.''

''Only the hounds my father kept for hunting. There was one in particular I was fond of as a boy.'' For a moment, there was a faraway look in his eyes; then he blinked. ''And you? Surely out in the country you owned a dog or a cat.''

She shook her head. ''My governess believed animals to be dirty, vile creatures. I wasn't allowed to keep one.'' Remembering how lonely she'd been, Isabel brushed her cheek against the puppy's soft head. "But now I have you, don't I, M'lord?"

Kern said nothing. She assured herself she didn't care if he disapproved of her rescuing a dog of mixed breed. She would do as she bloody well pleased. Yet when his hand settled against the small of her back and he guided her up the stairs to the town house, she found his touch oddly comforting, as comforting as the small warm body nestled in her arms.

Not that she needed comforting. She felt calm and in control this morning. In the light of day, she didn't understand why she had reacted with such melodrama the previous night. Her father meant nothing to her. She would conduct this interview as if Trimble were simply another suspect.

In answer to their knock, the housekeeper showed them into a small, spartanly furnished parlor. Isabel sat on a sagging chaise with M'lord perched in her lap. While they waited for their host, Kern paced in front of the darkened fireplace.

"From my preliminary investigation," he said in a low tone, "I've found out Trimble is a widower with no children. He lost money in several business ventures, but he's led a rather dull life otherwise."

"Excepting for his attachment to my mother, you mean."

Kern shrugged. "What did she write of Trimble? What manner of man is he?"

Denying the dull pain in her breast, Isabel busied herself with stroking the puppy. "Mama saw Sir John as more a gentleman than her other lovers. He treated her with respect and dignity. Or so she wrote."

"He might resent the fact that she stole *his* respect by writing about him in her memoirs," Kern said flatly. "If Trimble is our man, you are to let me handle him. And you are to comport yourself as a lady. Is that clear?"

Her fingers tightened around the dog. "I *have* behaved like a lady. And you may handle Trimble if and when I determine through *my* questioning that he is guilty. Is *that* clear?"

He gazed down his lordly nose at her. She thought he was going to spit out more commands at her, but after a moment, an odd little glint entered his eyes, and he extended his hand. "We can at least be civil. I'm willing to call a truce, if you are. Agreed?"

She stared at his hand, then slowly lifted her own. "Agreed."

His strong fingers closed around hers, and despite the barrier of his thin riding gloves, she could feel his warmth spreading up her arm and through her body, heating her blood and quickening her heartbeat. Strange, how he could have this mesmerizing effect on her with one touch, one glance of his cool green eyes. She ought to feel disgust, Isabel told herself. He had nothing to recommend him, this spawn of Lynwood. He was heir to a duke so depraved he might have murdered her mother.

Yet could she taint Kern with the sins of his father? Wasn't that as grossly unfair as deeming herself a whore because her mother had been one?

A noise out in the corridor caught her attention. At the same instant, Kern withdrew his hand and stepped back. In spite of her resolve to remain calm, she felt her muscles tense. In her lap, M'lord growled and alertly watched the doorway.

"Sshh." She petted the dog's spotted head and wished she could so easily soothe herself.

Assisted by a footman, Sir John Trimble limped his way into the room. He leaned heavily on the servant and settled into a wing chair, propping his foot on a stool. Pain tightened a face that could only be described as homely with its bulbous nose, the white scar that divided his cheek, and the dark eyes sunken in a terrain of wrinkles.

What had her mother seen in him? *Those who think him ugly have not looked deeply into his soul; they do not see how perfectly he understands a woman's heart.*

"Blasted gout," he grumbled, rubbing his left leg. "Forgive me, Miss Darcy, Lord Kern. 'Tis the effects of the long coach ride back to London yesterday, and 'twill ease in a day or so." He straightened in the chair. "But this is no way to greet my guests. May I offer you refreshment?"

"You needn't bother," Isabel said. "We won't keep you for long."

"You could never be a bother," he said, smiling gallantly. "Well. Has this visit to do with teaching you the finer points of whist? When last we met, at the Winfreys' ball, you said you wished to improve your game. I would be most happy to comply with my offer to help you."

He looked so hopeful that Isabel had a sudden glimpse into his life, living alone in reduced circumstances, having no wife or children to brighten his days. And so eager for a visitor that he would come downstairs even while feeling less than chipper.

Her compassion warred with resentment. If he was alone, it was his own fault. He could have wed her mother instead of marrying for money—he had ended up poor anyway. The thought intrigued Isabel. How different her own life might have been. She would have been born legitimate, treated as a lady, received by many respectable, genteel families. In time, people might have forgotten her mother's shady past. Isabel might even have aspired to wed a high-ranking nobleman like Lord Kern . . .

Banishing the childish fantasy, she said, "Thank you for your offer to tutor me, sir. But that's not why we're here. I'd hoped you would answer some questions."

His face sobered, and he glanced from her to Kern, who stood silently by the mantelpiece. "Ask away," Trimble said. "I confess, you have me curious."

She took a deep, steadying breath. "I am not who I

claim to be, Sir John. You see, once upon a time, before I was even born, you knew my mother.'' Isabel paused, gathering her courage. The confession never grew easier, no matter how many times she said it, and this one was the worst of all. ''I am—''

''Aurora's daughter,'' Trimble finished, his tone gruff.

Isabel sat unmoving, observing him even when M'lord nudged his cold, wet nose against her hand. *Aurora's daughter.* He had not laid claim to her, not even now. Trimble was studying her as well, an indecipherable shadow in his hooded eyes. She longed for his approval and hated herself for wanting it. Why should his opinion matter any more than the other men who had used her mother?

For all she knew, she could be looking into the face of a murderer. His face would be far less repulsive than the corruption of his soul.

Trimble's scarred features held a guarded interest. ''I thought you looked familiar when first we met. You resemble Aurora, and your names are similar. But you were staying with Lord Hathaway, and I simply couldn't believe . . .'' His words trailed off, though his shrewd gaze remained on her.

''I'm posing as Lord Hathaway's niece,'' she explained. ''I knew about his brother's association with my mother and thus persuaded Hathaway to give me a place in society. Not for my own gain,'' she hastened to add, with a defiant glance at Kern. ''But to have the chance to meet the men who once knew my mother.''

Kern said nothing. At least he seemed willing to let her handle the questioning.

''I believe,'' said Trimble, ''you had better tell me why you wish to meet these men.'' A soft, searching interest illuminated his gaze. ''Though I must warn you, my dear, that if you're hoping to find your father—''

"No," she said quickly. He must not say anything revealing, not in front of Kern. "I'm not."

"Yes, she is," Kern countered. He pushed away from the mantelpiece and walked to Trimble. "Aurora called him Apollo. Do you know his real name?"

Damn Kern! Holding M'lord in her trembling arms, Isabel jumped to her feet. "You are not obliged to answer him, sir. *I* am conducting the interview here."

Her gaze locked with Kern's. His clenched jaw showed his intense irritation. She doubted he was accustomed to being challenged by a mere woman. Well then, she would be the first to dare. She certainly had nothing to lose by it.

"What is going on?" Trimble asked, looking utterly confused. "I would never answer such a question, in any case. To do so would mean betraying a vow to Aurora."

"I see," Kern said. "What if the matter involved life-or-death consequences?"

"Life or death?" Trimble shook his head. "I *am* perplexed now. I assume you're involved in this . . . whatever it is . . . because of Lynwood?"

"In a manner of speaking. In due time, you'll understand." Kern bowed to Isabel. "Though I will defer to Miss Darling."

She couldn't believe it. He was actually backing off. Again. She had an inkling of what retreat must have cost him in pride.

Pleasantly surprised, she resumed her seat on the chaise and focused on Trimble. She looked into his face—were those dark eyes like hers? Ruthlessly, she stopped her foolish speculations. "Forgive me for being intrusive, Sir John, but when was the last time you saw my mother?"

"That would be a year ago." He gazed at a point above her head, and she sensed that he was lost in memory. "Not more than a month before her death."

"Was she ill then?"

"No. She was in the pink of health, though distressed in spirit."

When he hesitated, Isabel prompted, "Why? Please, this is very, very important."

"It seems several men had ordered her to stop writing her memoirs. That's why she sent for me, to tell me her troubles."

"*She* sent for you?" Kern broke in. "Hadn't you already heard about the memoirs?"

Trimble shrugged. "I'd heard, but they didn't matter to me. What have I to lose by the publication of her reminiscences?"

"Your reputation," Kern said, as if that were obvious. "Your honor. The ability to hold up your head in society."

Trimble laughed rather harshly. "Given my beastly face, I doubt anyone could say anything nasty that hasn't already been said a hundred times already. And at my age, I don't judge a man's honor by society's sanctimonious rules."

Kern cocked an eyebrow, but made no response. Clearly he disagreed, though he recognized that now was not the time to debate ethics.

A thought struck Isabel. "Who told you my mother was writing her memoirs?"

" 'Twas a sop named Terrence Dickenson. He proposed that we gentlemen who were described in such indelicate detail should band together to intimidate Aurora." Trimble worked his meaty fingers into a fist. "Needless to say, I threw the blackguard out on his ear."

A dizzying chill seeped through Isabel. To go to such lengths, Terrence Dickenson must have been desperate to stop her mother. She looked at Kern and saw the same grim realization in his eyes. Yet they could not be certain. Not yet. Trimble could be lying to throw suspicion off himself.

"Did you see my mother after that? Did you perhaps take her a gift?"

He shook his head. "I saw her only that once. She wanted comfort and reassurances, and then she wanted me to go away, to leave her in peace to finish her memoirs. I didn't even know she'd fallen ill until . . . afterward." He vented a strange, shuddering sigh. "Such a beautiful woman she was, Aurora Darling. Ever dreamy and hopeful, but strong and determined underneath all the feminine trappings. If you'll permit me to say so, you remind me of her."

Stunned, Isabel rested her fingers on M'lord's warm head. Trimble's observation touched her with an unexpected pleasure—and an answering surge of panic. She couldn't feel pleasure. She did not want to be like her mother. *She did not.*

At one time, long ago, she had hungered to grow up to be like the pretty, perfumed mama who summoned her to London at irregular intervals, who showered her with wildly lavish presents and took her out for ices and to Astley's Circus. But then Isabel had found out the ugly truth. She had discovered the source of the money that paid for the fancy dolls and frilly dresses and sugary pastries. And at that moment, she resolved to starve before she sold her body to any man.

Yet now she found her gaze lifting to Kern and her mind imagining his kiss, his caress, his lovemaking. If she didn't wish to be like her mother, then why did she want to lie naked in bed with this man? Why did she want to touch his hard male form? Why did she feel an ache in her breasts and a throbbing in her belly and a dampness between her legs?

Why did the pain of yearning tear at her heart?

She saw him glance at her, and prayed he could not read her thoughts. But his attention turned to Sir John. "I would hope you are more astute than others in seeing this resemblance," Kern said in a no-nonsense tone. "It's time you knew the truth. We've reason to believe Aurora Darling was murdered. By poison.''

All color fled Trimble's face. His cheeks turned as pale as the scar that disfigured his features. Hunching forward as if in pain, he gripped the arms of his chair. "No," he muttered. *"No."*

Kern went on, ''Minnie saw a man going into Aurora's chamber late on the night of May the tenth last year. Can you account for your whereabouts that evening?''

Trimble sat staring at the floor. Then he rubbed his hand over his eyes before looking back at Kern. "I cannot think. You are certain about this, my lord?''

"Unhappily so.''

"My mother recorded her fears in the final entry of her memoirs,'' Isabel added. She watched Trimble closely. Was his shock real? Or was he just an accomplished actor? "Unfortunately, she didn't specify any man in particular.''

"My God. *My God.* I should have gone to each of them who'd troubled her, as I'd wanted to do. I should not have let her dissuade me from that course of action.'' Trimble slammed his fist onto the arm of his chair. '' 'Twas foolish of me. Bloody foolish!''

"Give me the names of these men,'' Kern said, ''so that I may question them.''

"Nay.'' Resolve firmed Trimble's expression. With a grunt, he levered himself out of the chair and leaned against it. "With all due respect, my lord, I'll take care of the matter myself. As I should have done long ago.''

"With all due respect,'' Kern said, "I should like to accompany you. You're in no condition to be chasing after criminals.''

"I will manage. Whatever Aurora said to me was spoken in confidence. I will not betray her now. Or ever.''

The men exchanged a hard stare. Kern said, ''Then I will expect you to report to me whatever you find out. And I want you to consider Apollo a suspect, too.''

Trimble thinned his lips and looked away, before giving a curt nod. "Agreed."

Isabel could tell little from his expression. He had to be only pretending he would approach Apollo. *He had to be*.

She watched, aghast, as the two men shook hands. Clutching M'lord, she sprang up and stepped toward them. "Wait a minute. I am investigating the murder of *my* mother. You cannot shut me out of this. I want to confront these men. I want to be there to hear what excuses they have to offer."

Kern took her by the arm. "I'm sorry, but that is quite impossible."

"No, it isn't." Trembling with a sudden rage, she spun toward Trimble. Knowing he had lain with her mother and shared confidences cut Isabel to the quick. Knowing he had abandoned his only child robbed her of caution. "How do we know we can believe you? If you truly cared for my mother—and heaven knows we only have your word on that—then you'd realize she wouldn't wish you to harbor secrets from me."

"My dear, you cannot be allowed to endanger yourself. Please, consider what befell Aurora. Above all else, she would want you to be safe." With a paternal smile, Trimble reached out and brushed his fingertips over her cheek. "She did love you so. She told me the last time I saw her. She said she intended to move to the country and live with you at long last."

His gentle touch quenched the fire of her fury. Isabel felt abruptly drained and confused, at a loss for words. *She did love you so*.

Isabel had always known Aurora enjoyed playing the role of mama when it suited her. Aurora had made many declarations of love, effusive declarations befitting her extravagance in everything. Yet as she grew up, Isabel had come to doubt her.

She did love you so.

Buffeted by the conflicting emotions of confusion and yearning and frustration, Isabel made no objection when Kern guided her out of the town house. She clung tightly to the puppy, and M'lord seemed to sense her distress, for he nuzzled her cheek. Only as the carriage started down the street did she regain a bit of spunk. "Pull off on the side street there," she said, pointing to a narrow byway. "We'll wait and follow Trimble."

Snapping the reins, Kern sent her a black look. "I gave him my word of honor not to interfere. He'll contact the men and then report back to me. We'll have to be satisfied with that."

"Satisfied! How can you be so certain we can trust him?"

"Nothing is certain. But we've no other choice. If we'd badgered him until Christmastide, he'd not have betrayed your mother's confidence. That much was obvious."

Isabel turned to glance back at Trimble's brick residence. Of course, he wouldn't go anywhere. He did not need to seek out Apollo. And yet if he did leave the house . . . "We can't simply let him go. We can't!"

"Why are you reacting so strongly?" Kern gazed keenly at her. "It's the business about Apollo, isn't it?"

"I don't know what you mean."

"You do know. You claim you don't wish to contact your father, and yet you want to follow Trimble. What do you know about Apollo that you're not telling me?"

Her fingers tightened around the puppy. "Nothing."

"I wonder." Kern flashed her a fierce look. "Be stubborn, then, if you must. But Trimble is absolutely right on one count. You're endangering yourself. And I will no longer permit it."

His brusque tone shouldn't have surprised her. A dozen sharp retorts sprang to her tongue, but she saw the futility of arguing. She was also beginning to see that when it came to honor, men could be extraordinarily obstinate. Like Trimble, Kern wouldn't change his mind.

But that didn't mean she had to obey him.

❧ Chapter 13 ❧

"*A*re you going to tell her, Papa?" Helen asked, her blue eyes sparkling in the lamplight. She and Kern made a handsome couple, sitting side by side in the coach. "Oh, do tell Isabel what you've decided."

Lord Hathaway shifted as if the padded leather seat had grown uncomfortable. Tension radiated from him, and although he continued to look at Helen, Isabel sensed his attention was focused on *her*.

"No," he said in a gruff tone. "This is neither the time nor the place."

"It is the very place," Helen insisted with an excited smile. "And what better time than on a ride to the opera with all of us here together? Besides, my cousin deserves to know what you've decided, if only to set her mind at ease."

Isabel's curiosity bloomed brighter. What decision about her could make Helen's father appear so discomfited? He sat beside her, his posture rigidly upright despite the rhythmic sway of the coach. The small, interior lamp showed the strained expression on his profile.

Kern frowned at her, then at Hathaway. "Now you have me wondering. What is this decision?"

A muscle worked in Hathaway's jaw. Then he gave a curt nod. "A matter has come to my attention. Helen—

prompted by Miss Gilbert—informed me of a deplorable piece of gossip that circulated at the Wilkinses' ball the other night.''

Isabel's throat went dry. Had someone seen her and Kern locked in a passionate embrace? Had someone been watching from the shadows as they'd kissed and caressed like lovers? Shame weighed her with a sense of imminent doom. Her gaze locked with Kern's. By his grim visage she knew that he, too, was reliving their illicit encounter. They had violated Helen's trust, betrayed the tenets of honor. But if Helen knew their guilty secret, why did she look so animated?

''I simply could not believe it when Gillie told me what people were saying,'' Helen said, leaning forward confidentially. ''I was stunned by their viciousness. It is beneath the dignity of an aristocrat to be so mean-spirited. Had I not been ill that night, I would have put a stop to the tattling, once and for all.''

''What gossip did you hear?'' Isabel asked cautiously.

''It seems,'' the marquess said, ''that everyone has found out about your lack of funds, Miss Darcy. The rumors have spread rapidly throughout the *ton*, fostered by a cad named Charles Mobrey.''

Mobrey and his tattling tongue. A vast relief eddied through her. ''Oh, *that*. Well, it's no matter. Small-minded people may gossip, but they don't bother me.''

''You are admirably brave, Cousin.'' Helen reached across the coach to squeeze Isabel's gloved hand. ''But the problem goes beyond mere gossip. A lady must have an adequate dowry if she is to marry well. I told Papa so this very morning.''

''And I must concur,'' Hathaway said, glancing obliquely at Isabel. ''I've been remiss in tending to your financial situation. Helen has convinced me to settle the sum of five thousand pounds on you.''

''Five *thousand*—?'' Isabel echoed. A dizzying sense of

unreality rolled through her. Had she not been seated already, her knees would have buckled. She groped for the hand strap and clung tightly. *Five thousand pounds.* He was awarding her the princely sum as if it were a few pence tossed to a beggar. "But . . . why?"

Eyes narrowed beneath his thick white brows, Hathaway stared at her. "I should think the reason is obvious. So long as you live under my roof, you are under my guardianship. And I will not tolerate gossip tainting any member of my household."

His explanation sounded reasonable—and yet she sensed a hidden meaning behind his words. "Your offer is extremely generous," she murmured. "But you cannot be serious. I could never accept your money."

"You can. And you will."

A shadow haunted his grim gaze. His lips were taut, his expression stony. Why was he determined to give her this gift? A sum so enormous she could buy a spacious cottage in the country for her aunts, with plenty left over to live in comfort for the rest of their days. The prospect was infinitely tempting. Of course, to receive the bequest she would have to marry. And the money would go to her husband. She would have to persuade him to give her a portion of it for her own use . . .

Marrying also meant continuing the masquerade, hiding her disreputable past forever. Did the marquess believe she would feel no compunction about tricking an unsuspecting gentleman? He must. Dismay gnawed at her, although she had known from the start that he thought her amoral.

But still she couldn't fathom his purpose. Why would Hathaway risk having her remain in society, where as a purported relation of his family, they would encounter one another time and again?

Her skin prickling with suspicion, she glanced at Kern. She could see the shock in him, the tightness of his smooth-shaven cheeks as he looked from Hathaway to her. And she could see anger in his hard stare.

Five thousand pounds.

Then, in a cold flash, she fathomed the reason behind Hathaway's astonishing offer. Yes, it made a horrid, diabolical sense. He wanted her to stop investigating Lord Raymond.

Hathaway was buying her silence.

"What the bloody hell were you thinking?" Kern demanded. "Why would you promise her a marriage portion?"

He and the marquess stood in a little-traversed corridor of the Opera House in Haymarket while Hathaway puffed on a cheroot. They were waiting for Helen, who had vanished into the ladies' retiring room. It was intermission, and flocks of elegant theatergoers could be glimpsed in the foyer at the end of the passageway, sipping lemonade and discussing the performance. Pleading a headache, Isabel had remained in Hathaway's private box. Kern had had his doubts about leaving her alone there, but his drive to confront the marquess overruled any trouble she might court.

"Keep your voice down," Hathaway ordered. "Lest all of London overhear us."

Bracing his hand against the wall, Kern muttered, "Then give me your answer quietly."

"I already did. I want the gossip to stop, even if I have to buy her respectability."

Kern voiced the suspicion that had cudgeled his mind during the first half of the performance. "Did Isabel extort this money from you? Did she threaten to publish the memoirs?"

"Good God, no." Hathaway bent down to tap the ash from his cheroot. "She's never asked me for so much as a farthing, though I've paid for her wardrobe, of course. Can't have the girl going about in rags."

Kern despised himself for being glad she hadn't descended to more blackmail. "But *five thousand*? No one will expect you to grant so much to a distant relation."

"People may call me eccentric if it pleases them." Hathaway gave him a level stare. "That is far better than stirring questions about Isabel's background. Such gossip would reflect badly on Helen. Surely you realize that, Justin."

He did, yet outrage still sank its teeth into him. "So you'll all but invite Isabel to wed a gentleman," he said in a harsh undertone. "You'll let her dupe an honorable man."

"She may not take the offer. And if she doesn't marry, she won't get the money."

"But you know damned well she'll do it. You're taking a hell of a risk. She's the bastard of a courtesan."

Hathaway wore a stony expression. "She was taught by a governess, and she's comported herself well."

"And what happens when she's found out?"

"She won't be. She's a clever girl."

"Right. Just the other day, you said she's been gadding about London and asking questions of her mother's ex-lovers."

"Not anymore. You'll see to that."

Kern gritted his teeth. Nothing he said budged the marquess from his incredible, implacable decision. He couldn't imagine Isabel wedding—and bedding—one of the fops who buzzed around her.

No. By the devil, he *could* imagine it. He could imagine her opening her smooth white thighs to some rutting fool. He could imagine himself being plagued by her in the years to come, watching her swell with another man's child, seeing her grow soft and handsome with age. He could imagine he and Helen being obliged to entertain Isabel in their home, enduring her sensual smiles and acerbic wit.

"Bloody *hell*," he snapped. "You know what she is and

where she came from. Sooner or later she's bound to make a mistake. She'll bring shame on you—on all of us.''

''Nevertheless, the matter is settled.''

The marquess turned away to take another pull on his cheroot before stubbing it out in an ashtray. Kern had seldom seen him smoke, and never in public. He couldn't shake the gut feeling that something disturbed Hathaway, something deeper and darker than a monetary gift to the woman who had blackmailed her way into his household.

God! What would make Hathaway abandon all good judgment?

Lord Raymond. Hathaway had always protected his younger brother.

But that would mean Hathaway was bribing Isabel. Paying her to hold her tongue. Impossible.

At one time, Lord Raymond had been somewhat of a rake, squiring a variety of lower-class females until he'd made the mistake of seducing the wife of a wealthy merchant. He'd been discovered *in flagrante delicto* and challenged to a duel, which he barely escaped with his life. Since then, he'd led an exemplary existence devoted to the parishioners of St. George's Church.

Or had he? Was there a more sinister crime in his past? One that Hathaway hoped to silence?

No. *No.* Kern couldn't allow himself to think ill of Hathaway, the man whom he had known since boyhood, whom he considered far more a father than Lynwood. Hathaway was the most honorable man Kern had ever met. He had kept Kern on the straight and narrow path of propriety. He certainly wouldn't shield a murderer.

Unless the murderer was his brother . . .

Escorted by a gentleman, Helen approached them from the foyer. She seemed almost to float in her angelic white gown, her fair hair piled atop her head, her face wreathed in a smile. ''Forgive me for keeping you waiting. Look who I happened to meet in the foyer. I've been telling him the news about Isabel.''

Charles Mobrey made an elaborate bow, his corset creaking. ''Hathaway. Kern. How positively delightful to see you. I was just remarking to Lady Helen how pleasant it is to renew acquaintances with old friends. Is Miss Darcy here?''

Kern wanted to smash the ingratiating smirk from his face. ''Not for you,'' he said.

''Oh . . .'' Mobrey's mouth flapped like a fish's. ''I-I was so hoping to see her. We had a rather silly quarrel last time we met, and I wished to apologize—''

''You've said quite enough,'' Hathaway broke in, his expression freezing. ''Helen, we should return to our seats. The second act will be starting soon.''

''But . . . but . . .'' Mobrey stammered.

Helen slipped one hand around her father's arm, and the other through Kern's. Without so much as a good-bye, they left Mobrey standing alone in the corridor. As soon as they were out of earshot, Helen whispered, ''I knew I could count on the both of you to give him a setdown. What a self-important worm, to think we would permit him to court Isabel.''

''He shan't come near her,'' Kern said. ''I'll see to that.''

''And we must set to work on finding her a good husband,'' Helen added as they ascended the stairs to the upper corridor. ''Someone as wonderful as you, Justin.''

Her naïve smile struck Kern with guilt. She wouldn't think him so wonderful if she were to find out about the passionate kisses he and Isabel had shared. Helen would be hurt, terribly hurt. All because he had failed to control his dishonorable urges, his craving for a woman beyond the pale. The sordid secret weighed upon his conscience.

''Oh, I do hope Isabel has gotten over her headache,'' Helen went on. ''I should feel dreadful if she's caught the sniffles from me. Spending a week confined to the house is positively wretched.''

Kern thought a week of isolation would do Isabel a world of good. By then, he would have heard from Trimble and with any luck solved the mystery. He would convince her to renounce the marriage settlement and return to her own world, sparing him the torment of seeing her time and time again.

He opened the small door to their private box. ''I'm sure she's perfectly fine—''

The platitude died on his tongue as he followed Helen into the enclosure. No one occupied the row of four gilt chairs looking out over the lamplit theater. No one stood in the gloom behind the red velvet curtains.

Isabel was gone.

Taking a swift glance around, Isabel opened a door beside the stage.

A few minutes earlier, she had been sitting in the plush confines of the Hathaway box, gazing down on the audience. During the first act of the opera, she had spied a man sitting alone in the crowd, a man she needed to question. With her mind still reeling from the shock of Hathaway's bequest, it had been no hardship to pretend a headache. Helen had wanted to stay with her, and Kern had stared suspiciously at Isabel, but thankfully the party had left her alone during the half-hour intermission.

It was then that she had seen Terrence Dickenson leave his seat.

Rather than head back to the foyer, where the other patrons sought refreshment, he had gone up the aisle toward the stage. There, he'd furtively slipped through a small door in the side wall.

The very door Isabel now opened.

Unlike Kern, she wasn't content to wait for a report from Sir John Trimble. She couldn't trust the man. In the meantime, she needed to use this fortuitous opportunity to question another of the suspects. And perhaps, she admitted, she had a deeper reason. She needed to escape, even just for a few moments, the temptation of Hathaway's incredible offer.

Proceeding through the doorway, she found herself backstage. The area bustled with activity, and the smell of greasepaint and smoking lamps hung in the air. Behind the closed crimson curtain, a pair of stagehands hauled down a new backdrop, directed by a bald man in a baggy suit. Several minor performers changed costume behind a rickety wooden screen. A singer practicing her scales hit a sour note, much to the noisy amusement of the crew.

Isabel skirted the wall, careful not to trip over a bucket of water with a tin cup and a dead fly floating in it. Several people glanced her way, and she tried to act normal, as if she belonged back here. Not seeing Dickenson anywhere, she went down a passageway off to the side of the stage.

Compared to the elegance afforded the theatergoers, this brick corridor was dank and narrow and dirty. A meager light spilled from a lantern hung at the far end of the passage. Holding her hem above the rubbish-strewn floor, she hastened on her search, peering into rooms no larger than cubbyholes. In one, a plump woman sat before a dressing table and applied carmine to her cheeks. In another, a short, stocky man, naked to the waist, rummaged through a trunk of costumes. The next dressing room was deserted, lit by a guttering candle.

Perhaps he wasn't here. Perhaps he'd gone down a different corridor. Perhaps—for furtive reasons of his own—he'd left the Opera House through a rear exit.

The door of the last room was closed. Isabel hung back, debating whether or not to knock. Then the door opened and a lanky man emerged, thrust out by a feminine hand. The unseen woman trilled in a thick foreign accent, "*Come osa!* I must prepare for the second act."

Furtively, he drew her hand toward his crotch. "But I need you now, my dearest, my darling Lucia."

"Go." She gave him another shove and closed the door.

Terrence Dickenson turned, smoothing his thinning hair. His lusty smile died when he saw Isabel. "You," he snarled. "What the deuce are you doing backstage? Looking for a customer?"

"Hardly," Isabel said. "I wanted to have a word in private with you."

"Ah, so I was right. You do intend to milk me for money."

"I want information." She wouldn't deny the blackmail; better he should think her capable of exposing his filthy secrets to his wife. "I have some questions for you."

His upper lip curled, and he ran his hands down his plum-colored coat. Then he stepped toward her, and she felt a leap of fright. But he merely brushed past her and entered the empty dressing room. In the doorway, he turned and beckoned. "Well, come along. We cannot speak out in the open where any plebeian might overhear."

Isabel hesitated. There was no cause for alarm. She need only scream, and scores of people would come running. Besides, she might never have a better opportunity to find her mother's murderer.

She walked slowly into the room. In a saucer on the dressing table, a tiny flame shivered in a pool of melted wax. The feeble light played over the untidy surroundings, the remains of a meat pie, the uncapped jars of cosmetics, the clothing strewn over a trunk and chaise. A movement caught her eye, and she spun around to see Dickenson starting to close the door.

"Leave it open," she said.

Dickenson must have heard the severity in her voice, for he stopped with the door half shut. "Who are you to give me orders?"

"The owner of the memoirs." For safety's sake, she

added, "And should anything happen to me, I've left notice for the memoirs to be published. So cooperate."

Glowering, he went to the speckled mirror and adjusted his cravat, turning his head this way and that, admiring himself. "Where is your watchdog tonight? Or perhaps I should say, your fellow conspirator."

"If you are referring to Lord Kern, he is with Lord Hathaway and Lady Helen. They're waiting for me in our private box."

"So Kern has sent you to do his dirty work." Dickenson turned toward her, a sly look in his foxy eyes. "Mayhap the rotter thinks you'll coax some answers out of me." He crooked his forefinger. "Come here, my little ladybird, you're welcome to try."

Isabel stayed near the door. "You knew some of my mother's lovers. I should like to know who."

"Me? Why would you think *I* knew any of them?"

"Sir John Trimble told me so. It seems you tried to rally the men to stop my mother from finishing her memoirs."

In the uncertain light, Dickenson paled. He fussed with the diamond stickpin that anchored his cravat. "Trimble's a bloody liar. He was jealous of the rest of us who had the money to afford Aurora's services. He didn't like being put out of the club."

"Club? Do you mean White's? Or Boodle's?"

He chuckled. " 'Twas our own private fraternity, that's what. Those of us who'd caught Aurora's fancy at one time or another." His smile took on a carnal quality. "Ah, she was the best there was. The duchess of debauchery."

Isabel wanted to scratch his eyes out. Yet had not her mother earned the title on her back? Still, it was painful to hear the truth. "You can't mean you had meetings. Official gatherings of her current and former lovers?"

He shrugged. "We tippled the bottle and traded stories, but we certainly didn't pay dues or have any rules. Other than the obvious one."

"Give me their names."

"Why should I? 'Twas a secret society, no females allowed." Dickenson grinned, baring a set of pointed teeth. "Unless, of course, you want to continue in your mother's tradition. What say you? I'd set you up in your own house, buy you a fine carriage, hire servants of your own."

Bile stung Isabel's throat. How could her pretty, fanciful mother let herself be used by a league of lechers? "Give me the names, or I'll have *your* name before the magistrate at Bow Street Office. He'll be interested to hear how you incited these men in a conspiracy to murder my mother."

"A whore? Do you think the law would care?" Dickenson held up his hand. "Besides, we didn't kill her. And I'm cooperating, aren't I? I only thought it my gentlemanly duty to inform my friends that she was writing about us."

Isabel curled her fingers into fists and repeated, "Tell me their names."

Dickenson eyed her as if she were a rabid dog. "Don't suppose there's harm in you knowing. Besides me and Lynwood, there was Lord Raymond Jeffries—but he got religion and left the group." He ticked the names off on his fingers. "Lovejoy died at Waterloo. Blundell's been off to India these past five years. Who's left? Ah, yes, Paine shot himself back in 'thirteen after losing his fortune at the faro table."

Isabel released the breath she'd been holding. She knew those last three names from the memoirs, including the mythological name her mother had given each one: Mars, Hercules, Perseus.

She forced herself to ask, "You were Narcissus. Do you know what name my mother called Trimble?"

"How the devil should I? She never talked about any man but me when we were in bed together."

"Did you know the man she called Apollo?"

"Apollo?" Dickenson's face was blank. "Never heard of him."

To her bitter frustration, Dickenson had added nothing new. "So you went to Lynwood, Jeffries, and Trimble. And you told them that Aurora had to be done away with."

"That's a lie. I already told you there wasn't any conspiracy. You're putting words in my mouth." He looked her up and down, and his scowl transformed into a lusty leer. "Come to think of it, I've something to put in *your* mouth. Something big and tasty."

While Isabel watched in fascinated horror, he put his hand to his groin, rubbing slowly up and down, a glazed delight entering his eyes. "Come here, girl. I've been a good little boy, answering all your silly questions. Don't you think I've earned a reward?"

A great surge of anger rose in her. This coarse libertine had passed himself off as a gentleman, had acted the injured party when her mother had dared to record his randy exploits. "If you want your reward," she said, "then you come here."

He trotted eagerly to her, his fingers fumbling with the buttons of his breeches. "Did Aurora tutor you? Did she tell you how I like it done?"

"I have my own methods." Smiling secretively, Isabel let him get close enough to reach for her. Hiding her fist in her skirt, she drew back her arm. And she did what the aunts had advised her to do if a man ever assaulted her. She punched him in the groin.

Dickenson howled loud enough to wake the dead. Clutching himself, he staggered backward, momentum carrying him out the door. He fell in a pile of rubbish in the passageway. There, he lay whimpering, his lanky body curled around his injured part.

People rushed into the corridor. Cast and crew trotted from the direction of the stage. The fat woman came waddling out of her dressing room. From the other direction, the dark-haired Italian singer converged on him. "*Cuore mio!* What is zis? What 'as 'appened?"

Isabel shut the door on the hubbub. She leaned against the wood panel as the fury washed out of her, leaving her drained and shaking and ill. Dickenson had real cause to hate her now.

God help her if he was the murderer.

Kern made a quick search of the foyer and the box seats and the general admission audience. The second act would start soon; the orchestra was already tuning up their instruments. Isabel was nowhere to be seen. Surely she wouldn't have dared to leave the theater.

He didn't believe for a moment that Banbury tale about a headache. She courted trouble somewhere, he was sure of it. So much for any gratitude she might have shown Hathaway for granting her that dowry.

As a last resort, Kern strode backstage. Lamps flickered over the empty stage. The drop scene showed a moonlit night, the painted canvas anchored from behind by ropes and pulleys. He wondered why the place was deserted. Surely the crew should be preparing to open the curtains. The singers should be gathering to await their cues.

The buzz of voices drew him toward the rear of the stage. People crammed a narrow corridor, some standing on tiptoe as they strained to see over the others. Several of the women were giggling.

Bloody hell. He had the sudden strong certainty that he would find Isabel at the center of the fray.

He shoved his way through the throng. The stench of perfume and unwashed bodies stung his nose. "Get back to work," he said. "You've a show to get on."

Grumbling, the laborers and costumed performers heeded his command and headed in the direction of the stage. The crush lessened, and Kern found himself gazing down at a familiar face.

And he understood why Isabel had disappeared.

Terrence Dickenson lay with his head cradled in the lap

of the voluptuous soprano who had starred in the first act. Dickenson moaned piteously while cupping his groin, though he didn't look sorely wounded. He took full advantage of the singer's crooning sympathies by nuzzling his cheek to her pillowy bosom.

Kern seized Dickenson by his coat, hauled him to his feet, and thrust him against the brick wall. The soprano shrieked, rattling off what sounded like Italian curses. He ignored her. "Where is she?"

"She?" Dickenson sputtered. "Who?"

Kern tightened his grip. "Don't play the muttonhead. You know who I mean."

Dickenson's eyes bugged out as he gasped for air. "She's . . . in . . . there." He managed to nod toward a closed door.

Kern let go. Dickenson sank into an undignified heap. Changing allegiance, the soprano sidled up to Kern and rubbed herself against him like a çat in heat. "*Gioia mia.* You are a beeg, strong man. Come, you tell Lucia your name."

"You're wanted on stage," he said, giving her a push in that direction. The rejected singer spat out another string of invectives. He jerked Dickenson to his feet and shoved him after her. "I'd advise you to run home. Before I decide to make adjustments to your face."

His shoulders hunched as if anticipating a blow, Dickenson hurried away down the corridor after the soprano.

Kern rapped on the door. He tried to open it, but an obstruction blocked it. The knot in his chest twisted tighter. Had she been hurt? Had she collapsed in front of the door? "Isabel. Are you in there? Answer me."

For one terrifying moment he heard only distant music as the orchestra launched into the opening strains of the second act. Within, all lay silent. As silent as a tomb. He was preparing to hurl himself against the wooden panel when the knob rattled and the door swung inward.

He stormed into a cluttered cubbyhole lit by a single candle. Isabel hovered in the shadows behind the door. He seized her by the arms. "Are you all right?" he demanded.

"Of-of course, I'm all right," she said, though her voice shook. "I'm perfectly fine."

The relief that washed over him was so profound he forgot his anxiety, his anger. He forgot all but the feel of her, supple and warm, so close to him. He shaped his hands to her slender waist, the rounded bottom, the womanly hips and breasts. Her hair smelled faintly of roses, and the softness of it caressed his cheek. He imagined that dark hair strewn across a white pillow, and the light of a candle glowing on her pearly skin, and himself descending to her nakedness, kissing her, touching her, tasting her . . .

His mouth pressed down on hers, thirsting for her sweetness. She kissed him back without reservation, with all the ardor he had ever dreamed of in a woman. He couldn't imagine her belonging to any other man, kissing anyone else so passionately, though surely she must have done so. Her lips were soft and seductive, conveying a depth of feeling that enraptured him. He knew he should not be here with her, not like this. Though his heart hammered the truth, he held her close in his crushing grip, unwilling to let her go.

"Oh, Kern," she whispered against the madly beating pulse in his throat. "I'm glad you came looking for me."

He couldn't halt the lascivious turn of his mind. It was like a fever in him, burning out of control. He wanted to put an end to his torment. He wanted to make love to her—here. Now. In this murky little dressing room. While hundreds of patrons beyond the door listened to the opera.

The thought held an erotic appeal so powerful he forced himself to draw back. He pushed her away and held her at arm's length. With distance, a measure of anger returned to him. "What the devil are you doing here? Did you learn nothing from your first encounter with Dickenson?"

She thrust up her chin. Her sherry-brown eyes shone in the faint light. "I wasn't in danger. Didn't you see all the people out there? Besides, you might compliment me for disabling him."

So that explained why Dickenson had been clutching his crotch. Horror and fury overshadowed any admiration Kern might have felt. He skimmed his hands over her dainty shoulders to assure himself she was unharmed. "Tell me what that son of Satan did to you."

He felt a faint shudder run through her, and she glanced away. "It was nothing I couldn't handle. Though I'd feel safer if you returned my dagger."

"You shouldn't walk into situations where you need a weapon," Kern said through gritted teeth. "Now answer me. Did he force himself on you?"

"He made an unsavory offer." Bitterness tinged her voice and she held herself stiffly, with a pride that sliced into his heart. "Exactly the sort of offer gentlemen make to a woman of my background."

A fog of rage descended over Kern. His throat felt choked with venom. His chest throbbed with the need to draw blood. Dickenson's blood.

Releasing her, he swung toward the door. Visions of violence consumed his mind. He would make that bastard pay. He would send the rotter to hell . . .

Isabel darted in front of him, pressing her back to the closed door. "Where are you going?"

"To find Dickenson."

"What do you intend to do?"

"Give him his choice of pistols or swords."

She choked out a gasp. "Kern, you *mustn't*. You can't challenge him to a duel."

"I can, indeed. I'd kill him with my bare hands for touching you." His fingers flexed of their own accord. He saw himself throttling the life out of Dickenson, hearing him beg for mercy, watching his face turn purple . . .

Isabel's hands cupped his face, cool against his fevered skin. "*No!* That's out of the question. He didn't touch me."

"He insulted you, and that's enough."

"You can't kill a man over an insult to *me*. Think, Kern. Think of the scandal. Think of what it would do to Helen. She can't know what we feel for one another. She must never, ever know."

Helen. The pounding in his veins began to subside. The haze over his reason gradually dissipated. Reality slapped him with the truth of what he had almost done. He released a harsh breath.

He had almost forsaken his fiancée. He had almost betrayed the sweet girl who, for the past year, had planned their wedding.

He had almost declared himself the champion of a trollop.

Isabel gazed steadily at him, her eyes expressive with concern. Even with her dark hair mussed and her lips reddened from his kiss, she bore herself with dignity. No, he couldn't label her in derogatory terms. She was as much the natural daughter of a gentleman as she was the bastard of a whore.

Releasing her, he closed his eyes and leaned against the wall. Even now, she tempted him. His arms ached to hold her. The womanly scent of her lingered on his skin. She answered a dark need in himself, a need he dared not fathom. With a peculiar horror he realized he wanted her so much he had been ready to renounce Helen.

She can't know what we feel for one another.

What *did* he feel for Isabel? Lust, certainly. But his emotions went deeper than that, far deeper. And he could not allow himself to dive into the darkness lest he drown.

Dear Reader,

You might fancy the life of a courtesan is filled with endless pleasures. Certainly we indulge often in the delightfully wicked vices of the flesh. Yet like most ordinary souls, we also have the tedium of our daily lives, those times when our men have gone back to their world and we women are left to fend for ourselves.

It was shortly after Apollo forsook me that Minerva joined my household. I had lived alone until then, believing myself content, able to manage on ample funds left to me by Apollo. With the approach of my confinement, however, I realized the need for feminine company.

Upon advertising, I procured a companion, and when she found out my true vocation, she resolved to follow the same path, taking the name Minerva, or Minnie, as we so fondly call her. Minnie proved herself a great help upon the birth of my dear daughter. I do believe she was as proud as I to take the baby on outings to the park or to marvel at her first smile. And Minnie was as sad as I to say good-bye that dismal day we safely settled Apollo's daughter in Oxfordshire.

Over the years, other ladies joined our household: Diana, who fled from a brutal husband; Callandra, who sold her body to buy bread for her orphaned siblings; and Persephone, who was seduced by a footman and cast out by her merchant father. I have found great comfort in their friendships. We are Goddesses. And we are family . . .

—The True Confessions of a Ladybird

ᔕ Chapter 14 ᔕ

Her body burned for him. Shameless longing made her move restlessly. Her clothes melted away, and his big hands ravished her, stroking her breasts, then moving lower, to pleasure the aching place between her legs. At last, she could freely give herself to him. The joy of it carried her higher and higher. She felt him kissing her ear, her cheek...

Someone was licking her face. Isabel opened her eyes and blinked into the early morning sunshine streaming past the curtains. She lay in her bedroom at Hathaway House. And her enthusiastic assailant wasn't *someone*. It was M'lord.

The puppy snuffled eagerly against her ear, his tongue leaving a wet trail across her cheek. With a wry laugh, she scooted to a sitting position against the pillows and gathered him into her arms. Tail wagging, he continued to bathe her neck and chin in slobbery kisses.

"You stop that now, do you hear?" She moved him to her lap, petting his spotted gold coat until he rested quieter. "Silly dog. You ruined a perfectly wonderful dream."

It *had* been wonderful. Almost ecstatic. A residual heat throbbed within her, an eternal flame burning for Kern. Ever since he had kissed her at the opera house the previous night . . . nay, ever since she'd met him, she had been doomed to a purgatory of perpetual frustration. She could no longer deny that she wanted him, body and soul. She wanted what she had sworn never to take—a noble lover.

She wanted the one man who could cause her downfall.

Giving herself to Kern would send her down the immoral path her mother had taken. Worse, it would ruin Isabel's investigation, end her chance to find the man who had killed her mother. For if ever she let him make love to her, how could she remain here, knowing she had betrayed Helen, the girl who had become like a sister to her?

Isabel hugged the puppy closer, deriving comfort from his warmth. She had grown accustomed to the quiet elegance of this house. Her eyes drank in the spacious room with its hangings of pale-blue silk, the canopied bed, the dainty mahogany furniture. In the evenings, when the house lay silent, she liked to sit and read in the armchair by the marble fireplace. And in the mornings, she liked to lie here and fantasize about being a lady . . . enjoying comfort and respect . . . belonging in this world forever.

The thought lured her like a shining dream. She could have that life. She could accept Hathaway's dowry. Though it wasn't much by the standards of many members of the *ton*, five thousand pounds would secure her a fine gentleman as a husband.

But lately her flights of fancy had taken a dangerous turn. When she imagined sharing her marriage bed, she thought of Kern. Only Kern.

Even if he were free, he would never wed her. He knew her past. He knew the trickery she'd used to inveigle herself into this household. He knew she was not a lady. To him, she would always be the daughter of a whore.

Yet in the heat of the moment, he had kissed her with all the hunger of a man holding his beloved. He had been ready to fight Dickenson for insulting her. Until he'd remembered.

She gave M'lord another hug, pressing her cheek to his

soft coat. One radiant thought illuminated the gloom in her heart. Kern wanted her. Even if an illicit affair was out of the question, he still desired her. As much as she desired him.

As for Hathaway's offer, she wouldn't accept the money, of course. She couldn't. Even if it were freely given, without the disreputable price of bribery attached, she could never, ever take such a sum from any nobleman.

With one final pat, she set the puppy aside and threw back the counterpane. It was no use dreaming impossible dreams. The day would come when she had to depart this life. Though the dowry tempted her, she would return to her own world. Where she belonged.

The reason lay beneath her pillows.

Reaching beneath the feather-stuffed mound, she drew out the slim linen pocket that held her mother's memoirs. The familiar square of the book with its brass clasp reassured her. She followed the right course; she would find justice for her mother.

Padding into the dressing room, Isabel performed her morning ablutions, then slipped out of her nightdress and donned a fine chemise. Beneath it, she securely tied the long strings of the pocket around her waist. Then she rummaged in the wardrobe for a petticoat.

An ache lingered in her heart. Selfish or not, she wanted the loving husband and the respect due a lady. She did not need a palace, just a comfortable cottage in the country to raise a family of her own. Closing her eyes, she clutched the petticoat to her breasts. The dream wafted over her again, her children romping on the lawn with their father ... and when she ran to join them, the smiling man who greeted her with a kiss was Kern.

Was it love, this warm feeling she had for him? The thought made her shiver with desire and danger. How could she have fallen in love with the one man who was so wrong for her?

The outer door burst open. M'lord set up a loud yapping. Isabel peeked out into the bedroom to see Callie hurry inside. Though clad in a severe black gown covered by a crisp white apron, Callie managed to appear less than respectable. Her bosom strained against the seams of her bodice. Curls of brassy blond hair escaped her mobcap. She moved with a naturally seductive sway to her broad hips. No doubt she caused friction among the male servants, and Isabel could only hope Callie heeded her promise not to bed any one of them.

"So you're awake." Callie stalked to the window and jerked open the curtains. "Good. There's no time for lolling in bed this morning."

Her urgent tone startled Isabel. Quickly she stepped into the petticoat before Callie spied the pocket hidden beneath her chemise. "Does Helen wish to leave early for our shopping trip? She didn't mention it last night."

"'Tisn't her ladyship. There's trouble at home. Bad trouble."

The bottom dropped out of Isabel's stomach. Her fingers froze in the act of securing the tapes of her petticoat. "Aunt Persy? Has she—?"

"Nay, she's fine. 'Tis Minnie this time." Callie dug into the pocket of her apron, extracted a square of paper, and slapped it into Isabel's palm. "You'd best have a look at this. I don't read so good, so maybe I took it wrong."

Fingers shaking, Isabel unfolded the letter. She recognized Aunt Di's elegant script even before seeing the signature at the bottom. The message was painfully brief.

Aunt Minnie had been attacked during the night by a prowler.

Kern stood at the foot of the bed, staring down at his father.

The Duke of Lynwood twitched restlessly in his sleep. Curled up like an infant, he lay huddled on his side beneath the covers. By the light of a candle on the bedside table, his cheeks had a shrunken, yellow cast and his nose showed a webwork of spidery veins. He looked curiously defenseless in slumber. A sick old man far past his prime.

Though noon had come and gone, the heavy curtains were drawn, rendering the chamber as dark as night. The sweetish odor of laudanum lingered in the warm air. Lynwood had suffered another seizure the previous evening, while Kern had been at the opera. The physician had hopes for the duke's partial recovery, provided he was kept sedated for a few days to regain his strength.

His eyes closed, Lynwood quivered as if in pain. His lips moved as he groaned in his sleep.

Fighting an attack of compassion, Kern braced his hand on the bedpost. He shouldn't care what happened to the reprobate. He shouldn't wish he could ease his father's suffering. The duke had earned his place in hell. Lynwood epitomized all the reasons Kern resisted his lust for Isabel Darling.

Heat arrowed to his groin. The mere thought of her had that effect on him. She obsessed his mind and possessed his body. No matter how he tried, he could not cudgel his brain into forgetting her for more than a few minutes at a time. Whenever he turned his mind onto safer ground, the crooked path of his thoughts led inexorably back to her. Back to her slender form and laughing eyes, back to the pouty lips that could as easily curse him as kiss him.

Last night he had been ready to kill a man on her behalf. He assured himself his foolhardy impulse couldn't have been in defense of her honor. Rather, he abhorred the notion of any other man touching her. Even if he himself could not—should not—lay a hand on her tempting body.

He owed his allegiance to Helen. She was the lady of his choice, his future wife, the virtuous woman who would share his life. To Helen, he had pledged his word of honor. He had sworn not to be like other men, sowing his wild seed wherever he fancied. He had made that vow after the appalling incident on his fourteenth birthday.

Clenching his teeth, he resisted the plunge into dark memory. The past didn't matter anymore, except where it had been his teacher, shaping him into a man of honor.

He would not behave like Lynwood. He would not.

Turning on his heel, Kern stalked from the bedroom, giving a nod to the attendant waiting in the antechamber. Renewed resolve sustained Kern as he went down to his waiting carriage and set out for Hathaway House. This morning, he'd had another unproductive interview with the Reverend Lord Raymond Jeffries. Kern needed to inform Isabel that the clergyman still professed to know nothing about the murder.

Besides, he had promised Hathaway to keep a close watch on Isabel. For that purpose alone, Kern had to conquer his infatuation with her. He would begin by reminding himself of all the reasons why Helen suited him better than a beautiful, lying upstart.

And he would do so now.

Upon reaching the spacious town house in Grosvenor Square, he paced the drawing room while a footman scurried to announce his arrival. Kern felt restless, charged with energy as he waited for the two young women. Beyond a few words in private to Isabel in regard to the investigation, he intended to heed only his fiancée.

But when Helen breezed into the drawing room a few minutes later, she came alone. M'lord trotted at her heels, which surely meant Isabel would follow soon. She wouldn't have gone out without her precious mongrel.

Helen picked up the puppy and cuddled him in her lap. Her bright-eyed features made Kern feel guilty for neglecting her. "Justin! You've missed Papa—he's gone off to Parliament today. And you almost missed me, too. I'm going out shopping in a short while. Would you care to accompany me?"

He kissed the smooth back of her hand. "I'm afraid I haven't the time today."

"It's your father, isn't it?" The corners of her mouth drew downward in sympathy, and she touched his sleeve. "Papa told me the duke has had a relapse. I'm ever so sorry."

"He's resting now. There's nothing any of us can do."

"Our wedding is little more than a month away. Shall we delay it, do you think?"

The prospect tempted Kern, but just as swiftly, he denied the shocking impulse. He led her to a striped chaise and seated her beside him. "Of course we shouldn't delay. He'll recover within the fortnight. Dr. Sadler has assured me of it."

"Oh, I'm so glad." She leaned forward as if in confidence. "I would not wish the least unpleasantness to mar our nuptials. Oh, it is going to be the most perfect of all days. Let me tell you the menu I've chosen for our wedding breakfast."

She launched into an enthusiastic description of lobster salads and sugared raspberries and champagne sorbet. He listened for a time, offering comments where necessary, yet all the while he found himself looking at Helen, really looking at her. She had a small, pretty face framed by upswept fair hair, the classic English beauty. Her animated blue eyes and smiling mouth lent her an appealing, girlish quality, and she regarded the world as a garden perpetually bathed in sunshine, never seeing the dark side of night. Trivialities excited her—parties and shopping and mundane social duties.

Ten years separated them in age, yet he felt far older, almost ancient by comparison. Was this what his life with her would be like, endless chatter about menus and fashion and gossip, never delving deeper, always skimming the surface of matters? The prospect left him weary. Denying a restless unease, he reminded himself that Helen was chaste and loyal and modest, all the qualities of an excellent wife. She had a good heart, too—look at how she had convinced Hathaway to settle a dowry on Isabel.

Isabel. Kern felt a jolt of energy. The thought of her seared him with a powerful yearning. Where the devil was she? She had better be upstairs, primping herself for the shopping expedition.

If she'd gone haring off to question another suspect, he'd have to chase her down. If she'd foolishly endangered herself, then by God he would put her under lock and key. And let her argue till doomsday that she wasn't his to command.

After an elaborate accounting of the trouble Helen had gone through in deciding on the perfect wedding cake, he could contain his impatience no longer. "Is Isabel going shopping with you?"

"Oh, no. She isn't here today."

His muscles tensed. "Not here?"

"She went off in a hurry this morning to visit an acquaintance of her mother's who has fallen ill. I offered to go with her, or at least send Gillie, but Isabel insisted on having only her maid accompany her." Frowning in perplexity, Helen stroked the mongrel's ears. "She said she might be gone the night. Isn't that odd? I didn't realize she even knew anyone in London so well."

Kern set his jaw. He didn't find her disappearance odd in the least. Truth be told, he knew exactly where to find Isabel Darling.

Isabel balanced the tea tray on her palm while opening the bedroom door with her other hand. She walked into the shadowy chamber with its hangings of crimson velvet and placed the tray on the bedside table. "Here you go," she said in her cheeriest voice.

"Ah, there's my good, dear girl," Aunt Minnie said fondly. "Not too proud to fuss over your old aunties."

Minnie sat propped against the pillows. A mop of graying ginger hair straggled down past her shoulders, and a voluminous red nightdress encased a body that had gone soft and fleshy over the years. She looked like an enormous cherry tart.

"Of course I'm happy to fuss over you." Isabel poured a cup of steaming tea, adding a dollop of cream and a lump of sugar. She started to hand the cup to Minnie, then hesitated, eyeing the dressing that wrapped the length of Minnie's forearm. "Can you manage the cup?"

"I think so—only just." Using the fingers that poked out of the end of the bandage, Minnie carefully grasped the saucer that Isabel guided into her hand. With her uninjured arm, Minnie picked up the cup and lifted it to her lips. Her movements were slow and measured as if the pain and shock of the attack still lingered.

Watching her, Isabel felt stricken. She sat down on the edge of the bed. "How is your arm feeling?"

"Sore as the dickens. But it'll mend, don't you fear. 'Tis lucky I am the bastard took fright and ran. Only think, he might've stuck his sharp knife straight through my heart."

Isabel's own heart lurched at the grim possibility. In changing the dressing, she had seen the ugly gash that ran the length of Minnie's forearm. The sight had made her shudder. "I should have been here," she said for the umpteenth time. "I should have helped to chase him off. I could have called for the Watch. We might have caught the villain."

"Mother of God, there's nothing you could have done," Minnie said, wincing slightly as she set the teacup in its saucer. "Certainly we'd like you to come home, where you belong. But what's happened, happened. There's no sense in beating a dead dog."

Minnie's calm acceptance failed to boost Isabel's spirits. "I can't help feeling responsible. It's my fault that awful man came here. And . . . and he hurt you." Her throat seized up and she bent her head, her mind haunted by the destruction in Aurora's boudoir.

"There, there, dear." Minnie patted Isabel's back. "We'll set things to rights. You just go on back to your big fancy house and forget about us."

Isabel lifted her head. "I haven't forgotten you. I could never forget you."

"But maybe you'll get to liking the soft life of a lady so much you'll never want to return here." Minnie sighed, her bosom lifting and falling. "You can't blame an old woman for fearing so."

A fresh wave of guilt broke over Isabel. She thought of the dowry and her secret dreams. "I know where I belong, aunt. I *do*." Or did she? Was she letting her yearning for a prince overcome her good sense? *Kern. Oh, Kern.*

"Good afternoon, ladies." Callie posed in the doorway. She had discarded the white apron and unbuttoned the high neck of her gown, revealing the white half-moons of her breasts. Her blue eyes danced with delight. "Don't look so glum, you two. We've company, so put on your naughtiest smiles. Especially you, Isabel." In a stage whisper, she added with a wink, "It's Lord Kern."

As she vanished out the door, Minnie turned to Isabel. "What's this? You've a nobleman caller?"

Isabel knew she was blushing. She felt hot all over. As if she had conjured him, Kern was *here*. "I'll see him downstairs."

"Wait." Minnie grasped Isabel by the wrist. An age-old wisdom lit her hazel eyes, as if she could peer straight into Isabel's heart. "You've a hankering for this man—now don't deny it, I can see it on your face. Your Aunt Minnie's always known you better than anybody."

"Yes," Isabel whispered. "I do . . . have feelings for him."

"Ah, girl, 'tis nothing shameful, wanting to lie with a

man. You're a woman now, with a woman's needs. It's time you accepted that.''

Was Aunt Minnie urging her to succumb to Kern? Despite her astonishment, Isabel felt the tug of an exquisite longing. How glorious it would be to let him make love to her. To experience the delights she had heard her aunts gossip about . . .

Footsteps sounded out in the corridor and Callie reappeared, stepping inside to let their guest enter.

Kern stood in the doorway, a big, dark figure framed by the gloom of the corridor. His haughty green gaze swept over the gaudy crimson decor, then settled on the bed where Isabel sat with Minnie.

A chill descended over Isabel, and she felt exposed to him in all her vulnerability. She should have known he would show up; he had a knack for finding her, no matter where she went. But this time she wanted him gone before he saw the results of her wanton negligence, her headstrong foolishness. Her throat tightened again, and she swallowed hard. ''We can talk downstairs,'' she told him, rising from the mattress. ''If you'll excuse me, Aunt Minnie.''

''Don't run off with our gentleman caller,'' Minnie chided. ''First, I've a mind to have a nice chat with his lordship.''

''And so you shall.'' Kern walked to the foot of the bed and regarded the older woman. ''When I heard someone was ill, I assumed it was Persephone. But something's happened to you.''

'' 'Tis a dreadful tale,'' Callie put in, shivering deliciously. She settled herself on the stool before the dressing table and primped her skirts, artfully lifting her hem so that her trim ankles showed. ''I wasn't here, of course, but Diana told me all the screaming jolted her out of a sound sleep—''

''It's no concern of his lordship's,'' Isabel interrupted. Willing him to go away, she straightened the bedcovers and took the teacup from Minnie, placing it on the tray, all the while glowering at Kern. "Don't you have a speech to give at Parliament? Or an auction to attend at Tattersall's? If nothing else, Helen would love for you to take her shopping."

He frowned slightly at the mention of his fiancée. "My most pressing business is to find out what's happened here," he said. "Minnie? Will you be so kind as to enlighten me?"

"I'd be delighted," she said, as dignified as a grande dame holding court. "And do sit down, girl. You're making me nervous, hovering about so."

Only a few moments ago, Minnie had commended her for fussing. Feeling sick inside, Isabel lowered herself to a straight-backed chair near the bed. What else could she do, short of physically pushing Kern out of the bedroom? Not that she could succeed against his strength.

No, he would poke and pry until he'd heard the whole sordid story. And he would know how she had endangered the women who'd helped to raise her.

Minnie cradled her injured arm to her bosom. "A terrible event happened last night," she began in a dramatic tone. "A noise awakened me, though I couldn't tell you exactly what I'd heard. But seeing how Persy's been ill, my first thought went to her, that maybe she'd awakened and called for me, needing a dab of her tonic to help her back to sleep."

"What time did this happen?" Kern asked.

"In the wee hours—not too long before dawn. Soon's I heard the noise, I rose out of my bed and opened the door. The passage was black as Satan's heart, but I felt my way along as I'd done many a time before. That's when it happened." She paused, her face grim. "Near the staircase, a man rushed out of the darkness and knocked me flat."

"A man," Kern repeated. Scowling at Minnie, he

walked back and forth at a measured pace. "Did you get a look at him?"

She shook her fading ginger curls. "It was dark, like I said. I saw only his shadowy shape. When he pushed me down, I made a grab for him, hoping to catch the thieving bugger. I didn't know he had a knife till it was too late."

"Was he a big man? Or small? Stocky? Thin?"

"I can't say as I noticed." Wincing, Minnie eased her injured arm onto the counterpane. "The pain was so fearfully bad, I don't remember anything else. Except the blighter got clean away."

"You screamed," Callie reminded her. "Diana said the toffs likely heard you all the way over to Mayfair. And you near scared poor Persy out of her wits."

"Are they here?" Kern asked. "I'd like a word with them."

Callie rose. "I'll fetch them, m'lord."

As she minced out of the room, Isabel sat frozen with misery. Kern didn't know the whole story yet. He didn't realize the intruder was no common thief. That was the part she dreaded him finding out, the part that caused her such heartache, the part that implicated *her*.

A few minutes later, Callie returned, supporting a little gray-haired woman in a frilly pink dressing gown. Aunt Persy smiled and twittered upon seeing Kern, and he sprang to her aid, assisting her onto a chaise with all the care a gentleman might give his maiden aunt.

Isabel wanted to curl up into a ball. What if the prowler had attacked Aunt Persy instead? She lacked the strength to withstand the shock. She might have died. And it would have been Isabel's fault.

Diana sauntered into the bedroom, a waterfall of copper hair flowing to the waist of her honey-brown wrapper. Not even the fine lines of age could disguise her willowy beauty. She cast a resentful look at Kern and settled herself beside Minnie on the bed, making no move to draw down her hem when it rode up to her knees.

Isabel saw Kern glance at those long, slim legs. In the midst of her anguish, another fierce emotion invaded. She wanted to leap up and cover Aunt Di. The urge burned so shockingly strong, Isabel found herself gripping the seat of her chair. Especially when he walked closer to Diana.

"I understand," he said, looking down at her, "that you were asleep when Minnie was attacked last night."

"Yes."

"Before she screamed, did you hear any noises? Footsteps, perhaps? Someone moving about?"

"Nothing. I slept unusually well last night—at least until then." She spoke defiantly, with the suspicion she reserved for all gentlemen.

"When you came out of your room, did you see the intruder?"

Diana shook her head. "In the few minutes it took for me to light a candle, he got away. The front door was standing wide open. And Minnie was lying on the floor. Bleeding."

"Did you find the weapon?"

" 'Twas left on the stairs," Minnie offered. "Isabel, show it to his lordship."

Reluctantly, Isabel opened the drawer of the bedside table. She detested touching the blade, knowing it had been wielded in violence. She shuddered to think of the damage it might have inflicted.

Kern came closer, picking up the knife by the wooden handle and examining it. "An ordinary kitchen knife. No distinguishing marks."

"Aye, and I'll keep it right here," Minnie said, indicating he should return the knife to the drawer. "If the bugger ever comes back, I'll geld him, you can be sure of that."

Kern made no reply. He turned to Persy, who watched

with bright, birdlike eyes. "Ma'am, did you hear anything unusual?"

"Not a peep." She shivered as if the incident haunted her. "I'm sorry, my nightly tonic makes me ever so weary. I heard Minerva cry out, but nothing at all before that."

Kern returned to Diana. "Did you entertain anyone last night?"

"No. Don't you think I would have said so?" She made a moue of disgust. "I told you the last time you were here, I've little use for swine. Especially not in my bed."

Callie smiled slyly. "That's your own fault for never learning the difference between a pig and a cock."

"And you never cared what breed of animal shared your bed," Diana retorted. "So long as he had two balls and a limp stick for you to diddle."

"My customers always had harder cocks than yours," Callie said with a sniff. "If you want my advice, men might treat you better if you didn't lie there like a cold fish—"

"That's enough," Minnie snapped. "I'm sure his lordship doesn't care to listen to your squabbles."

Isabel bit her lip. Leaning against the wall, his arms folded over his elegant coat of forest green, Kern wore a look of pensive aloofness. What must he be thinking? Isabel didn't want him to form ill opinions of her aunts. She ached for him to see that in spite of their lack of virtue, they were loving guardians. As far back as she could remember, whenever she came to visit they had shunned men. Granted, Callie had had a lapse or two along the way, but they had kept to that pact of celibacy this past year, even when it meant doing without luxuries like wine and new gowns and jewelry.

Would their sacrifices matter to a nobleman like Kern? Not judging by the arrogance of his frown. She saw the tawdry scene through his eyes: Callie leaning forward to give him a look at her bosom, Minnie lolling in her red nightgown, Diana taunting him with a flash of naked legs, Persy looking frail from her battle against an unmentionable disease.

Never had Isabel been more keenly aware of the chasm between his life and hers. Yet these women were her family, the people she loved. She didn't have to suffer his disdain.

Isabel sprang to her feet. "Aunt Minnie's right. His lordship has heard quite enough. I'm sure he has better things to do with his time."

"On the contrary," he said, studying her with narrowed eyes, "I've another question."

"You want to know what the intruder was after," Minnie guessed. "Well, I can tell you it wasn't money or any other valuables. He was out to steal Aurora's memoirs."

Isabel couldn't move, though her heart pounded in painful strokes. Kern had warned her all along about the dangers of inciting the murderer. Now he would know that by her reckless disregard, she had risked the lives of her dear aunts.

"The blighter ransacked Aurora's bedchamber," Callie added. "You ought to see the mess. He ruined some perfectly fine dresses, too."

"And the memoirs?" Kern asked. "Were they stolen?"

"Ask Isabel," Diana said. "She has them hidden away somewhere. She won't tell even us where they are."

Little did they know, the small volume lay tucked inside its secret pocket. For once, Isabel wasn't proud of her cleverness, only sick at heart. "Mama's book is quite safe. That's all you need to know." She leaned down and hugged Minnie, careful not to jostle the bandaged arm. "I'm so sorry you were hurt."

"There now, my dear." Minnie gave her a quick squeeze. "Don't trouble yourself over me."

"With your permission," Kern said, "I would like to examine Aurora's bedchamber. Perhaps the intruder dropped something, or left a clue as to his identity."

"An excellent notion," Minnie said slowly. Her hazel eyes narrowed first on Kern, then Isabel. "My dear, you run along now and show Lord Kern to your mama's bedchamber. Stay with him while he looks around."

Isabel's spine went stiff. Was Aunt Minnie matchmaking? "I intended to tidy the room myself," she protested. "He won't know if there's something out of the ordinary, so there's no use bothering him."

"I'll go with him if you don't want to," Callie said, leaping up from the stool. "It would be my pleasure to keep his lordship company."

"But how much searching would he accomplish?" Diana asked, stretching languorously. "He'd be too busy fending you off."

Even as Callie let out a huff, Minnie said firmly, "This duty belongs to our Venus. It is her mother's things that were disturbed."

"Venus?" Kern asked. He turned and stared at Isabel.

A hot wave of mortification seared her cheeks. What a moment for Minnie to forget the preference Isabel had made clear years ago, when she had found out the erotic reputation of the goddess.

"It's the name Aurora gave her," Diana said. "Venus Isabel Darling."

"I think it's a lovely name," Persy piped up. "But we should honor Isabel's wishes, don't you think?"

Minnie cringed, a grimace on her plump face. "Forgive a tired old woman, my dear girl. 'Twas a stupid slip of the tongue. Perhaps I shall nap for a while, while you go on and help his lordship." She lifted her weary gaze to Kern. "I trust Lord Kern has no objection to your assistance."

His gaze burned into Isabel. The scorching heat descended to her belly. She knew she ought to protest, but no words came to her lips. She could only think about how badly she wanted to be alone with him.

Still watching her, he said in a low voice, "I have no objection."

ᥫ Chapter 15 ᥫ

*T*he odor of spilled perfume struck Kern at the doorway. The air smelled heavy and sensual as if he were entering a dark den of pleasure.

Yet the rose velvet draperies were drawn back, and the room was bright with sunshine. Unlike the decadent nest he recalled from his first meeting with Isabel, the boudoir showed a scene of reckless destruction.

Drawers had been pulled out of the highboy, and the contents lay strewn on the carpet. On the chaise, the pink pillows bled their stuffing. Even the cushion on the dressing-table stool had been slashed. Pots of overturned cosmetics littered the table and floor. Nothing had been smashed—the intruder had been careful to make no noise—yet the viciousness of the damage disturbed Kern.

"My God," he muttered. He picked a path through the chaos and walked into the bedroom, where more vandalism awaited him. A wardrobe had been emptied of its gowns. Crushed bonnets scattered the floor. High-heeled shoes and satin slippers lay everywhere.

He gravitated toward a dainty writing desk which was covered with papers. This must be where Aurora had written the reminiscences of her life as a courtesan. In his haste to find the memoirs, the intruder had dumped the quill pens and tipped over an inkpot, the black liquid staining the blank sheets of stationery.

Where had Isabel hidden the book? At Hathaway's? Or was it secreted somewhere else in this house? Tucked into a discreet cubbyhole known only to her?

She advanced slowly into the bedroom. The deep blue of her gown accentuated the paleness of her skin. Her brown eyes held a dazed disbelief as she surveyed the clutter. Yet when she turned to him, he could see the defenses going up in the squaring of her shoulders and the lifting of her chin. "Go on," she said. "Say it and be done. Tell me I asked for this to happen. Tell me it's my fault."

He should do just that. He should take her to task for provoking the murderer. But when he saw the faint quivering of her lower lip, he felt a treacherous softening in his chest. "Pointing the finger of blame would serve no purpose. I'd sooner spend my energy finding the culprit."

"And you think he conveniently left us his calling card?" Hugging herself, Isabel shook her head. "There's nothing here. Nothing but a colossal mess. He destroyed everything that belonged to my mother."

Kern resisted the urge to banish the sadness he sensed in her. "Then let's get to work tidying up. There's a chance we might find something to identify him." He cleared a place in the corner of the bedroom and tossed the ink-stained papers there. "Whatever is ruined beyond repair, put in this pile. Show me anything you find that's out of the ordinary."

Collecting a quill that had fallen to the carpet, he noticed that Isabel stood unmoving, her arms folded over her bosom. Her woebegone expression caught him. Her eyes held a suspicious sheen as she looked around the room, and he wondered suddenly what memories this vulgar room held for her. Even though she'd grown up in the country, she had visited her mother from time to time. Perhaps here, they'd chatted while Aurora applied her cosmetics or dressed for an evening of entertainment. Perhaps here, Aurora had given her daughter advice on how to please men.

Venus, the goddess of love.

Anger hit Kern like a fist to his gut. Aurora must have planned from the start to lure her daughter into her profession. Yet even as he cursed Aurora for corrupting an innocent girl, he burned to test the extent of Isabel's knowledge.

They were alone, unchaperoned. The door was firmly closed. Only a few steps away loomed the big canopied bed with its mirrored headboard and gaudy cherubs. He could lay her down and lift her skirts and sink into her softness . . .

"Well?" he snapped, more harshly than he'd intended. "Don't just stand there. Or do you want the murderer to get away with what he's done?"

Isabel blinked at him as if she'd forgotten his presence. "Of course not," she murmured.

Bending, she picked up a broken fan and dropped it onto the pile of papers in the corner. Then she began gathering the articles of clothing that were strewn over the floor. Her graceful movements fascinated him. He could spend hours watching her, glimpsing the shadow between her breasts as she leaned down, the curve of her derriere as she walked, the delicacy of her ankles whenever her hem shifted.

His eyes surreptitiously on her, he fumbled to put the pens back in their holder and stuck a sharp quill into his palm. His teeth clamped around a curse. So much for his powers of observation.

Yanking his attention from her, he focused on the task of sorting things out in the hopes of finding something significant—a man's cuff link, perhaps. Or a lost glove—anything to identify him. Had Dickenson come here last night? Or Lord Raymond?

Kern roved through the bedroom, collecting things which had belonged to Aurora, shoes and shawls, silver brushes and lace garters. With these he started another pile by the wall for someone to sort through later. He kept alert for anything unusual—not that silk stockings and flimsy feminine undergarments constituted the ordinary for him.

Then he saw it.

The small crimson object lay beneath the bed, near the bedpost. He scooped it up and rolled it in his fingers. "Look at this."

Isabel hastened to him. She leaned over his hand, so close he could smell the rainwater scent of her hair. "It's a button," she said, sounding disappointed.

"Yes, and it could have fallen off a man's waistcoat."

She plucked the button out of his palm and gave it a closer scrutiny. "No, it's from one of Minnie's gowns, I think. She comes in here from time to time to dust the place. I'll return it to her."

With a natural sway of her hips, Isabel walked away to put the button on the bedside table. She sank to her knees beside the bed and began to gather up an assortment of candles and books and papers that had been dumped out of the drawer.

"Where was your father last night?" she asked over her shoulder.

"At Lynwood House," he said absently, picking up a black chemise so sheer he could see his hand through it. His imagination draped the provocative garment over Isabel. She would be revealed to him in all her glory . . . full breasts . . . curvaceous hips . . . shadowy mound of Venus . . .

"Can you be sure of that?" Isabel asked. "Was someone with him?"

"With who?"

"Lynwood," she said, sounding exasperated. "I know

he's been ill, but has he recovered sufficiently that he might have come here last night?''

''No, in fact, he suffered a relapse late in the evening. He was sedated. The doctor stayed with him all night.'' With the suddenness of a tidal wave, relief poured over Kern. Why hadn't he thought of it before? ''You must realize what this means. My father couldn't possibly have done this.''

''He might have sent someone else to do his dirty work. He could have hired a lackey to search for the memoirs. The arrangements could have been made before he took ill.''

''No, the servants are loyal to me, and no one else has been to visit him.'' Buoyed by a satisfaction beyond belief, Kern dropped the skimpy chemise on the pile. It floated downward like the raiment of a wicked fairy. ''And if Lynwood did not do this, then he also did not poison your mother.''

She frowned as if reserving judgment. ''Then perhaps the intruder was the Reverend Lord Raymond. Perhaps he heard about the dowry and decided things had gone too far. He had to get the memoirs back.''

''I spoke with him this morning when he came by to pray at my father's bedside. I'd stake my life that he hadn't known about the dowry.'' In fact, upon hearing the news, Lord Raymond had uttered a colorful oath that would have shocked his more gently bred parishioners.

But was he a murderer? And if he was not, then why had Hathaway granted a marriage portion to Isabel?

Try as he might, Kern couldn't picture Hathaway's brother laying waste to this bedroom, then stabbing a woman. ''He's a respected clergyman. He wouldn't break into a brothel in the middle of the night.''

Isabel plucked an ostrich feather fan from the floor. She attempted to straighten one crooked white feather, drawing it through her fingers over and over. ''Yes, he would. He's done so before. My mother said as much in her memoirs.''

''He's done *this*?'' Disbelieving, Kern waved his hand around at the destruction. ''Give me the memoirs. Let me read that passage.''

''No, you misunderstand me.'' Isabel lifted the fan, her brown eyes peering over it like a concubine peeking out from behind a veil. ''Suffice it to say he preferred to visit my mother under cover of darkness. When no one of consequence would notice his sin.''

''A late-night assignation is a far cry from vandalism and assault. That brand of stealth belongs to a scoundrel like Terrence Dickenson.''

She dipped the fan until the feathery tips brushed her breasts. He found his gaze fixed there, found himself envying the fan. ''We cannot discount Trimble,'' she murmured in a curiously emotionless voice. ''I suspect he knows more than he lets on.''

He knows Apollo.

Kern refrained from reminding her of the father she so despised. ''There are plenty of men who would love to see the memoirs vanish.''

She lowered the fan to a place just below her waist. ''They won't find the memoirs,'' she said confidently. ''Trust me, they won't.''

Her coy maneuvering of the fan aroused Kern. In defiance of his willpower, heat scorched his groin. Was she deliberately enticing him?

He turned and slammed a drawer shut. ''There's another possibility to consider,'' he said. A thought gnawed at the edge of his mind. ''How well did your mother get along with Diana and Callandra?''

Isabel frowned. ''Well enough. They had their little spats from time to time, but no more than any close friends. What has that to do with the prowler?''

''The prowler could have been one of the women living here.''

The fan slid from her fingers and thunked to the floor. Her face frozen, Isabel took a step toward him. "You can't think . . . one of my aunts . . ."

"It seems far-fetched. But I noticed the enmity between Callandra and Diana. If either of them resented your mother for whatever reason, they might have turned their malice on her things."

"No. *No.*" Isabel shook her head for emphasis. The late afternoon sunlight picked out the fiery strands in her dark-brown hair. "That is utter nonsense. Aunt Callie and Aunt Di have always squabbled, but it doesn't mean they're sneaky and . . . and violent." She shuddered. "It's unthinkable. I've never seen any disloyalty between my aunts."

Much as it pained him to do so, he had to shatter her illusions. "Isabel, the first time we met, here in this room, someone left the back door unlocked for me. Someone informed me when the other women would be at dinner so that I would find you alone. Someone betrayed you in exchange for a gold sovereign. That someone was Callandra."

Isabel's lips parted in a soundless O. He could see her incredulity and the beginnings of hurt, and he regretted it fiercely.

"I'm sorry," he said gruffly. "But you may not know these women as well as you think. Can you verify Callandra's whereabouts last night?"

As if suddenly weak, Isabel sagged against the bedpost. "She waited for me to return home from the opera. Then she went up to her room in the servants' attic."

"Or perhaps she slipped out of the house and came here."

Isabel gave a snort of disbelief. "That's absurd. Why would Aunt Callie want the memoirs?"

"Perhaps there's something derogatory written about her. Or perhaps she wasn't looking for the memoirs at all, but something else entirely."

"Such as?" Isabel's tone conveyed skepticism.

"Such as an outlet for her resentment of Aurora." *She would have to be mad.* Kern didn't voice that thought. Instead, he motioned Isabel into the boudoir and picked up an empty flacon of scent. "If the intruder was looking for a book, he—or she—couldn't possibly have found it in this bottle. So why spill the perfume? And the cosmetics? Why slash your mother's gowns? Those are acts of wanton hatred."

"The prowler was frustrated by his failure to find the memoirs, that's all." Isabel reached for an empty jar on the dressing table. With jerky movements, she scooped powder back into the container. "I shouldn't be surprised that you would vilify my aunts. You'd rather not believe one of your own kind could be so malicious. It's much easier to blame a whore."

Without thinking, he moved forward to grasp her shoulders. "That's where you're wrong. Believe me, I know that with provocation, even a civilized gentleman can turn savage."

At the moment, he himself felt a feral urge that had nothing to do with violence—and everything to do with the instinctual act of mating.

Touching her was a mistake. The warmth of her skin seared him with desire. He wanted to slide his hands downward, to explore the slopes and valleys he had known only in his fantasies. He wanted to banish the tension in her, to shield her from the cold cruelties of hatred. Instead, he had added to her anguish by casting doubt on the women who had raised her.

"Dear God, the man who came here last night was a savage beast," she whispered, her eyes deep pools of misery. "He could have killed Aunt Minnie as he killed my mother. And it would have been my fault. I was too obstinate to see the truth."

Like a forlorn rag doll, she stood with her shoulders

limp. Kern couldn't bear to see her so desolate. It was all he could do to stop himself from shaking some sense into her. "Hindsight is always more accurate than foresight," he said. "You couldn't have known this would happen."

"But I should have foreseen the consequences of going after a murderer. I should have realized he might try to kill again."

"Are you saying you'll drop the investigation, then?" he asked, deliberately trying to provoke a reaction from her. "You'll stop seeking the villain who killed your mother? You'll let him get away unpunished?"

She bit her lower lip. "I don't know. Oh, Kern, I honestly don't know where to go from here."

The bewilderment in her voice tore at him, and once again her eyes showed the glint of tears. She had always been so strong, so dedicated, so ready to rise to a challenge. Now she looked pleadingly at him as if he knew the answers to all the questions inside herself. And with a fierceness that brutalized his self-control, he wanted to make her happy again.

"Isabel." He slid his arms around her, his hands moving up and down her slender back, over her sweetly rounded bottom. She snuggled closer to him like a kitten seeking comfort. He would hold her for a few moments, let himself revel in the dark, fathomless need she stirred inside him. It didn't matter that he was betrothed to another woman so long as he went no further. He concentrated on keeping his breathing even, his mind composed.

"Make me forget." Isabel slipped her hands inside his coat and lifted herself on tiptoe. "Help me, Kern."

His resolve wavered at the first forbidden brush of her lips on his. Despite all her experience, it was the kiss of a maiden, tender and questing, a compelling combination of innocence and immorality. On a groan, he succumbed to temptation. He would allow himself one kiss. And the pleasure of savoring the succulence of her mouth. The pleasure of touching her shapely form. The pleasure of holding her against his throbbing heat.

And the torture of anticipation. Oh, God. The torture of knowing he couldn't—shouldn't—take this embrace to its natural conclusion.

But he could venture to the edge. He could test the boundaries of his control and move into deeper waters. Nuzzling the smooth, fragrant skin of her cheek and throat, he unfastened the buttons down the back of her gown. He felt her small fingers at his coat and waistcoat, and realized she was performing the same task for him. Having fewer buttons to contend with, she succeeded first, reaching up to push both garments off his shoulders.

"This is wrong of me to want you so," she whispered, her palms warm through the linen of his shirt. "Yet why does it feel so right?"

"Because you," he muttered, "were made to be loved."

The bodice of her gown slithered downward, and she made quick work of the fastenings of her corset and chemise until she stood before him, bare to the waist. He released a harsh breath. Bathed by the soft light of early evening, her skin glowed like rich cream and her breasts formed coral-tipped mounds. He could not imagine a more perfect woman. She embodied her namesake: Venus, goddess of love.

She brought his palms up to cradle her breasts, then closed her eyes and sighed. "I adore your hands. I adore the way they make me feel, all warm and shivery inside."

She moved against him in the sinuous invitation of a siren. Desire blazed through his blood as she coaxed him closer to the limits of discipline. How could he not taste the feast she offered to him? He bent his head, closing his mouth around one taut nipple, then rubbing his cheek against the velvety hills, exploring the sweet-scented valley in between. He caressed her with his teeth and tongue, encouraged by her murmurings of delight.

He would stop in a moment. He would walk away from her. Honor demanded it of him.

But not yet. Not while her fingers tangled in his hair and moved down the column of his neck to loosen his cravat. Not while she unbuttoned his shirt. Not while she whispered his name and pressed a kiss to his bare throat. He could feel the trembling in her hands and in his, too, as he touched her. Isabel wanted him. As much as he wanted her.

Want. What a pale word to describe the pounding in his chest, the fever in his blood. His loins were locked in an everlasting purgatory, halfway between heaven and hell. He was no longer so certain that salvation held any worth or meaning. How could he aspire to a heaven without Isabel?

Let his soul be damned, then.

He gazed down at her lovely face and saw his own desperate desire reflected there. Paradise awaited him here. Now. With the one woman who set fire to his heart.

Ablaze with need, he guided Isabel out of the boudoir and into the bedroom. As they neared the bed, her steps faltered and she looked up at him with haunted eyes. "Kern, this is wicked. You know why—"

He pressed his finger over her soft, reddened lips. "If I'm doomed to burn, then by the devil, I'll burn with you."

She gave a little sigh. "Yes," she breathed. *"Yes."*

Their mouths met in another frantic kiss. Her breasts strained against him until he felt scourged by the erotic torture of flesh on flesh. Their partial nudity frustrated him. Groping inside her gown, his fingers tangled in the unfamiliar fastenings of undergarments, the myriad of tapes and hooks. His thumb snagged on a string circling the satiny curve of her waist. In one swift jerk he broke the cord, and an instant later his fevered brain registered a muted bump as if something had struck the floor.

She gasped and squirmed away. "Turn around," she whispered. "Please. Just for a moment."

"No." Like a stallion coaxing a shy mare, he nuzzled her throat, inhaling the musk of her arousal. Her attack of modesty baffled him. Unless she was still suffering doubts. "Isabel . . . I want to watch you undress."

He worshipped at the shrine of her bosom while her hands moved restlessly over his shoulders, his chest, venturing down to his waist and hips, skirting the swollen rod that strained against his breeches. *Oh God. Touch me. Touch me.*

Her fingers danced upward again, cradling his neck and clinging tightly. The teasing she-devil. With a growl of frustration, he tried to pull her toward the bed, but she remained stubbornly in place.

"Wait," she breathed.

He thought she meant to refuse him again, and he nearly howled with primitive male lust. Then she wriggled out of her gown and undergarments and dropped them where she stood. Only a garter around each slender thigh and a wisp of silk stockings saved her from nakedness.

His throat went bone dry. His mind went blank to all but the beauty of her. Alabaster flesh. Rounded hips. A tangle of dark curls.

His. All his.

She stepped out of the puddle of clothing, snuggled herself against him, and gave him a smile that was half seductive, half sweet. "Please. Will you take me to bed now?"

Mindlessly, he guided her down onto the linen sheets. He could wait no longer to touch her. His hand caressed a path up her thigh to skin as silken as her stocking . . . to feminine heat . . . and wanton wetness . . . to the satiny secrets of womanhood.

She tensed, but only for an instant. On a soft sigh of surrender, she opened fully to him and pressed herself against his fingers. When he found her most sensitive place, she twisted beneath him, her hands clinging to him. "*Oh* . . . dear heaven . . . please . . ."

He relished her pleasure as if it were his own. She was so small, so delicately made for his loving. Hot blood scalded his veins and roared in his ears. More fiercely than his own fulfillment, he wanted hers. He craved her complete surrender.

Her impatient hands roved over him, clutching at his opened shirt. Her hips lifted to him in the sweetest of invitations. "Yes. Oh, *yes*. Oh, Kern . . . I love this . . . I love *you*."

Even as her words fell like warm rain into his parched soul, she gasped his name once more and shuddered beneath him, convulsing against his fingertips.

I love you.

Exultation quaked through him, heightening his raging need. He wrested open his breeches, shoved them off, and sank down into the welcoming cradle of Isabel's body. When she closed her fingers around his throbbing shaft, he almost lost his battle for control. Her guiding hand led him to the brink of paradise, and in one fierce plunge, he met a barrier and breached it.

She stiffened, her nails digging into his back, her cry stifled against his sweat-slickened chest. He went still, fighting the urge to move within her incredible velvet tightness. "Isabel?"

He looked down at her, into the awed surprise on her face, and he knew. He was her first. The truth engulfed him with shock and a wild masculine triumph. "You're mine now. *Mine*." His voice sounded thick and guttural, his throat choked with an emotion too new to define.

Cupping her face, he kissed her with all the fierceness flooding his heart. Then he could restrain himself no longer; he delved deeper into the mystery of her. The sensual friction lured him ever closer to the darkness he now craved, to the black whirlpool that he could no longer resist. She found his rhythm and matched it, moving with him faster and harder, her small body arching to his. Her breathy moans stoked his fever and on her soft gasp of rapture, he tumbled over the edge, his seed pulsing into her. He plunged not into darkness but into a light so bright it blinded him with joy.

In the aftermath, he held tightly to Isabel and his labored breathing slowed. He rolled onto his back, bringing her half atop him. He found himself gazing up at the frilly pink canopy, each corner held by a fat, naked cherub gazing down blissfully at them.

He wanted to laugh, not in ridicule, but out of sheer satisfaction. The knot inside his chest had vanished. In its place he felt an immeasurable warmth and tenderness toward the woman lying in his arms.

The rich mass of her hair tumbled over her shoulders and onto him, as if to bind them together. He breathed in her fragrance mingled with the musk of their lovemaking. She lay with her cheek in the hollow of his shoulder, her fingers idly tracing the length of his collarbone. His skin heated wherever she touched him, and the feeling was a blend of sensual arousal and perfect euphoria. How long had it been since he'd felt so contented?

I love you.

His chest constricted with a yearning he could not fathom. He wondered if she truly meant those words, or if she'd spoken only in the heat of the moment. Passion was new to her. She might easily confuse it with deeper, more enduring emotions. Just as he himself might mistake the tenderness inside him as something heartfelt and lasting.

With effort, he blocked the direction of his mind. He wasn't yet ready to think about the future. He wanted to savor the moment.

Stroking the silken curve of her backside, he felt vastly pleased at the turn of events. He owed Isabel an apology.

He had misjudged her, tarred her with the same tawdry feather as her mother. But how could he beg forgiveness for making love to her? He couldn't express regret when he felt like crowing from the rooftop. He was her first, her only lover.

"Venus the virgin," he murmured.

Her hand went still. She lifted her head to regard him warily. Her reddened lips and tousled dark hair distinguished her as a woman who had been thoroughly pleasured. "I'm not one of the goddesses," she said defensively. "That's why I don't use the name."

"I know that now." He kissed the tip of her nose. "And I'm glad of it."

"And now I realize what I've missed," she continued with a sniff. "Chastity is overvalued."

"So is celibacy." She still looked vulnerable, so he confessed, "Isabel, contrary to your opinion about gentlemen, I've had only one sexual encounter before you. And that one was a gift for my fourteenth birthday. Courtesy of my father." He couldn't stop the brusque note that entered his voice.

Her fine eyebrows drew together in a frown. "A gift?"

"Yes." He could still feel the rage and pain of his adolescent heart. Yet if it helped Isabel feel more at ease, he'd tell her. "From the time I was very young, I hated the lecher my father was, and he knew it. Too often, he made my mother weep with his infidelities. She was nothing more than a breeding mare to him—and even motherhood brought her no peace since I was her only child to survive. She died when I was ten, from a fever after another stillbirth."

Isabel closed her eyes a moment, then looked at him again, sympathy softening her features. "Oh, Kern. I didn't know. I'm so sorry."

Uneasy with her compassion, he shrugged. "The point is that from the time I began to grow into a man, Lynwood was determined to corrupt me. He invited me to join his drunken orgies. He offered to lend me one of his many mistresses. But I was sickened by his excesses. And I resisted temptation until a house party at our estate the week of my fourteenth birthday.''

He paused, his throat rigid, the dark cloud of memory obscuring the hopes and dreams of an idealistic boy on the brink of adulthood. At the time, he had so wanted to believe in the triumph of love over evil.

"Please," Isabel said gently. "Will you tell me what happened?"

He took a deep breath. "My father invited his current mistress—a countess who brought along her daughter, a girl of about my age. As the only two juveniles in the party, Sarah and I spent much of the week together. She was pretty and friendly, and I fell madly in love with her."

He remembered those fine summer days, when she'd laughed and swung on the garden swing, her kicks giving him teasing glimpses of slender white legs.

"How lucky she was to have won your regard." Isabel feathered her fingertips up his cheek and over his temples. The affectionate gesture encouraged Kern to bare his soul to her, to relate the tale he had never revealed to any other person.

"By the second day, we'd shared a stolen kiss, which led to more daring caresses. Then on the last night, Sarah came to my bed, purportedly to say good-bye. You can imagine what happened next. Even when it became obvious she was experienced, I was blinded by my desire for her. I believed in her, trusted her." Recalling his reckless declarations of love, he grimaced and forced himself to go on. "The following morning, my father walked in and found us together. He wished me a happy birthday and gave Sarah a diamond bracelet, payment for services rendered. And she got out of my bed and went to him."

The echo of her laughter had haunted him for years afterward. But no longer. He felt strangely freed by the confession, as if a dark burden of shame and anger had been lifted from him.

Isabel's huffy breath feathered his chest. "That is appalling. How could your father plan such a thing? And how could that horrid girl possibly choose Lynwood over you?"

The implied compliment pleased him. He lightly ran his knuckles down the silky skin of her cheek. "It doesn't matter. I never saw Sarah again. And from that moment, I vowed to live an honorable life. I swore I wouldn't make love to any woman but my wife."

Until now. Until you.

The unspoken words hovered in the twilight air. By seducing Isabel, he had complicated his future. There would be consequences to face later, decisions to make. But for now, he wanted only to go on holding her, savoring her warmth and softness. One night of passion wouldn't make him a profligate.

Her velvety brown eyes still looked troubled. "You thought . . . I was like Sarah."

He couldn't deny it. He had believed the worst of Isabel. By way of atonement, he kissed her brow. "I was wrong. I saw only what experience taught me to see."

"And what do you see now?" Her voice held a thread of defiance that touched him deeply even as it made him smile.

"I see a woman who is beautiful inside and out." He smoothed his palms down the back of her, feeling himself stir in response to her feminine shape. "A woman who knows her own mind." He caressed the globes of her breasts. "A woman who had the discernment to save herself for me."

"And I see an arrogant man who did likewise." She

stretched languidly, her fingers playing with the hair on his chest. "I trust you won't wait so long for your next intimate experience."

She gave him a coy half-smile that instantly roused him to hard, raging need. He turned her onto her back, letting her feel how much he wanted her. "I trust you're right."

While the rays of the setting sun bathed the room in gold, they kissed and caressed, exploring all the secrets of their bodies. He took his time with her, pleasuring her with his mouth and hands until she lay panting, clutching at him. "Kern . . . *oh* . . . that's wicked . . . but don't stop . . . please don't stop."

"Say my name, then. Justin."

"Justin." She smiled at him, her eyes dreamy with something greater than passion. "Justin, I do love you."

This time, he had to choke back a declaration of his own. He couldn't love her; he didn't dare. "Ah, Isabel. I've never wanted any woman as much as I want you."

He slowly entered her until she fit him like a tight sheath, then moved in rhythm with her as if they were one body, one soul. And when she reached the peak, he came with her, the world exploding on his fierce cry of exultation.

Dusk spread a deep purple veil over the room. Isabel lay snuggled against him. Her eyes were closed, her breathing peaceful. A throat-catching tenderness stole over him as he realized she had fallen asleep. And he felt not a whit of regret for exhausting her.

He wanted to sleep beside her, to hold her for a little while longer. But she might take a chill now that her passion had cooled.

He eased himself free, his gaze on the rumpled coverlet, which dangled crookedly over the side of the bed. As he leaned over to tug it up, he noticed a linen-covered square sticking out from beneath the pile of her clothing on the floor.

Nudged by curiosity, he reached down and picked it up. The booklike shape made his blood run cold with suspicion. He opened the drawstring and pulled out a slim, leather-bound volume. For a long moment, he stared down through the half-darkness at the title.

The True Confessions of a Ladybird.

Apollo and I despised each other on first sight.

*On that fateful night of our meeting, I was per-
suaded to attend a gathering of gentlemen at a private club off St. James's Street. They wished to give
me as a special gift to a friend on the eve of his
betrothal. Being intrigued by the notion, I allowed
myself to be conveyed inside a covered silver platter
borne by two footmen.*

*There, clad in a diaphanous dress, I emerged like
Venus from her seashell. And found myself facing the
most compelling man I had ever met in my illustrious
career as a courtesan.*

*Apollo was furious, of course. I understood why
later, when I came to know his noble character. But
at that moment when he took one contemptuous look
at me, denounced me for a whore in front of the party
of gentlemen, and then walked out of the room, I
hated him.*

*And I was determined to have him. No general
could have waged a campaign more boldly than I
did that spring. I dressed as a lady and called on
Apollo. I conspired to meet him riding in the park.
When at last I crept into his bed, the glorious experience ended our animosity and awakened our
tender affections for each other.*

*Oh, what a vain and foolish creature I had been
until then! I thought I knew what it was to love a
man. All that summer I devoted myself to Apollo,
remaining faithful until our last night together, the
night before his wedding. The night I conceived our
love child . . .*

—The True Confessions of a Ladybird

✄ Chapter 16 ✄

*I*sabel awoke to darkness and an empty bed.

For a moment she could not imagine why she was snuggled beneath the covers in her mother's room, or why her body felt so marvelously replete, a pleasant ache lingering deep in her belly. Her eyes still closed, she stretched, aware of the smoothness of the linens against her sensitized skin. Then she caught a whiff of musk and the joyous episode came back to her in a wonderful wave of memory.

She and Kern had made love. Not once but twice their bodies had been joined in the most intimate way. She fancied she could still feel the tender touch of his hands and mouth, arousing her to an ecstasy she had not dreamed possible. The mere thought of it made her long for him again.

Had he left her already?

She lifted her head from the pillow, her gaze drawn to a small circle of light across the room. The bereft feeling inside her changed to unabashed pleasure. Half in shadow, he sat in an armchair by the hearth. A candle flickered on the small table beside him. He had donned his clothing, though he looked deliciously virile with his white linen shirt open to his bare chest. One of his feet was propped on a footstool as he gazed down at a book in his lap. An absorbed expression dominated his strong features, and she remembered the raspy sensation of his cheek against her breasts. Her flesh tingled at the memory.

She loved him. The first time she had said so, she had surprised herself with the unexpected power of her feelings. The words had come straight out of her heart, a revelation as inevitable as the tides. What they had shared was more than mere lust, more than the satisfaction of a mutual physical urge. She loved Justin Culver, Earl of Kern and heir to the Duke of Lynwood. She loved his strength of character, his sense of honor, his determination to seek out the truth. Despite his exalted status, he was a good man, a man worthy of her favor.

But, oh, what a tangled skein they had woven. Their relationship had altered irrevocably. Where would they go from here? He was not a profligate to use a woman and then abandon her. Nor was he free to offer his heart to her. He was betrothed to Helen.

Pain throttled Isabel's throat. She couldn't yet think about facing the girl who had become like a sister to her, the girl she had betrayed in the most vile way possible. She felt sick inside at the thought.

Not that her treachery had been cold-bloodedly planned. In the heat of the moment, she and Kern had been swept into a storm of passion. Instinct and emotion had overpowered logic and reason. Now, her heart ached at the utter impossibility of their situation. Like her mother, she had fallen in love with a lord who was engaged to wed a lady.

A page rustled as he turned it. He could have gone away while she was sleeping. Instead, he sat reading, waiting for her to awaken, and his very presence opened a bright window of hope, letting in fairy-tale dreams of happily ever after.

I've never wanted any woman as much as I want you.

It was not a declaration of love, but the utterance of a truth she craved nonetheless. Awash with yearning, she slipped quietly out of bed and padded toward him. From the edge of her vision, she noticed the signs of vandalism in the gloom, but nothing could mar the shining image of her beloved.

"Justin?" It felt strange and wonderful using his given name, an intimacy still new to her.

He looked up sharply, his gaze boring into her. He did not return the smile she flashed at him. His face was solemn, his expression chiseled from granite. She sensed immediately that something in him had changed, though she could not say what. His shadowed green eyes traveled from the crown of her tumbled hair down over her unclothed body.

Feeling suddenly shy, she paused by the bedpost. It had seemed perfectly natural to walk naked toward him. But under the force of his frown, she crossed her arms over her breasts in a hopelessly inadequate attempt to cover herself. Anxious to decipher his mood, she stared back at him, taking in the charmingly rumpled black hair, the noble cheekbones and inflexible jaw, the unbuttoned shirt that showed the hair on his flat abdomen, a dark arrow that pointed straight down to his . . .

Her gaze landed on the opened book in his lap.

The rivulets of heat inside her chilled to icicles. Her lips parted, but only a thin gasp emerged.

He sat reading *The True Confessions of a Ladybird*.

In a horrifying flash, she remembered him undressing her, inadvertently breaking the string that secured the hidden pocket. She had been frantic lest he realize what he'd done. So frantic, she had wriggled out of her gown and petticoat and drawers, letting them drop over the fallen memoirs. She had enticed him into bed, and from the moment he'd come down on her, she had forgotten everything but Kern.

Until now.

She flew across the room. "Give that back to me."

"It's too late." He snapped the slender volume shut. "I've already read it."

"Give it back," she said through gritted teeth.

"No." He sat unmoving, infuriatingly calm as he regarded her. "First we talk."

She was tempted to lunge at him, to wrench the memoirs out of his thieving hands. But she was stopped by a vision of herself, naked and wrestling with him for the book. She cursed the involuntary pulse beating in her loins. At the moment she wasn't feeling amenable to letting him touch her.

She spun around and marched to the bed. With trembling fingers, she snatched up her chemise and yanked it over her head. The crumpled linen garment floated down to her knees, giving her a modicum of modesty as she stormed back to face him. "That book belonged to my mother. You have no right to steal it."

"I haven't stolen it. And I have every right to know exactly what the memoirs say. There might have been a clue that you missed."

"Then tell me what it is and give the book back."

She held out her hand. He ignored it. Still holding the dainty volume, he cocked his head to regard her. "You think Trimble is your father."

She told herself to deny it, but no words came to her tongue. Now he knew. Knew the name of the scoundrel who had set so little value on his own daughter. Trimble had tossed her away as if she were a bit of rubbish. It shouldn't hurt. And yet it did. *It did.* In her heart dwelled that lonely little girl who pretended her father was the king.

"I understand now," Kern went on, "why you acted so strangely around him. He's the man who shared your mother's secrets. The only man she didn't call by the name of a god. The only man she truly trusted."

Through dry lips, she found her voice. "Promise me . . .

you won't demand an explanation from him. I wish to do that myself.''

"I'll make you no such promise."

"Why not?" she cried out.

"Because you may have come to the wrong conclusion about Trimble. He might *not* be your father."

Isabel took a step backward. "I beg your pardon? I've had far longer to think about this than you have."

"It's just a feeling I have. Something I need to investigate."

"Your investigation is over." She didn't want him asking questions of Trimble. If Trimble didn't wish to acknowledge her, then so be it. Praying her voice wouldn't shake, she said, "Now give me the book."

Leaning back in his chair, Kern arched one eyebrow. "That isn't all I learned. I also found myself enlightened about your mother."

"Oh? Did you realize how justified you are in ridiculing her?" Pacing before him, Isabel hugged her midsection, trying to ease her pain. It was no use. She felt stripped raw by his poking and prying into her past. "Did you enjoy reading about all her encounters with men? Quite titillating, isn't it?"

He frowned. "I'd already seen one of the passages pertaining to my father—the copy you sent to him before we met. The rest is no more explicit."

"Don't try to spare my feelings," Isabel snapped, anger overheating her. "It's one thing to know Mama was a whore, and quite another entirely to read about her and her lovers in exquisite detail. Everything they did together, where they did it, when they did it." She took a shuddering breath. "The memoirs only confirm how indiscriminate she was, how far removed from *your* definition of a lady . . ." To Isabel's horror, her voice broke. A hot moisture stung her eyes and spilled down her cheeks.

Mortified, she swung away, but Kern tossed the memoirs

onto the side table and caught her by the waist, tumbling her onto his lap. The stiffness drained out of her and she latched tightly onto him. He pressed her face to his shirt while she sobbed out her rage and grief. All the while, he stroked her hair and whispered soothing words she dared not heed. Surely he understood that her mother's misdeeds tainted Isabel, too. How could she ever hope he might regard her as more than a mistress? No woman of her background could marry a nobleman.

Marry.

In her heart, she acknowledged the wrenching, impossible truth. She wanted to be his wife, to bear his children, to sleep beside him each night, and to walk proudly by his side at *ton* functions. She wanted him to know her ill-favored upbringing and to cherish her nonetheless. With all the fierceness of yearning, she wanted to be Lady Kern.

With his thumb, he lifted her face and gently caught a stray tear that clung to her lower lashes. "Isabel, I'm sorry for hurting you," he said gruffly. "Believe me, that was never my intention. And you're wrong about my reaction to the memoirs. For the first time, I can see Aurora as a person with hopes and dreams." The admission sounded halting as if he still wrestled with the truth of it.

The conflicting feelings inside Isabel poured out. "Many viewed her as a disgusting creature. But she was my mother, Justin. She did try to do her best for me."

"Yes, I can see that now. And she loved your father, whoever he was. What they shared was more than a sordid, meaningless affair."

"She let him use her. She deliberately seduced him."

"Praise God she did. Else you might never have been born."

His hard mouth quirked into a half-smile, lending a rakish quality to his heartbreakingly handsome features. His hand lay heavily on her shoulder, his fingers massaging away her tension. The bitterness lost its power over her, burned to cinders by the steady flame of her love. And by the gratifying certainty that Kern did not regret their tryst.

Her insides curled into a sweet knot of erotic longing. She lolled half naked in the lap of a muscled, virile male. A possessive look darkened his eyes, and she thrilled to the heat prickling over every inch of her skin. His gaze dipped to her breasts, and he surely saw the coral points straining against the fine fabric of the chemise.

His hand descended slowly. She held her breath in delicious anticipation of his caress. But he cupped his palm over her belly instead, his touch warm and firm.

"Isabel," he said in a strange, gravelly voice. "You may be carrying my child."

She could only stare at him as his meaning sank in and filled her with irrepressible joy and overwhelming panic. "Merciful God. I hadn't even considered . . ." Her voice trailed away as she grappled with the awesome possibility of nurturing his baby inside her body, of giving birth to his son or daughter. And she remembered her loneliness as a girl, the empty feeling of never having known the love of a father.

She clutched his shirt and informed him, "If indeed I'm pregnant, then I'm not letting you walk away as my mother did my father. Our child will never suffer as I suffered."

"Of course not," Kern said. "Apollo was a cad for abandoning you. Before God, I could never do as he did. I could never, ever cut myself off from my own child."

Her heart thrummed against her rib cage. Was he saying he would marry her, then? And what if she weren't pregnant? Would he still cleave to her, make love to her, ask her to be his wife? A hundred questions crowded her mind, and she ached to know the answers. "What about Helen?" she whispered. "What will we tell her?"

His fingers flexed around Isabel's waist. His features tightened with guilt and regret, and his gaze shifted to the shadows of the bedroom. He shook his head. "I don't know," he admitted in a low, tortured voice. "I honestly don't know."

Isabel forced out, "Do you love her?"

He brought his brooding gaze back to her. "I'm very fond of her. Though not . . . like this." His hands moved caressingly over her hips, then stilled. "But it isn't a question of love. It's a question of honor."

Her heart constricted as she understood his indecision. They were trapped in a quandary, loath to hurt Helen and yet realizing Helen stood squarely in the path to their own happiness. Kern had to be suffering the torment of the damned for breaking his betrothal promise. He was not a man to shrug away a vow—and she could not admire him were he so cavalier.

What had happened tonight had not been just another sexual romp for him; he had led a monastic life, a life of true nobility. Yet he hadn't said he loved her, either. Isabel drew a painful breath. No man had ever spoken those three magical words to her, and her soul hungered to hear them from Kern.

He touched her cheek, the darkness of regret glittering in his eyes. "I must go now," he said.

Panicked by the fear that he might never return, she snuggled closer to him. "We have this night," she whispered. "Oh, Justin. Don't leave me yet. I couldn't bear it."

"Don't you know I want to stay?" he said in a gritty voice. "But I cannot in all conscience—"

He sucked in a harsh breath when she swung her leg over and shamelessly straddled him. She sat facing him, her hands on his chest, registering the thunder of his heartbeat. She could feel his heat, his hardness swelling beneath her. A rush of sensual longing almost made her swoon. "You were saying?" she prompted coyly.

"Minx," he muttered. But he didn't push her away. His fingers wove into her hair, and she needed no urging to lean closer to his tantalizing mouth. Their lips were a breath away from the kiss that would keep him with her, perhaps win his affections forever—

A loud rapping on the outer door broke the erotic spell. His hands squeezed possessively around her waist. "Bloody damn," he snarled.

Isabel jerked around and stared into the gloom of the boudoir. "My aunts. Oh, dear heaven. I forgot all about them. They mustn't find us together like this."

She scrambled off his lap, but he caught her wrist before she could dash for her clothes. "Isabel, wait. Do you trust me?"

Tenderness welled in her breast. "Of course."

"Then let me take the memoirs."

"No!"

"Listen," he commanded. "The book should be locked in a bank vault. If you don't believe me, take a look around you. There's someone who will stop at nothing to find it."

She glanced uneasily at the destruction in the shadowed bedroom. The intruder had stabbed Aunt Minnie . . . Isabel swallowed hard. "But it's all I have left of my mother."

"I know. I'll keep it safe for you." His thumb rubbed gently along her inner wrist. Then the chilling aspect of a stranger iced his eyes. "I shall inform each of the men that I now possess the memoirs. It's the least I can do to protect you."

Without taking her gaze from him, she groped on the table for the small book and pressed it into his hands. "As you desire, my lord."

Just as quickly as it had appeared, his dangerous look vanished, replaced by one of moody intensity. He lifted her hand to his mouth and kissed the back. Her knees wobbled, and at that moment she would have promised him the sun and the moon and the stars if she could.

But all she could offer was her heart.

The rapping sounded again, and she dove for her gown, skipping her petticoat in her haste to dress. Kern pulled on his coat and tucked the slim volume into an inner pocket. As he knotted his cravat, she thought with a pang that he had never looked more elegantly handsome. Or further beyond her reach.

He came to her and swiftly buttoned the back of her gown, then turned her for a brief, stirring kiss. "Isabel, I wish . . ." He paused, his voice tortured. "I can't make you any promises. It would be wrong of me. You do understand that."

"Yes." The admission chafed at her. In the days ahead, she would have to sustain herself on the crumbs of memory.

The muffled sound of quarreling voices came from the passageway. Bracing herself for an awkward scene, Isabel opened the door.

Diana stood in the murky corridor, a flickering oil lamp held in her hand. The other aunts crowded in behind her. They fell silent at Isabel's disheveled appearance, her hair tumbling around her shoulders. Four sets of accusing eyes looked from Isabel to Kern, who stood just behind her. His hand closed, warm and reassuring, around her shoulder, and she had to resist the urge to lean back into his protective strength.

Diana's elegant mouth pinched tight. "Well," she said, her tone grating. "We came to check on your progress in finding out the identity of the prowler. Too late, it would seem."

"I told you not to bother her," Minnie snapped, gingerly clasping her bandaged arm to her pillowy bosom. "She's old enough to watch over herself. 'Tis none of your concern what she chooses to do in private."

"None of my concern? We raised her to behave better than the rest of us." Diana brushed past Isabel and Kern and marched into the bedroom. Isabel reluctantly followed and the other aunts trailed along, whispering like a flock of gossiping geese.

Halting by the bed, Diana held the lamp high, illuminating the small, rusty brown spots on the sheets. The women gathered around, exclaiming to one another.

"No wonder they had the door shut for so long," Callie said, casting an envious look at Isabel.

"Our dear little Venus is a woman at last," Minnie murmured. She shook her head as if in wistful wonder.

"Oh my," Aunt Persy said in dismay, wilting onto a stool. "Your lordship, we had thought to invite you to sup with us. But I don't suppose that would be wise now."

Diana curled her fingers into fists and spun around toward Kern. "Blackguard! You seduced her. You've ruined any hope she had of marrying well."

He stood square-shouldered and grim-faced in the shadows, offering no excuses for his actions.

Mortified, Isabel yanked the covers over the telltale stain. She didn't want Diana's defense or Persy's anxiety or even the approval of Minnie and Callie. "Enough, all of you," she snapped. "Lord Kern did nothing I didn't want him to do. And that is all I intend to say on the matter."

Silence shrouded the lamplit room. The aunts stared uncertainly at Isabel, and she knew they must be shocked by her vehemence. Yet she felt not a fragment of regret. It was time they realized she had grown up.

Callie trotted forward to put her arm around Isabel in a soft, motherly embrace. "You're right, we shouldn't pry," she said. "I only hope you were careful. Did you use a French sponge?"

"A . . . what?"

"We'll explain in a moment," Minnie said. Pointedly staring at Kern, she added, "For now, I'm sure his lordship would like to take his leave of us."

His arms folded across his chest, Kern appeared discomfited by the discussion. He made a formal bow. "If you will excuse me." He aimed one last intense glance at Isabel, and for a moment her spirit soared with the hope that he would come and kiss her, give her some sign of his affection. But he turned and strode out the door.

As the sound of his footfalls faded away, Isabel wanted to run after him. She wanted to recapture their glorious sense of closeness. She wanted him to hold her in his arms and never let go.

Yet with wrenching awareness she knew she could not be sure he would return to her. Ever.

I can't make you any promises. It would be wrong of me.

"You look worn out, my dear," said Aunt Persy in her quavering voice. "I remember being rather sore after my first time. You should soak in a hot bath."

Isabel managed a smile. If only the remedy could ease the pain in her heart as well. "Thank you. Perhaps I shall."

The other women gathered around, clucking over her. "Do sit down," Aunt Di advised, guiding Isabel to a chair. "I'll set the water to boiling in the kitchen." She hastened out the door.

"Don't add too much cool to the tub," Callie called after her. To Isabel, she confided, "The heat of the water can also help prevent conception. Though the sponge works best."

"How . . . so?"

" 'Tis soaked in vinegar to stop the man's seed from taking root," Minnie said. She went on to explain in a practical, efficient manner how to place the device over the inner mouth of the womb.

Isabel listened with wary fascination, and her fingers crept surreptitiously over her belly. Even while her logic could see the sense in taking precautions, she felt the leap of a wild, instinctive yearning. Did her body already nurture Kern's baby? A little boy with black hair and an impish smile . . . or a daughter with elfin green eyes . . .

Had her mother wished so much for Apollo's child?

Isabel suddenly did not want a hot bath. She did not want fussing, either. She needed to escape from the well-meaning advice of her aunts. She needed time to think, to sort through the new and myriad emotions crowding her heart.

She shot to her feet. ''I'm afraid I've tarried here long enough. I really must return to Hathaway House.''

''Diana has upset you, hasn't she?'' Aunt Persy asked. ''My dear, you mustn't run away because you feel you've done something wicked. We aren't angry with you, only concerned because we love you.''

Isabel bent down and hugged Persy's frail form. ''I love you, too. All of you.''

Minnie sat down heavily on the bed, the ropes creaking. ''Then stay here with us,'' she urged. ''Everything's changed now. You can't pretend to be a lady anymore. You should move back with your family, where you belong.''

Isabel's throat seized up. *Did* she belong here in this shabby house with the kind women who had raised her? Or did she belong in Kern's glittering realm of high society? Aunt Minnie was right; everything *had* changed. Yet Isabel felt caught between two worlds, and somehow she had to feel her way through the darkness. ''I have no choice but to go back,'' she said. ''How else will I find the man who murdered Mama?''

Callie picked up a frilly pink gown from a heap of ruined clothing. The lace had been ripped, the skirt gored by a knife. ''I don't suppose you and his lordship figured out who did all this.''

''Not yet.'' On a cold nudge of memory, Isabel recalled what Kern had said. *The prowler could have been one of the women living here.*

The possibility horrified her. She looked at Callie, who poked through the litter of shoes and fans and undergarments. With a chill, Isabel remembered another revelation Kern had told her.

Someone betrayed you in exchange for a gold sovereign. That someone was Callandra.

↝ Chapter 17 ↜

For the first time in his twenty-eight years, Kern was drunk. He sat in the library at Lynwood House, his bootheels propped on the mahogany desk where ofttimes he studied bills proposed in Parliament or scrutinized the account books for his estate in Derbyshire. Now, by the light of a branch of candles, he leaned back in his chair and counted the cracks in the ceiling.

The mindless act was more productive than contemplating the wreck he had made of his life. Or worse, the wreck he had made of Isabel's life.

Blackguard. You've ruined any hope she had of marrying well.

Diana's accusation rang in his mind, worsening the drumbeat of guilt pounding in his head. He groped for his glass. His fingers closed around the fine crystal and he brought it to his lips. Empty.

"Bloody *hell*," he said through gritted teeth.

His feet came crashing to the floor. Pushing back the leather chair, he rose rather unsteadily and wove his way to the sideboard. He disliked the woozy drift of his mind, his inability to employ logic rather than rash sentiment. He disliked the way his thoughts kept circling back to Isabel, back to the incredible moment when he had stroked her to climax and she had cried out to him from the depths of her heart.

I love you.

Heat prickled behind his eyelids as he stared down into his empty glass. No wonder he never got drunk. It didn't dull his pain. It made him maudlin, dangerously so. Nevertheless, he poured another generous draught of whiskey from the decanter and tossed back a burning gulp.

He had ruined Helen's life, too, though she didn't know it yet. In the long hours since he'd left Isabel, the other women clucking around her like mother hens, he had come to a difficult, inevitable decision. He must alter his plan for his life. He could not marry Helen.

He felt no lifting of relief, only the dread of hurting her. She admired him, trusted him as only a naïve girl could. And no matter that he would take full responsibility for breaking their betrothal, she would suffer the humiliation of rejection before all the *ton*.

He could do nothing to ease her pain. Though the news of his philandering would devastate Helen, he could not stand before God and vow to honor and cherish her. Not while another woman enslaved him, body and soul.

I love you.

Desperate to stifle his longing, he hurled the glass at the marble hearth. His aim was off and the crystal shattered against the wall, shards spewing over the floral carpet. But he could not destroy the aching need inside himself. The need for Isabel.

He stumbled to a chair and sank down, raking his fingers through his hair. He could almost smell the rainwater freshness of her skin. He could almost see her sensual smile. He could almost feel the hot velvet glove of her body enclosing him. One night of passion had not sated him; it had increased his desire a hundredfold. He could not live without her.

I love you.

Her soft words battered his heart. She deserved a good husband, but Kern could never be that man. He could never take her to wife. Such a *mésalliance* simply wasn't done. Yet for her, he would abandon his integrity, his principles. For her, he would become like Lynwood.

Honor be damned. Though she would be the ruin of him, he would possess her.

He would make Isabel Darling his mistress.

"You are a lazybones," Helen declared.

At the laughing comment, Isabel opened her eyes to see the blond girl standing by the bedside, M'lord in her arms, his tail wagging madly. A dull daylight blanketed the bedroom, and the breeze through the opened casement carried the cool portent of rain.

"M'lord and I have been awake for *hours*," Helen went on, ruffling the dog's ears. "Callie says you returned rather late last night. Did your acquaintance recover from her illness?"

Nothing in her smiling face revealed any knowledge of the momentous events that had kept Isabel away for the evening. Her breast clenched with guilt and dread and fierce, shameful envy. Oh, to be Kern's betrothed! Did Helen fathom how very lucky she was?

She realized that Helen awaited a reply. "My acquaintance? Oh, the friend of my mother's." Thinking of Aunt Minnie's ordeal, Isabel concealed a shiver. "She . . . suffered a minor accident, but she's better now. Thank you for being so understanding in letting me go."

Helen made a playful grimace. "I've no hold over your time, Cousin. But certainly I missed your company yesterday. Shopping with Gillie can be rather tame, though I found the most cunning pink bonnet for my trousseau."

As she described the items she had purchased in anticipation of becoming Kern's bride, Isabel waged silent war with jealousy and despair. The intimacy of the previous night seemed like a wistful dream now. Reality was Helen, chattering of her wedding clothes in blissful ignorance.

Dear God. If Helen knew the truth, she would hate Isabel.

Her throat tight, Isabel rose from the bed. She caught herself before reaching for the small pocket she kept under her pillows, remembering she'd given the memoirs to Kern for safekeeping.

It's the least I can do to protect you.

His words shone through the cloud of her misery, and her heart thrilled to his masculine guardianship. Not because she thought herself weak and incapable, but because he cared enough to shield her from harm. He made her feel wanted. Cherished. Her body glowed in the aftermath of his lovemaking. She felt utterly transformed today, a girl initiated into the mysteries of womanhood. And she dared say nothing about it to Helen.

"I ordered five more traveling gowns for our honeymoon trip to the Continent," Helen said. Holding the dog, she twirled around, her blue skirts flying. "Oh, I can scarcely wait to see Paris and Venice and Rome, all the places I've longed to visit. Did you know that bandits still roam the passes through the Alps? And that brave men fight bulls in Madrid?"

Helen had never looked more animated. Isabel struggled to keep a pleasant look on her face when she was dying inside. The honeymoon. She would sell her soul to know such happiness with Kern.

Going into the dressing room, she only half listened to the girl's cheerful prattle about the journey. As she donned her clothing, she couldn't stop her quick, furtive thoughts of Kern: the feel of his big warm hands caressing her curves, the keen pleasure of his mouth on her breasts, the joyous ecstasy of being one with him. And afterward, he'd held her in his arms as if he couldn't bear to let her go.

I've never wanted any woman as much as I want you.

"You're smiling," Helen accused from her seat on the dressing table stool, M'lord ensconced in her lap. "I can't think there's anything amusing about missing breakfast."

"Missing breakfast?" With a guilty start, Isabel realized she'd lost the thread of their conversation.

"Silly, you haven't been listening," Helen chided on a giggle. "I said, it's nearly time for luncheon. Come here, I'll put up your hair for you."

Isabel sank onto the dressing-table stool that Helen vacated. Helen deftly wound Isabel's hair into an elegant chignon, securing it with tortoiseshell pins. Her manner of friendly affection twisted the knife of remorse more deeply into Isabel. How could she have betrayed the girl who had become like a sister to her?

Yet how could she have denied her boundless love for Kern?

She had tossed and turned for most of the night, torn between yearning for Kern and anxiety over the future. The burden of their secret weighed heavily on her conscience. Should she admit the truth to Helen?

I hope you don't mind, but I've fallen madly in love with your fiancé. Last night we consummated our passion for each other.

The words stuck like thorns in her throat. Helen would be shattered. She would call off the betrothal. Was it fair of Isabel to destroy the happiness of a dear friend?

No. She could confess nothing. That decision belonged to Kern. But would he, too, keep silent?

The unpalatable thought sat sourly in her stomach. Perhaps upon reflection he would realize he needed a lady for his wife. Perhaps, like so many other noblemen, he would decide that love didn't matter in a marriage. Perhaps he would go on with the wedding and the honeymoon. He might disappear from her life forever.

"Oh, piffle, you have that faraway look in your eyes again," Helen said, her expression rueful in the mirror.

"Forgive me for babbling on too much. It's a bothersome habit of mine."

"Please, you needn't apologize." Isabel rose from the stool and hugged Helen's slender form. "I happen to like your babble. You're lively and happy and a joy to be around."

Helen glowed. "Papa always says so, too. Speaking of Papa, he's returning home for luncheon. I thought while we were waiting for him, we could go down to the library for a few moments. I've something to show you there."

Linking their arms, Helen pulled Isabel out into the sumptuous corridor that led to the grand staircase. As they descended to the foyer, a flash of lightning illuminated the gray clouds. The long windows flanking the door showed a gloomy day. It was so dark that a footman was lighting candles in the wall sconces. Isabel fancied she could feel the tingle of sparks in the air, and the approaching storm only added to her sense of unease.

Helen drew her into the library. The stately room was vacant, scented by the leather of calf-bound books. "I was sitting here last night with Papa," she confided, "addressing the wedding invitations. That's when I noticed it."

"It?"

"Come here." With the eagerness of a conspirator, Helen led Isabel to one of the portraits lining the wall above a bookcase. She nodded up at the painting of a smiling, bewigged lady clad in a lavish green satin gown of a fashion fifty years outmoded. "That's Papa's mother—the dowager marchioness, my grandmama. Do you notice anything about her?"

Frowning, Isabel studied the lady's fine bone structure, the cool patrician smile and the etching of dark brows over brown eyes. A spaniel lolled at the gentlewoman's feet. "She's very pretty."

"Pretty, bah," Helen bantered. "She's *beautiful*. And she looks just like you."

"Like me?" Isabel said dubiously. "She's wearing a huge white wig."

Helen laughed. "You have to imagine her without the wig. I never knew her, but Papa said she had brown hair with a hint of red, just like you. And look at her eyes. They're the color of sherry, and tilted up ever so slightly, identical to yours. You have her love of dogs, too."

"Along with thousands of other ladies," Isabel scoffed lightly. She picked up M'lord and hugged him to her bosom as she stole another glance at the portrait. How refined the marchioness appeared. Yet benevolent and amiable, too. Isabel's heart wrenched. Was that how Helen saw her, a kind and loving friend? Little did she know the truth. "What did your father say to your assessment?"

Helen looked a little sheepish. "He just harrumphed. But after I pointed out the resemblance, he did stare at the portrait for quite a long while. As if he were looking for similarities."

"Or simply reminiscing about his mother," Isabel said. She could imagine Hathaway's chagrin at the suggestion that the marchioness was ancestor to a whore's bastard. Yet Isabel could summon no worldly amusement today, only a wistful sadness. "Well, everyone back home says I take after *my* mother. So any resemblance is purely coincidental."

"Perhaps so." Helen pursed her lips. "But I still say—"

A light rapping sounded on the door, and a liveried footman stepped inside, bowing to them. "Beg pardon, m'lady. Lord Kern has come to see you."

Helen clapped her hands. "Oh, famous. We shall ask Justin for his opinion on the matter. He has a sharp eye for detail, so no doubt he'll agree with me."

The rumble of thunder sounded closer. Isabel stood still, her heart racing with joy and trepidation. M'lord squirmed as she tightened her arms around the puppy.

Kern was here. *Here.*
And he'd come to speak to Helen.

When Kern walked through the doorway of the library, he came face-to-face with Isabel on her way out. She stopped as if frozen, her beautiful dark eyes riveted to him.

He couldn't halt the involuntary leap of his pulse. Nor could he discipline his thirst for Isabel. The sight of her poured like warm rain into the desert of his soul. She looked pale and fragile in a gown of deep wine silk. The faint lavender shadows beneath her eyes gave proof that she had slept as little as he. He fisted his fingers to keep from touching her. Had she suffered regrets about giving him the gift of her virginity?

"Hello, Justin," Helen called gaily from the far end of the library. "Perhaps you can persuade Isabel to stay."

Isabel gave him an intent, unreadable stare that didn't waver, even when the puppy licked her chin. "I need to take M'lord to the kitchen," she murmured. "If you'll excuse me."

Turning her gaze downward, she hastened past Kern and out the door, leaving a torturous trace of her feminine scent.

He released a long breath. Resolutely he closed the door and walked toward Helen. His temples throbbed from more than an excess of whiskey. He'd gone this morning to secure the memoirs in the vault of his bank; then he'd had no other excuse to delay this moment of reckoning.

"Oh, piffle," Helen said, her brow wrinkling. "I fear I've embarrassed my cousin. She's admirably modest, but I never thought she'd feel so shy about me pointing out the resemblance."

"Resemblance?"

"To Grandmama," Helen said, waving her hand at the old-fashioned portrait of a lady. "Don't you agree they look alike? I noticed it last night, when I was sitting at the desk, addressing the invitations to our wedding.''

He barely glanced at the painting. His mind focused on his loathsome duty. If only he could be like other gentlemen, keeping a mistress hidden away and a wife for all the world to see. But he could not treat Helen—or Isabel—so shabbily.

He found himself hesitating and cursed his cowardice. Better to get this onerous task over with and done.

He took hold of Helen's arm and led her to a chaise. He seated her, though he remained standing. With the bafflement of the innocent, she gazed up at him. ''Is something wrong, Justin?''

He wanted to bellow out his aversion to hurting her. Instead, he said in a heavy tone, ''Helen, I'm very sorry to have to say this. But there will be no wedding.''

Her lips parted. She blinked rapidly as if trying to assimilate his words. ''No wedding? You can't mean . . . ours?'' She placed her small, white hand over her bosom.

''Yes, ours,'' he said as gently as he could manage. ''I am obliged to cry off the engagement.''

''But . . . why?''

He recited the speech he'd rehearsed through the long, dark hours of the night. ''Please understand, it isn't your fault whatsoever. A man could never ask for a more lovely and virtuous lady. But—'' He paused, knowing the words would seal his fate. ''But I've become involved with another woman. It was not something I'd intended to happen. Yet it did, and under the circumstances, it would be dishonorable of me to continue our betrothal.''

Helen's wounded gaze tormented him. ''Another woman? But only yesterday we were discussing our wedding breakfast. And our cake. You said nothing then . . . not a hint . . .'' Her voice broke and tears glossed her blue eyes.

Fumbling in his pocket for a handkerchief, he sank to one knee before her. He pressed the neatly folded square into her palm. "I said nothing because I had not yet come to a decision." *Because I'd not yet made love to Isabel. I'd not yet accepted how much she means to me.*

Helen clutched the handkerchief, but made no attempt to check the slow spill of her tears. "Who is this other woman? Tell me her name."

Kern shook his head. "I cannot. It's best you forget about her."

God forbid Helen should learn the truth and suffer that unspeakable pain. As soon as the murderer was found, Isabel would move quietly out of this house. She would sever all ties to Helen. Then, and only then, would he proceed with his plan for Isabel.

"How can I forget about her?" Helen asked in a shaky voice. "She stole your affections. What happened between yesterday and now? After you left me, you must have gone to her."

He could not deny it. Nor could he bear to see Helen so distraught. "Don't torture yourself, please don't. Just realize that you are utterly blameless in the matter. I shall make certain people know that the wrongdoing lies with me."

Helen gave a violent shake of her head. "No, Justin. Don't speak as if it's too late." Her face damp, she reached out and grasped his hands. "You feel honor-bound to end our betrothal. But you had a flirtation, that's all. Many men do so. I forgive you."

Kern released a sharp breath. He felt pushed into a corner, forced to dash her last hopes. "My God. I despise causing you grief. But it was more than a flirtation. I've . . . been intimate with her."

For a moment she stared at him with the guilelessness of a girl. Then comprehension widened her eyes and she drew her hands back, her fingers twisting in the folds of her skirt. Taking a quavering breath, she turned her head away as if the shock was too great to be borne. "You did with her . . . what a husband does with his wife.''

''Yes.''

Lightning flashed outside, followed by the scolding of thunder and the drumming of rain against the windows. Tears dripped soundlessly down Helen's pale cheeks. ''How could you?'' she whispered. *''How could you?''*

He could not explain any further without deepening her wound. That would require describing the incredible, loving attachment between himself and Isabel. ''Helen . . . you've been as dear to me as a sister. I remember holding you in my arms not long after you were born. And thinking I would protect you forever.'' Words of contrition choked his throat. ''I loathe hurting you. And I'm sorry. Truly sorry.''

She sat stiff and still. Without returning her gaze to him, she said in a grating undertone, ''Go away from here. *Go*.''

The coldness in her voice shook him. He knelt before her, reluctant to leave her in pain. If only he could hold her close and comfort her, stroke her hair. But by his contemptible act of betrayal, he had forfeited that privilege. Forever.

Kern slowly rose to his feet. Though Helen did not look at him, he bowed to her. Except for her tears, she might have been an alabaster statue. Had she really loved him so much?

The question only worsened his self-disgust. He wanted to extend his best wishes for her future happiness, but feared any attempt at good will would only make a mockery of her anguish. His chest tight, he pivoted on his heel and strode out of the library.

His footfalls rang out on the marble floor of the passageway. He felt as if he had kicked a kitten. In his black mood, he could think only of departing from this house which he had regarded as a second home. Henceforth, he would no longer be welcome here. And he had thrown it all away for a woman who did not fit into his world. A woman he wanted more than life itself.

As if his despairing thoughts had conjured her up, Isabel appeared before him. She waited by the gilded newel post of the staircase, the mongrel in her arms. On seeing Kern, she set down the dog and hastened forward, her skirt rustling against the patter of the rain. He told himself to walk past her, to stride out the door without looking back. Yet she brought to his dark spirit the forbidden light of hope.

"Justin?" she said in a breathless, questioning voice. Her fingers twined together, she sent a speaking glance toward the impassive footman stationed by the front door.

Kern addressed him. "Tell my groom to wait the carriage for me. I'll be out shortly." The groom already had been given his instructions, but the footman's absence would buy them a moment alone.

"Yes, m'lord." Picking up an umbrella, the liveried servant opened the door and disappeared out into the rainstorm.

Kern reached for Isabel's hand and drew her just inside the drawing room. His thumb stroking over her delicate wrist, he spoke in a harsh, intimate whisper. "We can't be seen together. Not now."

"You told her."

"Yes. But I took care not to identify you by name."

"Dear God. She must be devastated."

Isabel leaned back against the doorjamb, a sigh shuddering from her, lifting her smooth white bosom. All of his fiercely suppressed need broke free to taunt him. He wanted to lose himself in her soft, scented womanhood, to forget his sins in the sweet affirmation of her love. His untimely passion was reprehensible, making him a cad of the worst kind.

Yet an eternity would pass before he could make Isabel his own again, and his craving for her was too strong to bear. He could not leave her without a kiss of farewell. He bent closer, brushing his lips across hers, letting his mouth convey all the turbulent emotion in his heart. She too felt the poignancy of desperation, for she leaned up on tiptoe to return his kiss.

A small sound jarred the melody of the rain. Jolted, he drew back sharply.

Helen stood in the foyer.

The puppy trotted to her, tail wagging. She paid the animal no heed. Her hand to her throat, she stared at Kern and Isabel. His mouth went utterly dry. He could see awareness dawning in her eyes ... the disbelief, then the starkness of shock as she realized the identity of his lover.

"You?" she whispered, her appalled gaze focusing on Isabel. *"You?"*

A soft cry of anguish escaped Isabel, but she did not move or speak. The three of them stood frozen in a tableau like a tragedy on the stage of a theater.

He did not think the moment could be any worse. But then the front door opened and Hathaway walked inside, the footman holding an umbrella over him.

The marquess removed his rain-dampened greatcoat. "'Tis weather for ducks," he said in a jovial tone. "If this storm keeps up, I daresay the streets shall be flooded." As the footman bore away the wet coat, Hathaway looked at his daughter and frowned, as if noticing her distraught state for the first time. "Helen? You're weeping. Has something happened?"

She ran to him. "Papa. Oh, Papa."

He hugged her to his side. "My dear, what is troubling you?"

"Justin has cried off our engagement," she said. "We aren't getting married."

Hathaway's astonished gaze swung to Kern. "Is this true?"

"Yes."

"Tell Papa the rest." Helen dashed away her tears, then

clenched her hands at her sides. In a voice raw with grief and anger, she went on, "Tell him the vile secret you tried to hide from me. That all those times when I was ill and sent the two of you off together, you were defiling her. Tell him that you took my cousin Isabel to your bed."

His act of dishonor sounded all the more horrifying when uttered by a faultless girl. A grayish cast came over Hathaway's noble features. His disbelieving stare bored into Kern. "You seduced her?"

With a sense of fatality, Kern admitted, "Yes."

"No," Isabel said in a low, urgent tone. "That isn't true. He didn't force me. God forgive me, but I-I love him."

Kern only half heard her declaration. No matter what she said, the blame lay solely with him. He had permitted his loins to rule his head. In one reckless act of debauchery, he had taken the virtue of one woman and destroyed the dreams of another.

Disillusionment and disgust twisted Hathaway's granite features. Kern braced himself for a tirade of rebukes. But he wasn't prepared for the blaze of fury.

"Lecher." In a flash of movement, Hathaway sprang across the foyer. His fist met Kern's jaw with a *crack*.

Kern staggered backward under the numbing impact. His vision darkened for an instant, and he stumbled over a chair, collapsing into a sprawled heap on the floor of the drawing room. The puppy yapped excitedly.

His posture menacing, Hathaway loomed over him. Kern lay unmoving, aware of the pain. By instinct, his fingers balled into fists, but he could not strike back. He could not trade blows with the man whom he regarded as a father. Especially when his punishment was richly deserved.

Isabel thrust herself in front of Hathaway. "No! Don't touch him again."

Hathaway glowered fiercely. His look could have curdled milk, but Isabel faced him without flinching. After a moment, he turned on his heel and strode away.

She sank to her knees. "Justin! Are you all right?"

By way of reply, he picked himself up from the rug and rose to his feet.

In the doorway to the foyer, Helen stood with her hands to her mouth, her blue eyes wide and tragic. Beside her, Hathaway regarded him with undisguised loathing. "Get out," he snapped.

It was the second time Kern had been told to leave, and this time, he would comply. He should have done so when Helen had sent him away, and not stopped to kiss Isabel one last time. Yet perhaps the disclosure of his sins was for the best. Now, at least, he and Isabel would be spared the burden of living a lie.

That thought was cold comfort.

Isabel knelt in a puddle of wine-colored skirts. As if sensing her unhappiness, the puppy nudged at her hands, and she picked him up, cuddling his small form against her. She gazed up at Kern with such loving concern, he was tempted to sweep her away in his carriage, to carry her on a wild dash northward to Gretna Green, where he could bind her to him forever with the ties of matrimony.

Madness.

He could never marry Isabel. Nor could he leave her here to suffer the censure of Hathaway. She had endured enough already.

Kern extended his hand and helped her to her feet. As he led her past Helen, he met Hathaway's icy gaze. The words of apology that sprang to his tongue seemed a cliché. Yet he had to say them. "I'm deeply sorry for the distress I've caused you and Helen." *But not for loving Isabel. Never for that.*

Hathaway said nothing. His arm supporting Helen, he narrowed his eyes at Isabel. The brooding intensity of that stare shook Kern. He had the distinct impression of dark, roiling emotions in Hathaway. A thought struck Kern harder than a fist. How well did he really know Hathaway?

Had the marquess vandalized Aurora's chambers in an attempt to find the memoirs? Was he so desperate to protect Lord Raymond from a charge of murder?

All the more reason to take Isabel away from here. His jaw aching, Kern gripped her arm and guided her toward the front door. But she broke free and ran back to Helen, carefully placing the wriggling puppy in Helen's arms. "Please," she said in a broken murmur, "will you keep M'lord safe? He's all I have left to give you."

Helen scowled at Isabel; then the animosity left her eyes and she looked sadly down at the dog she cradled against her bosom. Ever so slowly, she pressed her cheek to his head. "Of course I'll watch over him."

Isabel reached out as if to give the puppy one last pat. But she curled her fingers at her side and spun around toward Kern. Holding her chin high, she walked toward him, unshed tears glazing her brown eyes.

To console the girl she regarded as a friend, Isabel had given away her most prized possession. Kern felt stunned by her selfless act, and the sudden fierceness of emotion in him rivaled the storm outside. He'd been prudent and responsible all his life. But ever since that fateful day when he had stolen into the brothel to confront a blackmailer, Isabel had turned his life upside down.

And with the desperation of the damned, Kern knew he could deny the truth no longer. For better or for worse, he loved Venus Isabel Darling.

⮾ Chapter 18 ⮿

*I*sabel gazed out the window of the carriage. The rain wept down the glass, obscuring the city streets and mimicking the sorrow inside her. She pressed her cheek to the damp smoothness of Kern's coat and felt the strong beating of his heart. Without making any sexual overtures, he held her close as the vehicle rumbled over the wet cobblestones, carrying her away from her life as a lady.

She needed his warmth and his comfort. With only the clothes on her back, she had left Hathaway House forever. She had forfeited the glittering world of the *ton*, the world she had dreamed about since girlhood. What was infinitely worse, no more would she laugh with Helen or listen to her blithe chatter. No more would they walk arm in arm to the shops on Regent Street. No more would they sit in bed to giggle and gossip after a fancy ball. By indulging her love for Kern, she had caused immeasurable pain to the girl she had come to think of as a friend, the sister she'd always wanted.

As punishment, she would never see Helen again.

The image of Helen's unhappy face haunted Isabel. It had been wrenching to give away M'lord, yet she would have offered her soul as atonement if it were possible. How could she ever forgive herself for being the cause of such grief?

Yet how could she have denied her powerful feelings for Kern? It would be easier to dam the tides.

The pattering of the rain made a lonely sound. She wondered what Kern was thinking as he gazed moodily out into the storm. Did he suffer regrets over losing Helen?

He had lost so much. He had cut himself off from the respected life he so valued. Lord Hathaway had acted as a father to Kern when Lynwood had failed to do so. The two families had maintained close ties. Now Kern had made himself a pariah.

For her sake.

Somehow she would make it up to him. She would love him forever. All was not lost. They had each other, and their bond transcended physical lust. Kern felt affection for her too, else he would not sit with her like this, holding her close to his large, sheltering body as if she were the most precious woman in the world to him.

The thought lifted her flagging spirits. After a time, when he had overcome the catastrophic events of this day, he would realize how much they meant to each other. He was not a rake who kept a string of mistresses. Surely he would want her for his wife.

He turned to her suddenly and asked, "What is your birth date?"

The question caught her off guard. "June the twelfth."

"You'll be nineteen?"

"Yes. Why do you wish to know?"

He stared at her for so long, she thought he had not heard. "It's nothing," he said finally. "I merely wondered."

He was concerned about her age. Likely he blamed himself for ruining her young life. Instead, he had brought her a joy she had not dreamed possible. Her hand sought his broad shoulder, and she pressed a kiss to the redness on his jaw where Hathaway had struck him. "Oh, Justin," she murmured. "I do love you."

His arm tightened around her; then he released her, setting her away from him. "No," he said in a grating voice. "You can't love a man who is like Lynwood."

Horrified by the comparison, she sat up straight and faced him. "You are *not* like your father. How *can* you be, when you've taken only one woman to bed in more than a decade?"

"Honor isn't measured in numbers. I either have principles, or I don't."

"Balderdash. You did an act of supreme honor today, an act of good conscience. You could have remained silent—as other so-called gentlemen would have done. But you were honest, and that I can only admire."

"In the eyes of the *ton*, I behaved like a cad."

"A pox on what other people think. You are the most decent and proper gentleman in society—quite possibly all of England. And let anyone dare say otherwise, and I shall set them straight posthaste."

A gleam entered his green eyes. "Now that I should like to see."

Isabel was far from done. "And furthermore, *I* shall not heed those small-minded people who judge our behavior. We cannot demean the beauty of what happened between us by calling it dishonorable or disgraceful."

"Does that mean you still want me?"

Her pulse fluttered at the husky thread of yearning in his voice. Did he think she would refuse him? She burrowed into his arms until the masculine scent and warmth of him surrounded her. "Of course I want you, Justin. I'll always want you."

For a heartbeat, he did not move. Then he embraced her tightly and pressed his lips to her hair. "I warn you, my honor is tarnished. Perhaps forever."

"So is mine. So you see, we're a perfect match."

Their lips met with mutual need and tender promise. He kissed her slowly, searchingly, with passion and something greater, something steadfast and loving. She relaxed against him, her arms sliding around his lean waist as the feelings inside her blossomed into the ripeness of desire. His hand cupped her breast, pampering the sensitive peak until she felt lush and full, yet empty and aching. She wanted to belong to Kern, to pledge her life to him. She wanted to call him husband . . .

A sudden jouncing broke them apart as the carriage rolled to a stop. Glancing out the wet window, Isabel saw the pale stone of the town house where her aunts lived. She'd come back here to stay. "Don't leave me, Justin," she whispered against his firm mouth. "Not yet."

"As you wish." He briefly held her close, then let go an instant before the footman opened the door.

She stepped down from the carriage and into the blustery, windblown day. The tree branches swayed, the dark green leaves fluttering against the gray clouds. The rain had slowed to a drizzle, but a maze of huge puddles inundated the pavement, and she stood there shivering as she searched for a pathway to the front steps. She was lifting her hem in preparation to leap across a pool of water when Kern swept her into his arms and carried her up to the porch.

Flooded by warm excitement, she clung to his neck. He cradled her close to him on a public street. Surely that was an unmistakable declaration of his regard for her. A glorious sense of freedom washed through Isabel as she realized she no longer had to hide her love for him. She could be unreserved in her affections. And she wanted to demonstrate how much she loved him. Again and again.

The front door opened and Aunt Minnie stepped aside to allow them entry. "Mother of God, whatever is going on here?" she asked as Kern set Isabel down. "I thought you'd moved back to Lord Hathaway's house."

Isabel sobered. "Everything has changed. I-I couldn't remain there."

Cradling her injured arm against her purple gown, Minnie looked keenly from Isabel to Kern and back again. "Well, now. This is the best news I've had all morning. Welcome home, my girl."

She enfolded Isabel in a one-armed hug to her cushiony bosom. The embrace brought back fond memories of visits here when Minnie had smothered her with attention, advising her on how to defend herself against bullies or answering a hundred questions on life in the city. "How are you feeling, Auntie? Is your arm bothering you?"

" 'Tis only a nuisance, nothing more." Minnie glanced out the still-opened door. "Where is that laggard maid of yours?"

"Aunt Callie!" Isabel's hand flew to her mouth. "Dear heaven, I forgot all about her."

Kern's palm settled warmly over her shoulder. "Callandra has surely heard of your departure by now," he said. "And no doubt she'll set out on her own when the rain stops. But if it would make you feel better, I'll send my coachman after her."

"Yes, thank you."

He went outside, and heedless of the cold rain, Isabel stood in the doorway watching him. He cut a fine figure in his dark-green morning coat and buckskin breeches, and she felt another tingle of pleasure to know that he had chosen her above all others.

"Such a considerate man he is," Minnie said from close beside her. "To send his carriage away at your whim. He must be intending to tarry awhile with you."

Anxiety wrenched Isabel. "Is it wrong of me?"

Minnie's lined face softened. "No, it is not wrong to want pleasure, my dear. You're a grown woman now, like your aunties." She narrowed her eyes at Kern as the carriage pulled away and he strode back toward the porch. In a low voice, she added, "His lordship appears quite smitten. He should be generous with you."

The cold prickling of gooseflesh swept over Isabel. She meant to protest that she didn't want riches, she craved only the treasure of his love. But he leaped up the steps and came within earshot, and she could do no more than smile at him.

"I wonder if your coachman will even find Callandra there," Minnie said, as she shut the door behind him. "You should know that a man came here this morning, looking for her."

"A man?" Kern asked, frowning. "Who?"

"Sir John Trimble was his name. He was one of those who courted Aurora, though I never understood how she could abide so hideous a face as his."

The news jolted Isabel. "Why was he looking for Aunt Callie?"

Minnie shrugged. "He said he wished to ask her a few questions. That was all he would admit to me. I sent him off to Hathaway's not half an hour ago."

Isabel shared a stunned look with Kern. The grim curiosity in his eyes reflected her own puzzlement. Sir John was supposed to be questioning the men who had romanced her mother. Why had he come here? Surely he didn't think Aunt Callie knew more than she admitted about the murder.

Someone betrayed you in exchange for a gold sovereign. That someone was Callandra.

In all the upheaval, Isabel had not had the chance to question Callie. Now, an icy foreboding lurched in her belly. "Should we go after them?"

Kern shook his head. "My coachman will find Callandra and bring her back here. I'll have a word with her then, and Trimble, too."

"A capital notion, m'lord," Minnie said. Smiling shrewdly, she made a shooing motion toward the staircase. "You two go on upstairs and get out of those damp clothes before you catch a chill. And do not fear being disturbed.

Persy is napping, and Diana went to Billingsgate Market this morning. She's likely waiting out the storm in one of the fishmongers' shops. I'm down to the kitchen to fix myself a nice cup of tea." She lumbered away toward the door that led to the basement rooms.

Feeling a flush of embarrassment, Isabel lowered her gaze to the floor, where the wood planks bore the wet imprint of Kern's boots. Why should Minnie's approval of their dalliance lend it a sordid air? Isabel knew the mortifying answer in an instant. It illustrated the difference between her world and his. No aristocratic aunt would speak so openly of a romantic tryst, let alone give her permission for the affair to take place.

Kern's fingers nudged up her chin. "Isabel. Look at me."

She reluctantly complied, aware of the color in her cheeks that he surely must see. The warmth in his eyes traveled straight to the cold place within her.

"Do you wish me to leave?" he said gently. "You have but to ask, and I'll go. No matter how much I want to stay."

He loomed over her, his hair attractively windblown. Deep inside, she feared that if he left her now, he might have second thoughts about honor and duty. He might never come back. She reached up on tiptoe to brush a black lock from his forehead. "If I were a lady," she whispered, "I would tell you to go. But I cannot."

"You are a lady," he said with feeling. "The lady of my heart."

He feathered a kiss across her brow, then caught her by the waist and urged her up the stairs. The firmness of his grip erased the last of her misgivings. She could scarcely walk for wanting him. Her legs had all the substance of melting butter.

When he would have turned toward Aurora's chambers, Isabel drew him down to the end of the corridor and into a smaller bedroom, closing the door behind them. The decor was extravagantly girlish with pink draperies and lace-trimmed linens. An assortment of dolls sat on a shelf by the canopied bed. Schoolbooks marched across a white-painted desk. In a corner of the chamber, a wooden rocking horse waited patiently for a rider.

Kern took in the surroundings with one contemplative sweep of his gaze. "This is your bedroom."

"Yes. Mama always kept it ready for my visits." Her back straight, she wondered if he scorned her for her upbringing. But she held herself proudly. She could not change who she was, a trollop's daughter. He would have to accept her less-than-illustrious antecedents.

"I thought you had taken over your mother's chambers," he said. "You were in her boudoir when first we met."

"I often stayed there when I felt lonely for her." Isabel remembered the mixture of love and resentment she had felt for her mother for so long. Softly she added, "I wish I could tell her that I understand her so much better now. She, too, was searching for love."

"And I believed the worst of you. Can you ever forgive me?" Before she could reply, he moved his hands to frame her face, his thumbs stroking her cheekbones. "Isabel," he added roughly, "I need you so much. God knows I should wait, to give us both time to adjust to the changes in our lives."

She couldn't bear to think of all the heartache that lay behind them. Her body hungered for another taste of the rapture he had shown her the past night. She wanted to lose herself in the splendor only Kern could give to her.

Pressing herself to him, she let her hands wander freely over his tautly muscled form. "My dearest lord," she whispered, "all that matters is here and now. I need you, too. More than I ever imagined possible."

His eyes filled with an ardor so precious she feared she

might have dreamed it. He plucked the pins, one by one, from her hair. The long, curling tendrils tumbled downward to her waist. "Beautiful," he murmured, rubbing the rich, red-brown strands between his fingers. He leaned closer to inhale deeply, his eyes closed as if to savor her essence, and she swallowed hard to contain the ascent of sweet emotion.

Bending his dark head to her, he put his mouth to the madly beating pulse in her throat while his hands skimmed over the curves of her waist and hips. He made short work of the fastenings of her gown, letting it slither to her feet. Within moments, she found herself held naked against a fully clothed male, enjoying the erotic friction of his rain-dampened clothes against her sensitive flesh.

Pleasure ignited wherever he touched her, leaving a flush of fever that encompassed her body. She could no longer resist the lure of temptation. Her fingers crept down to the buttery smoothness of his buckskin breeches and found the ridge of his arousal. Emboldened by love, she took the liberty of undoing the buttons of his breeches until he sprang free into her hand, thick and hot and velvety to her questing fingers.

The breath left him in a sharp hiss. "Not yet." He pressed her against the bedpost, stretched her arms up over her head, and imprisoned her wrists while he caressed her with his other hand. "First, let me touch you . . . taste you. All of you."

He lowered his eyes to her slim body, and her senses reeled under his frank scrutiny. His lashes at half-mast, he cupped the rounded swells of her breasts and played with the pearly peaks. Then he bent his head and put his mouth to her, giving rise to the wild beauty of passion. Excitement sang over her skin, and she could not stop herself from twisting against him. She ached to caress him, to welcome him into her body, but he held her arms captive, enslaving her to his sensual assault.

His hand slid downward, brushing her hips and belly in light, teasing strokes until she edged her legs apart in wanton greed. "Please," she begged. "Oh, please."

He kept his eyes on her face as he moved his hand to the dark cluster of curls that crowned her thighs. "You're mine," he said thickly, even as he dipped his callused fingertip into her moist font.

"Yes." She tilted her head back against the bedpost as her entire being responded to the glory of his touch. Her body moved to the rhythm of his stroking, and when he stopped, she cried out in frustration.

Without any awareness of how it happened, she realized he had released her hands. Like a supplicant adoring a goddess, he knelt before her, cradling her hips. The intimate heat of his breath scandalized her. She tensed in surprise at the thrilling roughness of his cheek against her soft inner thigh. Before she could do more than gasp, his tongue delved deeply, commencing an exquisite tempo that caused her knees to tremble and her resistance to vanish like smoke.

To keep herself from falling, she steadied her hands upon his broad shoulders, letting the wicked sensations carry her higher and higher. And then she did fall, tumbling with a cry of ecstasy into wave upon wave of perfect pleasure.

He stood up and she felt him lifting her, spreading her legs wide to prepare her for the solid, invading force of him. On an upward thrust he filled her completely, and she wrapped her legs around his waist while his masterful arms supported her against the bedpost and his hands gripped her bottom. In a daze of delight, she closed her eyes and rested her cheek against his damp shirt, her hands clasping hard to the back of his neck. He groaned her name as he moved within her, reawakening the marvelous urgency. Craving all he could give to her, she took him more deeply into herself, again and again. Even as she sobbed out her love for him, her flesh tensed around him, then released her into another luxurious rain of rapture. With a fierce growl of completion, he held her tightly as his body shook with powerful spasms.

He exhaled a ragged sigh into the cloud of her hair. His chest heaved with the effort to draw air into his lungs. For long moments, they slumped against each other as their breathing slowed. Isabel felt utterly drained of strength, even while her heart overflowed with contentment.

Kern gently lowered her to the floor, but the moment her toes touched the soft carpet, the world tilted as he lifted her into his arms and laid her on the bed. Then he stepped back. Though her limbs were deliciously relaxed, she wanted him close, and with a small sound of protest, she reached for him. He pressed her back down against the pillows. "Lie still, my love."

Isabel caught her breath. Dare she hope he'd spoken from his heart? She felt utterly vulnerable, helpless against the sweet rise of optimism. Yes, she could hope. He had shown her without words the strength of his feelings, and she already knew the constancy of his character. He was not a man to use a woman merely to satisfy his own selfish needs. Only a deep, abiding devotion could have enticed him into her bed for a second time.

He looked incredibly appealing, fully clothed with only the flap of his breeches undone. He shrugged off his coat and cravat and shirt, letting the garments drop to the floor. All the while he watched her, his burning gaze sweeping over her nakedness. As he peeled down his breeches, the intensity of his stare ignited a slow heat within her, even though she felt too replete to move.

She wanted to feel his weight on her. Wordlessly, she lifted her arms, inviting him to lie down with her. He obliged, stretching out beside her and tucking her head into the crook of his shoulder. His arm settled heavily beneath her breasts and his bended knee rested in the vee of her legs. Her fingers threading through the crisp black hairs on his chest, she sighed from sheer happiness. "I love the way you feel, covering me."

He tilted up her chin. In a voice vibrant with candor, he said, "And I love you."

The declaration transported Isabel to the summit of her romantic dreams. She could have wept with joy. "Justin. Oh, Justin."

They made love again, a slow, sweet mating that took her to the edge of enchantment and beyond. He held her close in the aftermath, their breath flowing together, their bodies relaxing as one. The rain tapped against the window and made their bower all the more cozy, sheltered from the rest of the world.

He gazed steadily at her, his green eyes deep and soft. "We took no precautions again." His hand caressed her belly. "Not that I'm sorry. I want you to bear my child, Isabel. I want a son or a daughter to be born of our love."

"Yes," she whispered. "I want that, too."

He gathered her close, stroking the tangle of her hair. "I shall find a house for you, so that we can have our privacy. Or better yet, we'll leave London. You wouldn't mind moving to my estate in Derbyshire, would you?" Without awaiting her answer, he went on, "You'll love living there, especially in the summer when the wildflowers are in bloom. The hills are beautiful and green, and there's a fine old rose garden beside the dower house."

A flurry of raindrops struck the windowpanes. Dazzled by the radiant picture he painted, she repeated, "The dower house?"

"Yes. That's where you'll stay. It's only half a mile from the main house, set in a stand of beech trees." He brushed a tender, fervent kiss across her brow. "Believe me, my love, I'd like nothing more than to have you in my house, to sleep beside me each night. But at least we'll see each other every day, take our meals together, go for long walks. Are you accomplished at riding a horse?''

Suspicion prickled across her skin, and she could only numbly shake her head. What was he asking of her?

"Then I'll teach you," he said. "We'll ride to a place deep into the forest where I used to go as a boy. There's a glade beside a stream where we can lie together, laze away the afternoon. I'd like to see your hair spread out on the grass, the sunlight dappling your beautiful skin." As he spoke, his hand moved over her, touching her in idle, possessive strokes. "And don't spare a worry for intruders. There won't be anyone around to disturb our tryst. The *ton* will be barred from the premises. That way, I can devote all of my time to pleasing you."

His low, mesmerizing voice aroused her even as his meaning sank like talons into her heart. "You want me to be . . . your mistress."

"Yes." He cupped her face in his big hands. "I want you to be a part of my life, Isabel. A permanent part. I'll take care of you always. For the rest of our lives."

She slowly shook her head. "I don't want an affair."

He frowned. "Don't you? But I thought you wanted to be with me. You said you loved me." He looked deeply into her eyes, and a stillness came over him. The darkness of understanding shadowed his features. "My love," he said hoarsely. "Did you think we would marry?"

She couldn't speak. She could only lie there, cold and aching as her dream castle came crashing down in ruins around her.

He squeezed his eyes shut for a moment. When he looked at her again, regrets tautened his handsome face. "God! I'm sorry. So sorry I misled you. But surely you can see that marriage is impossible."

"No," she whispered. "I can't see."

"I've a duty to uphold, a seat in Parliament to fill some-day, a responsibility to society. As much as I wish circum-stances were different, I can't change who I am. I can't change my station in life." His fingers skimmed over the delicacy of her jaw. "Neither of us can."

She struck his hand away. "To you, I'm the bastard of a trollop. I'll never be anything more."

"That isn't true. You're much more. Or I wouldn't be here with you like this. I wouldn't have thrown away everything I believe in."

"Oh, am I now to blame for ruining your life?"

A muscle jumped in his jaw, and he took hold of her shoulders. "Isabel, you *are* my life. I'll never abandon you; you have my word on that. Let there be no doubt as to my complete devotion to you."

She sat up and scooted away, wanting so badly to accept his sordid offer that she had to remove herself from his tempting touch. "And when you need an heir?" she choked out. "What will you do then? You'll take a lady to wife. You'll leave me for her."

He looked away, his jaw set, as if he were contemplating a grim future. "I've a second cousin who can inherit. I'd always intended to do my duty and produce an heir, but that's impossible now." He fervently kissed her hand, his expression raw with longing. "I love you, Isabel. I can't imagine sharing my life with any other woman but you."

She had longed to hear those words from the man she cherished above all others. But with his shameful proposition, Kern had robbed the joy from her.

She slipped from the bed and snatched up her chemise, her fists clenched in the fine linen, holding it to cover her breasts. "I'm afraid, my lord, that you'll have to survive without me." Her voice grew ragged with unshed tears. The overpowering grief suddenly made her furious. "You see, I won't be like my mother. I won't squander my life pining for a man who sets himself beyond my reach. Nor will my children be born bastards as I was."

Her declaration struck Kern like a blow. She didn't understand; perhaps she could never understand. For as long as he lived, he would never forget the look of disgust on Hathaway's face. The ache in Kern's jaw was a reminder of how the world would view his actions.

Hathaway had raised him to abide by strict rules of propriety. From boyhood, Kern had never questioned his responsibilities as lord and master of his people, his obligation to be the model of moral behavior. Out of love for Isabel, he'd already bent those unwritten laws of decorum. He had offered to dedicate himself to her, to sacrifice his duty to take a blue-blooded wife and to sire an heir of impeccable lineage.

Damn! Couldn't she see? He wasn't setting himself above her so much as acknowledging the cold realities that life imposed on them. Though his rank forbade him to marry her, surely he could give her no greater vow than absolute fidelity.

Or could he?

Could he turn his back on all the principles Hathaway had drummed into him, all the precepts that had guided him along the rocky path to manhood? Could he, who had pledged to bring respect back to the name of Lynwood, take the natural daughter of a courtesan as his wife?

The desire to do just that tempted him mightily. He got out of bed and snatched up his clothing. Tormented by fantasy, he fastened the buttons of his breeches. Isabel whirled around, presenting her back to him as she drew the chemise over her head and then stepped into her petticoat. She looked so small and vulnerable, he wanted to seize her up in his arms and carry her away to a place where the censure of the world could never hurt her.

To you, I'm the bastard of a trollop. I'll never be anything more.

How wrong she was. He didn't know quite how it had happened, but he regarded Isabel Darling as the center of his existence. Without her, the future stretched out like a bleak, endless darkness. He needed time to think, to determine what to do.

Walking to her, he curved his fingers around the tender warmth of her forearm. "Come with me, Isabel."

Her chin shot up. "No. I won't be your whore."

Her anger cut him, but it was no less than he deserved. "I'm not suggesting you should be. I'm concerned about your safety. Look at what happened to Minnie."

She stared down at his hand with such freezing contempt that he let loose of her. "I'm perfectly capable of taking care of myself," she said. "I've managed to do so for years."

"For pity's sake, don't be foolish." Anxiety roughened his voice. "It's far too dangerous for you to remain here without my protection. You can stay at Lynwood House for the time being. At least until we find out who killed your mother."

"So you can try to seduce me again? I think not, my lord." She gave a firm shake of her head, causing her unbound hair to swirl around her half-clothed form. "I'd sooner stay among those who respect me."

He deserved her reproof. It reminded him that he lacked the right of a husband to safeguard his wife. Yet neither could he let her come to harm. "I'll send several of my footmen here to watch over the house."

She leaned down to pick up her gown. "Don't bother yourself. I don't intend to be alone for long."

"What the devil is that supposed to mean?"

"Exactly what you think." She held the wine-colored silk to her breasts and regarded him with maddening aloofness. "It means I'll find another man to protect me. A man who regards me as worthy of his name."

⚘ Chapter 19 ⚘

"*S*ir John can't 'ave no visitors, m'lord." Her eyes red-rimmed raisins in a pudding face, the old housekeeper peered out through the crack of the half-closed door. " 'E's took ill, God save 'im."

Kern pressed his hand to the wooden panel when she would have shut it in his face. "I must see him, whether he's ill or not. It's a matter of vital importance."

She snuffled loudly. "Ye don't understand, m'lord. The poor man's dyin' on 'is deathbed. The doctor's wid 'im now."

Dying?

Kern thrust the door open and stepped past the startled housekeeper. He strode through the dim foyer to the narrow staircase that hugged the wall.

"Ye mustn't go up there. Ye mustn't disturb the master."

Ignoring her wail of protest, he took the risers two at a time. Bloody damn, he shouldn't have waited until morning to call on Trimble. But yesterday he had been trapped in torment over losing Isabel. He'd spent the night pacing, aching for her, imagining her in the arms of an admirer.

I'll find another man to protect me. A man who regards me as worthy of his name.

She had spoken out of pain and anger, out of the need

to strike back and hurt him. She could not have meant those words. Isabel was too scrupulous, too honorable to invite another man into her bed so soon.

Yet what would happen over the course of days, weeks? She lived in a brothel. The other whores would encourage her to take lovers. God knew, Isabel had been so devastated by his infamous offer, she might seek solace in the most elemental human closeness . . .

He found himself standing in the upper corridor, breathing hard, his fists clenched. He had to get a hold on himself. What mattered now was to eliminate the threat to her safety.

Four closed doors faced him. It took him all of three seconds to find the right one.

As he entered the spartan chamber, the odor of sickness struck him. On a narrow bedstead, his scarred face yellowish-pale in contrast to the dark coverlet, lay Sir John Trimble. His breathing was shallow, his eyes closed, his body as still as death.

Was this man Isabel's father? The man who had forsaken his bastard daughter all those years ago? It was hard to believe. Kern had judged him an honest man, not given to subterfuge.

A gaunt man with wispy white hair bent over the patient, carefully removing the small leech from Trimble's limp arm and dropping it into a jar. The man straightened and wearily regarded Kern.

Kern strode to the doctor. "I am Lord Kern, a friend of Sir John's. Tell me how he fares."

The smaller man gravely shook his head. "Poorly, I fear. He's fallen into a stupor. I cannot rouse him, though five times already today I've bled the ill humors from him."

The housekeeper lumbered into the room, her gnarled fingers twisted in her apron. " 'E come 'ome yesterday afternoon, complainin' of a bellyache. Afore I knew it, 'e'd collapsed in the entry."

"What precisely is the nature of his illness?" Kern asked the physician.

" 'Tis peculiar, the sudden severity of his symptoms." The doctor scratched his balding head. "Retching all day and night. A yellow cast to his skin and a quickened pulse, even now while he lies senseless. I suppose he might have eaten something putrid."

"But you think otherwise."

The man shrugged. "In all my years, I've treated but a single other case that exactly matched this one. 'Twas a housewife who tried to do away with herself by ingesting a quantity of arsenic."

Poison.

Kern's blood ran cold. Yesterday, Trimble had visited the brothel, then left to look for Callandra. Kern had spoken to Callandra on his way out. Newly arrived from Hathaway's, she had expressed surprise that Trimble was looking for her.

Now Kern wondered. Was she lying? Had Trimble found her and confronted her about the murder? Had she then somehow poisoned him to keep her secret safe?

Frustrated, he turned to the housekeeper. "Did Sir John say where he'd been yesterday? To whom he'd spoken?"

She shook her mobcapped head. " 'E were too weak an' sick to talk. I 'astened to fetch the doctor, an' when I come back, 'e were in a bad way."

"Did he say anything at all? A name, perhaps? Callandra or Callie?"

She started to deny it again; then the doctor intervened. "My lord, I do remember him muttering something last evening. I remember wondering why he kept babbling the name of a Greek god."

Kern stepped forward. He only just stopped himself from seizing the physician by his lapels and shaking him. "Which god? Tell me, man."

" 'Twas Apollo."

Apollo.

Perhaps Minnie was mistaken. Perhaps Trimble had not gone after Callandra because he thought *her* guilty, but because he believed she knew some incriminating evidence about Isabel's father. That meant Trimble was not Apollo, after all. If Trimble then had gone to confront Apollo . . .

Apollo could have poisoned Trimble.

Kern took his leave and hastened out to his carriage. Before he went back to the brothel to question Callandra again, he intended to test the theory that had occupied him since reading the memoirs and spotting the clue written there. He would have followed up on his conjecture already had he not been distracted by his love for Isabel.

He sprang into his waiting phaeton and snatched up the ribbons, hurrying the horse down the street. With any luck, he might have the means to deduce Apollo's identity.

Isabel carried her tray down the steep steps to the basement kitchen. The odor of cooked cabbage from the luncheon meal eddied over her as she entered the long room with its stone walls and familiar rows of dainty rose plates displayed on the shelves. As a girl, she'd loved this kitchen. She had pretended it was a secret cave where she could hide from wicked witches and fire-breathing dragons. Now it was a sanctuary for her troubled spirits.

Aunt Minnie stood at the chopping block in the center of the room. She was slicing onions, her plump fingers awkwardly wielding the knife, her injured arm hugged to her bosom. Seeing Isabel, Minnie put down the utensil and wiped her hands on the stained apron that encompassed her broad form. Her gaze sharpened on the tray Isabel carried to the dry sink.

"Here now, you scarcely touched the cabbage soup. 'Twas the same treatment you gave my coddled eggs at breakfast." A wounded look entered her hazel eyes. "I'm beginning to think you got spoiled by the fancier fare at Hathaway's."

"It isn't that. I'm just not very hungry today."

"Mother of God. You ate like a bird yesterday, too. Even Persy does better. Sit down there, and I'll fetch you a scone. Fresh-baked by these two old hands."

Too weary to argue, Isabel sank onto a high stool. The thought of eating left her indifferent, but she'd make the attempt to please her aunt. She really didn't want to return to her lonely bedroom anyway, to lie on the bed where she and Kern had made love. She didn't want to suffer the anguish of loss or remember the endearments he had whispered in her ears.

I love you . . . I'll take care of you always . . . for the rest of our lives.

Minnie plunked a plate in front of Isabel, then dropped a generous dollop of butter onto the china. "Have you a bellyache?" she said shrewdly. " 'Tis too soon for you to be showing signs of breeding."

Isabel froze in the act of buttering the scone. A soft yearning assailed her breast. Very slowly, she lowered the knife to the table. "Oh, Aunt Minnie. Do you truly think I might have conceived already?"

"It's possible," Minnie said, her face grave. " 'Tis easy to let your passions carry you away, then afterwards you pay the price. You must promise me to be careful henceforth."

Minnie didn't know that Kern had left for good. There would be no next time. Isabel would never see him again— unless she had the courage to take the step she had pondered all night. With all the fervency in her heart, she admitted, "But I love Justin. I want his child."

"Nay, dearie." Minnie shook her mobcapped head, the stray ginger strands plastered to her neck. "You mustn't entertain such fairy-tale notions. You'll only be disappointed. Did I ever tell you about the babe I lost?"

Isabel paused, a piece of the scone poised at her lips. ''No,'' she said in surprise. ''What happened?''

'' 'Twas right before your mama took me in.'' Minnie settled her bulk onto a chair. ''I was an orphan, lucky to have a post as upper maid in the household of a viscount. The master's son took a fancy to me, and he tempted me into lifting my skirts. What a feast was that first taste of pleasure! I wanted more, and so we carried on blissfully for a few months.'' She smiled, staring into the distance; then her features hardened. ''His parents guessed the truth, but they pretended not to notice till my belly began to swell. Then they lost no time tossing me out into the gutter.''

Isabel swallowed convulsively. She could see Minnie as a frightened girl having no one to turn to, forced to cope with pregnancy on her own. ''Oh, Aunt Minnie. What did you do? Where did you go?''

'' 'Twas summertime, so I survived on the streets. Nobody would hire me, of course. For food, I had only a few pence I'd saved from my earnings. 'Tis no surprise the babe was born too soon and too puny.'' A look of immeasurable sadness came over her face, and she hugged her immense bosom. ''My poor, wee daughter died in my arms.''

Tears sprang to Isabel's eyes. Rising from the stool, she hugged the woman who had been like a mother to her, aware of her familiar warmth. ''I'm so very sorry. I never imagined . . .''

''Ah, 'twas for the best. It made me determined to raise myself up, and when I heard your mother was seeking a companion during her confinement, I called on her. Soft-hearted she was, Aurora. She was taken by the similarities in our stories and hired me. And then you were born and 'twas like a blessing, for I had another little girl to replace the one I lost.''

Isabel perched on the edge of the stool. "Did you love him? The father, I mean."

Minnie shrugged, getting up from the chair to scour the countertop with a rag. "Love's but a pretty word for lust. Anyhow, he's dead now. He and his parents died not a year later of a sickness, God rot their black souls. From him, I learnt my lesson. To take my pleasure of men and to take their money, too."

At the cynicism in the older woman's voice, Isabel shuddered inwardly. She sensed depths in her aunt that had been hidden before now. How strange that she had known Minnie all her life, yet Minnie had never breathed a hint of the tragedy in her past. Isabel wondered if she herself would become so embittered if she stayed here.

"Justin isn't like that," she said. "He wouldn't abandon his own child. He told me so."

"All gentlemen make promises in the bedroom. No doubt your own father did so to Aurora. Has he sent you so much as a ha'penny since her death?"

"No."

"See there? Men don't care a whit for their by-blows."

Isabel bowed her head, determined to conquer the pain of her father's abandonment. As a child she had dreamed of being invited to the castle to meet the king. He would welcome her with open arms, declare that he'd been searching for his little lost princess, and they would be together forever . . .

Now that she was grown, Isabel knew there would be no happily ever after. Not with the heartless stranger who had sired her. If Sir John Trimble didn't wish to acknowledge her, then it was his loss.

But she might find happiness with Kern.

The thought shone like a light at the end of a long, dark tunnel. How much better to turn her face to the radiance of the future than to flounder in darkness. With a sudden outpouring of hope, Isabel realized she had been given a chance denied to Minnie and Aurora. Unlike them, she had a man who truly cherished her, who wanted her to be a permanent part of his life. And she had denied him for the sake of prideful scruples.

"Justin isn't like Apollo. And he isn't like the rake who seduced you," she said slowly. "He wants me to be his mistress."

Minnie's hand stilled around the rag. Her eyes narrowed. "He's asked you to service only him?"

Put so bluntly, his proposal sounded sordid and shameful. Isabel stared down at her crumbled scone. "I did want to marry him, Auntie. I still do. But I realize now that our circumstances are too different. I cannot hope for the impossible. I can only seize the happiness he offers me."

In a rustling of starched petticoats, Minnie came closer to pat Isabel on the back. "Ah, dearie, don't fret. Of course his lordship cannot marry a girl of your background. Such is the way of life. You'll stay right here with your aunties, and we will make sure his lordship pays a pretty penny for the privilege of visiting you. You'll be set for life—"

"No! I don't want his money. And I don't want you asking him for any." Sickened by the thought, Isabel pulled back from Minnie's comforting touch.

"Because if you took his money, you'd feel like a whore," Minnie said flatly. "Tell me, is it better to let him use you for free?"

"Only his love matters to me. I want nothing more from him."

Minnie frowned in concern. "Be practical, dearie. Every girl loves the man who introduces her to pleasure. But I thought you were more sensible than Aurora. She spent her life pining for a man who scorned her."

Isabel understood her mother so much better now. Aurora wasn't a vain, foolish creature, but a woman longing for love. "She felt about Apollo the way I feel about Justin. Except for me, things will be different. I'll be with the man I love. Forever.''

Minnie made a grunt of disgust. ''If you believe his lies, you'll only be hurt when he leaves you.''

I'll take care of you always. For the rest of our lives.

''Justin won't leave me. I know he won't.'' Remembering how tenderly he had held her, how steadfast he had been in declaring his affections, Isabel felt the ice around her heart melt into a puddle of longing. The certainty of his love gave her the courage to make her choice. In a voice firm with conviction, she said, ''I am going with him.''

''Going?'' Minnie said in a hoarse whisper. ''Where?''

''To his estate in Derbyshire. He wants me to live in the dower house. That way, we can be together often.'' A tremulous smile lifted her lips as Isabel thought of devoting herself to Kern, away from the censorious gossips of London. When she told him of her decision, his face would light up and he would take her into his arms . . .

The excitement spilled over into nervous anticipation. ''I must tidy myself,'' she said, aware that she wore the same crumpled gown as the previous day.

Darting to the hearth, she filled the cauldron with water from the tall can and then stirred up the glowing coals. When she whirled around, she saw Minnie standing by the chopping block, her arms crossed, a stricken expression on her face.

''You're leaving again. Just like that.''

''Oh, Auntie. You haven't lost me. I'll convince Justin to buy you and the aunts that cottage in the country. So be happy for me. Please.''

''How can I be, when you may be gone for months?''

''Or a lifetime,'' Isabel whispered. Though regrets tugged at her, she felt the thrill of stepping boldly into the future. ''I'm grown up now, and it's time for me to go. Don't you see? I love Justin with all my heart. And he loves me. He's going to devote himself to me, like a husband to his wife.''

''It won't last. You're Venus, the daughter of a courtesan.''

Isabel swallowed her lingering doubts. ''That doesn't matter to him. He knows I'm not promiscuous, that I've never had any other man. And he knows I'll be faithful to him, as if we'd spoken vows before God.''

For another long moment, Minnie stood staring, an unreadable expression on her motherly face. Then she turned away. ''Run along upstairs, child. Send Callie down to fetch the hot water. Meanwhile, I'll bring you a pot of tea to calm your high spirits. It won't do to have his lordship thinking you're naught but a silly girl.''

The gruff resignation in her voice touched Isabel's heart. How she would miss dear Minnie and Persy and Callie and Diana.

Isabel's only regret was that she couldn't find the murderer now that she had been barred from society. The mystery was no clearer to her than when she had started. Perhaps it was for the best. She had been caught too long in dark dreams of revenge.

She pressed a kiss to Minnie's familiar, doughy cheek. ''I'll come to visit you and the aunts. I promise I will.'' Isabel felt good about her decision. Her life here lay behind her now. At last she had found her own future, her own love.

Turning, she ran lightly up the steep steps, already pondering which gown to wear. She wanted to look her best for Justin. She would go to him like a bride, perfumed and pretty and pure at heart.

Her breast thrummed with joyous anticipation. Wouldn't he be surprised when she showed up on his doorstep?

Kern paused inside the nave of St. George's Church.

A watery sunlight shone through the tall windows and

onto the empty pews. On this midweek afternoon, the chandeliers were unlit, the choir loft deserted, the rector's podium vacant. The cool air held a mystical hush, an unmistakable spiritual presence.

Kern's footsteps echoed as he walked to the front of the church. Obeying an urge more compelling than his mission, he sank to his knees before the altar. Here, in the space of a few weeks, he would have taken his vows to Helen.

It seemed incredible that he had almost bound himself to her forever. Now he could see what a terrible disservice he would have done to Helen, promising to love and cherish her while his heart belonged to another. For the first time since breaking the news to her, he felt a measure of peace. Though he would always regret causing her pain, he had acted in her best interests. He prayed she would someday understand that and find the happiness he'd found with Isabel.

Isabel.

He bowed his head and closed his eyes. But he couldn't stop the image of her gliding up the aisle to join him at the altar, a dark-haired beauty in her wedding finery. She would slip her small fingers through his. Her smile would be radiant, her voice firm as she spoke her vows.

I, Venus Isabel Darling, take thee, Justin Culver, Earl of Kern, to be my wedded husband; to have and to hold from this day forward; for better, for worse; for richer, for poorer; in sickness and in health; to love, cherish, and to obey, till death us do part, according to God's holy ordinance; and thereto I give thee my troth.

As he stared down at the marble steps, a sense of rightness settled over Kern. He knew then with crystal clarity that nothing else mattered—not duty, not society, not guilt—nothing but pledging himself to the woman he loved. As soon as he finished his business here at the church, he would go to Isabel and ask her to be his wife. He would wed her before all the *ton* . . .

"Praying for forgiveness?" a sharp voice queried.

Kern's head shot up. In the shadows to the side of the altar stood the Reverend Lord Raymond Jeffries.

He walked closer, leaning on his cane, his hawk-nosed face showing disdain. "Well?" he prompted coldly. "I trust you're here to beg God's mercy for breaking the heart of my young niece."

Kern rose to his feet. "How is Helen?"

"She and Hathaway are preparing to leave for the Continent. Because she cannot bear the pain of being cast aside for a hussy."

Kern felt a tightness in his chest even as he curled his fingers into fists. "Miss Darling is not a hussy. Should you speak ill of her again, I shall be forced to silence you."

Lord Raymond halted his advance. "To what depths have you fallen? Threatening a man of God in front of the altar." He shook his head, a brown curl drooping onto his brow. "I cannot believe you're the same lad who vowed never to be like Lynwood."

Kern gave him a sarcastic look. "We all have our hidden depths. At least I am willing to openly acknowledge mine."

That boyish face took on an ugly glower above his cleric's collar. "I've done penance for my sins, not that it's any concern of yours. 'Judge not, lest ye be judged.' "

Kern studied the man whom Aurora had called Icarus. Lord Raymond had visited her in the dark of night, draping himself in her frilly undergarments and fancying himself a fallen angel. Reading that passage in the memoirs had disgusted Kern, made him aware of how little he knew of Lord Raymond.

Had the clergyman murdered Aurora? Had Hathaway helped his brother conceal the truth? Had Lord Raymond broken into the brothel and vandalized Aurora's bedroom?

"You should know," Kern said, "that Isabel no longer has the memoirs in her possession."

Lord Raymond turned deathly pale. *"What?"* He swayed, his knuckles whitening around his ivory-knobbed cane. His impassioned voice echoed off the stone walls. "She hasn't given the book to a publisher, has she? You must stop her! I'll never become bishop if that filth is brought to light."

"Perhaps a man who is ruled by personal ambition should never lead the faithful." Kern paused, deliberately prolonging Lord Raymond's fear for another moment. "But you're mistaken. *I* have the memoirs."

"You? Oh, praise God! Where is the book?"

"In a safe place. Where no one but myself can touch it."

"Then you must destroy the pages that refer to me." Lord Raymond hobbled forward and grasped Kern's sleeve. "I beg of you, Justin, for the sake of our long association, you must do this."

"I will. But only when I determine that you did not poison Aurora Darling."

A stillness came over the pastor. His middle-aged features took on a granite harshness that Kern usually associated with Hathaway. "So," Lord Raymond said. "Isabel has charmed you into doubting even me. There was a time when you would have taken me at my word."

The truth of that knifed into Kern. But he could feel no remorse, not when someone wanted the memoirs so badly he would murder Aurora and attack Minnie. And now that same villain had poisoned Sir John Trimble.

A sense of purpose galvanized Kern. Apollo was the key to the mystery. Once Kern found Isabel's father, he might have a chance to unlock the secrets of the past.

"I should like to examine the marriage registries for this parish," he said.

"Why?"

"Never mind. Just pray that whatever I find helps to clear your tarnished name."

Though eyeing him with suspicion, the Reverend Lord Raymond escorted Kern to a small antechamber. Rows of leather-bound books lined the shelves, records of births and deaths and marriages.

Kern dismissed the cleric and closed the oak door. Then he scanned the dates marked in gold tooling on the spines until he found the volume that encompassed the appropriate year.

The clue had been in the memoirs all along.

All that summer I devoted myself to Apollo, remaining faithful until our last night together, the night before his wedding. The night I conceived our love child . . .

Moving to a table near a high window, Kern opened the book. A faint musty smell eddied to him, and the old pages whispered as he turned them. He skimmed row upon row of names penned in spidery handwriting, the ink faded to brown. Countless brides and grooms had signed their names here at the close of the ceremony, to record their nuptials in the official registry.

His pulse quickened when he found the month he sought. *September 1803.*

Isabel had been born on June the twelfth, 1804, which meant she had been conceived the previous September— the night before Apollo's wedding. Since the marriage had taken place in London, and the vast majority of the gentry attended St. George's Church, there was an excellent chance that one of the bridegrooms registered here was Apollo.

Luckily, September was not so popular a month for weddings as June or December. There were no more than forty or fifty marriages listed. Still, the size of the task daunted Kern.

He slowly moved his forefinger down the row of names, committing each one to memory. He recognized a number of men from the *ton*, mostly well-respected, middle-aged lords. But he did not discount anyone, except those he knew had died.

At best, he hoped to compile a list of suspects. From there, he could question the men and determine who among them knew Aurora Darling. He could enlist the aid of the whores in identifying which of these gentlemen had visited the brothel—

His finger stopped on one name.

Kern sat there staring, reading the inscription over and over, resisting the truth that crept over him. It could not be. *It could not.*

But he knew with cold certainty that his search had come to a close.

He had found Apollo.

❧ Chapter 20 ❧

*I*sabel awoke to the hum of bees.

No, *voices*.

Blinking into the dimness of dusk, she wondered what had happened to the afternoon. Her brain felt sluggish, thick-witted. Her limbs lay heavily at her sides. Her body throbbed with a languid warmth.

Slowly she absorbed her surroundings. The gold cherubs holding up the canopy. The frilly rose draperies. The gilded furniture.

Why was she lying in her mother's bed?

Before she could fathom an answer, the whispering came again. From the boudoir.

Kern?

Summoning all her strength, she tried to lift herself up, but her head swam giddily. The doorway doubled, then tripled. She collapsed back onto the pillows. It took several minutes for the room to stop spinning.

Not Kern. That had been another time. The time when he had made love to her in this bed. Oh, how she had gloried in the way he had stroked her body. He had touched her until she cried out with sheer bliss. Even now, her loins pulsed with the resonance of desire, and she drifted deeper into the lovely memory . . .

But something made her resist. She groped for the thought before it floated away.

Kern had left her. Forever. Because she'd refused to become his mistress.

But she *did* want to be his mistress. She had meant to go after him.

Hadn't she?

Isabel frowned, her temples aching. The last thing she recalled was scrubbing herself in a hot tub. Aunt Callie had brought up the water and laid out Isabel's clothes. Aunt Minnie had coaxed Isabel to drink a pot of tea. She remembered stepping out of the tub, then swaying from the rush of an irresistible weariness.

The world had faded to black, leaving only the sound of quarreling voices. The sharp one had been Aunt Callie . . .

That voice didn't resemble the murmuring she heard now. A faint glow came from the boudoir. Who was there? Isabel tried to call out, but only a dry croak emerged.

She had not dreamed the bath. Her unbound hair felt a bit damp to her cheek. The strands smelled fragrant, scented by rosewater. She had been preparing herself for Kern. Yes. She'd meant to don her best finery and go to Lynwood House. To tell him that she'd changed her mind.

But now she wore only a flimsy night rail. Had she fallen ill?

She certainly felt woozy. It was difficult to string two thoughts together. A pleasant lassitude filled her body. She relished the coolness of the sheets, the softness of the pillow. Utterly relaxed, she fancied herself a wilted rose, her arms like drooping petals.

The sound of footsteps came from the boudoir. A man's heavy tread.

A drowsy smile curved her lips. Perhaps Kern had come back to her, after all. Perhaps he wanted them to marry. The golden dream enveloped her. He would take her into his strong arms and kiss her and love her . . .

A man entered the bedroom. Tall and gangly, he held a lighted candlestick in his hand. The flame cast weird shadows over his aging, patrician features and thinning gray hair.

Terrence Dickenson.

Her muddled brain could make no sense of his presence. Hazy with confusion, she tried to speak. "Whaaaat . . . ?" *What are you doing here?*

Her voice sounded slurred. Her tongue felt thick, and her mouth tasted as dry as straw.

Dickenson placed the candlestick on the bedside table. Then he sat down, the feather mattress sinking under his weight.

He bent closer to her. One corner of his mouth curled upward, baring his teeth. "You're awake. Just as well. I'd sooner you knew it was me."

Alarm slithered into the disorder of her mind. The heat of his breath fanned her face. What did he intend?

"Go . . . awaaaaay," she said in a hoarse whisper.

His sinister chuckle raised goose bumps on her skin. "Ah, this is an unparalleled delight, Miss Darling, having you at my mercy. I do believe I shall enjoy our little encounter even more than I had anticipated."

He spoke as if this assignation had been arranged. But how had he known she was here?

The question vanished beneath a surge of anxiety. He stood up, unknotted his cravat, then placed it over the seat of a chair. Methodically he stripped off his fancy coat and waistcoat. As he removed his shirt, he watched himself in the mirrored headboard. He sucked in his slight paunch and lovingly ran his hands over his pale chest. Turning to and fro, he admired his reflection.

A paralysis of fear gripped Isabel. Despite her befuddlement, she grasped an unspeakable horror. He meant to rape her.

She jerked her head toward the boudoir. Her senses reeled sickeningly, and she blinked several times to bring the darkened doorway into focus. She must flee. Find one of her aunts. They would save her . . .

Isabel tensed her slack muscles. Her arms and legs felt mired in treacle. Summoning all of her meager might, she threw herself toward the side of the bed.

A weight slammed onto her. The jarring impact quaked through her, and she gasped for breath. Dickenson pinned her to the sheets. ''Not so fast, my pretty. We haven't had our amusement yet.''

He ground his groin into the cradle of her hips. Through his pantaloons, she could feel his arousal.

Panic bubbled up inside her. His body pressed like an andiron onto hers. He smelled of too much cologne, and nausea rose in her throat. Heedless, she struggled to bring her knee up.

He laughed at her futile efforts. ''Don't think I'll fall for that trick again. This time, you'll do as I say.''

Easily confining her, he seized her hand, brought it down to the placket of his trousers, and proceeded to rub her fingers against him. Delight glazed his eyes, and he groaned out his pleasure.

''*Nooooo!*'' The scream tore from her, harsh and low. At the same moment, she pinched his rod through the cotton of his pantaloons. She put all of her flagging strength into a grinding twist of her fingers.

He howled. His grip slackened. Sobbing, she tried to scramble free, but the night rail hobbled her legs.

He slapped the side of her head. ''Bitch!''

She cried out in pain. Her ears rang and her senses careened. She fell back panting, her eyes squeezed shut against the whirling darkness.

A flurry of footsteps approached. Someone shoved Dickenson away. His weight left her, and she found herself gathered against a pillowy form, rocked in a warm, comforting embrace.

"There now, child. Calm yourself. Your auntie's here for you."

Aunt Minnie. *Oh, thank God!*

Shaking and weak, Isabel clutched at the older woman. "Hellllp . . . meee."

"Of course I'll help you, dearie. Never doubt that. Haven't I always done what's best for you?"

She stroked Isabel's hair and with each loving caress, the frenzy of fear seeped from Isabel. Her death grip slowly eased. She felt drained and lethargic, safe even though Dickenson sat slumped at the foot of the bed.

Aunt Minnie seemed to possess some magical power over him. He made no move to fight her. Instead he glowered at the two of them, while gingerly rubbing his injured member.

"She should be punished," he said venomously.

Minnie stopped her crooning and lifted her head. "Clumsy bastard," she snapped. " 'Tis what you deserve."

"She wouldn't cooperate."

"Of course not. You came at her like a rutting bull."

"I'll have you know, other women appreciate my skills in the bedchamber."

"Skills, bah. I was out there, listening. A girl likes to hear soft words and compliments, not crude threats and bullying."

In a swirling fog of disbelief, Isabel absorbed the exchange. *No.* She must be dreaming . . . this was a nightmare. Aunt Minnie could not have known Dickenson was here. She would not let him perform this act of violation.

"Perhaps I did overwhelm the chit," Dickenson said in a grudging tone. "But I thought you'd given her a potion of opium to make her cooperate."

Minnie's arm tightened around Isabel. "So I did. But

that doesn't give you leave to treat her like a common trollop. She requires gentler care.''

Drugged? She had been drugged? By Aunt Minnie?

The notion staggered Isabel with the blow of betrayal. Her head pounding, she tried to make sense of the madness. The tea. It had tasted sweeter than usual . . .

"Wwwhy . . . ?" *Why did you do this to me?*

"Sshh, now there's a good girl," Minnie said, petting Isabel's cheek. "Just lie quiet and let your auntie do the fretting. I shan't allow him to hurt you. You'll feel only pleasure, the sweetest pleasure you've ever known.''

"I'll make sure she enjoys it this time." Grinning, Dickenson put his hands to the buttons of his pantaloons. "Now let's get on with it. You did want the deed done tonight, didn't you?''

Renewed panic rushed over Isabel. She latched onto Minnie's arm and tried to pull herself upright. The room dipped and rolled. The edges of her vision turned black. "Stoooop . . . hiiiim. *Pleeeease.*" Each word emerged, thick and slow, as she struggled to keep from falling into an endless inky pit.

Minnie leaned closer to massage the back of Isabel's neck. "There now, dearie, you mustn't work yourself up into a state. You must relax and lie still. I'll sit right here and protect you from harm. You're safe with me." Her voice was soft, honeyed, persuasive. "Let your fears float away, my girl. Close your eyes now and let yourself dream. 'Tis your Justin making love to his Venus, that's all. He'll touch you gently . . . stroke you . . . love you . . . and the pleasure will come if you don't fight it. Just let yourself drift to Justin, let yourself remember how wonderful he makes you feel . . .''

Despite Isabel's resistance, the mesmerizing tone lulled her, the words flowing through her with a hypnotic power, luring her into a soft cloud of inertia. Her eyelids grew impossibly heavy. *Justin.* A dizzying fervor swept over her. Yes, Justin would be here. She craved his loving, the clever pampering of his hands.

"In a moment, he'll touch you, arouse you. There's no sensation quite so fine in all the world. So let him come to you. Let him caress you, join himself with you. Let the pleasure carry you higher and higher. The lovely, lovely pleasure . . ."

The hissing of her conscience faded to nothing, drowned out by the liquid excitement pulsing through her veins. Her loins throbbed with erotic heat. She felt soft and damp with longing, hungry for relief from the ache deep inside herself. Someone eased up the hem of the night rail, and she heard herself whimper at the delicious coolness of air against her bare legs.

Justin. She moved restlessly against the smooth sheets. Her skin felt highly sensitized. He would touch her now. He would make love to her again and transport her to paradise. She wanted him so badly . . .

And with sweetly carnal warmth, his hand settled onto her thigh.

"It's about bloody time," Kern snapped. "I've been here twice already today, looking for you. Where the devil have you been?"

Lord Hathaway had just stepped into the library. A short yet stately aristocrat, he glared with piercing dark eyes that might have skewered a lesser man. "You have brass to show your face in this house." With a jerk of his head, he indicated the open door. "Now get out."

Kern strode to the door and shoved it shut. "Not until I have my say."

His lips thinned, the marquess looked him up and down. "You've said quite enough already. Because of you, Helen has suffered a terrible blow. Because of you, she has withdrawn from society lest she be humiliated before all the *ton*. I've been out settling my business affairs so that I can take her to the Continent for the summer.''

The thought of Helen's anguish penetrated the storm of Kern's anger. ''I shall make certain everyone knows the broken betrothal is solely my fault.''

''And should that salve your conscience for the grief you've caused her?'' Hathaway shook his fist. ''Pray God she quickly realizes she is better off without a vile lecher like you. A man who has proven himself to be Lynwood's bad seed.''

The fury rushed back into Kern. ''Are you referring to my relationship with Isabel Darling?''

''You know bloody well I am.'' His cheeks flushed with rage, Hathaway took a step toward Kern. ''How dare you seduce a young girl living under my guardianship? You have no scruples. No honor.''

Kern deliberately goaded him. ''Tell me, why should you care so much about what happens to the bastard daughter of a whore?''

The marquess spun away, striding to the sideboard to pick up the decanter of whiskey. ''I was responsible for her welfare,'' he said over his shoulder. ''While Isabel lived here, she comported herself as a lady—until you led her astray.''

In four furious steps, Kern reached Hathaway and knocked the glass out of his hand. The crystal shattered. Whiskey spilled over the sideboard and dripped onto the carpet.

''Isabel Darling blackmailed her way into this house,'' Kern said coldly. ''She tricked Helen into believing they were cousins. And after all that, you offered Isabel five thousand pounds if she would marry a gentleman. I want you to tell me why.''

Stone-faced, Hathaway averted his gaze. ''There's nothing to tell. We've been over all this before.''

Kern seized the marquess by his lapels and shoved him

up against a bookcase. Several volumes crashed to the floor. "God damn you for a lying coward. You are going to acknowledge her. You are going to tell me who she really is. Now."

Hathaway's chest heaved. But he made no attempt to free himself. His eyes stark with shock, he stared at Kern. "You've guessed," he said hoarsely. "How—?"

"That doesn't matter." Kern gave Hathaway a shake. "Just say it. Speak the truth for once in your hypocritical life."

"All right, then! Isabel . . . is my natural daughter."

The agonized declaration echoed inside Kern's skull. He had known the truth upon seeing Hathaway's bold signature in the church registry. Yet now Hathaway's villainy jolted him anew. This was the man Kern had admired all his life.

Kern released his hold and walked away. Pacing the library, he fit all the facts together. "You are Apollo. Isabel was born of your affair with Aurora Darling. An affair which ended the night before your marriage."

Hathaway stumbled to a chair and sank down, bowing his head and raking his fingers through his salt-and-pepper hair. "Yes."

"At the time of your wedding I was only nine years old," Kern said. "But I recall watching you take your vows at St. George's. And thinking you were the sort of gentleman I wanted to be someday." His tone hardened. "But the man I revered had left the bed of his mistress only hours before."

"I did what I believed was right."

"Right? You led me to think you were better than Lynwood. That you were a moral man, a man with a conscience. When all the while you were carrying on a flaming affair with a courtesan."

"I loved Aurora. Leaving her was the most difficult decision I have ever made."

"What about abandoning Isabel?" Kern's voice vibrated with repugnance. "You had a daughter who needed you."

"I didn't know Aurora had become pregnant." Hathaway lifted his head. "And for pity's sake, she was a strumpet. To stay with her was unthinkable. I had no choice but to marry as I'd planned."

As much as he hated to admit it, Kern understood Hathaway's dilemma. Too well. Though Kern had broken his engagement to Helen, he had offered Isabel the dubious stature of his mistress. How did that make him any more noble than Hathaway?

"Once I found out about Aurora's delicate condition," Hathaway went on heavily, "it was too late to make other choices. By then my wife was also with child. I had to keep Isabel's birth a secret. Lest Helen be tainted by my public disclosure of a bastard."

"You could have visited Isabel without announcing it to the world."

"I paid for her house, her clothes, her governess. I made certain she was raised far from the brothel."

"She needed a father, not a bloody bank account."

"Dammit." Hathaway brought his fist down onto his knee. "Do you think her welfare has not weighed upon my conscience all these years? Why else do you suppose I brought her into my own household? It had little to do with those infernal memoirs. That was merely an excuse, a God-given opportunity to know my own daughter." His voice broke and he buried his face in his hands.

Kern felt a grudging sympathy for the man. Clearly Hathaway had suffered for his sins. Yet there were too many unanswered questions. "So you and your brother Raymond had an affair with the same woman."

A muscle jumped in Hathaway's jaw. "I despised him when he took up with her, though I hadn't seen her in many years. But I couldn't blame him for being enticed by her beauty."

''When you found out Isabel was searching for her mother's murderer, you asked me to stop her. Was it only the discovery of your secret that you feared?''

Hathaway frowned at him. ''If you think I believed Raymond had committed the crime, then you're wrong. My brother is at times a weak man, but he did not poison Aurora.''

''Ah,'' Kern said quietly, his gaze piercing the marquess, ''but did *you* do the deed?''

Hathaway's face went ashen. The mantel clock ticked softly into the silence. In the passageway beyond the closed door, muffled footsteps approached, then faded as a servant went by on his duties. ''You would ask such a monstrous thing . . . of me?''

Kern hated himself for these suspicions. But if he hoped to protect Isabel, he had no choice. ''You had ample reason to want Aurora dead. She knew your secret. She and one other confidant. Sir John Trimble.''

''He contacted you?''

''No. This morning, I visited Trimble. He's been poisoned.''

Hathaway half rose out of his chair, his hands gripping the arms. ''Good God! Are you quite sure?''

''The doctor said as much. He also said that in his delirium, Trimble mumbled the name Apollo.''

Hathaway gave a jerky nod. ''Trimble came to visit me yesterday morning. He asked me a number of questions about my activities on the night Aurora took ill. I admit, I was furious with him.'' Gazing steadily at Kern, the marquess added, ''When he left here, Trimble mentioned that he felt queasy. You may believe that or not. I shan't defend myself against so base a charge as murder.''

Kern believed him. Hathaway had not poisoned Trimble. Nor did Kern seriously think he had done away with Aurora. An affair with a courtesan did not rob a man of all honor.

Then who? Who was the culprit?

"While Trimble was here, did he visit Callie, Isabel's maid?"

Hathaway shook his head. "Not to my knowledge. He came by shortly after you and Isabel left. I spoke with him, then he took his leave."

Strange. Minnie had claimed Trimble wanted to question Callie. Had he done so without Hathaway's knowledge? Was that when Callie had poisoned Trimble? Something didn't quite fit—

Hathaway stood up, his granite glare fixed on Kern. "Speaking of Isabel, I demand to know your intentions toward her."

"My intentions," Kern said absently.

"Yes, by God. I despise the notion of Isabel being your mistress." Breathing hard, Hathaway clenched his fists. "Even if she could never aspire to a nobleman, I had hoped for her to marry a man of means so that she might lead a life of decency and virtue. Now you have ruined her."

"But—"

"I'm not finished. You have robbed Isabel of her future. Though the deed is done and it seems I must tolerate this affair, I insist that you treat her well. Or you shall answer to me."

That fatherly fury had a curious effect on Kern. He felt his own anger slipping away. "Isabel will not be my mistress," he said. "She'll be my wife."

"Wife?"

"I love her," Kern said, a husky note entering his voice. "She's taught me to heed my heart rather than the rules of propriety."

Hathaway's thunderstruck expression gave way to guarded relief. "Marriage. I would never have thought . . . But, yes, it might work. The two of you can move to the country for a while. The scandal will die down eventually. And Helen will accustom herself to the idea. I do believe she sorely misses her friendship with Isabel even more than she misses planning the wedding." He walked to the old portrait of the beautiful, bewigged lady and gazed up at it. "Do you know, Helen is the only one who noticed the resemblance? And I couldn't tell her how astute she was, that Isabel is her half sister. That is why Isabel looks so much like my mother."

Kern joined him in studying the picture of Lady Hathaway. For the first time, he noticed the haunting similarity in the eyes and cheekbones, in the serenely smiling mouth. His chest ached. Isabel possessed that same refinement and proud will. Why had it taken him so long to see it?

"Isabel will be a duchess someday," Hathaway went on. "Her Grace of Lynwood. No one will dare to snub her. And if they do, I shall take care of them."

"No," Kern stated. "*I* shall."

Hathaway's gaze took on the darkness of regrets. "Yes. You've earned that right." He walked to the window and stared out into the gathering dusk. "She does not yet know who I am."

I have no father. And should you seek to prove otherwise, I shall never, ever forgive you.

Kern remembered the tears glittering in her eyes. Now he understood why she had not wanted him to delve more deeply into her past. She was ashamed for him to see that her father regarded her as an embarrassment to be hidden away. "She will not be told, either," he said. "Not yet, anyway. Perhaps in time, once all this trouble is past, she'll be ready to accept the truth."

Without turning, the marquess gave a curt nod. "I defer to your judgment on the matter. Let us hope that Minerva has the sense to keep her counsel, too."

The statement jolted Kern. "Minnie knows your identity?"

"Yes, she and Trimble were the only ones. After Aurora

died, I needed a way to get money to Isabel. So I contacted Minerva.''

"Money?'' Baffled and angry, Kern stared at Hathaway's back. "You've given no money to Isabel in the past year.''

The marquess pivoted around. "I have, indeed. Every quarter, I've deposited a thousand pounds to an account in Minerva's name. She is to use the funds to provide for Isabel's needs.''

Four thousand per annum—a comfortable fortune. Yet the house was run-down. The women had little to eat. Isabel had been forced to wear outmoded clothes. "Minnie didn't give the money to Isabel. Minnie acted as if they were destitute.'' Kern spoke aloud, his suspicions leaping. "Minnie was also the last person to see Sir John Trimble before he came here.''

"What are you saying?'' Hathaway demanded. "That Minerva poisoned Trimble? But why?''

"Perhaps he asked her too many questions about Aurora's death,'' Kern said grimly. "Perhaps Minnie knows more than she'll admit. Far more.''

A wild fear flashed in Hathaway's eyes. "Isabel can't stay there,'' he said, striding toward the door of the library. "I shall bring her back here.''

Kern caught up to him. "She'll know who you are, then. It's best I go alone.''

"No,'' the marquess said in a voice that brooked no argument. "I failed Isabel too often while she was growing up. This is one time I shan't let her down.''

❧ Chapter 21 ❧

*I*sabel felt his hand creep up her thigh. His palm left a clammy dampness on her flesh. His fingers latched too tightly, almost pinching her.

Justin?

She squirmed, trying to rid herself of the uneasiness, desiring to sink back into the hot well of arousal. But her body refused to cooperate. Gooseflesh scurried over her skin. His touch felt foreign somehow, disgusting. Acting on instinct, she clamped her legs together, locking him out before he reached his goal.

"Demned cold fish," a man muttered.

Not Justin.

Stabbed by alarm, she forced open her heavy eyelids. And found herself looking into the foxy features of Terrence Dickenson.

Her lassitude vanished under a flood of awareness. A single candle illuminated her mother's bedroom. The night rail had been drawn up to her waist.

Aunt Minnie held Isabel close, stroking her hair, crooning soft words in her ear. "There now, my little Venus, don't take fright. You're a ladybird now, just like your aunties. You'll stay right here with us, enjoy the pleasures of many men . . ."

Aunt Minnie meant to turn her into a whore. Kern would

not want her then. He would not take her away from this brothel. The horror of it resonated inside Isabel, emerging in a choked cry.

She threw herself toward the edge of the mattress. With her night rail hiked up, she moved quicker than before. The room pitched and swayed. She tumbled off the bed, landing hard on her shoulder. Too dazed to stand, she scrambled onto her hands and knees, heading for the boudoir.

Hurry. Get out. Find help.

Dickenson latched onto her legs. She fought him, kicking and scratching. Her nails gouged flesh. He fell back with a howl.

Sobbing and dizzy, she lurched toward safety. But Aunt Minnie blocked the darkened doorway.

"You cannot escape, child," she said. "There's nowhere to go."

Isabel struggled to focus her whirling thoughts. "Aunnnt . . . Callllie." *Aunt Di. Aunt Persy.*

Minnie smiled gently. "The other whores can't help you. They're fast asleep. I made certain of that."

Hope trickled out of Isabel. Crouched on the floor, she pulled the skimpy night rail down around her ankles. It was all she could do to protect herself.

Justin. Oh, Justin.

But she knew he would not come for her. She had sent him away. Forever. She pressed her hands to her head, trying to steady the sway of her senses. Dear God. She had only her drugged wits to rely upon.

"You should have made certain of her compliance," Dickenson complained, blotting the blood from the scratches on his face. "I tell you, she's ill-natured enough to wither a man's cock."

"She's more beautiful than you deserve," Minnie retorted. "But never fear, her lack of cooperation can be remedied."

Reaching into the pocket of her apron, Minnie drew out a spoon and a small vial. She uncorked the vial and walked slowly toward Isabel. "Don't be frightened, my child. I'm not going to harm you. Only help you to feel better. A wee draught of this medicine and you'll drift into dreamland, where only pleasure awaits you."

Isabel waited until Minnie carefully lowered her bulk to her knees. As the older woman measured out a spoonful, Isabel lashed out and struck Minnie, aiming for her bandaged arm. Minnie shrieked. The vial and spoon went flying.

Isabel scrambled for the boudoir.

As she reached the doorway, someone caught a fistful of Isabel's hair. Sparks of pain flashed through her skull. She fell backward against Minnie's cushiony form.

Favoring her injured arm, Minnie called out to Dickenson, "Help me, you lout. Hold her."

Dickenson wrestled Isabel down onto the floor. She continued to wriggle, but the attempt at escape had drained her reserve of energy. When Minnie tried to poke a spoonful of liquid into Isabel's mouth, she resorted to her last line of defense.

She clamped her lips shut.

Minnie pinched Isabel's nose. "You're making this so difficult," she muttered. "I only want you to stay here so that I can take care of you, be your mother. It's what I've always wanted. But you won't cooperate, and neither would Aurora. She wanted to move away with you, leave me here."

Mama?

Isabel tried to capture the fleeting thought. Blackness encroached on her vision. The lack of air made her chest burn. When she could hold out no longer, she parted her lips for a breath.

Minnie pushed in the spoon. Isabel gagged as the sweetish elixir rolled to the back of her throat.

* * *

Built of the same pale stone as its neighbors, the town house loomed through the dimness of dusk. Tall fluted columns flanked the front porch. Three granite steps led up to a discreet white door. The windows were dark except for the glimmering of candlelight in one upstairs room.

Aurora's old bedchamber.

Who was in there?

Kern lifted his hand to the brass knocker, thought better of it, then tried the knob. Locked.

"We'll go to the back door," he said.

Hathaway gave a grim nod, falling into step beside Kern as they rounded the corner. He, too, must have felt the prick of foreboding on seeing that light. Was Minnie in there again?

Minnie must have done that vicious destruction. She had mutilated Aurora's possessions and then pretended a prowler had attacked her. Why? There was nothing in the memoirs to implicate her.

Unless she hadn't been looking for the memoirs. Unless her knife wound was self-inflicted, designed to lure Isabel back home.

Despite the mildness of the evening, a chill shook Kern. He should never have let Isabel stay here. He was a damned fool for allowing her out of his sight. He would not rest until he had her safely in his arms again.

Gloom lay thickly in the mews. A horse snuffled in one of the small stables. The dampness from the previous day's rain sharpened the stench of rubbish. Their footsteps tapped an urgent tattoo on the cobblestones.

Reaching the servants' entrance, Kern opened the door. Hathaway followed him inside. Their eyes needed a moment to adjust to the unlit passageway. Strange, he could smell no sign of dinner preparations, only a trace of musk, the scent of this house.

Had everyone gone out?

Kern started up the narrow back staircase. They slowly

felt their way through the darkness. He would find Isabel safely in her bedroom. She would be napping perhaps. That would explain why no light shone in her window.

Or perhaps she and her aunts were congregated in Aurora's bedchamber. God knew, they could be chatting over old times. Or consoling Isabel in her heartache.

Yet he couldn't shake the urgency that gripped him. Henceforth, he would keep her close to him always. He would marry her. And let her dare to defy her vow to honor and obey him.

Shadows shrouded the upstairs passageway. Hathaway pointed to the closed door of Aurora's boudoir. Kern walked down the corridor and put his ear to the white-painted panel. He could discern the murmur of voices inside. He quietly tried the knob, but it did not turn.

Locked.

Isabel spat out the potion. Right in Minnie's face.

Cursing, the old whore jumped back. She lifted a corner of her apron to wipe her eyes. "Ungrateful girl. I'm doing what's best for you. That's what I've always done."

Isabel curled up in a ball on the floor. Despite her act of defiance, a small amount of the drug trickled down her throat. She knew that when it took effect her fate would be sealed.

Dickenson could use her however he liked. Aunt Minnie would encourage him. And Isabel would be defenseless to stop them.

A weapon. She had to find a weapon.

Her senses swam as she scanned the room. But except for the furniture, the place was virtually barren. Aunt Minnie had seen to that.

The realization wormed its way into Isabel's mind. Aunt Minnie had destroyed Mama's things. She had ripped gowns, spilled perfume, overturned the inkwell onto the desk. She had hated Mama.

She had killed Mama.

The horrid thought hammered at Isabel. Aunt Minnie
wanted Isabel to stay here. She had said so again and again.
And according to the memoirs, Aurora had intended to
move away to the country, to live with Isabel, leaving the
ladybirds behind.

*God willing, the proceeds from my book will permit me
to leave this house of assignation forever and join my dear
daughter in Oxfordshire. There at last we shall live together, she and I . . .*

Mama had feared that one of her ex-lovers had poisoned
her, to stop her from completing the memoirs. But the murder had had little to do with *The Confessions of a Ladybird.*

It had everything to do with Aunt Minnie's determination to keep Isabel here at the brothel.

A fog drifted over Isabel's consciousness. The opium.
She struggled to think, to hold on to her reason, but a warm
mist clouded her mind until only a vague sense of danger
lingered. More than anything, she wanted to snuggle up
and close her eyes. Her limbs seemed to weigh a hundred
pounds apiece. She grew hazily aware of a heat glowing
in her belly, a soft and languorous desire. *Justin.* How she
wanted him to hold her. She moved restlessly, the carpet
chafing her tender skin.

Minnie's voice came from a long way off. "There, my
child. I can see that you swallowed enough of the medicine
to put you in a happier humor. 'Tis for the best, you'll
soon realize."

"Move aside. She's ready for me to have a go at her."
Dickenson.

He towered over her. Isabel tried to focus her bleary
eyes, but his lofty image split in two. She mustn't let him
touch her . . .

"Pick her up and carry her to the bed," Aunt Minnie
told him.

"What do you take me for, your servant?"

"Do it. I won't have my girl humped on the floor like a bitch dog."

Grumbling, Dickenson approached Isabel with care, as if he expected her to erupt into violence again. She had little strength left. The soporific effects of the opium flowed through her veins, rendering her weak and torpid.

He crouched down, shoved his arms beneath her body. His cold, sweaty hands jolted her out of her daze. She flinched from him, and a low cry of terror burst from her lungs.

"Noooo!"

Kern and Hathaway had just had a whispered debate on whether or not to knock when they heard the muffled scream.

Like a sliver of ice, the sound pierced Kern. *Isabel.*

"Stand back," he ordered.

Hathaway barely leapt clear when Kern thrust his shoulder at the door. The wooden panel groaned. He came at it again and this time the latch gave way and the door flew back on its hinges.

He pounded into the boudoir, Hathaway on his heels. The room was dark. Vacant. A meager light trickled from the bedchamber.

He ran there, fear squeezing his chest. In one quick sweep his gaze took in the candlelit scene.

Naked to the waist, Terrence Dickenson stood beside the canopied bed. Minnie squatted near the headboard. She pillowed Isabel's head and stroked her hair, crooning to her.

Like a virginal offering, Isabel lay unmoving, her eyes closed, her slender form draped in a sheer white negligee.

"Good God!" Hathaway exploded.

A red mist of rage descended on Kern. Uttering a savage growl, he launched himself at Dickenson. The older man retreated swiftly, stumbled over a stool and sprawled onto the carpet.

He cowered in terror and held up a hand to forestall
Kern. "I-I can explain. Minnie put me up to this. B-but
nothing happened. It-it was all a m-mistake."

"Bloody right it was a mistake."

Kern yanked Dickenson up from the floor and landed a
fist to his jaw. With a satisfying crack of bone, Dickenson's
head jerked back. He hit the wall and slid down, landing
in a heap, a crumpled marionette. His eyes were shut, his
body limp.

Kern strode to the bed. Minnie tried to throw herself
over Isabel, but the marquess wrested her away, pulling
her arms behind her back. "Ow!" she protested. "Watch
how you treat my poor arm."

"You'll get the treatment you deserve. In Newgate
Prison."

"Newgate! On what charge?"

Hathaway wore a look of merciless severity. "The murder of Aurora Darling."

Kern sat down on the bed. Muttering incoherently, Isabel
moved her head back and forth on the pillow. The dusky
points of her breasts pressed against the gown, and the
gossamer fabric skimmed her feminine curves. God, Minnie had invited Dickenson here. To rape Isabel.

Fury flooded Kern anew, along with a fierce tenderness.
He touched her cheek. Blessedly warm, smooth as swans-
down. "Isabel."

Her eyelids fluttered. She squirmed restively, her hands
clutching at him. "Jusssstin?"

"I'm here, dearest." His throat tight, he brushed aside
a lock of hair and kissed her brow. "I'm here."

She opened her eyes. Dark and sultry, her gaze drifted
over him, and her lips curved into a slow, sweet smile.
"I'mmm not . . . dreaming?"

Her words sounded slurred. Jolted by panic, he jerked
toward Minnie. "What the devil did you give her? Poison?"

"Of course not," she said huffily. " 'Twas only a wee spot of opium. I love her more than you ever could."

"Love? You know only selfishness and spite." He gathered Isabel up into his arms. Lifting her from the bed, he held her close, rejoicing in her nearness. "It's not a dream," he murmured in her ear. "I'm really here. And I'll never leave you again."

"No!" Minnie shouted. "You can't have her."

"He can, indeed, madam," Hathaway said grimly. "And if I have my way, you will never see Isabel again."

He pulled Minnie toward the door. She dug in her heels, yanking ineffectually at his hold. "How dare you! You've no right to take me from her! You of all men."

"I've every right. And well you know it."

"Hah. Tossing the dear girl a few coins now and then, that's all. I made sure she didn't get your paltry offerings. So that she wouldn't mistake money for love."

Pinning her arms behind her back, Hathaway hissed in her ear, "Thievery. There's another crime to put before the magistrate."

"You won't dare. You'd have to tell the world about your tryst with Aurora. You'd have to admit you're Isabel's father."

Isabel blinked in confusion. "Faaather?"

Hathaway's gaze locked on hers. Though Minnie tugged at his grip, he kept his eyes fixed on his daughter. The starkness of vulnerability softened his stony features. "Yes, it's true," he said, the words sounding wrenched from a place deep inside him. "I am your father."

Isabel slowly shook her head, her unbound hair swirling against Kern. "Yooooou . . . and Mama . . . ?"

"I loved her. With all my heart. If I'd had half your Justin's courage—" Hathaway's voice broke off. His eyes glittered, and he turned his head to the side.

In a sudden flurry, Minnie wrenched herself from him. She ran for the door, but Hathaway grappled her and

brought her down. This time, he snatched up a scarf and
secured her hands behind her back. A foul stream of curses
erupted from the whore.

Isabel shuddered, and Kern pressed her face into the
crook of his shoulder, sheltering her from sight and sound.
Her hands clung tightly to the back of his neck. He could
think of nothing he wanted more than to take her away
from here, to help her forget the betrayal she had suffered
this night.

Hathaway hauled Minnie to her feet. "I'll send the
coachman back to fetch that one." He nodded toward
Dickenson, still out cold on the floor of the bedroom.

"I should take them to the Bow Street Office," Kern
said. "You'll want to stay clear of this mess."

"No. It's high time I did what was right." Hathaway
lifted a bemused eyebrow at Isabel, his face softening.
"Besides, it would seem you are otherwise occupied."

Isabel moved sinuously in Kern's arms. With maddening
sensuality, she pressed her breasts to him, making him
more keenly aware of her feminine shape. Clearly, the drug
had caused her to lose all inhibitions. Her soft lips drifted
over his throat, and he felt the teasing dampness of her
tongue. And his own swift, untimely reaction.

Hathaway aimed a flinty look at Kern. "Young man, I
would suggest you act immediately to legitimize your relationship with my daughter."

Kern couldn't stop a broad smile. "As you say, my
lord."

Two hours later, the Lynwood coach set forth on the Great
North Road.

Snug within the plush interior, Kern cradled Isabel close
to his side. She lay curled sweetly against him, her slender
body wrapped in a warm mantle that covered her from
neck to toes. Beneath, she wore the nightdress; he had

lacked the heart to disturb her when she'd fallen asleep during his hasty preparations.

The servants at Lynwood House had scurried to do his bidding, the valet packing a valise, the cook loading a hamper with delicacies, the grooms hitching the team of horses. Despite their questioning glances, no one had dared to ask why the master was setting forth on a long journey at night—and in the company of an unchaperoned young lady. He had offered them no explanation. They would find out why within a few days' time.

The *ton* would find out, too. And the small-minded gossips. Kern smiled into the darkness. Devil take them all. He had everything he wanted right here beside him.

Isabel stirred, stretching herself and releasing a luxurious sigh. Her eyelids lifted, and in the faintness of starlight, she blinked at him. Her hand crept up his coat as if to reassure herself of his presence. "Justin?"

He kissed her brow. "How are you feeling?"

"A little better . . . not so dizzy." She glanced around as if just realizing they occupied a coach. "Are you taking me to Lynwood House?"

"No, sweetheart. I'm abducting you."

She frowned. "Abducting? But . . . I'll gladly go with you anywhere. I was getting ready to come and tell you so, but then Aunt Minnie—" Isabel paused, her white teeth sinking into her lower lip. "I can scarcely believe what's happened. All those years . . . she was like a second mother to me . . ."

Sensing her anguish, Kern threaded his hand into her silken curls. "Don't torture yourself, my love. You didn't know her true character. None of us knew."

Isabel drew a deep, shuddering breath. "Remember when Aunt Persy became ill? Aunt Minnie must have poisoned her. To try to convince me to leave Hathaway's house and return home." Suddenly she stiffened. "My other aunts—"

"Are all sleeping soundly," he finished. "I checked on them myself. And I left instructions for Dr. Sadler to stop by at first light, to ensure none of them suffer any ill effects. He'll see to Trimble, too."

"And Sir John . . . isn't my father after all."

"No, he is not."

She sat very still, watching him. "Lord Hathaway . . . is he truly . . . ?"

I have no father. And should you seek to prove otherwise, I shall never, ever forgive you.

Kern steeled himself. "Yes, darling, Hathaway is your father. I only just discovered the truth before we came to you." He framed her face in his hands. "Isabel, I'm sorry if that news causes you pain. But I do think if you give him time, he'll show you that he does care—he always has. He went through a lot of anguish over you."

She turned her gaze out the window of the coach, where the night rushed past with only the occasional twinkle of candlelight in a cottage or house. "It's strange. I find . . . I cannot hate him, after all. He's given me a sister—the sister I've always wanted." Her voice went husky. "The sister whom I hurt so badly."

Kern gathered her close. "Helen needs time to realize she and I weren't right for one another. She'll understand that when she finds a great passion of her own."

A sigh whispered from Isabel. She turned fully toward him, pressing her body to the length of him. Her hand burrowed inside his coat, stroking idly up and down his side. With tempting allure, she wriggled into a more comfortable position against him. They were alone in the semi-darkness of the coach with many hours of traveling ahead of them. He thought of the nightdress beneath her mantle and the way the gauze clung to her breasts and hips. He had only to part her overgarment and delve inside . . .

But Isabel had suffered a terrible shock this night. He

ought to have more respect for her than take advantage of her vulnerable state.

She caressed his cheek. "Justin, I spoke hastily when I refused your offer. I do want to be your mistress. With all my heart."

Arousal shimmered through him, along with a deep, abiding love. She didn't yet know their destination. "There's something I need to tell you—"

His voice broke off as her fingers brushed intimately against him. She reached inside his breeches to find the buttons hidden there, undoing them one by one. "But if you truly want me, I have certain rules you must abide by," she continued.

He couldn't think. "Rules."

"Yes. You will dedicate your life to me—and any children we might have. You will forsake all other women. No one else shall ever touch you like this."

When her dainty fingers closed around him, he bit back a groan and struggled to keep his sanity. "Isabel, my love . . . listen. About you being my mistress—"

"Mmmm. And if you do as I say, I shall devote my life to pleasing you, my lord." With a suddenness that transfixed him, she slid off his lap and knelt between his legs. All coherent thought fled his mind as her hands gently cupped him. In the darkness, her fingers explored him with slow reverence. "You are mine," she whispered fiercely. "Mine alone."

A furnace of heat ignited in his groin. He could feel the warm breath of her parted lips. So near.

Her finger found a glistening drop of liquid and smoothed it over the tip of him. Struck by a bolt of sensation, he clenched his fists to keep from urging her mouth closer. Softly, she went on, "Did you know that sometimes I would listen secretly while my aunts gossiped? I found their stories shocking—yet fascinating. And I never thought I would want to do such things with a man . . . until I met you.''

She rubbed her cheek against his hard length. And then she turned her head and gave him the most intimate kiss of all.

He very nearly exploded.

Digging his fingers into the cushions, he fought for mastery of himself. His heart thundered in his chest. Fire sizzled through his veins as she loved him with her mouth and hands. Harsh groans hissed through his gritted teeth. When he could bear no more of the exquisite torture, he hauled her onto his lap and frantically hiked the gown and cloak to her waist. His hands sought her smooth backside. Her breathing quick and shallow, she straddled him, clinging to his shoulders.

He touched her in a swift caress, found her moist and ready. With little urging from him, she lowered herself until the heat of her body sheathed him to the hilt. He put his hand between them to stroke her and she moaned with uninhibited pleasure, her hips undulating. Within moments, she cried out his name, her inner muscles convulsing around him. Seized by a rapture of sharp, white intensity, he shared her delirious joy, spilling his seed and his soul into her.

The aftermath released him into perfect contentment. He came back to the gentle rocking of the coach, the fragrance of her rose-scented hair. In a voice raspy with emotion, he said, ''I love you, Venus Isabel Darling.''

''And I, you.'' Soft and relaxed, Isabel nestled against him. ''Mmmm. I don't think I could ever be happier.''

''You might be if you found out our destination.''

Her fingers skimmed the length of his jaw as if she could not yet believe he was real. ''Your estate in Derbyshire, of course. I'm to live in the dower house.''

He shook his head. ''Take another guess.''

Isabel straightened slowly. She peered out the window

at the blackness of night, pierced only by a faint light cast by the outside lamps. "I can't imagine. Where?"

"To a little town on the border of Scotland."

"Scotland!" she exclaimed. "But why . . . ?" Her words trailed off and he sensed her anxiety, the sudden stillness in her.

He could tease her no longer. "We're off to Gretna Green, my love. It's the nearest place where we can wed without being bothered by banns or a license." When she remained silent, unmoving, he went on huskily, "I haven't officially asked you to be my wife. Will you marry me?"

She did not answer at first. Then with a glad cry, she fell into his arms. "Oh, Justin. I never thought . . . Of course I will."

Replete with satisfaction, he wove his fingers through her mussed hair. "Now I have some rules of my own. First and foremost of which is having your promise to stay safe with me and out of trouble."

"Agreed. I don't ever want to live apart from you, my dearest." A tender smile curved her lips. "It feels extraordinary to be so happy. Extraordinary and wonderful."

"There's more of that to come." He brought her face closer for a warm, fervent kiss. "You see, I intend to spend my life making you happy."

Relishing the steady beat of his heart, Isabel tucked her head into the crook of his shoulder and sighed in pleasure. She felt blessedly free from the secrets of the past. Kern had given her so much—pride in herself and the power of lasting love. Most of all, he had made her believe again in happily-ever-afters.

PROPERTY OF
KINSMAN FREE PUBLIC LIBRARY

Dear Reader,

I hope you enjoyed Isabel and Justin's journey to happiness. May their compelling, unconventional love story live on in your heart as it does in mine.

When I finished writing *Her Secret Affair*, something still nagged at me. I ached to know what would happen to Lady Helen Jeffries, who had become as real to me as a best friend. Would she survive the disastrous end to her betrothal? Would she find her own happily ever after?

One of the nicest aspects about being a writer is imagining wonderful new stories. So I moved time ahead five years and made Helen a world traveler who likes her independence and considers herself too sophisticated for romance. She's ridden a camel in Egypt, fed the monkeys on Gibraltar Rock, and toured the ancient wonders of Baghdad. Yet there's one area in which she woefully lacks experience: sexual intimacy.

When her coach goes off the road during a blizzard, Helen is stranded in a ruined castle with her rescuer, a fierce Scotsman with a shadowed past. Helen decides he's the perfect man to show her the mysteries of lovemaking. After they spend their one night together, she'll never see him again.

Or so she believes!

Set in the rugged Scottish Highlands, "Beauty and the Brute" will appear as a novella in the *Scandalous Weddings* anthology published by St. Martin's Paperbacks, on sale in the fall of 1998.

I hope you'll be as eager as I was to know Helen's story. In the meantime, may you always have an exciting romance to brighten your life.

Barbara Dawson Smith